Public Image, Private Heart

A Workplace Slow-Burn Romance

Trevor Jensen

Copyright © 2026 by Trevor Jensen

All rights reserved.

No part of this publication may be reproduced, distributed, or transmitted in any form or by any means, including photocopying, recording, or other electronic or mechanical methods, without the prior written permission of the publisher, except as permitted by U.S. copyright law. For permission requests, contact [include publisher/author contact info].

The story, all names, characters, and incidents portrayed in this production are fictitious. No identification with actual persons (living or deceased), places, buildings, and products is intended or should be inferred.

Dedication

For the women who were told being indispensable was the goal.

For the ones who learned how to hold everything together so well that no one ever thought to ask if they were tired.

This story is for you.

May you build a life that doesn't require you to burn out to deserve it. May you find work that challenges you without consuming you. And may you meet someone who doesn't compete with your ambition—

but steadies it.

— Trevor Jensen

Contents

1. Chapter 1: The Moment That Wasn't Supposed to Happen   1
2. Chapter 2: Optics   16
3. Chapter 3: Lunch   29
4. Chapter 4: The Shadow   44
5. Chapter 5: The Soft Spot   57
6. Chapter 6: The Almost Break   71
7. Chapter 7: The Dress Rehearsal   91
8. Chapter 8: Flashbulbs   104
9. Chapter 9: The Terrace That Lied   120
10. Chapter 10: Damage, Controlled   136
11. Chapter 11: The Morning After   152
12. Chapter 12: The Choice, On Camera   169
13. Chapter 13: Elevator Rules   182
14. Chapter 14: Ma'am, This Is a Hospital   200

15. Chapter 15: The Meeting That Definitely Wasn't a Date — 212
16. Chapter 16: Hot Mic, Cold Hands — 230
17. Chapter 17: The Price of Being Seen — 245
18. Chapter 18: Rehearsal in an Empty Room — 259
19. Chapter 19: The Line Between Help and Control — 277
20. Chapter 20: The Shape of Distance — 293
21. Chapter 21: The Calm Before the Spotlight — 309
22. Chapter 22: Under the Lights — 323
23. Chapter 23: Off Script — 335
24. Chapter 24: Terms of Engagement — 349
25. Epilogue: The Cameras Are Off — 362
26. Acknowledgements — 373
27. About the Author — 374

Chapter 1: The Moment That Wasn't Supposed to Happen

The microphone was still live.

Avery Sloan realized this at the exact moment she said, "If morale were measurable in caffeine intake, we'd be a top-tier institution."

a beat.

A laugh.

Then the faint, unmistakable echo of her own voice coming back through the overhead speakers.

Still live.

She closed her eyes for half a second—not in panic, not in defeat, but in calculation.

The town hall auditorium was full. Staff in scrubs. Administrators in business casual. A few board members scattered in the back row like silent auditors of the human experience. The stage lights were warm, forgiving. The banner behind her read:

Transparency. Accountability. Excellence.

She was good at all three.

Usually.

"Let me clarify," she continued smoothly, stepping closer to the podium as if this were all part of a measured plan. "While caffeine may be our unofficial fourth pillar, we are actively addressing workload distribution across departments."

A few more laughs.

The tension shifted, but not entirely.

Someone in the third row—surgical nurse, mid-forties, crossed arms—called out, "So you admit we're exhausted?"

The question wasn't hostile.

It was tired.

And tired is harder to deflect than hostile.

Avery adjusted her stance.

"I admit," she said evenly, "that healthcare is demanding. And I admit that when we see patterns of burnout, we're responsible for addressing them."

A murmur of approval.

She saw Natalie at the side curtain, eyes wide, mouthing something that looked suspiciously like *the clip is trending*.

Of course it was.

Because that was how the world worked now.

Avery's mouth tightened. Her list of things she didn't do in public was already long. Lose composure. Admit exhaustion. Make jokes that sounded like weakness. She could feel herself drafting a new item as she spoke: Do not become a meme.

Then she saw him in the back row, half in shadow, standing with the easy stillness of someone who didn't need to take up space to be noticed. Miles Carter. Crisp suit. Unhurried gaze. The sort of man who looked like he'd read every rule and decided which ones mattered.

He wasn't smirking at her. He wasn't recording. He was simply watching, like he was taking the temperature of the room and, oddly, of her. When her eyes flicked toward him, he gave a small, almost imperceptible nod, as if to say: Keep going. You've got it.

You could manage a multimillion-dollar system flawlessly for years, but one off-script moment with a hot mic and suddenly you were a headline.

She smiled at the nurse in the third row.

"We are reviewing staffing allocations this quarter," she added. "And I am aware that caffeine is not a sustainable morale strategy."

This time the laughter was warmer.

Relieved.

The moment passed.

The Q&A continued.

She fielded questions about billing transparency, patient wait times, the upcoming expansion of the pediatric wing. Her answers were crisp. Measured. Steady.

By the time she stepped off the stage forty minutes later, you would never have known there had been a flicker.

Except there had.

Avery stepped into the side corridor and paused. A younger nurse leaned against the wall, eyes closed, the sort of stillness that meant she'd been running on adrenaline and fumes.

Without thinking, Avery pulled a sealed water bottle from the event cart, twisted the cap, then stopped. She handed it over unopened instead, letting the nurse keep the dignity of doing it herself.

"You did good in there," Avery said, voice low. She adjusted her collar once—an old tell—and forced her jaw to unclench. "If you have a specific shift pattern that's breaking you, email my office. Not Natalie. Me."

The nurse blinked, surprised, then nodded. "Yes, ma'am."

Avery gave a small, almost uncomfortable nod back and kept walking, as if compassion were another item on a checklist she was learning how to live with.

"You joked about exhaustion."

Natalie did not whisper.

Natalie did not believe in whispering.

They were in the hallway behind the auditorium, and Natalie's heels clicked at an anxious tempo as she walked beside Avery.

"It was human," Avery replied.

"It was viral."

Avery handed her the wireless mic. "Those are not mutually exclusive."

Natalie stopped walking and turned her phone around.

The clip was already circulating.

Avery Sloan, COO of St. Catherine's Medical Center, jokes about staff burnout.

The caption beneath the clip read:

"If morale were measurable in caffeine intake…"

The comment count was climbing.

"That was a controlled remark," Avery said calmly.

Natalie stared at her.

"Controlled? You ad-libbed."

"I refined."

"You blinked."

"I blink."

"You paused."

"I breathe."

Natalie groaned. "The board is going to call."

"Of course they are."

As if summoned by story inevitability, Avery's phone buzzed.

Gerald Whitmore.

Board Chair.

Of course.

She answered before the second ring.

"Gerald."

"Avery." His voice was measured but not sharp. "I saw the clip."

"I assumed you might."

"… candid."

"I was contextualizing workload."

Another pause.

"We'll discuss spotlight tomorrow."

"Of course."

The call ended.

Natalie looked at her expectantly.

"Well?" Natalie asked.

"He would like to discuss spotlight."

Natalie inhaled deeply, as if oxygen itself were insufficient.

"This is not how you want to enter a succession review cycle."

Avery smoothed the lapel of her blazer.

"No," she agreed. "It's not."

And yet.

Somewhere beneath the surface, something else stirred.

Not fear.

Not exactly.

Something closer to... relief.

Because for one brief second, she had said something real.

By the time she reached her office, the clip had crossed fifty thousand views.

By the time she sat down, it was one hundred twenty-three thousand.

She watched it once.

Not to self-flagellate.

To analyze.

She looked steady. Controlled. Slightly dry.

no tremor in her voice.

No defensive edge.

a flicker of fatigue that most people wouldn't notice unless they were looking for it.

She closed the video.

Her reflection in the darkened laptop screen looked composed.

Competent.

Impenetrable.

"You're trending."

She didn't jump.

But she did exhale.

Miles Carter leaned casually against the doorframe, sleeves rolled to mid-forearm, tie slightly loosened as if the day had already negotiated with him and lost.

"I was informed," she replied.

"You were funny."

"That was not the objective."

"Still."

He stepped inside and closed the door gently behind him.

"Do you enjoy watching minor crises unfold?" she asked.

"Only when they're not actual crises."

"This is not a crisis."

"No," he agreed. "It's momentum."

She raised an eyebrow.

"That's a generous interpretation."

"You humanized yourself in front of five hundred employees."

"I referenced caffeine."

"You admitted exhaustion."

"I did not admit personal exhaustion."

He tilted his head slightly.

"You didn't have to."

Her jaw tightened almost imperceptibly.

She stood.

"I do not have the luxury of appearing fragile during a succession review."

"You didn't appear fragile."

"I appeared unscripted."

"That's different."

She walked around the desk, creating distance.

"Unscripted is unpredictable. Unpredictable is unstable. Unstable is disqualifying."

"That's dramatic."

"That's accurate."

He studied her.

"You think perfection is the job requirement."

"It is."

"No," he said softly. "Consistency is."

She hated that it landed.

Consistency meant you could be exhausted and still show up. It meant you could have a rough day and still be reliable. It meant you could be human and still be trusted.

Avery's mouth tightened. "Perception doesn't reward human."

Miles's gaze stayed on her, calm. "Then stop trying to win with perception."

That made something sharp flare in her chest. "Easy for you to say."

"Is it?" he asked, and for the first time she heard the edge under his warmth. "Because I built a career on managing it."

Avery's eyes narrowed. "Then why are you here."

His mouth quirked, but it wasn't a joke. "Because your board asked for help. Because Montclaire is panicking. And because the clip isn't the real issue."

What is, then, hovered between them.

Avery crossed to the window, looking down at the city. "They want a replacement."

"They want options," Miles corrected gently. "And right now the option they can't stop talking about is you."

That should have felt like power. Instead it felt like a spotlight searching for a crack.

Avery turned back. "I'm not losing this job because someone made a meme."

Miles's expression softened. "You won't. But you are going to get squeezed."

Before she could respond, the door banged open without a knock, because of course it did.

"Okay," Natalie announced, breathless, coat half off, phone in hand like it was a weapon. "Bad news: the clip has crossed fifty thousand views. Good news: half the comments are people admitting they also live on cold brew and spite."

Avery didn't look at her. "Natalie."

Natalie saw Miles and froze. "Oh. Great. The Crisis Guy is here."

Miles offered a mild smile. "Hi, Natalie."

"Do not 'hi' me," Natalie said, pointing at him. "I have three group texts, two board members and one resident who just DMed me the clip with thirteen skull emojis."

Avery exhaled slowly. "You're not helping."

"I am always helping," Natalie said, then looked directly at Miles. "Is he helping?"

Miles held up his hands slightly. "I'm trying."

Natalie's eyes narrowed. "Trying is what people say before they send an email that ruins my weekend."

Avery stepped back toward the desk. "What does the board want."

Natalie flipped her phone around. "Gerald Whitmore wants a call. In ten minutes. The board chair wants 'a path forward.' And Patrick Ames wants you to 'lean into authenticity.'"

Avery's jaw tightened. "Of course he does."

Miles's gaze sharpened at the name. "Patrick's already framing this as a messaging opportunity."

Natalie scoffed. "Everything is a messaging opportunity to Patrick. He'd monetize a sneeze."

Avery's mouth twitched in spite of herself, then flattened again. "We don't have time for this."

Miles stepped closer to the desk, voice steady. "We do, actually. Because this is the first move. If you try to bulldoze past it, it becomes the story."

Avery's shoulders tensed. "I refuse to let a joke become my legacy."

"Then we make sure the joke is about something else," Natalie said immediately. "Like Patrick."

Miles's mouth twitched. "Tempting."

Avery pinched the bridge of her nose. "Focus."

Miles nodded. "Here's what happens. Gerald calls. He offers support while measuring you. Patrick recommends a public-facing adjustment. And you feel like you have to prove you're unshakable."

Avery's eyes lifted. "I am unshakable."

Miles's gaze held hers. "You're disciplined. That's different."

The words hit too close to something private. Avery's jaw tightened.

Natalie made a small sound. "Okay, I hate that he's right."

Avery shot her a look. "Natalie."

Natalie lifted both hands. "I'm just saying: you're not a robot. And if the board wants a robot, they can buy one."

Miles's voice stayed calm. "We give them steadiness, not perfection. We set boundaries. We don't apologize for being human. We redirect to mission."

Avery stared at him. "Boundaries with the board."

Miles nodded. "Politely. Firmly. And we build a thirty-day plan that turns this into proof of leadership, not a liability."

Natalie blinked. "Thirty days."

Miles glanced at her. "The campaign window. The board's review window. The media cycle. We align them."

Avery's pulse ticked. Forced proximity, she realized. A schedule. A plan that would put this man in her orbit every day while the entire city tried to turn her face into a headline.

Avery's voice went cool. "I don't need a babysitter."

Miles's expression didn't change, but the warmth in his eyes sharpened. "Good. Because I don't babysit."

Natalie made a pleased noise. "Oh, I like him. That's unfortunate."

Miles ignored her. "I'm here to build a shield while you do your job. You keep leading. I handle the noise."

Avery's throat tightened. She didn't like needing a shield. She liked being the shield.

"And," Miles added, softer, "I'm here because you shouldn't have to do this alone."

Avery hated how that landed too.

Natalie's phone buzzed again. She glanced at it and groaned. "Gerald is calling me now because he thinks I'm you."

Avery's eyes narrowed. "Why would he think that."

Natalie shrugged. "Because I answer my emails."

Avery exhaled, then looked at Miles. "Ten minutes."

Miles nodded. "We'll be ready."

Natalie pointed two fingers at both of them. "Okay. Ground rules. No charming the board. No flirting. No making me the third wheel in a corporate romance."

Avery deadpanned. "This is not a romance."

Natalie stared at her like she'd lost her mind. "It's Manhattan. Everything becomes a romance if there's eye contact."

Miles's mouth twitched again, almost a smile. "Noted."

Avery's phone buzzed in her palm, the screen lighting with Gerald's name like a countdown.

She looked at Miles once more. "If this goes badly—"

"It won't," he said quietly.

Avery hated how sure he sounded.

She hit accept. "Gerald."

She crossed her arms.

"And what do you think that clip showed?"

"That you care."

She blinked.

"That's not what it showed."

"It showed you listening to a tired nurse instead of reciting a policy memo."

"I did both."

"You prioritized the human."

"That is called leadership."

He smiled faintly.

"Yes. It is."

Silence settled between them.

The air felt different in her office today. Charged in a way she couldn't quite define.

"You're calm," she observed.

"I try to be."

"Why?"

"Because you're not."

Her chin lifted.

"I am calm."

"You're controlled."

She didn't respond.

He walked closer, stopping a respectful distance from her desk.

"For what it's worth," he said, "if the board disqualifies you over a caffeine joke, they're not evaluating the right metric."

"That is not how boards operate."

"I know."

"Then you know spotlight matter."

"spotlight matter," he agreed. "But authenticity compounds."

She let out a quiet laugh.

"Are you always this philosophical when someone's trending?"

"Only when it's interesting."

"And this is interesting?"

"Yes."

"Why?"

"Because you don't like being seen."

The statement landed without accusation.

observation.

"I am seen every day," she replied evenly.

"No," he corrected gently. "You are observed."

The distinction irritated her because it was precise.

She stepped closer.

"Let me be clear," she said. "I do not require emotional analysis today."

"Noted."

"And I do not need reassurance."

"Also noted."

"And I am not destabilized."

He didn't respond immediately.

Then:

"You blinked twice before answering that."

Her jaw tightened.

"That means nothing."

"It means you're tired."

The word pressed somewhere beneath her sternum.

"I am efficient," she corrected.

He held her gaze.

"That's not the same thing."

Her phone buzzed again.

Three new emails.

Two from board members.

One from communications requesting an official statement "for the party line."

She inhaled slowly.

"I will handle this," she said.

"I know."

"Then why are you still here?"

He smiled slightly.

"Because you matter."

The words were simple.

Unadorned.

And entirely inconvenient.

She looked at him longer than necessary.

"That is not part of your consulting brief."

"No," he agreed. "It isn't."

The silence stretched.

Something unfamiliar moved between them—not flirtation, not quite tension.

Recognition.

She broke eye contact first.

"There will be an spotlight review tomorrow," she said. "You should prepare your recommendations."

"I already have."

"Of course you do."

He moved toward the door.

"Avery?"

"Yes."

"You didn't lose control out there."

"I know."

"You showed it."

The door closed behind him.

She stood alone in the quiet.

Showed it.

The phrase lingered.

She moved back to her desk and opened the clip again.

Watched the moment.

The pause.

The flicker.
The almost-smile.
She looked human.
Not fragile.
Not unstable.
Human.
Her father would have called it a misstep.
Perception is leverage, he used to say. You show cracks, you invite pressure.
She had lived by that doctrine.
Refined it.
Perfected it.
But today, when the nurse asked if she admitted they were exhausted, something in her had refused to deflect entirely.
She had answered.
And people had responded.
Her phone buzzed again.
A text from Natalie.
Natalie: Board member #3 says your comment was "refreshing."
Avery stared at the word.
Refreshing.
Not reckless.
Not unprofessional.
Refreshing.
Another buzz.
Miles: Don't overcorrect.
She frowned at the screen.
Avery: I don't overcorrect.
Three dots.
Miles: You do.
She almost smiled.
Avery: That's an interpretation.
Miles: It's a pattern.
She set the phone down.
Walked to the window.

The city stretched below her—moving, breathing, imperfect.

Her entire career had been built on controlled ascent.

Predictable output.

Measured tone.

Today, for half a second, she had let something unscripted slip through.

And the world had not collapsed.

If anything, it had leaned closer.

Her calendar reminder chimed.

Succession Evaluation: Preliminary Metrics Review – Tomorrow 8:00 a.m.

She stared at it.

Then back at the clip.

Then at her reflection in the glass.

"You cannot afford cracks," she murmured to herself.

But the conviction felt thinner than it had yesterday.

Her phone buzzed one last time.

Miles: For the record, caffeine is a morale strategy. not a sustainable one.

She let out a soft, reluctant laugh.

Avery: That's not funny.

Miles: It absolutely is.

She stared at the screen longer than necessary.

Then typed:

Avery: We discuss spotlight at 8:00 tomorrow.

Miles: I'll bring coffee.

She shook her head.

Put the phone down.

And for the first time since the clip began climbing view counts, she allowed herself a single, dangerous thought:

Maybe being seen wasn't the threat.

Maybe hiding was.

The thought unsettled her more than the trending counter ever could.

And tomorrow, when she sat across from the board to discuss "spotlight," she would have to decide which version of herself she intended to protect.

The flawless one.

Or the real one.

The microphone had been live.

And now, so was everything else.

Chapter 2: Optics

By 7:42 a.m., Avery had already reviewed the clip twelve times.

Not because she was spiraling.

Because she believed in data.

The view count had crossed 312,000 overnight.

The comments were still climbing.

Half praised her candor.

Half speculated that "executive humor" was code for institutional collapse.

The internet did not believe in moderation.

Natalie stood at the small conference table in Avery's office, armed with coffee and controlled panic.

"Board member number five used the phrase 'story vulnerability,'" Natalie said. "Which I believe is polite for 'this could go badly.'"

Avery adjusted the cuff of her blazer.

"Board member number five also once described a Wi-Fi outage as an existential threat. Context is important."

Natalie squinted at her.

"You're calm."

"I am prepared."

"That's not the same thing."

Avery did not dignify that with a response.

a knock on the door.

Not rushed.

Not hesitant.

Deliberate.

"Come in," she said.

Miles entered with two coffees balanced in one hand.

"Peace offering," he said.

"I did not request caffeine."

"You didn't need to."

He handed one to Natalie first.

Strategic.

Then he placed the second on Avery's desk.

"I said I'd bring coffee," he reminded her.

She glanced at it as if it were contraband.

"I do not want the spotlight of you being right."

"That ship sailed yesterday."

Natalie made a strangled sound that might have been a laugh and retreated toward the door.

"I'll wait outside," she said quickly. "Preferably somewhere without live microphones."

The door closed.

Silence settled.

Miles leaned against the wall, not taking a seat without invitation.

"You've built three contingency statements," he said.

She didn't look up from her tablet.

"Four."

"Overcorrection."

"Preparedness."

"Anxiety."

She looked up sharply.

"Efficiency."

He didn't argue.

He stepped closer and rested his hip against the edge of her desk.

"You're not in danger," he said.

"That is not the assessment I would use."

"Then what would you use?"

"Exposure."

He tilted his head.

"That's interesting."

"It's factual."

"You answered a nurse honestly."

"In front of a board chair."

"In front of staff."

She inhaled slowly.

"The board evaluates predictability."

"They evaluate leadership."

"And leadership is predictability."

"No," he said softly. "Leadership is credibility."

She met his gaze.

"And credibility comes from control."

He studied her.

"You believe that."

"Yes."

"Even when the control costs you?"

"That's irrelevant."

He straightened.

"Why?"

"Because the cost is mine."

The words landed harder than she intended.

Silence stretched.

"Is it?" he asked quietly.

She frowned.

"What does that mean?"

"It means the cost isn't only yours."

She blinked.

"Explain."

"You carry everything alone. That affects the people around you."

"I delegate."

"You isolate."

Her jaw tightened.

"That is not an accurate assessment."

"It is."

She stepped away from the desk.

"This conversation is not strategic."

"Not everything has to be strategic."

"Yes," she replied evenly. "It does."

At 8:00 a.m. sharp, the board assembled in the executive conference room.

Mahogany table.

Muted lighting.

Strategic neutrality.

Gerald Whitmore sat at the head, fingers laced.

"Avery," he began, "let's discuss spotlight."

Of course.

She folded her hands neatly in front of her.

"I anticipated we would."

A screen flickered to life, displaying the clip.

Again.

Her own voice filled the room.

If morale were measurable in caffeine intake...

The board members watched as if observing a specimen.

When the clip ended, Gerald cleared his throat.

"Unscripted."

"Yes."

" too candid."

"Possibly."

A murmur around the table.

Board member three leaned forward.

"However," she said carefully, "engagement metrics are unusually positive."

Avery blinked once.

Positive?

Board member five adjusted his glasses.

"Staff survey responses spiked overnight. Voluntary feedback increased."

Another pause.

Gerald looked at her.

"Can you explain why?"

She considered the room.

Every instinct told her to pivot.

To emphasize messaging discipline.

Instead, she heard her own voice from yesterday.

I admit that healthcare is demanding.

"I listened," she said simply.

Silence.

"You listened," Gerald repeated.

"Yes."

The nurse in the third row had not asked for policy.

She had asked for acknowledgment.

"I addressed workload realities without deflecting," Avery continued. "Staff do not need perfection. They need credibility."

Miles, seated two chairs down as an advisory observer, did not react.

But she felt it.

The shift.

Gerald leaned back slowly.

"And do you intend to continue in that... tone?"

Tone.

There it was again.

"I intend to lead authentically," she replied.

The room stilled.

It was a risk.

Small.

But real.

Board member three smiled faintly.

"Refreshing," she murmured.

The same word Natalie had texted.

Refreshing.

Not reckless.

Not unstable.

Refreshing.

Gerald nodded once.

"well," he said. "Proceed carefully."

Proceed carefully.

She almost laughed.

That was her entire packaged.

When the meeting adjourned, Avery walked back to her office with measured steps.

She did not hurry.

She did not exhale visibly.

She closed her door.

Then leaned back against it.

Her pulse was steady.

But something else wasn't.

A knock.

She opened the door before he could repeat it.

"You used the word authentically," Miles said.

"Yes."

"That's new."

"Is it?"

"Yes."

She moved past him into the hallway.

"I did not implode."

"No."

"I did not get disqualified."

"No."

"You were right about engagement metrics."

"I know."

She stopped walking.

"You knew?"

"I checked them last night."

"You didn't tell me."

"You weren't ready to hear it."

She stared at him.

"That is an extraordinary claim."

"It's accurate."

She narrowed her eyes slightly.

"You are confident."

"I am observant."

"That's not the same thing."

He smiled faintly.

"It often is."

They resumed walking.

Halfway down the corridor, she said quietly, "I do not isolate."

He didn't answer immediately.

Then:

"You didn't let anyone see you exhale after that meeting."

She blinked.

"I didn't need to."

"You did."

They stopped outside her office.

"You don't get to tell me what I need," she said.

His gaze softened.

"I don't want to."

"Then don't."

Silence hung between them.

Charged.

Not hostile.

close.

Too close.

"You mattered in there," he said quietly. "Not because you were perfect. Because you were real."

The word again.

Real.

She felt something flicker low in her chest.

Dangerous.

Unmeasured.

"I am always real," she said.

"No," he replied softly. "You're usually impenetrable."

The honesty struck deeper than criticism would have.

She looked at him longer than was strictly professional.

"This is a workplace," she said.

"Yes."

"And you are a consultant."

"Yes."

"And this dynamic remains within those parameters."

A faint smile curved his mouth.

"Of course."

"Good."

She turned to open her office door.

"Avery."

She paused.

"You don't have to carry it alone."

The phrase again.

Alone.

Her hand stilled on the door handle.

"I am not alone," she said.

"You don't let anyone stand next to you."

She entered her office without responding.

Closed the door.

And stood there, staring at the wood grain as if it held answers.

Her phone buzzed.

Natalie: Board member #3 said she'd follow you anywhere after that.

Avery stared at the message.

Follow.

Leadership wasn't about control.

It was about credibility.

And credibility, apparently, sometimes came from admitting the obvious.

Her phone buzzed again.

Miles: You didn't overcorrect.

She stared at the text.

Avery: That's not a victory.

Miles: It is.

She hesitated.

Avery: I cannot afford instability.

The response came quickly.

Miles: Authenticity isn't instability.

She stared at the words.

Her father's voice echoed faintly in memory.

Perception is leverage.

Show cracks, invite pressure.

But today, she had shown something else.

Not a crack.

A pulse.

And instead of pressure, the room had leaned closer.

She sat down at her desk and took a slow breath.

For the first time in a long time, the pressure felt different.

Less like something she had to outrun.

More like something she might be able to share.

Her phone buzzed again.

Miles: Lunch?

She stared at the single word.

That was not in her schedule.

That was not strategic.

That was not controlled.

Avery: I have metrics to review.

Three dots.

Miles: You also have a pulse.

She exhaled slowly.

Then, because she was still an executive and not a character in someone else's story, she opened the pediatrics deck and began rewriting the first slide.

Avery stared at the coffee longer than necessary.

Miles left. Natalie followed, still muttering about polls and soup.

Avery's throat tightened. She hated that she felt seen.

Miles's voice dropped slightly. "Your public image cracked. It didn't shatter. You're still you."

Avery lifted a brow. "Yes."

Miles stepped toward the door, then looked back at Avery. "One more thing."

Natalie nodded sharply. "Okay. Great. I'm going to go commit mild violence against the scheduling app. Avery, drink the coffee. Miles, keep being annoyingly correct."

Avery's chest tightened, irritated by the way that landed like something she wanted.

Miles's mouth curved faintly. "If you wobble, you look at me. Not for rescue. For reality."

"I won't," Avery said automatically.

Miles's gaze steadied. "Then you hold. And if you wobble -"

Avery swallowed. "And if they push."

Miles picked up his folder and paused. "I'll be in the conference room at nine. You'll walk in with the data, not the apology."

Avery didn't deny it.

Miles stood, smoothing his sleeves. "You don't hate the city. You hate being seen."

Avery's face went blank. "I hate this city."

Then Natalie's phone pinged again and she groaned. "Okay. New development. Someone made a poll. 'Would you trust Avery Sloan to run your life?' The options are 'Yes, she scares me' and 'Yes, she's hot.'"

Avery stared at him, the word boundary settling somewhere uncomfortable and necessary.

Miles's eyes held hers. "It's boundary-setting."

Avery exhaled, almost amused despite herself. "That's manipulative."

Natalie's grin sharpened. "Yes. Starve them."

Miles's smile was small. "You make them wait. You remind them your time is valuable."

Avery's eyes narrowed. "Which is."

Miles shook his head. "If you chase it, they'll assume fear. There's a third option."

Avery didn't respond. She set the phone down and looked at Miles. "If I ignore it, they'll assume guilt."

Her phone buzzed again. Another board member text. Another "Checking in." Another subtle probe.

Avery's throat tightened at the quiet certainty in his voice.

Miles's gaze softened. "You don't have to become someone else to survive this."

Avery inhaled slowly. "That was situational."

Natalie stared. "You literally went viral for joking."

Avery shot her a look. "I don't joke."

Natalie nodded. "Which means you can't joke. I know. Tragic."

Miles tapped his folder. "We control the internal narrative. You show up, you're prepared, and you refuse to be baited into either defensiveness or charm."

Avery's fingers tightened on the coffee cup. "How."

Miles leaned back slightly. "Here's the point. The internet is doing what it does: turning complexity into a story. We can't stop it. But we can keep it from steering the mission."

Natalie held up both hands. "I'm not saying anything. I'm just observing the ecosystem."

Avery shot her a look. "Natalie."

Natalie made a delighted sound. "Oh. Interesting. He knows your sick behavior."

Avery looked at him. "How would you know that."

Miles's mouth twitched. "You do when you're sick."

Avery's voice went flat. "I do not want soup."

Natalie scrolled. "One person said, 'She's grumpy but in a way that makes you want to bring her soup.'"

Miles's face stayed neutral. "They did."

Avery felt heat climb her neck. "They said that."

Natalie's expression tightened with solemnity. "I read all of them. Including the one that says you're 'obviously a secret softie' and the one that says Miles has 'golden retriever energy' and the one that says you should 'kiss already.'"

Avery stared. "You read them."

Natalie pushed the door open wider and walked in fully, holding her own phone like it was evidence. "I volunteer as tribute. I have already suffered so you don't have to."

Miles didn't flinch. "Not publicly. Internally. You need to know what narrative you're walking into."

Avery's eyes narrowed. "No."

"One more thing," Miles said, voice calm. "We should address the comments."

She took the coffee anyway. It was the exact roast she liked, which meant either Natalie had told him or he had paid attention. Both options were unacceptable.

Avery's pulse ticked. She hated how easily he read the crack beneath her armor.

Miles looked at her. "You do. You just don't like it when people notice."

Avery's jaw tightened. "I don't do human language."

"Good," Miles said. "Then we frame it in human language. Not board language. Not PR language. Human."

Avery kept her face neutral. "We already have the data."

Natalie, still hovering in the doorway, sighed dreamily. "He's such a problem. I hate that he's right."

Miles's eyes flicked to her screen. "Like the real story: pediatric outcomes, staffing retention, the expansion timeline. Make the clip irrelevant by making the substance irresistible."

Avery's gaze sharpened. "Like what."

Miles nodded, unbothered. "They won't. So we give them something else to chew on."

Instead she said, "I want the board to stop asking if I'm 'okay.'"

I want it to look like yesterday, Avery thought. Before the microphone. Before the internet decided I was a character.

"Okay," Miles said, opening his folder. "Tell me what you want the day to look like."

Miles pulled a chair closer without asking and sat like he belonged there. He didn't. The audacity was irritating. Unfortunately, the audacity was also competent.

Avery's eyes narrowed. "They already are."

Miles set the coffee on the edge of Avery's desk. "Due diligence would be confirming the board members aren't about to weaponize a video clip into an existential crisis."

Avery looked up, deadpan. "It's called due diligence."

Natalie opened the door enough to stick her head in. "Says the woman who's currently running sentiment analysis on her own face."

Avery clicked her trackpad with deliberate calm. "Natalie has an unhealthy relationship with drama."

Miles's mouth twitched. "That too."

From the corner, Natalie's voice drifted in from behind Avery's door like a stage whisper. "I did not. I said she was about to do something decisive and emotionally repressed."

"Because your assistant told me you were about to do something heroic and ill-advised."

Avery didn't look up from her laptop. "Then why are you in my office."

"I'm not here to interfere," he said, which was exactly what a person interfering would say.

At 8:11 a.m., Miles Carter appeared in her doorway without knocking, holding a paper cup of coffee like a peace offering and a folder like a threat.

The corner of her mouth betrayed her.

Avery: Thirty minutes.

Miles: I'll take it.

She set the phone down.

And for the first time since the microphone had stayed live, she allowed herself to make a decision that wasn't about spotlight.

It was about choice.

Which, she was beginning to realize, might be far more destabilizing than perfection ever was.

Chapter 3: Lunch

Avery did not do spontaneous.

She did scheduled. She did structured. She did optimized.

She did not do "Lunch?"

And yet at 12:03 p.m., she found herself standing in the hospital lobby beside Miles Carter while Natalie stared at her like she'd witnessed a solar eclipse.

"You're... leaving?" Natalie asked cautiously.

"For thirty minutes."

Natalie blinked. "Voluntarily?"

Avery straightened the cuff of her blazer. "I am capable of leaving a building."

"Historically debatable."

Miles held the lobby door open. "We'll return her intact."

Natalie narrowed her eyes. "That is not the phrasing I wanted."

Avery shot her assistant a look that meant we will discuss this later, then stepped outside.

The air was brisk. Clean. Unfiltered by hospital ventilation systems and quiet executive pressure.

She hadn't realized how stale the air inside had felt.

"Where are we going?" she asked.

"There's a café three blocks down," Miles replied. "Actual food. Requires chewing."

"That seems unnecessarily physical."

"It builds character."

"I have character."

"You have control."

She exhaled.

He did this on purpose.

They walked side by side down the sidewalk. Not touching. Not crowding. close enough to register each other's presence.

People passed them without recognition. No one pointed. No one whispered.

She wasn't "trending" here.

She was another woman in a navy blazer walking with a man who looked annoyingly calm about everything.

"This is reckless," she said.

"Lunch?"

"Yes."

"It's noon."

"It's unscheduled."

"That's not the same as reckless."

She stopped at the crosswalk, turning toward him.

"Do you deliberately destabilize me?"

He didn't hesitate.

"Yes."

The honesty caught her off guard.

"That is not reassuring."

"I don't mean in a harmful way."

"Destabilization is inherently harmful."

"Not when the structure is too rigid."

The light changed.

They crossed.

She walked a half-step ahead of him now.

"I am not rigid."

"You plan your breathing."

"I optimize my breathing."

He laughed softly.

"That's not a normal sentence."

"Define normal."

"Unmeasured."

"I do not aspire to unmeasured."

"Why?"

"Because unmeasured is unpredictable."

"And predictable is safe?"

"Yes."

He studied her profile as they walked.

"And safe is fulfilling?"

She didn't answer.

The café was narrow, warm, filled with the smell of roasted coffee and bread that had known an oven.

Avery hesitated at the door.

He noticed.

"You don't like not knowing what the seating layout looks like," he said.

"I prefer familiarity."

"You've never been here?"

"No."

"Good."

She narrowed her eyes slightly.

"That was not a compliment."

"It was."

They stepped inside.

The place was small enough that proximity was unavoidable. Wooden tables. Low lighting. A chalkboard menu written in enthusiastic handwriting.

No one bowed. No one evaluated. No one cared who she was.

She didn't realize how much she needed that until it happened.

They ordered.

He chose without hesitation.

She studied the menu like it was a merger document.

"You don't trust menus," he observed.

"I trust information."

"It's a sandwich."

"It's an unknown sandwich."

He smiled faintly. "You're exhausting."

"I am thorough."

"That's not what I meant."

They sat near the window.

She removed her blazer, draped it neatly over the chair.

He noticed.

"You're relaxing," he said.

"I removed a layer."

"That counts."

She folded her hands on the table.

"You were calm in the board meeting," she said.

"I wasn't the one being evaluated."

"You always look calm."

"I'm not always calm."

She raised an eyebrow.

"When are you not calm?"

"When someone I respect is carrying more than they should."

The words landed quietly.

She looked out the window.

"I am not carrying more than I should."

"You are."

"That is an assertion."

"It's an observation."

"You observe a great deal."

"It's part of my job."

"No," she said softly. "It's not."

Their food arrived.

He pushed her plate toward her gently.

"You need this."

"I do not require monitoring."

"I'm not monitoring."

"You are."

"I'm noticing."

The distinction again.

She picked up the sandwich.

Took a bite.

Paused.

"See?" he said.

"It's adequate."

He laughed.

"That's the most enthusiastic praise you've given anything all day."

She swallowed.

"You enjoyed destabilizing me earlier."

"I enjoyed watching you choose not to overcorrect."

"That is not destabilization."

"It is for you."

She set the sandwich down.

"Do you believe I am fragile?"

"No."

"Then what?"

"Human."

The word again.

It threaded through everything.

"You use that word strategically," she said.

"No."

"Yes."

"It bothers you."

"It's imprecise."

"It's accurate."

She leaned back in her chair.

"You recommended me."

"Yes."

"Why?"

He didn't hesitate.

"You ask better questions than anyone in the room."

"That is a skill."

"It's a value."

She studied him carefully.

"And you don't think the board will penalize authenticity?"

"They might."

"That's not comforting."

"You didn't hire me to comfort you."

"No," she agreed. "I hired you to optimize perception."

"And perception shifted."

"Because of a caffeine joke."

"Because you listened."

Silence settled between them.

The café noise hummed softly around them.

For the first time in days, she wasn't bracing for impact.

She was just... sitting.

"You don't like being seen," he said quietly.

"I am seen constantly."

"No," he corrected gently. "You are evaluated."

Her chest tightened slightly.

"That is part of leadership."

"Not all of it."

She looked at him steadily.

"What do you think leadership is?"

He didn't look away.

"It's choosing not to hide when it would be easier."

The words lodged somewhere uncomfortable.

"I do not hide."

"You armor."

"That is different."

"Yes," he said softly. "It is."

She felt it then.

Not attraction exactly.

But awareness.

Of him. Of herself. Of the space between them.

"You're certain," she said.

"About what?"

"About me."

"I pay attention."

"That's dangerous."

"Why?"

"Because you might be wrong."

He smiled slightly.

"Or you might be."
The air shifted.
Not heavy.
charged.
She reached for her water, buying a second.
"You leave in twenty-seven days," she said.
"Twenty-six."
She frowned.
"You're counting?"
"Yes."
"Why?"
"Because this matters."
Her pulse flickered.
"That is not professional language."
"No," he agreed. "It isn't."
She looked down at her plate.
"You are a consultant."
"Yes."
"And this remains within those parameters."
"For now."
The words were quiet.
Measured.
But not dismissive.
She felt something unfamiliar bloom low in her chest.
Anticipation.
Unwelcome.
Unscheduled.
She stood abruptly.
"We should return."
"You've eaten half."
"That is sufficient."
He rose slowly.
"You're running."
"I am managing time."
"You're avoiding something."
"I am not."

He stepped closer—not touching, near enough that she could feel the warmth of him.

"You don't know how to let someone stand beside you without calculating the risk," he said.

"That is not true."

"It is."

Her breath hitched, slightly.

"That is an extraordinary assumption."

"It's not an assumption."

Silence stretched between them.

Too close.

Too aware.

The café noise blurred.

She took a step back.

"This is inappropriate."

"No," he said gently. "It's honest."

Her jaw tightened.

"I do not have space for this."

"For what?"

"For variables."

His expression softened.

"I'm not a variable."

"You are."

"I'm a choice."

The distinction hit harder than she expected.

Choice.

She was excellent at strategy. At inevitability. At building outcomes.

Choice was different.

Choice was personal.

She turned toward the door.

"You are dangerously calm," she said.

"I'm not calm."

"No?"

"I'm trying hard not to move closer."

Her breath stalled.

For a split second, she imagined what that would look like.
Then she opened the door and stepped outside.
Cold air hit her face.
She walked back toward the hospital without looking at him.
He matched her pace.
Not pushing. Not retreating.
there.
At the entrance, she paused.
"You destabilize me," she said quietly.
"I know."
"That is not strategic."
"Maybe not."
She met his eyes.
"But it's real."
The word lingered between them like something newly alive.
She stepped inside the building.
Back into fluorescent lighting and structured air.
Miles laughed softly, and Avery hated how much she liked the sound.
Natalie called back, delighted, "It's called due diligence."
Avery groaned. "Natalie."
Natalie, from down the hall, shouted, "I heard that. I'm documenting the growth."
Avery rolled her eyes, but she couldn't stop the small curve of her mouth.
Miles's smile widened, enough to feel dangerous. "Now who's negotiating outcomes."
Avery's cheeks warmed. "Maybe fries."
Miles raised a brow. "Next time."
Avery cleared her throat. "Next time..."
Miles was watching her, steady.
But when she reached her office door, she paused and looked back at him.
Avery stepped out first, the old rhythm returning.
The elevator chimed and opened onto the executive floor.
Avery's pulse ticked. She hadn't.

Miles's voice dropped. "And you didn't look at your phone once."

Avery stared at the elevator numbers like they could save her from this conversation. "It was thirty minutes."

Miles smiled. "About you leaving the building voluntarily."

Avery's lips twitched, then she sighed, as if giving in to something inconvenient. "You're going to be insufferable about this, aren't you."

Miles shrugged slightly. "It might be a hobby."

Avery's chest tightened. "That's not your job."

Miles's eyes softened. "I was trying to make you breathe."

Avery shot him a look. "Were you."

Miles glanced at her. "Is that what you think I was doing."

Avery nodded once. "No one tried to impress anyone."

Miles's mouth curved faintly. "Lunch."

Avery paused. Then, because the elevator was a sealed box and because she was tired of pretending, she said, "It was nice."

Miles tilted his head. "Are you."

Avery exhaled. "I'm fine."

"You okay," he asked quietly.

Miles stood beside her, close enough that his shoulder brushed hers when the elevator shifted. He didn't move away.

Avery stared at the mirrored wall like it had suddenly become an emotional liability.

The elevator doors closed.

The resident laughed and vanished down the hall.

Natalie gasped. "How dare you."

The resident stepped out to let them in. "Also, please tell whoever runs comms not to make us do TikToks."

"Thank you," Avery managed.

Avery's throat tightened unexpectedly.

The resident shrugged. "My mom sent it to me. She hates hospitals. She said you made her laugh."

Avery blinked.

Then a resident in scrubs, no older than twenty-five, grinned and said, "Hey. Nice joke at the press thing."

Avery's spine stiffened automatically.

Every head turned. Not because of her title. Because of the clip. The internet had leaked into the building like a draft.

They reached the elevators. Avery pressed the button. The doors opened to reveal a packed car full of staff.

Miles's eyes were warm. "It's a little funny."

Avery glared. "That's not funny."

Miles coughed a laugh.

Natalie shrugged. "Because you have a face that says 'I could fire God.'"

Avery went still. "Why."

Natalie held up her phone. "I am not starting. The internet is starting. Someone posted a meme of you titled 'When the CEO says no' and it has seven million views."

Avery shot her a look. "Do not start."

Natalie blinked. "Miracles."

"She fed herself," Miles said.

Natalie narrowed her eyes at Miles. "Did you feed her."

"Thirty minutes," Avery said, as if time itself had been the mission.

She looked them over. "You're alive."

Back in the lobby, Natalie was waiting like a disappointed parent at pickup.

But something in her chest stayed warm anyway, like she'd tucked the soup in there for later.

They left. Outside, the hospital rose in the distance like a responsibility Avery usually carried alone.

Miles glanced at his watch. "We should go. Before Natalie sends a search party."

Avery felt her mouth curve again, small and involuntary, like stepping onto ice that might hold.

"Exactly," Miles said. "Low stakes. High discomfort."

Avery blinked. "Like lunch."

Miles's voice softened. "Then we practice. In small, inconvenient ways."

She wanted to say she didn't need anyone. That needing was weakness. Instead she said, quieter than she intended, "I don't know how to do that."

Avery's chest tightened.

"You were good in that room yesterday," Miles said. "But you don't have to be alone in it."

Avery waited, wary.

"Good," Miles said. "Then I'll just say one thing."

Avery's mouth tightened. "This is lunch, not therapy."

Miles held her gaze. "Your body thinks it does."

"My life doesn't end."

Halfway through, Miles asked, "Do you always run like your life ends if you stop."

Their food arrived, interrupting the moment like mercy. They ate. It was absurd how normal it felt, how the soup smelled like something from childhood Avery hadn't had time to remember.

Miles didn't push. He said, quietly, "You don't have to win lunch."

Avery's breath caught.

"Control," Miles said softly.

Avery stared at him. "Win what."

Miles nodded. "Yes. You just do it like you're trying to win."

Avery's jaw tightened. "So what. Everyone copes."

"It was coping," Miles said gently.

Avery's cheeks warmed. "That was accidental."

"You reorganized your pens while we walked here," Miles said. "In your pocket. I watched you do it."

"I do not."

Miles continued, "But mostly you tell on yourself."

Avery narrowed her eyes.

Miles smiled faintly. "Some of it."

Avery froze. "Natalie told you."

Miles's voice stayed calm. "I know what you do when you're stressed."

"You don't know me," she said automatically.

Avery's throat tightened. She hated the accuracy.

"Good," Miles said. "Boundaries are healthy. Walls just keep you lonely."

"It's a boundary."

Miles leaned forward slightly. "No questions is a wall."

She rolled her eyes. "Fine. People are dramatic."

Miles stared at her. "Avery."

"I'm not intimidating."

"At lunch," he asked, amused, "or at being around someone who isn't intimidated by you."

Avery exhaled. "I'm not good at this."

Miles's mouth twitched. "That's not how conversations work."

"No questions," Avery added.

"Thirty," Miles agreed.

When the server left, Avery tapped the edge of the menu. "So. Thirty minutes."

They ordered. Miles asked for soup and a sandwich. Avery ordered a salad because it was safe, and because she refused to admit she wanted fries out of spite.

Avery raised a brow. "Spreadsheets are useful."

"You were technically human," Miles said. "Emotionally, you were a spreadsheet."

"I was human five minutes ago."

"The part of you that's human."

Avery's expression went neutral. "There what is."

Miles's gaze softened. "There it is."

Avery huffed a laugh, then immediately felt betrayed by her own body for making that sound.

Miles leaned back slightly. "I've lived a full life."

Avery lifted her eyes. "You talk like you've been betrayed by potatoes."

"You're right. Sometimes it's disappointment."

Avery's mouth twitched. "Fries are not a guarantee."

"The outcome is usually fries," Miles said.

"Menus are contracts," Avery said. "You agree to a price in exchange for an outcome."

Miles watched her with faint amusement. "You're reading it like it's a contract."

Avery opened the menu and stared at it as if it might contain a hidden clause.

Miles said yes. Avery said yes. The server vanished again like a magician who only specialized in hydration.

A server appeared, cheerful. "Water?"

They slid into a booth. Miles took the seat across from her, not beside, like he understood she needed space even when she didn't want it.

Avery felt her shoulders drop half an inch without permission.

Inside, no one recognized her. The room was full of regular people doing regular lunch things: laughing too loudly, arguing about sandwich choices, eating like they weren't on a deadline.

"Then we'll be fast," Miles said, and held the door open like he wasn't aware simple gestures could be dangerous.

"I want it to be fast," she said, which was the closest she could get to admitting she wanted it at all.

No, Avery thought. But wanting something and allowing it were different sports.

Miles glanced at the modest awning. "Do you want it to be."

Avery paused on the sidewalk, suspicious. "This isn't a power lunch."

It was a small corner place with worn wood tables and a chalkboard that advertised soup with the confidence of someone who had never been online.

The restaurant Miles chose was not trendy. No neon. No influencer lighting. No menu described as a "curated experience."

But something had shifted.

Not externally.

Not visibly.

Internally.

And as she walked toward the elevators, she realized something deeply inconvenient:

For the first time in years, she wasn't calculating how to control the next moment.

She was wondering what she might choose instead.

Chapter 4: The Shadow

Avery told herself lunch was a one-time lapse.

A controlled deviation.

A strategic anomaly.

She told herself this while standing in the elevator, watching the floors tick upward, and absolutely not thinking about the way Miles had said, I'm trying hard not to move closer.

She also told herself this while adjusting the fall of her blazer as if fabric could restore equilibrium.

The elevator doors opened.

Natalie was already waiting.

Natalie's expression was neutral in the same way a cat is neutral right before it knocks something expensive off a counter.

"You're back," Natalie said.

"Yes."

"In one piece."

"Yes."

Natalie's eyes flicked to Avery's hands. "You brought nothing."

"I brought myself."

Natalie's smile widened. "You didn't bring coffee."

"I did not purchase coffee."

Natalie leaned forward slightly. "Did he buy you coffee?"

Avery kept walking. "I do not discuss coffee procurement."

"That's a yes."

"It is not a yes."

Natalie trailed her down the hall like a determined journalist. "You were gone thirty-eight minutes."

"It was thirty."

"It was thirty-eight."

"That is within acceptable variance."

Natalie gasped. "You used the phrase acceptable variance about lunch."

Avery stopped outside her office and turned. "Natalie."

Natalie snapped to attention immediately. "Yes?"

"Do not make this weird."

Natalie blinked, then looked delighted. "I was going to say the same thing."

Avery opened the door, stepped inside, and closed it firmly.

Natalie's voice floated through the wood.

"For the record, you looked less like a robotic competence machine when you came back!"

Avery stared at her desk.

Robotic competence machine.

She would have objected, but it was inconveniently accurate.

She sat down.

Opened her laptop.

Pulled up the afternoon agenda.

And discovered she had two new calendar invites.

Both marked urgent.

Both titled with words that made her temples ache.

spotlight the party line: Messaging DisciplineSite Walk-through: PR Visibility Sweep

She exhaled slowly.

Her phone buzzed.

A text from Gerald Whitmore.

Gerald: Communications wants a refreshed media posture memo by end of day. Carter will assist.

Assist.

That word implied choices she did not approve.

Her office door opened.

Miles stepped in without knocking, like this had already been negotiated.

He held a folder.

And a coffee.

Of course.

He placed the coffee on her desk gently.

"I didn't ask," she said.

"You didn't have to."

"That's not an excuse."

"It's not," he agreed. "It's a morale strategy."

She stared at the cup.

Natalie had been right. This was becoming a motif.

"If you keep doing that," she said carefully, "people will assume... things."

Miles's expression shifted subtly. "What things?"

Avery looked at the folder. "We have work."

"Yes," he said. "We do."

He opened the folder and slid out a printed document.

Media Posture: Human Credibility Without Loss of Authority

Avery read the title once, then looked up.

"That's not a memo. That's a philosophy essay."

"It's a strategy," he corrected.

She scanned the first paragraph and immediately saw the problem.

It was good.

Worse, it was accurate.

"You want me to lean into authenticity," she said.

"I want you to lean into credibility," he replied.

"That sounds like rebranding exhaustion."

"No," he said quietly. "It's letting people see you breathe."

"I do breathe."

"You micro-breathe."

She looked up sharply.

"Are you always this committed to my respiratory patterns?"

"Only because they're alarming."

She stared at him.

Then she did something she almost never did.

She laughed.

It was brief.

But real.

Miles's mouth curved slightly, like he'd witnessed a rare and valuable event.

"Don't," she warned.

"Don't what?"

"Look pleased."

"I can't help it."

"That's dangerous."

He leaned lightly against the chair across from her desk. "Why?"

"Because you'll start expecting it."

"I don't expect anything from you," he said. "I notice."

That word again.

Notice.

It didn't feel like evaluation.

It felt like proximity.

She refocused on the memo. "We have a site walkthrough."

"Yes."

"Communications will be there."

"Yes."

"Which means cameras."

"Yes."

She looked up. "And you'll be there."

"Yes."

"That is unnecessary."

Miles shrugged. "Gerald requested it."

Avery's jaw tightened.

Of course he did.

Because the board loved layers of oversight disguised as collaboration.

"Fine," she said. "But we keep this clean."

Miles's eyebrows lifted slightly. "Clean?"

"Professional. Neutral. Controlled."

"Ah," he said, voice faintly amused. "We're back to controlled."

"We never left."

He didn't respond immediately.

Then: "You did. For thirty-eight minutes."

Avery's eyes narrowed. "Natalie told you."

"No," he said. "I have a clock."

She glared.

He smiled.

It was not a wide smile.

It was worse.

It was the small, private kind.

Avery hated it.

Mostly because she did not hate it.

The pediatric wing expansion site was on the east side of the campus, fenced off behind temporary barricades and optimism. Hard hats waited in a neat row like a staged photo op.

Communications director Marla Greene greeted Avery with a bright smile that belonged in a brochure.

"Avery! So glad you're here. We're doing a quick visibility sweep, and then we'll grab a few images for internal comms."

Avery accepted a hard hat without comment. She did not enjoy being photographed in protective gear. It made her look... approachable.

Which was apparently the goal now.

Marla's gaze flicked to Miles. "And you are?"

"Miles Carter," he said smoothly. "Consulting."

Marla's smile widened. "Ah. The calm one."

Avery glanced at him.

He didn't react.

Of course he didn't.

They walked along the perimeter of the construction zone, stepping carefully over temporary plywood paths. The air smelled like sawdust and fresh paint.

Avery's heels were not designed for this terrain.

Miles noticed immediately.

He didn't comment.

He simply slowed his stride by a fraction so she wouldn't have to choose between dignity and speed.

It was subtle.

It was also infuriating.

Because it felt like care.

And care was harder to manage than criticism.

Marla gestured toward a section of framing. "This will be the new family waiting area. We're thinking a donor plaque wall right here."

Avery nodded. "Good. We'll need to keep sightlines open."

Marla smiled brightly. "And we'll want some photos of you in the space. Maybe you looking thoughtfully at the plans."

Avery kept her expression neutral. "Thoughtfully."

Miles's voice drifted in. "She's good at thoughtful."

Avery's head turned slightly. "Do not narrate me."

"I'm assessing tone," he replied.

Marla laughed. "You two have great energy."

Avery's stomach tightened.

Energy.

That was not the packaged.

Miles said smoothly, "We're aligned on priorities."

Marla beamed. "Love that."

Avery mentally drafted a resignation letter.

Halfway through the walkthrough, a construction manager led them into an unfinished corridor. Exposed wiring. Bare studs. The space echoed with their footsteps.

Marla hung back to take photos.

Avery stepped carefully around a coil of cable.

Her heel caught.

Not dramatically.

enough for her balance to shift.

For one humiliating half-second, she teetered.

Miles's hand shot out instinctively and caught her elbow.

Warm.

Firm.

Supportive.

Avery froze.

Miles froze.

Marla's camera shutter clicked.

Avery's breath stalled.

Miles released her immediately as if contact had rules.

"You're fine," he said quietly.

"I am fine," she snapped, too quickly.

Marla looked delighted. "That was... adorable."

Avery turned. "It was not adorable."

Marla lifted her hands. "Sorry. Sorry. I meant... human."

The word again.

Human.

Avery's pulse did something unhelpful.

Miles's expression was unreadable, but his ears were faintly pink.

Avery had never noticed his ears before.

She hated that she was noticing now.

They continued walking.

The corridor narrowed.

The air shifted.

Cooler.

A draft moved through the unfinished space like a sigh.

Then the lights flickered.

Once.

Twice.

And went out.

The corridor dropped into dim emergency lighting. Red EXIT signs glowed faintly.

Marla's voice echoed from behind. "Oh. That's... probably normal, right?"

The construction manager cursed softly under his breath and fumbled for his radio.

"Power blip," he muttered. "Happens sometimes. Elevator's down too, looks like."

Avery's head snapped up. "Elevator?"

"We'll take the service stairs," the manager said, already moving. "Everyone stay close."

Marla hesitated. "Are we... safe?"

"Yes," the manager said. "annoying."

Avery watched him disappear into the dim light, then looked toward the direction he'd indicated.

The service stairwell was at the end of the corridor.

Which meant walking through a dark unfinished hallway full of cables and exposed framing.

Avery did not like dark unfinished hallways.

Avery also did not like that her heart had started beating faster.

"Not a crisis," Miles murmured beside her.

She shot him a look. "Do not."

He held up his hands slightly. "I won't."

Marla called, "Avery, can you stand right there for a photo with the red exit sign behind you? It's sort of dramatic."

Avery stared at her. "No."

"But it's good spotlight," Marla insisted. "Leadership in the face of adversity."

Avery's voice sharpened. "The adversity is a power outage."

Marla pouted.

Miles leaned closer, voice low. "If you stand under that sign, you'll look like you're auditioning for a corporate thriller."

Avery's eyes narrowed. "Thank you."

"You're welcome."

They started toward the stairwell.

The emergency lighting cast everyone in slightly sinister shadows.

Marla hung back, still taking photos.

Avery's heel clicked on the plywood path, echoing.

She hated how loud it sounded.

She hated how aware she was of Miles beside her.

Not in front.

Beside.

She kept her gaze forward.

"Are you afraid of the dark?" Miles asked quietly.

"No."

"Are you afraid of unfinished spaces?"

"No."

"Are you afraid of losing control?"

Avery stopped walking.

Miles stopped too.

The emergency lighting made his face look sharper, his eyes darker.

"No," she said.

He waited.

The silence stretched.

Then she said, more quietly, "I don't enjoy unpredictability."

"That's more honest."

She exhaled. "Stop coaxing truth out of me like I'm a nervous witness."

He smiled faintly. "You're not nervous."

"Correct."

"And you're not a witness," he said. "You're a leader."

"That doesn't help."

"It does."

"Why?"

"Because leaders can admit when something is inconvenient."

Avery's jaw tightened. "This is inconvenient."

He nodded once, as if satisfied.

They reached the stairwell door.

Miles opened it and stepped aside.

"After you," he said.

Avery hesitated for a fraction of a second.

Then stepped in.

The stairwell was narrow. Concrete. Bare. Lit by dim emergency bulbs.

Not claustrophobic.

Just... close.

Marla came in behind them, breathing too loudly.

"Okay," she said, trying for cheerful. "We're fine. This is fine."

Avery began descending.

The stairs were steep.

Her heels clicked.

Miles descended one step behind her, close enough that she could feel his presence like heat.

"Do you always wear heels to construction sites?" he asked softly.

"No."

"Do you always pretend you're fine when you're not?"

Avery's grip tightened on the handrail. "I am fine."

"Sure."

She shot him a look over her shoulder.

He was smiling.

Not smug.

Amused.

"Stop," she whispered.

"I didn't do anything."

"You're enjoying this."

"Maybe."

"That's not strategic."

"No," he agreed. "It's human."

She glared at the stairwell wall, as if concrete could offer guidance.

They reached the landing.

Marla stopped and fanned herself. "This is unexpectedly intense."

Avery said, "It's stairs."

Marla pointed at Miles. "He's not even breathing hard."

Miles replied smoothly, "I'm micro-breathing."

Avery's head snapped toward him.

Marla burst out laughing.

Avery did not.

Avery wanted to.

Which was worse.

They continued downward.

When they finally emerged onto the ground floor, the power was still out in half the building.

Avery checked her watch.

They were ten minutes behind schedule.

Which meant everything else would compress.

Which meant her day would become a math problem.

Marla said brightly, "Well! That was exciting."

"It was stairs," Avery repeated.

Marla checked her phone, then frowned. "Oh no."

Avery's stomach tightened. "What."

Marla held up her screen.

The photo.

The one where Miles caught Avery's elbow.

It was already in the internal comms Slack channel.

And someone had added a caption.

"Our COO getting support from the mysterious consultant"

reactions.

Many reactions.

Too many reactions.

Avery stared at the screen as if staring hard enough could delete it.

Miles leaned in slightly to see.

His expression didn't change.

But his voice went quieter.

"That's... fast."

Avery's pulse spiked.

"That is unacceptable," she said tightly.

Marla looked panicked. "I didn't post it! Someone must have grabbed it from my camera roll when I AirDropped the site shots."

Avery's jaw tightened. "We need that removed."

Marla nodded rapidly. "Yes. Yes. Of course. I'll—"

Natalie's voice cut through from behind them, breathless.

"Avery."

Avery turned.

Natalie held up her phone with the sort of dread usually reserved for medical test results.

"It's not internal," Natalie said.

Avery's stomach dropped.

"What do you mean."

Natalie swallowed.

"Someone posted it on Midtown Pulse."

Avery stared at her.

Midtown Pulse was a local gossip account that specialized in "executive sightings" and "hospital drama."

It was not major press.

It was worse.

Because it was shameless.

Natalie held up the screen.

There it was.

Avery. Miles. The hand on her elbow.

A caption beneath it:

"St. Catherine's COO spotted getting 'support' from consultant Miles Carter after viral town hall. New power couple?"

Avery's vision narrowed.

"Power couple," she repeated flatly.

Miles's voice was calm beside her. "This is what happens when a microphone stays live."

Avery turned slowly toward him.

Her expression was controlled.

Her tone was not.

"This," she said, "is exactly why I do not do unscheduled."

Miles didn't flinch.

Natalie looked like she might faint.

Marla looked like she might resign.

Avery inhaled slowly, forcing her pulse back into compliance.

Then her phone buzzed.

A new text.

From Gerald Whitmore.

Gerald: Come to my office. Now. Bring Carter.

Avery stared at the message.

Now.

Bring Carter.

She lifted her eyes.

Miles was already watching her, steady and unreadable.

"What," she asked tightly, "did we walk into."

Miles's gaze held hers.

"spotlight," he said quietly. "But louder."

Avery's heart beat once, hard.

Then she turned toward the main building entrance.

"Fine," she said. "Let's go discuss spotlight."

And as she walked, she realized something deeply inconvenient.

The microphone had stayed live.

Now the entire city felt like it was listening.

Chapter 5: The Soft Spot

The studio lights were not bright.

They were interrogative.

Avery decided this at 8:37 a.m., seated upright in a low velvet chair that had clearly been selected for aesthetic rather than spinal integrity. The greenroom smelled faintly of citrus cleaner and ambition. A wall-mounted screen replayed a teaser clip of the segment she was about to walk into.

"Leadership Under Pressure."

She would have preferred "Competent Executive Continues Being Competent," but apparently that did not test well.

Miles stood near the coffee station, sleeves rolled, speaking quietly with the anchor. He wasn't leaning in. He wasn't performing. He looked... comfortable.

That irritated her.

"You're charming them," she said as she crossed the room.

Miles glanced at her. "I'm assessing tone."

"That looked suspiciously like charming."

"Charm," he said mildly, "is a tone."

The anchor laughed. "He's good at it."

Avery offered a tight smile. "I'm sure he is."

Miles's mouth twitched. He enjoyed this. Not the spotlight. The calibration.

He handed her a cup of water. "You're steady."

"I'm vertical," she replied. "That's sufficient."

"You're more than vertical."

She did not dignify that with a response.

A production assistant appeared at the door. "Thirty seconds."

Avery stood. Adjusted her blazer. Smoothed a nonexistent wrinkle. She did not feel nervous. She felt alert. Focused. Precision always felt like this.

"Remember," Miles said quietly, stepping closer but not touching, "don't answer the headline. Answer the room."

She met his eyes.

"I don't answer rooms."

"You did Friday."

She held his gaze a second longer than necessary.

Then she walked onto the set.

The lights hit first.

Then the sound.

Then the awareness that no podium, no desk, no shield—two chairs angled toward each other and a camera that seemed to blink expectantly.

The anchor smiled warmly. "Avery Sloan, thank you for being here."

"Thank you for having me."

They began predictably: billing corrections, compliance review, internal safeguards.

Avery answered cleanly. Efficiently. She did not rush. She did not ramble.

Midway through, the anchor leaned in slightly.

"The viral clip last week—did it rattle you?"

There it was.

Not accusatory. Not hostile. Curious.

Avery considered the question.

"Yes," she said.

The word hung there.

The anchor blinked, clearly not expecting it.

"Yes?" she prompted.

"It ruffled me," Avery clarified. "Not because of the speculation. Because of what it suggested. That one moment of fatigue could outweigh years of stability."

"That's a lot of pressure."

"It's leadership."

"People are rooting for you," the anchor said gently. "You know that, right?"

There it was again.

You.

Not the hospital. Not the board.

You.

Avery felt the reflex to pivot.

I hope they're rooting for the organization.

She could feel the sentence forming.

Instead, she inhaled slowly.

"I hope they're rooting for clarity," she said. "And for a leadership culture that allows people to be both strong and human."

The word slipped out before she could over-engineer it.

Human.

The anchor smiled. "And are you human, Avery?"

a flicker of amusement in that.

"Yes," she said evenly. "Though I try not to advertise it too loudly."

The audience chuckled.

It was small. But real.

And for a brief, disorienting second, she felt it—not scrutiny.

Connection.

Back in the hallway afterward, Miles fell into step beside her.

"You said yes," he observed.

"Yes to what?"

"To being rattled."

"I contextualized it."

"You admitted it."

She exhaled. "It was strategic."

He stopped walking.

She took two more steps before noticing and turned back.

"Was it?" he asked quietly.

She opened her mouth.

Closed it.

"Everything is strategic," she said finally.

"Not everything."

"It should be."

His expression didn't change.

"You're good at absorbing impact," he said. "You're less good at letting anyone see it."

"I don't see the benefit."

"The benefit is you don't have to carry it alone."

She resumed walking. "I am not alone."

"No," he agreed softly. "You behave like you are."

Back at the hospital, the executive floor felt almost tranquil in contrast to the studio's artificial brightness.

Natalie intercepted her near the elevators.

"You were phenomenal," she said, eyes wide. "The board chair already emailed."

"That was fast."

"He used the word 'composed.' Twice."

Avery nodded. "Good."

Natalie hesitated. "Also... this came."

She handed over a small cream envelope.

Handwritten.

From the nursing staff.

Avery raised an eyebrow.

Natalie smiled knowingly. "I didn't open it."

"Thank you."

Once inside her office, Avery closed the door and sat down.

She opened the envelope carefully.

Inside was a card, filled edge to edge with signatures.

Thank you for speaking plainly. It meant something.

No corporate phrasing. No agenda.

gratitude.

Her throat tightened unexpectedly.

It was easier to manage criticism. Easier to absorb suspicion. Easier to handle expectation.

Gratitude was... destabilizing.

A knock at the door.

"Come in."

Miles stepped inside.

"You look like someone handed you a live wire."

She held up the card. "The nursing staff."

He read it quietly.

"That's dangerous," she murmured.

"What is?"

"Being appreciated."

He looked at her carefully. "Why?"

"Because appreciation becomes reliance. Reliance becomes expectation."

"And expectation already exists."

She set the card down.

"My father used to say that if you let people see you tired, they'll assume you're weak."

Miles didn't interrupt.

"He believed perception was leverage," she continued. "You show cracks, you invite pressure."

"And do you believe that?"

"I used to."

"And now?"

She didn't answer.

The silence stretched.

"You weren't weak today," he said quietly.

"I wasn't weak Friday either."

"No," he agreed. "You weren't."

She looked at him.

"I was tired," she admitted.

"You were human."

"That word again."

"Yes."

She stood and moved toward the window, needing space.

The city below moved with indifferent efficiency.

"You leave in twenty-four days," she said.

"Yes."

"That's good."

"Why?"

"Because this is becoming complicated."

His voice softened. "Complicated doesn't mean wrong."

"For me, it does."

She turned to face him.

"You're calm," she said.

"I try to be."

"Why?"

"Because you don't get to be."

That caught her off guard.

"I am calm."

"You are controlled."

Her jaw tightened.

"Control works."

"Yes."

"And?"

"And it's heavy."

The honesty of it lingered.

She exhaled slowly.

"Stay," she said.

He paused. "For what?"

"For five minutes. Without strategy."

He sat in the chair across from her desk.

They did not discuss succession metrics.

They did not dissect the interview.

They talked about the anchor's aggressively cheerful blazer, which Avery described as "a motivational highlighter."

They debated whether hospital coffee should legally be classified as a mood suppressant.

They laughed—softly, then genuinely.

The sound surprised her.

It felt foreign in this room.

Miles watched her carefully.

"That," he said quietly, "is the tone you don't use enough."

"What tone?"

"That one."

She sobered slightly.

"You're invested for a contractor."

"I prefer to leave things better than I found them."

"And you think I need improving?"

He held her gaze.

"I think you deserve ease."

The word landed somewhere deep and inconvenient.

Ease.

She had optimized for competence. For inevitability. For indispensability.

Ease had never been part of the formula.

"You don't have to prove you're indispensable every hour," he said.

"Yes," she replied quietly. "I do."

But even to her own ears, it sounded thinner.

He stood.

As he moved toward the door, she spoke again.

"Why did you recommend me?"

He turned.

"I've answered that."

"No. You've given me the polished version."

He studied her.

"The real version?"

"Yes."

"Because you were the only candidate who asked how the decision would affect staff morale."

She blinked.

"That was procedural."

"It was human."

The word again.

"You see things," she said.

"It's my job."

"No," she replied softly. "It's not."

He didn't argue.

At the door, he paused.

"You don't have to carry everything alone," he said.

"I'm not alone."

"No," he agreed gently. "You don't let anyone stand beside you."

The door closed behind him.

Avery remained seated.

The card lay open on her desk.

Thank you for speaking plainly.

It meant something.

She stared at the words.

Then she did something reckless.

She slipped the card into her desk drawer—not hidden, not displayed.

Saved.

Natalie, in the opposite seat, made a satisfied sound and said to absolutely no one, "Due diligence."

Avery stared out the window, heart beating too fast.

He simply laced his fingers through hers as if it was the most natural thing in the world.

Miles didn't react like it was a victory.

She moved her hand the final inch and let her fingers rest against his.

Then she made a decision that wasn't about spotlight.

Avery looked at it for half a second.

Miles shifted slightly, his hand near hers on the seat. Not touching. Waiting.

, Avery watched the city slide by and felt the strange sensation of being both exposed and safe. Like the spotlight had been harsh, but the person beside her had made it survivable.

They climbed in. The driver pulled away from the curb.

Natalie opened the door to the car. "I'm saving you from yourself. Again."

Avery groaned. "Natalie."

Natalie cleared her throat loudly. "Okay! Great! Emotional growth! Love that for us! Now please get in the car before a reporter recognizes you as Warm Deposition and asks for a quote."

Avery inhaled slowly. Let it land. Like praise was something she had to permit herself.

Miles didn't move closer. He softened his tone. "Then let it land."

"She doesn't usually..." Avery began, then stopped. Her voice tightened. "She doesn't usually say proud."

Avery stared at him, the same question from lunch echoing in a new place. She hated that he asked it in a way that made it answerable.

Miles tilted his head. "Are you."

Avery swallowed. "I'm fine."

Miles's gaze stayed on Avery. "You okay."

Natalie sniffed. "I'm not starting. I'm observing the ecosystem."

Avery shot her a look. "Don't start."

Natalie made a tiny sound and pretended she was adjusting her tote bag. "I'm not crying."

Avery's chest went tight in a way that was not convenient in public. "She said that."

Miles read, then his expression softened. "She said, 'Tell Avery I saw it. I'm proud. Also tell her to eat lunch like a person.'"

Avery's throat tightened. "What did she say."

Miles lifted a brow. "She does now."

Avery froze. "My mother doesn't text."

Miles's phone buzzed. He glanced down, then smiled faintly. "Your mother texted."

Natalie nodded, relieved. "Thank you. I would like one day without the phrase 'content strategy.'"

Avery exhaled slowly. "We are not leveraging anything."

He was watching her, steady, like he could see the reflex and wasn't afraid of it. Like he was quietly reminding her she didn't have to obey it.

Then she looked at Miles.

Avery stared at the message and felt something in her chest tighten. The old reflex: clamp down, correct, control.

Natalie held up her phone like evidence. "He did."

Avery stopped. "He did not."

Natalie resumed walking. "Unfortunately, memes now count as work. Gerald already emailed asking if we can 'leverage Warm Deposition into a mission-forward content strategy.'"

"Yes," Miles said. "To do actual work. Not be memes."

Avery exhaled, annoyed at the flutter it caused. "We're going back to the hospital."

Miles's gaze flicked to Avery, soft. "It sort of was."

Avery's cheeks warmed. "It was not."

"It was romantic," Natalie said, disgusted.

Miles looked mildly wounded. "That was accurate."

Natalie narrowed her eyes. "You absolutely did. With your little hurricane compliment."

Miles held up both hands. "I didn't start the approachable campaign."

Avery stared. "Approachable is not a goal."

Natalie pointed the lint roller at Miles. "Because he brought you coffee and now the universe thinks you're approachable."

Avery pressed her lips together. "Why is my life like this."

Miles's mouth twitched. "Also, it would enjoy the attention."

"You can't sue the internet," Natalie said, voice solemn. "The internet has no assets and no conscience."

Avery went still. "I will sue the internet."

Natalie stopped walking. "NO." She looked down at her screen, then gasped. "Oh my God. They are."

Miles kept his tone neutral, which was never a good sign. "They're calling you 'Warm Deposition.'"

Avery shot him a look. "What."

Miles glanced at his phone, then slid it back into his pocket. "Too late."

Avery rubbed her temple. "I didn't authorize sunsets."

Natalie walked beside Avery, still clutching the lint roller like it was a security blanket. "Okay. Immediate debrief. You said 'tired of perfect' and now twelve people are making inspirational graphics out of it. One of them put it over a sunset. I hate them."

In the hallway outside the studio, the air felt cooler, as if it hadn't been heated by stage lights and collective judgment.

And that, Avery realized as they walked into the blessed anonymity of the hallway, was the most dangerous part of all.

But his eyes said something else: I see you. I like you. I won't use you.

His mouth curved. "I'm not."

Avery shot him a look. "Don't."

Miles leaned in, voice low, for her. "We already did. Apparently."

Avery's cheeks warmed. "We are not."

As they stepped offstage, the host called after them, smiling, "You two are going to make the internet explode."

Avery took it before she could overthink.

Miles stood and offered Avery his hand as if they were leaving a normal room instead of a televised set.

Avery exhaled. "Give it time."

Natalie rushed in from off-camera, whisper-hissing, "You did it. No lawsuits. No proposals. No one cried."

Avery's muscles unlocked all at once.

The segment ended. The cameras cut. The lights softened.

Avery added, softer, "But thank you. Truly. For caring about something real."

The host laughed again. "There she is."

She exhaled. "Yes. Stop making this about me. Make it about the kids."

Avery blinked. Not a trap. Not yet.

The host grinned. "Is there anything you want to say to the people who've been cheering you on this week."

Avery's stomach dropped.

The host's eyes sparkled. "Okay, I have to ask what everyone's asking."

Avery's throat tightened.

"It is," Miles said, still smiling. "She cares. She just refuses to dramatize it."

Avery's mouth twitched. "I don't know if that's a compliment."

The host laughed. "That's the nicest insult I've ever heard."

Miles didn't flinch. "It's like standing next to a hurricane with excellent posture."

Avery froze half a heartbeat. The question wasn't about messaging. It was about them.

Then she turned to Miles, casual as a blade. "What's it like working with Avery Sloan."

"Of course," the host said.

Avery smiled. "I'm focused on pediatrics."

Natalie's warning echoed in Avery's skull.

The host tilted her head. "And how are you holding up, Avery."

Avery added, calm, "But I wasn't surprised people are hungry for honesty. They're tired of perfect."

"Fair," the host said, laughing.

She kept her face composed. "I was surprised the mic stayed live."

Avery felt the old instinct to armor up. Under the coffee table, Miles's fingers brushed lightly against her knee - a small, grounding touch that sent a jolt through her system.

The host leaned in. "That clip. The mic. The joke. Were you surprised by the reaction."

"Because it's needed," Avery said. "And because our staff doesn't quit on kids."

The host nodded. "And the community response has been huge."

Avery exhaled and let the mission take the wheel. Infusion chairs. Family lounges. Mental health support that didn't require parents to beg. Her voice steadied because this part was real.

The host turned earnest. "Pediatrics. You have an expansion underway. Tell us what this does for families."

Avery felt her cheeks warm. Next to her, Miles's shoulder shifted like he was holding back a laugh.

The host laughed, delighted. "You are just as dry as the clip promised."

Avery smiled with lethal politeness. "That's unfortunate."

The host smiled into the camera. "Today we're joined by St. Catherine's CEO Avery Sloan and crisis strategist Miles Carter. Avery, the internet can't stop talking about you."

Avery sat. Miles sat beside her, angled slightly toward her without crowding. Supportive without claiming.

They walked toward the set. The lights hit Avery like interrogation beams. The couch looked too soft to be trustworthy.

The stage manager waved. "Places!"

We. The word landed like a hand at Avery's back.

Miles added softly, "If she tries to make it personal, we redirect."

"If she asks you how you're feeling," Natalie whispered, "you say: focused on the mission. If she asks if you're okay, you say: grateful for the team."

Avery's throat tightened. Simple was a trap disguised as a compliment.

The anchor laughed. "Quick rundown. We'll open with pediatrics, touch on the viral moment, then end with the fundraiser preview."

Avery's eyes narrowed. "Traitor."

Miles smiled politely. "It's the lighting."

The anchor, already camera-ready, breezed over with a grin. "Avery, so glad you're here. And Miles, we love having you. You look dangerously calm."

Avery shot him a look. "Stop helping."

Miles leaned in slightly. "Friendly oath."

"Exactly," Natalie said. "So try for warm deposition."

Avery stared at her. "Everything I say sounds like a deposition."

Natalie appeared at Avery's shoulder with a lint roller like a weapon. "Okay. Breathe. Smile. Do not say anything that sounds like a deposition."

"I want none."

Miles's mouth twitched. "Do you want fewer."

Avery kept her face neutral. "Ninety seconds is excessive."

"You're live in ninety seconds," the producer said brightly, as if live television wasn't a human rights violation.

The producer clipped a mic pack to the back of Avery's dress with the reverence of someone handling explosives.

And for the first time since the viral clip, she allowed herself to sit back in her chair without bracing.

Not because the pressure had lifted.

But because someone had noticed it.

And that was infinitely more destabilizing than criticism ever could be.

Twenty-four days.

She could manage twenty-four days.

She wasn't entirely sure she wanted to.

Chapter 6: The Almost Break

Today was board subcommittee day.

She did not lose composure.

The subcommittee meeting ended at 11:47 a.m.

Gerald Whitmore clasped his hands as if closing a prayer. "Excellent clarity, Avery. The board appreciates your steadiness."

Steadiness.

There it was again.

She smiled. "Thank you."

He studied her longer than usual. "Make sure you're pacing yourself. This is a marathon."

"I am well-conditioned," she replied.

A flicker of amusement crossed his face. "I'm sure you are."

She left the room with her spine straight and her jaw tight.

She leaned back in her chair and closed her eyes for three seconds.

One.

Two.

Three.

"You look like you're negotiating with gravity."

She opened her eyes.

Miles stood in the doorway, not smiling but not concerned either. Observing.

"I'm fine," she said automatically.

He stepped inside and closed the door gently behind him.

"You always say that first."

"It's usually accurate."

He walked toward her desk, hands in his pockets. Casual. Controlled. Infuriatingly calm.

"When was the last time you ate something that required chewing?" he asked.

She stared at him.

"That is not relevant."

"That's not an answer."

She inhaled slowly. "I had a protein bar."

"When?"

She glanced at the clock.

He raised an eyebrow.

"Unclear," she admitted.

He nodded once, as if confirming a theory.

"Sit," he said.

She blinked. "I am sitting."

"Differently."

Her spine straightened on instinct.

"That is not a command you're authorized to give."

"I'm not commanding. I'm suggesting."

She crossed her arms. "I do not require posture coaching."

"You're not breathing."

"I am breathing."

"You're micro-breathing. That doesn't count."

She almost smiled.

Almost.

"I have projections to finalize."

"And you'll do them better in ten minutes."

"I don't take ten-minute breaks."

"That's not something to be proud of."

She stood abruptly, circling around the desk.

"I am in the middle of a succession evaluation cycle," she said. "Every output matters. Every tone shift matters. Every data point matters."

"And you matter," he said quietly.

She stopped.
"That is not the same thing."
"It is to me."
The words landed heavier than she expected.
She turned away, walking toward the window.
The city below moved with indifference. Traffic flowed. Ambulances cut through intersections. People lived their lives without caring about her board metrics.
"I stay necessary," she said, almost to herself. "That's how this works."
"And if you stopped?"
"I won't."
"That wasn't the question."
She turned back.
"What are you asking?"
"I'm asking when you decided exhaustion was proof of worth."
Her mouth opened.
Closed.
"That is not what this is."
"No?"
"No."
"Then what is it?"
She held his gaze.
"I am not allowed to slip," she said evenly. "Not now. Not when I'm this close."
He stepped closer, but not close enough to crowd.
"You're not slipping."
"Not yet."
Silence pressed between them.
He studied her carefully, as if evaluating a fragile structure he did not want to destabilize.
"Say it," he said softly.
"Say what?"
"That you're tired."
The word lodged somewhere beneath her sternum.

She looked at the floor.
Looked at her hands.
Looked back at him.
"I am tired," she said.
It was quiet.
Not dramatic.
real.
He did not rush to respond.
He did not look triumphant.
He simply nodded once.
"I know."
The relief that followed was almost offensive.
She hated that it felt good to say it.
"That doesn't change anything," she added quickly.
"It changes you not pretending."
She laughed once, brittle.
"That's not strategic."
"No," he agreed. "It's honest."
Her phone buzzed.
Dinner reminder. Two board members. Private dining room. 7:00 p.m.
She glanced at it.
"You have dinner," he said.
"Yes."
"Cancel."
She looked at him sharply.
"Absolutely not."
"You need sleep."
"I need momentum."
"You need both."
"I don't get both."
He studied her.
"Who told you that?"
She didn't answer.
He stepped closer.
"Your father?" he asked quietly.

Her jaw tightened.

"That's not your territory."

"You brought him up."

She exhaled sharply.

"He believed perception was leverage," she said. "He believed if you let people see you tired, they'd assume you were weak."

"And do you?"

She hesitated.

"I don't know."

"That's progress."

"That's destabilizing."

He smiled faintly.

"Same thing."

She shook her head.

"You're comfortable in ambiguity."

"I'm comfortable with reality."

"And what reality is that?"

"That you are carrying a weight you don't have to carry alone."

The word alone again.

She turned back toward the desk, gripping the edge lightly.

"That's leadership."

"That's isolation."

"It's the same thing."

"It doesn't have to be."

Her throat tightened unexpectedly.

"Stop," she said quietly.

"Stop what?"

"Seeing me."

He did not step back.

"I can't."

"Why?"

"Because you matter."

The room felt smaller.

Quieter.

More dangerous.

"You leave in twenty-three days," she said.
"Yes."
"And then this ends."
"This changes."
She met his gaze.
"You're falling," she said.
It wasn't accusatory.
It was observational.
He didn't deny it.
He didn't dramatize it either.
"Yes," he said simply.
Her breath caught.
"You're not panicking," she observed.
"No."
"Why?"
"Because I don't think this is something to run from."
"And I do?"
"Yes."
The honesty made her laugh softly.
"That's inconvenient."
"It usually is."

She sank into her chair, exhaustion finally visible in the angle of her shoulders.

, neither of them spoke.

Then he did something unexpected.

He stepped closer.

Not aggressively.

enough that he could reach out and gently adjust the collar of her blazer where it had twisted slightly.

The contact was brief.

Accidental, almost.

Her breath stalled.

He seemed to realize what he'd done at the same moment she did.

His hand stilled.

Their eyes met.

It would have been easy to step back immediately.

He didn't.

She didn't either.

The space between them narrowed to something charged and deliberate.

"This," she whispered, "is what I meant by complicated."

His hand dropped slowly.

"Complicated doesn't mean wrong."

"For me, it does."

"Why?"

"Because I don't mix trajectory with distraction."

His gaze sharpened slightly.

"You think I'm a distraction?"

She hesitated.

"You're... destabilizing."

He nodded once.

"That's fair."

The lack of defensiveness unsettled her more than argument would have.

"I cannot afford variables," she said.

"I'm not a variable," he replied quietly. "I'm a person."

The correction landed.

She looked at him differently then.

Less like an obstacle.

More like a choice.

"That's worse," she murmured.

He smiled faintly.

"I know."

By the time she arrived at dinner that evening, she had regained composure.

She discussed growth projections. Community engagement. Long-term stability.

She smiled.

She answered.

She impressed.

She returned home at 10:18 p.m.

Her heels came off by the door. Her phone buzzed almost immediately.

Miles: Did you get home?

She stared at the message.

It was unnecessary.

It was simple.

It was... grounding.

Avery: Yes.

Three dots appeared.

Miles: Eat something real.

She huffed out a small laugh.

Avery: That's not a directive you're authorized to give.

Miles: I'm assessing tone.

She shook her head.

Avery: It still sounds like charming.

Miles: Charm is a tone.

She stared at the screen longer than she should have.

Then:

Avery: I am tired.

a pause.

Long enough that she wondered if she'd overstepped.

Then:

Miles: I know.

No advice.

No solution.

acknowledgment.

She sat on the edge of her bed, the city lights filtering through the curtains.

For years, exhaustion had felt like proof.

Proof she was working hard enough.

Proof she deserved the seat.

Proof she was necessary.

Tonight, for the first time, it felt like something else.

A signal.

Not of weakness.

Of limit.

Her phone buzzed again.

Miles: You don't have to prove it every day.

She typed back before she could reconsider.

Avery: Yes, I do.

The response came quickly.

Miles: No. You don't.

She stared at the words.

Her instinct was to argue.

To defend.

To assert.

Instead, she set the phone down.

Lay back against the pillows.

Closed her eyes.

And allowed herself,, to not prove anything at all.

Twenty-three days.

She could manage twenty-three days.

The question was no longer whether she could hold the pressure.

It was whether she wanted to keep holding it alone.

And that realization—quiet, steady, undeniable—was far more destabilizing than any board evaluation.

For the first time in a long time, the almost-break felt less like collapse.

And more like choice.

***

Avery knew the moment she stepped into Gerald Whitmore's office that someone had rehearsed outrage.

Not Gerald. He was too old-school to rehearse. His outrage came preloaded, like a board packet: tabbed, annotated, and delivered with a polite smile.

Miles walked beside her, unhurried, holding his hard hat under one arm like a prop he refused to be embarrassed by.

Gerald looked up from behind his desk. "Avery. Mr. Carter."

"Gerald," Avery said, tone even.

Miles nodded. "Chair Whitmore."

Gerald gestured. "Sit."

Avery sat. Miles followed with infuriating calm.

Gerald slid his phone across the desk.

On the screen: the Midtown Pulse post.

St. Catherine's COO spotted getting 'support' from consultant Miles Carter after viral town hall. New power couple?

Avery's mouth tightened.

Gerald watched her carefully. "Care to explain why our COO is being shipped by an account that also posts 'best brunches for cardiologists'?"

Avery chose restraint. "The post is inaccurate."

"And yet it exists," Gerald said. "Which makes it, in the eyes of the public, half true."

Miles's voice stayed steady. "It's a photo of me preventing a fall."

Gerald's gaze flicked to him. "The internet is not known for nuance, Mr. Carter."

"No," Miles agreed. "It's known for momentum."

Avery shot him a look. Momentum was his favorite euphemism for chaos.

Gerald interlaced his fingers. "Avery, we are in the early phase of a succession evaluation. We are also fundraising for pediatrics. Donors don't like distractions."

"I'm aware," Avery said.

"Then you're aware this is a distraction."

Avery's mind ran solutions: takedown requests, internal comms lock, PR statement, a shinier story to bury the headline.

Gerald continued, "There's more."

He swiped to a screenshot of the internal Slack thread. Reactions. Comments. Emojis. The caption about the "mysterious consultant."

Gerald's voice stayed level. "Staff engagement is high. But it's high in a direction we did not authorize. Donors are forwarding this to my inbox like it's a soap opera."

Avery's tone sharpened. "This is not a soap opera."

"No," Gerald agreed. "It's a hospital. Which is why we cannot look like we're playing."

Miles's jaw tightened subtly at that.

Gerald leaned forward. "We will not respond directly to Midtown Pulse. We will not dignify gossip. We will flood the zone with competence."

Avery nodded once. "Agreed."

"And," Gerald added, gaze steady, "we will put you where people can see you in a context that reads as leadership. Not... whatever this is."

Avery's mouth tightened. "A construction site."

Gerald didn't blink. "Tomorrow evening we have the St. Catherine's Children's Gala kickoff at the Montclaire. Donors. Press. Photographers. The board wants you there."

Avery had planned to send Natalie with talking points. Galas were soft power. She preferred hard outcomes.

"I can attend," she said.

Gerald nodded. "Good. And Mr. Carter will attend with you."

Avery turned her head slowly. "Excuse me?"

Miles's brows rose a fraction.

Gerald's voice was patient. "He's associated with your spotlight now. If you arrive separately, the gossip account has a field day. If you arrive together with a clear professional frame, it becomes boring."

Miles's tone stayed even. "I'm a consultant. Not an accessory."

Gerald smiled without warmth. "Welcome to spotlight, Mr. Carter."

Avery's fingers tightened against her knee. "This is unnecessary."

Gerald's gaze sharpened. "Avery, you want this role. The board is not looking for a brilliant technician. They're looking for a figure who can hold the room. This is part of holding the room."

Avery nodded once. "Understood."

Gerald stood, ending it. "Natalie will coordinate with communications. I want a revised media posture memo by end of day. And Avery," he added, voice low, "the public loves a story. The board loves control."

Avery rose. "Yes."

Gerald's gaze held hers. "Do you still have it?"

The question was quiet. Dangerous. Not about the gossip. About her.

Avery met his eyes. "Yes."

Gerald nodded once. "Then show me."

They left his office with the sort of silence that could crack glass.

In the hallway, Miles spoke first. "He assigned me as your plus-one."

"He assigned you as a prop," Avery said tightly.

Miles's eyes narrowed. "And you're okay with that?"

Avery turned, irritation sharp. "I am okay with whatever protects my trajectory."

"At what cost?" Miles asked.

"Stop."

"Stop what?"

"Making this about feelings."

"It is about feelings," he said, voice low. "His feelings. The donors' feelings. You're being forced into a story you didn't choose."

"And you're being dramatic," she snapped.

His calm didn't budge. "Did you hear him say 'influenced'? He thinks I'm controlling you."

Avery's laugh was sharp. "No one controls me."

Miles stepped closer, enough to make her aware of the air between them. "Then why did that land?"

Avery's throat tightened. Because it did.

She pushed open the stairwell door. Concrete walls, quiet air. No eyes. No performance.

Miles followed.

Avery exhaled. "This is why I hate visibility."

"You don't hate visibility," he said. "You hate being misread."

"Same thing."

"No. Being misread is fixable. Being invisible is lonely."

Avery's spine stiffened. "Do not psychoanalyze me in a stairwell."

"I'm noticing," he said.

"That word again."

"It's still accurate."

Avery stared at the wall. "We are not going to the gala together."

Miles didn't move. "We are."

"You don't decide that."

"You do," he said. "But you already decided in Gerald's office."

Damn him.

Miles continued, voice steady. "If we do this, we frame it. Two professionals. One mission. Zero romance."

Avery's stomach did something unhelpful. "Do you think they'll believe that?"

Miles's expression warmed. "I don't care what they believe."

Avery's breath caught. "Then why are you doing it?"

He hesitated, then chose honesty. "Because you matter. And I don't like watching people rewrite you into a story you didn't choose."

Avery's mind kept snagging on Gerald's phrase: influenced.

She hated that implication more than the gossip itself.

"You heard him," she said, keeping her voice flat as they stepped out of the stairwell and into the corridor again. "He thinks I can be softened."

Miles walked beside her. "He thinks softness is weakness."

"And he thinks you're the cause," Avery added.

Miles's gaze flicked to her. "Do you?"

Avery's steps slowed by half a beat. "I don't think in causes. I think in outcomes."

"That's not an answer."

"It is. You don't like it."

He didn't push further, but the silence between them shifted, more charged than comfortable.

Avery watched the laugh for one second too long.

Miles noticed. Of course he did.

"You're thinking about pediatrics," he said.

"I'm thinking about donors," she corrected.

He didn't call her on it. He said, "Same thing, sometimes."

That irritated her. Mostly because it was true.

They headed back.

Natalie waited outside Avery's office, phone in hand, eyes wide. "Please tell me I'm hallucinating the words 'gala kickoff' on my calendar."

"You're not," Avery said.

Natalie's gaze flicked between them. "And Miles is coming too."

Miles's expression stayed calm. "Apparently."

Natalie's mouth opened, delighted and horrified at once. "Okay. Great. Fantastic. No notes."

Avery entered her office and shut the door. Natalie followed anyway, because boundaries were a concept she considered optional.

"I pulled two outfits," Natalie announced, holding up two garment bags like evidence.

Avery stared. "Why."

"Because press line," Natalie said, as if that was self-explanatory. "We need credible, not cold. Powerful, not... armored."

Miles coughed, which might have been a laugh trying to escape.

Avery shot him a look. "Do not."

Natalie ignored both of them and continued, "Also, Miles, don't wear a suit that screams 'secret boyfriend.'"

Miles blinked. "That's... specific."

Natalie shrugged. "The internet is specific."

Avery's temples ached. "Five minutes. Then I have work."

Natalie nodded briskly, unzipped one bag, and held up a deep blue dress. Structured, but softer than Avery's usual armor. "This says competent but approachable."

Avery's gaze narrowed. "It says medium risk."

"Perfect," Natalie said.

Miles looked away, but not quickly enough to hide the warmth in his expression.

Avery caught it. "Stop being calm."

"I'm trying," he said, voice dry.

Natalie clapped once. "Okay. Great. We'll survive."

Avery turned back to her laptop, grounding herself in work. "Memo. Internal comms. Press line plan. I want it warm without being soft."

Miles nodded. "Credible."

"Credible," Avery repeated.

Natalie pointed at her. "You said credible. That's growth."

Avery ignored her.

Avery's gaze sharpened. "No denial."

"Denial makes it real," Miles said. "Deflection makes it boring."

Avery exhaled. "Fine."

Natalie hustled out to "coordinate with Marla" which meant, in practice, that she would terrify the communications team into efficiency.

The door clicked shut.

Avery's office returned to its usual quiet, except now it held the faint aftershock of Gerald's office and the stairwell, like the air had been rearranged.

Miles moved to the side chair across from her desk, opened his laptop, and started typing without being asked.

Avery watched him for one second before forcing her attention back to her own screen.

"Internal first," she said, more to herself than to him.

When she finished, she read it twice.

Then, against her instincts, she read it a third time as if she were one of the nurses in the third row.

It landed differently.

Not softer. Just... closer.

She sent it.

Avery swallowed and closed the window like it might burn her.

Miles glanced up. "That was good."

"That was functional," she said.

He didn't argue. "Functional and good can overlap."

Her phone rang. Unknown number.

She frowned and answered anyway. "Avery Sloan."

A man's voice, smooth and practiced. "Ms. Sloan, this is Patrick Ames with the Montclaire Foundation. I'm calling about tomorrow's kickoff."

Avery's posture straightened instinctively. "Of course. How can I help?"

"We've had... questions," Patrick said delicately. "Nothing formal. Just... chatter. We want to ensure tomorrow remains focused on the children."

Avery felt her jaw tighten. Chatter. Another polite synonym for gossip.

"Tomorrow will be focused on the children," she said evenly. "You have my word."

"Yes," Avery replied. "Understood."

"Excellent. And, if I may," Patrick added, voice dropping slightly, "it may help to have your consultant present. Professional continuity, and all that."

Avery held her expression neutral even though no one could see it. "He will be present."

"Perfect," Patrick said. "See you tomorrow."

The call ended.

Avery stared at her phone, then set it down slowly.

Miles's eyes were on her, steady. "They called."

"Yes."

"To make sure you're not a scandal."

Avery's laugh was brief and humorless. "To make sure their donors aren't."

Miles's gaze softened. "That's pressure."

"I know what pressure is," she said.

He didn't move. "Do you know what support is?"

Avery's fingers tightened around her pen. "I do not need support."

Miles's voice stayed calm. "Avery. Yesterday you made a joke and the internet turned it into a referendum. Today you tripped and they turned it into a romance novel. Tomorrow you'll breathe wrong and they'll call it a breakdown."

Avery's eyes flashed. "Don't."

"Don't what?"

"Don't say breathe. Don't say breakdown. Don't narrate my body like it's a headline."

Miles's expression tightened, the first sign of real irritation. "I'm not the one making headlines."

Avery stood abruptly. "You're enjoying the fact that I'm exposed."

Miles stood too, slower, careful. "No."

"Yes," she snapped. "Because it proves your theory. That I should be 'human.' That I should show cracks."

Miles's gaze held hers. "I never said cracks. I said breath."

"Same thing," she shot back.

"No," he said, voice low. "Cracks are damage. Breath is life."

The words landed and she hated them for being right.

She turned away, moving to the window, staring down at the city as if she could out-stare the noise.

Behind her, Miles's voice softened. "He called you influenced."

Avery's shoulders went rigid.

Miles continued, quieter. "That's what this is, isn't it. That word is what hit."

Avery's throat tightened. She didn't answer.

Miles took a careful step closer, stopping behind her, not touching. "Tell me what it hit."

Avery's laugh came out sharp. "You don't get to ask that."

"I do if you want me to stand beside you tomorrow night and not misstep."

Avery's hands curled into fists on the windowsill.

She heard her father's voice, clear as if he were in the room.

Perception is leverage. You show weakness, you invite pressure. You let people see you need someone, and they'll use it.

She swallowed.

"It hit..." She stopped, jaw tightening. She tried again. "It hit the part of me that was trained to believe dependence is failure."

Miles was quiet.

Then he said, softly, "That's not training. That's cruelty."

Avery spun to face him. "Don't."

"Don't what?" he asked, and his voice wasn't calm now. It was contained.

"Don't talk about my father."

"I didn't," he said. "You did."

Avery's breath came faster than she liked. She forced it down. "We are not doing this."

Miles looked at her. "Okay."

The single word should have been a relief.

Instead it made something inside her sink.

Because he didn't argue. He didn't push. He stepped back, giving her exactly what she claimed to want.

Space.

And the space felt like punishment.

Avery's phone buzzed again.

A message in the same unknown thread.

Unknown: Your chair wants control. I wonder what he'll do when he learns what you want.

Avery's blood chilled.

Miles saw her face and moved instantly. "What now?"

Avery held the phone out, hand steady even though her pulse wasn't.

Miles read the text, jaw tightening harder. "That's personal."

Avery's voice went flat. "Someone is watching."

Miles's eyes lifted to hers. "And they're close enough to know your chair."

Avery's stomach twisted. "This is not about gossip anymore."

Miles shook his head slightly. "No. This is someone playing with you."

Avery forced her breath even. "We can handle it."

Miles's gaze sharpened. "How?"

She chose the only strategy that fit the romcom pressure cooker: refuse the bait, control the stage, keep the tone bright enough to hide the teeth.

"We handle it by not reacting," she said. "We handle it by staying boring."

Miles's mouth twitched, almost a smile. "Boring is your love language."

Avery shot him a look. "Don't."

But her voice had lost some of its bite.

Miles's tone softened. "We go to the Montclaire. We control the frame. And we quietly find out who thinks they can talk to you like that."

Avery stared at the message again.

What you want.

Her chest tightened. She didn't know if she wanted to delete the text or throw her phone out a window.

Miles's voice was gentle now. "Avery."

She looked up.

He held her gaze, steady, present. "You don't have to do this alone."

The phrase hit her in the exact place she guarded most.

She swallowed. "I know."

It wasn't surrender.

But it also wasn't denial.

Miles's expression softened, relief flickering for half a second before he masked it.

Avery exhaled slowly.

Then she did something she almost never did.

She asked for help.

"Draft the gala remarks," she said quietly. "Two minutes. Warm. Credible. No fluff."

Miles blinked, then nodded. "Done."

Avery's mouth tightened as if she regretted it already.

Miles sat back down, typing fast.

Avery returned to her desk, opened her calendar, and stared at tomorrow evening's block of time.

Press line. Donors. Cameras. A man beside her who noticed everything. And someone in the shadows texting like they owned the script.

She was good at scripts.

She had never been good at improvisation.

And yet the microphone had been live.

Now everything felt live.

Outside the door, the hospital hummed on, indifferent.

Inside, the story had shifted.

And tomorrow night, at the Montclaire, the cameras would be waiting.

Chapter 7: The Dress Rehearsal

By 4:11 p.m., Avery had accepted three uncomfortable truths:

1. The gala was happening whether she liked it or not.

2. The internet was going to interpret her facial expressions like they were a courtroom exhibit.

3. Natalie had entered a state of "crisis stylist," which made her both more efficient and more terrifying.

Avery stood in her office while Natalie marched in with two garment bags and the focused expression of someone defusing a bomb in couture.

Natalie slapped the bags onto the couch. "Okay. We are not getting 'Power Couple' trending again."

Avery's eyes narrowed. "We didn't get it trending the first time."

Natalie pointed a finger at her without looking up, already unzipping the first garment bag. "Do not argue with me. My nervous system cannot take it."

Avery glanced toward the door. "Where is—"

As if on cue, Miles knocked once and stepped in like he'd been summoned by the word where.

He had changed since the morning. No suit jacket. Crisp button-down, sleeves rolled. Dark trousers. No tie. The sort of outfit that said I'm professional while also whispering I could carry you out of a burning building without wrinkling anything.

Avery hated that her brain noticed.

Natalie noticed too. Natalie's eyes flicked to him and then back to Avery with the satisfaction of someone watching a chess piece land exactly where she wanted.

"Oh good," Natalie said. "You're here. This is a three-person problem now."

Miles blinked. "I didn't know we were doing group work."

"We are," Natalie said brightly. "Because neither of you is fully capable of being normal."

Avery stared. "Natalie."

Natalie held up a dress, structured and deep blue. "This is the one. It says 'executive' but not 'robot.'"

Avery's mouth tightened. "I am not a robot."

Miles murmured, "You are... optimized."

Avery turned slowly. "Do not assist."

Natalie's face lit up. "See? That's the banter we need. Keep doing that. It reads as chemistry but plausible deniability."

Avery's gaze sharpened. "We do not want chemistry."

Natalie looked at her like she'd said the sky was fictional. "Avery. The internet already thinks you're dating. We want controlled chemistry. Not chaotic chemistry."

Miles said mildly, "Is there a chemistry spectrum?"

Natalie clapped once. "Yes. And you two are currently oscillating."

Natalie nodded solemnly. "Fine. But if anyone asks, you are now medically cleared for warmth."

Avery's cheeks warmed. She adjusted her collar again, trying to hide the softness like it was a breach. "Can we please return to the agenda."

Natalie froze, eyes shining with triumph. "That. That laugh. Bottle it. Put it in the gala."

Miles's thumb hovered over the phone screen. "Sincerity: two point three seconds. Excellent."

Avery's eyes widened a fraction. Then, against her will, a laugh slipped out—quick, surprised, real.

Miles glanced at Avery, voice low. "If it helps, I have never eaten an intern either."

Natalie leaned in. "Avery. You joked about caffeine like it was a morale metric and the entire hospital applauded. You can handle one ridiculous smile."

Avery stared at her. "Absolutely not."

"Welcome to my life," Natalie said. "Smile three. 'I promise I don't eat interns.'"

Miles took it like it might explode. "Timing sincerity feels unethical."

Natalie shoved her phone at him. "Timer app. You're timing sincerity."

Miles blinked. "I don't have a—"

Natalie pointed at Miles. "You. Stopwatch."

Miles said, deadpan, "Tragic."

Avery's mouth twitched despite herself. "I do not own a throw blanket."

Natalie nodded, pleased. "Okay. That one says, 'I might own a throw blanket.' Good."

Avery inhaled through her nose, counted four beats the way she did in elevators, and tried again—softer this time. Less armor, more person.

Natalie clapped once. "Great. The threat is present. Smile two. Human."

Avery turned slowly. "Do not make this worse."

Miles murmured, "If a spreadsheet could judge me, it would look like that."

Natalie squinted. "That's not a smile. That's a quarterly report."

Avery set her shoulders and lifted the corners of her mouth into a neat, controlled expression.

"That's exactly what an intern-eater would say," Natalie replied. "Smile one. Executive."

Avery's eyes narrowed. "I have never eaten an intern."

Natalie reached into her tote and produced a tiny kitchen timer. "Not yet. But don't underestimate them." She clicked it on with a cheerful beep. "Okay. Avery. Three smiles. Executive. Human. And 'I promise I don't eat interns.'"

Miles lifted a brow. "Is 'secretly a lizard' trending right now."

"A warmth drill," Natalie repeated, as if this were standard medical protocol. "You will be photographed within five minutes of stepping out of that door. The internet will freeze-frame your face and decide whether you're secretly in love, secretly furious, or secretly a lizard. We are giving them none of those."

Avery stared. "We are doing a what."

Natalie snapped her fingers. "Before anyone changes clothes, we're doing a warmth drill."

Avery's head began to ache behind her eyes. She glanced at the agenda on her desk. Media posture memo. Gala remarks. Security coordination. A dozen things she could control.

This wasn't one of them.

Natalie shoved the dress toward her. "Change. We need to see the silhouette in real lighting."

Avery stared at the dress. "In my office."

"Yes," Natalie said. "We are not doing a dressing room. Dressing rooms invite feelings. We are doing logistics."

Miles cleared his throat and pivoted toward the window like a gentleman who had been raised correctly but dropped into the wrong meeting.

Avery looked between them. "This is absurd."

Natalie smiled. "Correct. Now change."

Avery muttered something unprintable and went into the small adjoining restroom.

She locked the door, stared at herself in the mirror, and took one slow breath.

Her phone buzzed.

A text.

Unknown: Blue suits you. But the dress will break your armor.

Avery froze.

Not because the text was poetic. Because it was specific.

Blue suits you.

She stared at the screen until her pulse settled into something like order.

Then she typed, deleted, typed again, deleted again.

Finally she did what she was best at.

Nothing.

She took a screenshot, turned her phone face down on the counter, and stripped off her blazer as if fabric could absorb panic.

When she stepped back into her office, the atmosphere had shifted. Natalie was still bustling, laying out accessories like she was staging a military operation. Miles stood near the bookshelves, hands in his pockets, gaze deliberately elsewhere.

Avery crossed to her desk and slid the screenshot toward him without a word.

Miles glanced down.

His face didn't change much, but something in his posture tightened.

"That's the unknown number again?" he asked quietly.

"Yes."

Natalie's head snapped up. "Wait, what?"

Avery kept her voice level. "Someone is texting me. They referenced the board chair earlier."

Natalie's eyes widened. "Why are we not calling security?"

"We are not turning this into a procedural," Avery said.

Miles looked up. "We can handle it without making it a spectacle."

Natalie's mouth opened. "Isn't the entire concept of a gala a spectacle?"

Avery shot her a look. "Not now."

Miles's gaze flicked between them. "I'll ask IT to trace the number. Quietly. No drama."

Natalie pointed at him. "Okay, see, that's hot. Competence is hot."

Avery stared. "Natalie."

Natalie held up her hands. "Sorry. But it is."

Avery turned away, inhaled, and reminded herself that she was not losing control. She was managing variables.

Natalie, apparently, was not a variable. Natalie was a hurricane.

"Change," Natalie repeated, as if they hadn't discussed a stranger texting psychological commentary about Avery's wardrobe.

Miles turned more fully toward the window.

Avery slipped into the dress.

The fabric was smooth, heavier than she expected. Structured at the waist. Clean lines. Professional, but less armored than her typical suits. It didn't cling. It didn't flirt.

It did, however, feel like it exposed her collarbone more than she was used to. Which was ridiculous. She had a collarbone. It wasn't classified.

She stepped out.

Natalie stopped mid-motion.

Miles went still.

Avery's first instinct was to smooth invisible wrinkles. To adjust. To correct.

Natalie exhaled slowly. "Okay. That's... unfair."

Avery narrowed her eyes. "Define unfair."

Natalie circled her like a stylist assessing a high-value asset. "You look like you could fire someone with a smile and then donate a wing in their name."

Avery's mouth twitched despite herself. "That's horrifying."

"It's powerful," Natalie corrected. "And it reads warm."

Avery turned slightly toward the mirror on the wall.

Warm.

She looked like herself, but... softer at the edges. Like someone who might laugh in public. Like someone who might sit at a table and not be calculating exit routes.

Miles's gaze was fixed on a point somewhere near her shoulder, like he was trying hard not to look too directly.

Avery's pulse did something inconvenient.

Natalie clapped again. "Perfect. Shoes."

Avery stared. "I am not changing shoes."

"You will," Natalie said, already kneeling by the garment bags. "Not heels. We are not repeating the construction site elbow-catch."

Miles murmured, "Thank you."

Avery turned sharply. "Excuse me?"

Miles's expression was calm but his ears had gone faintly pink again. "I'm grateful we're not repeating it."

Natalie's eyes went wide with delighted horror. "Oh my god, you're blushing."

Miles blinked. "I'm not."

Natalie pointed. "That's the face you make when you are."

Avery's cheeks warmed slightly, which was a betrayal of her entire packaged.

Natalie handed her a pair of sleek flats. "These. Trust me."

Avery slipped them on and immediately hated how comfortable they were.

Comfort was suspicious.

Natalie stepped back, assessed the full look, then pointed at Miles. "Now you. What are you wearing?"

Miles blinked. "A suit."

Natalie grimaced like he'd said "I plan to wear Crocs." "Not a funeral suit. Not a wedding suit. Something that says 'professional support' and not 'secret boyfriend.'"

Miles looked to Avery as if asking for rescue.

Avery said evenly, "Do what she says. It will end faster."

Miles stared. "Is this how you lead?"

"Yes," Avery replied. "By strategic surrender."

Natalie beamed. "Exactly. Okay. Avery, hair."

Avery's eyes narrowed. "My hair is acceptable."

Natalie sighed. "It is. But it's also 'I could cross-examine God.'"

Avery opened her mouth.

Natalie held up a hand. "Not a bad thing. But tonight we want 'I could cross-examine God, and I'd bring him a glass of water afterward.'"

Avery stared in silence.

Miles, in a voice that suggested he was fighting for his life, said, "That's... oddly specific."

Natalie nodded. "You get it."

Avery closed her eyes briefly and counted to three.

When she opened them, she said, "We have remarks to finalize."

Miles stepped forward slightly. "I drafted a version. Two minutes. Warm, credible, focused on pediatrics. No fluff."

Natalie pointed at him. "Hot."

Avery deadpanned. "Stop saying hot."

Natalie's grin widened. "No."

Miles handed Avery a printed page.

Avery read quickly.

It was good. Clean. Grounded. It framed the pediatric expansion as a promise rather than a project. It spoke to donors without pandering, to staff without begging. It sounded like her voice, but... reachable.

She looked up. "This is accurate."

Miles nodded. "It's you. Without the armor."

Natalie's eyes gleamed. "Armor. Yes. Great. New motif."

Avery's gaze sharpened. "We are not adding motifs."

Natalie waved that away. "We already have coffee and armor. It's fine."

Avery took one slow breath. "We need to discuss arrival."

Miles nodded. "We arrive together. Press line. You lead. I stay half a step behind."

Avery's eyes narrowed. "Half a step behind."

"That signals support without dominance," Miles said.

Natalie nodded vigorously. "Yes. It says 'he respects her power.' important."

Avery looked between them. "This feels... staged."

Miles's voice stayed calm. "It is staged. That's what spotlight are."

Avery exhaled. "Fine."

Natalie clapped again. "Okay! We're done here. Miles, go change. Avery, I'm coming with you to the car, because I do not trust you not to put a blazer over that dress like it's a moral obligation."

Avery's mouth tightened. "It's cold outside."

Natalie pointed at her. "You will not sabotage warmth."

Avery stared at her assistant. "How are you employed."

Natalie smiled sweetly. "Because you secretly like me."

Avery opened her mouth, closed it, and chose silence. That was essentially a confession.

Miles stepped toward the door, then paused. "Avery."

She looked up.

His gaze was steady. But a flicker there, too. Something restrained.

"Don't read the texts alone," he said quietly.

Avery's jaw tightened. "I'm not afraid."

"I didn't say you were."

The phrasing was careful. Not accusing. Not paternal.

Just... present.

Avery nodded once.

Miles left.

Natalie watched him go, then turned back to Avery with the expression of someone watching a storm form over the ocean.

"Okay," Natalie said softly. "He's in deep."

Avery's throat tightened. "Natalie."

Natalie lifted a hand. "I know. Professional. Parameters. Controlled. But he's in deep. And you're pretending you don't feel anything, which is your favorite hobby."

Avery's voice was flat. "My favorite hobby is efficiency."

Natalie smiled. "Liar."

Avery picked up her phone, glanced at the screen, and felt her stomach tighten again.

The unknown number hadn't messaged again.

That was almost worse.

She slid the phone into her purse and stood.

"Car," she said.

Natalie nodded, grabbed her own bag, and marched Avery out like a bodyguard escorting a dignitary through hostile territory.

The Montclaire was one of those spaces designed to make you feel underdressed no matter what you wore.

Even the air felt expensive.

The entrance glowed with soft amber lighting. Valets in black coats moved like choreography. A small press line was already forming, cameras angled toward the arriving donors like hungry birds.

Avery sat in the backseat of the car, staring out the window.

Natalie adjusted Avery's earring with the seriousness of surgery.

"Okay," Natalie whispered. "Remember: one smile longer than you're comfortable with. Do not look like you're about to issue subpoenas."

"I do not look like that."

Natalie stared at her.

Avery sighed. "Fine."

Natalie squeezed her hand once, surprising both of them. "You've got this."

Avery blinked. That was... supportive.

Natalie opened the door. "Showtime."

Avery stepped out.

The night air was crisp.

And immediately, the world felt like it was watching.

Miles was already there near the entrance, exactly as promised. Suit, but not severe. Tie loosened slightly. Hair neatly in place. He looked like he belonged without trying.

He turned as she approached.

For a fraction of a second, something softened in his face. Not surprise. Not admiration that was obvious.

Something quieter.

And then it was gone, replaced by calm professionalism.

He offered his arm.

Not to grab.

Not to claim.

Just... available.

Avery hesitated.

Every instinct told her not to. Touch in public was a headline waiting to happen.

Then she remembered the photo. The elbow. The story.

If she refused his arm now, the cameras would read it as tension.

Or worse, denial.

spotlight.

She took his arm.

His hand tightened slightly at her fingertips, a barely-there pressure that said, I'm here.

Natalie disappeared into the background, satisfied and terrifying.

Miles leaned slightly closer, voice low. "You okay?"

Avery kept her face neutral for the cameras. "I am composed."

Miles's breath warmed her ear as he murmured, "That wasn't the question."

Avery's pulse jumped.

"Don't," she whispered.

"Noted," he replied softly. "But I'm still here."

They stepped onto the carpet.

Camera shutters clicked.

Avery lifted her chin and smiled.

A donor couple greeted them. A board member waved. A photographer called Avery's name.

She angled her face, held the smile, offered a brief remark about the pediatric wing, then moved forward.

Miles stayed half a step behind, exactly as planned.

It should have felt controlled.

It should have felt safe.

Instead it felt like walking a tightrope while someone whispered your secrets from below.

As they reached the doors, her phone vibrated inside her purse.

Once.

Twice.

Avery's stomach tightened.

She didn't stop walking. She didn't react.

Miles's hand stayed steady on her arm.

Inside the lobby, the noise rose. Laughter. Glasses clinking. The hum of money and attention.

Avery's phone vibrated again.

Miles glanced at her face, reading micro-signals with irritating accuracy.

"You got another," he murmured.

Avery kept her smile in place as a donor greeted her.

She responded with practiced warmth.

Then, the moment the donor moved on, she slipped her phone out.

One new message.

Unknown: Smile. They love you. Now watch what happens when you stop being perfect.

Avery's blood chilled.

She felt Miles shift closer.

"What is it?" he asked quietly.

Avery held the phone so he could see.

Miles read it once.

His jaw tightened.

Then he looked up, scanning the room with new focus.

"Okay," he murmured, calm but edged now. "We stay together tonight."

Avery's voice went flat. "We already are."

Miles's eyes met hers.

"No," he said quietly. "I mean truly. No gaps."

Avery's pulse hammered, but her face stayed composed.

Across the room, Gerald Whitmore lifted a glass, already searching for her.

The press line was behind them.

The donors were around them.

And someone unseen had promised a moment when she would stop being perfect.

Avery tightened her grip on Miles's arm by a fraction.

Not a cling.

A choice.

Miles leaned in, voice low enough that only she could hear.

"Give me your hand," he said.

Avery's eyes flashed. "Why."

"Because I'm not letting anyone rewrite you tonight."

The words hit.

Not romantic.

Not dramatic.

Protective.

Steady.

Avery slid her hand into his.

His fingers closed gently around hers.

The contact grounded her in a way she resented.

And then Gerald Whitmore's voice cut through the hum as he approached, smiling like a man who loved control.

"Avery," he said warmly. "There you are."

Avery lifted her chin.

Miles's hand stayed in hers.

And somewhere in the room, hidden behind champagne flutes and expensive smiles, someone watched and waited for her to slip.

Chapter 8: Flashbulbs

Avery had walked into a thousand rooms like this one.

Rooms that smelled like money and restraint. Rooms where laughter was curated and every glass of champagne had an agenda. Rooms that existed to reassure powerful people that everything was fine.

Tonight, the Montclaire lobby felt different.

Not because it was bigger or richer, though it was both. Not because cameras were pointed at her, though they were.

Different because her right hand was inside Miles Carter's.

It wasn't a grip. Not a claim.

Just... contact.

Warm fingers around hers, steady pressure that said I'm here without making a speech about it.

Gerald Whitmore approached with a smile that had never once been captured in an unflattering photograph.

"Avery," he said warmly, then let his gaze flick to their hands for a fraction of a second before returning to her face. "Excellent. You made it."

He didn't say anything about the handhold.

That, in itself, was a comment.

"Chair Whitmore," Miles said politely.

Gerald nodded at him the way men nodded at useful objects. "Mr. Carter."

Avery lifted her chin. "We're on schedule."

"Good," Gerald replied. "The press line is behind you. The donors are ahead of you. In the middle is where you live tonight. Visible, but not consumed."

Avery's smile held.

Inside, her stomach tightened.

Gerald leaned in slightly. "Your remarks are at seven. Keep them brief. Keep them warm. Keep them uncontroversial."

"Warm," Avery repeated, as if it were a performance metric.

Gerald's eyes slid again toward her hand in Miles's. "And keep it... aligned."

Aligned.

Avery's smile sharpened.

She wanted to say, I'm not a puppet.

Instead, she said, "Of course."

Gerald nodded once, satisfied, and moved away toward a cluster of board members as if he had placed a chess piece.

Miles's hand remained steady around hers.

Avery didn't look at him. She couldn't, not yet. Looking would make it real, and real was the enemy of composure.

"Don't let him dictate your breathing," Miles murmured.

Avery's head turned slightly. "You're doing it again."

He didn't pretend not to know what she meant. "I'm reminding you that this is your room too."

"This is the Montclaire's room," she replied. "I'm renting it."

Miles's thumb pressed lightly against her knuckles, a barely-there reassurance. "Then take up space."

Avery exhaled slowly through her nose.

She could do space. She could do rooms. She could do cameras.

She could not do anonymous strangers promising to watch her stop being perfect.

Her phone buzzed inside her purse like a pulse.

Avery ignored it.

Miles's eyes scanned the lobby with quiet focus, as if he were measuring risk the way she measured metrics.

"Are you looking for the texter?" she asked softly, keeping her smile in place as a donor couple drifted toward them.

"I'm looking for anyone who looks too interested in you," Miles replied.

"That's everyone," Avery said.

Miles's mouth twitched. "Fair."

The donor couple arrived. A woman with diamond earrings and the faint air of someone who'd never been told no in a restaurant. Her husband wore a cufflink set shaped like tiny anchors, which Avery could not stop noticing.

"Avery Sloan!" the woman exclaimed. "We've been eager to meet you."

"Thank you for supporting the pediatric expansion," Avery replied smoothly.

"Oh, of course," the woman said, waving a hand as if children were a charming hobby. "And this must be Miles."

Miles smiled politely. "Miles Carter."

The woman's gaze sparkled. "The consultant from the photo."

Avery's smile didn't falter. "Miles is supporting our communications the party line."

The woman leaned in conspiratorially. "He's handsome."

Avery's eyelid twitched once. Not enough for cameras. Enough for Miles to feel it, because his hand tightened a fraction.

"Thank you," Miles said, tone pleasant. "We're focused on the kids tonight."

The woman laughed like he'd told a joke that confirmed her world view. "Of course. Of course."

Her husband clasped Avery's hand with damp enthusiasm. "We saw your town hall clip. Refreshing."

Avery's spine straightened. "I'm glad it resonated."

"It did," he said. "My daughter's a nurse. She sent it to me with five exclamation points."

Avery's throat tightened unexpectedly. She let her smile soften, slightly. "Please tell her I appreciate that."

The woman squeezed Avery's forearm. "You're so... relatable."

Avery resisted the urge to glance at Miles like, Do you hear the nonsense I have to endure?

"Relatable is good," the woman continued. "People love a woman who's powerful but still, you know, real."

Avery's stomach dropped a half-inch.

Miles's tone cut in gently. "Avery's leadership is the reason this expansion is possible."

The woman blinked, then smiled again. "Oh yes. Of course. We're thrilled."

They moved on.

Avery kept her smile until their backs were turned.

Then she exhaled sharply.

"I hate this," she said under her breath.

Miles leaned closer. "Which part?"

"All of it."

"That's not specific."

Avery's eyes narrowed. "Stop making me name feelings."

Miles's voice went quieter. "I'm not making you. I'm offering you a way through it."

Avery's phone buzzed again.

This time she couldn't ignore it. Not with Miles watching the room like a hawk and Gerald's phrase echoing in her head.

She eased her hand out of Miles's with controlled movements. She didn't want anyone thinking she was pulling away from him specifically, just... adjusting.

She pulled the phone from her purse and angled it toward herself.

No new message.

a calendar reminder: REMARKS – 7:00 PM.

Her pulse didn't slow.

Miles's hand hovered near hers, not touching, a question.

Avery slid her phone away and re-took his hand, more firmly this time.

It was a choice.

And it made her feel steadier in a way she didn't want to examine.

"Okay," she murmured. "We do this."

Miles's gaze met hers briefly. "Together."

Avery didn't answer. But she didn't let go.

Natalie appeared from nowhere like a glittering tactical unit.

She wore black, sleek, professional, and the sort of shoes that suggested she could run if necessary. In one hand, she held a small clutch. In the other, she held her phone like a weapon.

"Okay," Natalie said briskly, appearing at Avery's left side. "We're doing the rounds, we're avoiding the press traps, and if anyone asks if you two are dating, you laugh like they suggested you're joining a circus."

Miles blinked. "What if they ask if we're joining a circus?"

Natalie narrowed her eyes at him. "Then you say yes. But professionally."

Avery's mouth twitched.

Natalie saw it and looked thrilled, then immediately hardened again. "No smiling. Not yet. Save it for the cameras."

Avery stared at her. "That doesn't make sense."

Natalie pointed toward the press line. "Those cameras are looking for moments. They're not looking for your operational excellence. They want micro-drama."

Miles murmured, "That's depressing."

Natalie nodded. "Yes. Welcome to visibility."

Avery's stomach tightened at the word.

Natalie turned to Avery, voice lower. "I had Marla scrub the internal Slack thread. Midtown Pulse is still up, but it's being drowned by gala content. We're burying it."

Avery nodded. "Good."

"And," Natalie continued, "IT says the unknown number is masked through a burner service. So we can't trace it cleanly."

Avery's jaw tightened. "Of course."

Natalie's eyes softened a fraction. "But we can limit the story tonight."

Avery's throat tightened. She swallowed it down. "We will."

Natalie pointed a finger at Miles. "You. You are half a step behind. That is the frame."

Miles glanced at Avery. "She's confident."

Avery said, "It's her coping mechanism."

Natalie gasped. "Excuse me, it's my superpower."

Avery's mouth twitched again.

Natalie nodded approvingly. "Yes. Great. We're alive."

She steered them forward.

The gala space opened into a massive ballroom where the ceiling glittered with chandeliers and the walls were draped in soft gold fabric. Servers floated with trays. Donors clustered in elegant groups. A string quartet played something expensive.

Avery felt the room look at her.

Not hostile.

Interested.

That was worse.

Natalie guided them toward a group that included Patrick Ames from the Montclaire Foundation.

Patrick's smile was polished. "Avery. Wonderful to see you."

His gaze flicked to Miles, then back to Avery with a fraction too much ease.

Avery's skin prickled.

"We spoke earlier," Avery said evenly.

"Yes," Patrick replied. "And I'm reassured."

Avery's smile stayed in place. "That was the intention."

Patrick's eyes lingered on their hands for the briefest moment. "The photographers will do a quick arrival shot in five minutes. We'll keep it tasteful."

Miles's tone was pleasant. "Appreciated."

Patrick smiled. "Of course."

Avery's phone buzzed.

Once.

Avery's stomach clenched.

She didn't move.

Miles's grip tightened slightly, as if he felt it through her.

Natalie's eyes darted to Avery's purse. "Do not check it."

Avery whispered, "I wasn't going to."

Natalie's face said she did not believe that.

Patrick continued speaking, unaware or pretending not to notice. "We're thrilled about the pediatric wing. The donor response has been exceptionally positive. Your remarks will be... important."

Avery's smile deepened. "They will be brief."

Patrick laughed. "Music to a foundation director's ears."

Avery's phone buzzed again.

Two vibrations, close together.

She couldn't keep ignoring it. Not with her heart beating like this.

She gently loosened her hand from Miles's and slid her phone out under cover of turning toward the drinks table.

Natalie stepped into her peripheral vision like a bouncer.

Avery angled the screen.

Unknown: He's good at playing calm. You're better at playing cold. Let's see who wins.

Her throat tightened so hard she almost coughed.

A second message popped up.

Unknown: Tell him you don't need him. Watch his face.

Avery's fingers went cold around the phone.

Natalie's voice was a whisper at her shoulder. "What."

Avery didn't want to show her. Didn't want to widen the circle.

But Natalie had already become part of it.

Avery angled the phone so Natalie could read.

Natalie's face went utterly still.

Then: "Okay. That's not cute."

Miles appeared at Avery's right side like he'd sensed gravity shift. "What happened."

Avery didn't have time for denial. She held the phone where he could see.

Miles read it once.

His jaw tightened, but his voice stayed level. "We don't react."

Natalie hissed, "I want to react."

Miles's eyes flicked to her. "I know."

Avery's pulse hammered. "They want you to look hurt."

Miles's gaze met hers. "Then we don't give them that."

Natalie leaned closer. "Do we know who it is."

Avery shook her head slightly.

Miles's eyes scanned the room again, sharper now. "But they're close enough to see us."

Avery slid the phone back into her purse.

A donor approached, beaming.

Avery forced her smile back on like a mask.

The donor said, "Oh! Avery Sloan. I loved your clip."

Avery said, "Thank you for being here tonight."

Her voice did not tremble.

Her hands did not shake.

Miles stayed close, an anchor she refused to name.

The donor glanced between them. "And this must be your..."

"Consultant," Avery said smoothly.

Miles added, "We're focused on pediatrics tonight."

The donor laughed. "Of course. Of course."

He moved on.

Natalie exhaled slowly. "Okay. We stay boring."

Avery's mouth tightened. "Boring is survival."

Miles's gaze softened. "You're doing great."

Avery's eyes flashed. "Don't praise me right now."

Miles's mouth twitched. "Noted."

Natalie muttered, "Oh my god, the chemistry is going to kill me."

Avery shot her a look. Natalie gave her an innocent shrug.

The press line was a short corridor near the ballroom entrance, flanked by photographers and two local reporters who looked thrilled to be within champagne range.

Avery's pulse steadied as she approached.

This, she could do.

This was performance, but it was a familiar performance.

Natalie leaned in. "Smile longer than you want to. Don't say anything that could be turned into a quote about executives being exhausted."

Avery murmured, "Yes, Mother."

Natalie glared. "Do not be funny with me."

Miles said softly, "She's already funny."

Avery shot him a look that should have decapitated him.

It didn't.

They stepped into the line.

Cameras flashed.

"Avery! Look here!"

"Avery, a quick comment on pediatrics!"

"Avery, who's your guest?"

Avery smiled. Held it. Warm. Credible. Not soft.

"This evening is about expanding care for children who need it most," she said. "We're grateful for the community's support."

A reporter leaned in. "And Miles Carter, crisis strategist, is here with you tonight. Is he working on the aftermath of your viral moment?"

Avery's smile did not falter.

Miles answered calmly, "I'm here to support St. Catherine's mission."

The reporter's eyes sparkled. "And to support Avery?"

Avery's heartbeat spiked.

Miles turned his gaze toward her, expression neutral enough for cameras, but his voice softened a fraction. "Avery's leadership speaks for itself."

Avery's pulse did something that felt like betrayal.

She lifted her chin. "We're a team tonight."

It came out clean.

Professional.

A sentence Gerald would approve.

A sentence Midtown Pulse could misread into romance, if they wanted.

The cameras flashed faster.

Natalie's eyes widened slightly.

Avery kept her smile in place.

Then, without warning, a photographer stepped closer.

"Can I get you two closer together?" he called.

Avery's skin prickled.

Miles didn't move immediately. He waited for Avery, giving her the choice.

Avery's spine straightened.

Closer meant headline fuel.

Further apart meant tension.

spotlight.

She stepped half a step nearer.

Miles mirrored her, calm, subtle.

The photographer nodded. "Perfect. Avery, tilt your chin. Miles, just... look like you like her."

Avery's eyes widened.

Natalie muttered, "Oh my god."

Miles, voice polite, said, "We're here for pediatrics."

The photographer waved him off. "Sure. Sure. But the internet loves a story."

Avery's smile tightened.

Miles leaned slightly toward her, voice low enough only she could hear. "I'm sorry."

Avery whispered back, "Don't apologize. Stand steady."

Miles's mouth curved faintly. "Yes, ma'am."

Avery's pulse jumped.

The photographer snapped the shot.

"Great," he said. "Okay, thank you."

They stepped away from the press line and back into the ballroom.

Avery's smile dropped the moment they were out of the lights.

Natalie exhaled loudly. "We survived."

Avery murmured, "Barely."

Miles's voice was quiet. "You did well."

Avery shot him a look. "Stop praising me."

Miles nodded as if she'd given a reasonable directive. "Okay."

The fact that he didn't argue made her chest tighten.

She hated that she noticed.

At 6:58, Avery stood near the stage steps with her printed remarks in one hand and a glass of water in the other. The room's attention drifted toward her like a tide.

Gerald Whitmore approached, smiling. "Ready."

Avery's smile held. "Yes."

Gerald's gaze flicked to Miles. "Mr. Carter."

Miles nodded.

Gerald's voice lowered. "Keep her on message."

Avery's eyes flashed. "I am on message."

Gerald smiled. "Of course. That's what I mean."

He moved away.

Avery stared after him, the old anger rising like a familiar pressure.

On message.

As if her voice belonged to them.

Miles stepped closer, not touching, but near enough that she could hear him clearly over the rising hum.

"You don't have to be anyone else," he said.

Avery's throat tightened. "Yes, I do."

Miles's eyes held hers. "No. You have to be effective."

Avery swallowed.

She wanted to snap back.

Instead, she looked down at her remarks.

She could do effective.

She stepped onto the stage.

The lights warmed her face. The room quieted.

Avery stood at the podium. Smiled. Let the silence settle.

"Good evening," she began. "Thank you for being here."

The words came easily at first. Gratitude. Mission. Children. Care.

She saw faces: donors, board members, staff.

She saw a pediatric nurse she recognized from the third row at the town hall.

The nurse lifted her chin, as if to say, I'm here.

Avery's chest tightened.

She continued. "This expansion isn't a building. It's a promise."

The room stilled slightly.

Her voice warmed.

She talked about families in waiting rooms, about parents who counted minutes, about doctors who stayed late, about nurses who did too much and still showed up.

Her tone was controlled, but something underneath it softened into truth.

Then, mid-sentence, the microphone popped.

A small, sharp crack of feedback.

Avery's breath hitched.

Not because of the sound.

Because of the memory.

Live mic. Viral clip.

The room shifted. A ripple.

Avery steadied herself at the podium.

She could feel her heartbeat.

She could feel the eyes.

She looked out and found Miles in the crowd, near the aisle, watching her with calm focus.

Not telling her what to do.

Just... there.

Avery inhaled slowly and said, without losing her smile, "The microphone is reminding us that nothing in healthcare works perfectly on the first try."

A laugh rippled through the room.

Warm.

Not cruel.

Avery continued, "But what matters is what happens next. We adjust. We steady. We keep going."

The room leaned in.

Her voice held.

Her hands did not shake.

She finished strong, thanked donors, thanked staff, and stepped away from the podium to applause that felt genuine.

She walked offstage with her spine straight and her heart pounding.

Gerald Whitmore met her at the steps, smiling like a man who'd watched his investment rise.

"Excellent," he murmured. "Warm. Controlled."

Avery's smile stayed polite. "Thank you."

But she didn't feel controlled.

She felt... alive.

It unsettled her.

Miles met her near the side corridor, away from the crowd.

"You were great," he said quietly.

Avery exhaled. "I almost had a second viral moment."

"You handled it."

"I made a joke."

Miles's mouth curved faintly. "You're learning."

Avery's eyes narrowed. "Don't."

Miles held his hands up slightly. "Noted."

a beat of silence.

Then Avery's phone buzzed again, heavy inside her purse.

Avery's stomach tightened.

She didn't want to look.

She had to.

She pulled the phone out.

A new message.

Unknown: Good recovery. But you're still performing.

Avery's fingers went cold.

Another message immediately followed.

Unknown: Look to your left. I'm the one clapping slow.

Avery's breath stopped.

Slow clap.

That was... specific. Visual. Close.

Miles saw her face change. "What."

Avery turned her phone toward him.

Miles read it once, then his eyes lifted, sharp scanning the room beyond the corridor.

"Don't panic," he murmured.

"I'm not panicking," Avery whispered. "I'm furious."

Miles's gaze flicked to hers. "Fury can look like panic if you move too fast."

Avery's jaw tightened.

She looked to her left.

The ballroom was visible through the open archway.

People were applauding and chatting as the emcee transitioned to the next segment.

Avery scanned faces quickly.

There. Near the bar.

A man in a charcoal suit clapping slowly, deliberately, eyes on the stage.

Not smiling.

Just... watching.

Avery didn't recognize him as a donor.

She recognized him as staff.

Montclaire.

Then she saw the lapel pin: Montclaire Foundation.

Patrick Ames.

He finished the slow clap and lifted his glass, the smallest tilt, like a toast.

Avery's blood chilled.

Miles followed her gaze. His face tightened.

"That's Patrick," Miles murmured. "The foundation director."

Avery's throat tightened. "He called me earlier."

Miles's jaw tightened. "And he wanted you reassured."

Avery stared at Patrick as if staring could force answers out of skin.

Her phone buzzed again.

Unknown: You wanted control. I want truth.

Avery's pulse hammered.

Miles's voice was low, steady. "We don't confront him here."

Avery's eyes flashed. "Why not."

"Because this is his stage," Miles said. "And because if he wants a scene, he'll get one. Not on your terms."

Avery's breath came shallow.

She looked at Patrick again.

He turned away as if he'd never been watching at all, blending into the crowd with practiced ease.

Avery's fingers curled around her phone.

She felt Miles move closer, not touching but near enough that his presence steadied her.

"We leave?" she whispered.

Miles's eyes stayed on the room. "Not yet. We shift. We stay together. We watch."

Avery swallowed.

Her phone buzzed one last time, a final punch.

Unknown: Meet me by the terrace doors in five minutes. Come alone. Or I'll send the next photo to Gerald.

Avery's blood turned to ice.

Miles's gaze snapped to her face. "What did it say."

Avery held up the phone.

Miles read it.

His jaw tightened hard. "No."

Avery's voice went flat. "They're threatening me with Gerald."

Miles's eyes held hers. "You are not going alone."

Avery swallowed. "If I don't—"

"We'll control it," Miles said, voice firm but quiet. "We'll go together. We'll keep it professional. And if someone tries to corner you, they'll have to go through me."

Avery's pulse hammered.

The terrace doors were visible across the ballroom, glass framed in gold, leading to a shadowed outdoor space.

Five minutes.

Alone.

Or a photo to Gerald.

Avery lifted her chin.

Her instinct was to handle it. Alone. Clean. Quiet.

The harder instinct, the new one, was to let someone stand beside her.

She looked at Miles.

His expression was steady. Protective without being theatrical.

"Okay," Avery whispered. "Together."

Miles nodded once. "Together."

And as they moved through the crowd toward the terrace doors, Avery felt the room's glittering noise fade into a single sharp awareness:

Someone here thought they could control her.

And tonight, she was done being a story other people told.

Chapter 9: The Terrace That Lied

The terrace doors were heavier than Avery expected.

Not physically. The weight of them was familiar, the sort of thick glass built to suggest security and exclusivity. It was the symbolic weight that caught her. The feeling that stepping outside meant stepping off-script.

Miles stayed close, not pulling her, not guiding her like a handler. moving with her through the crowd as if their orbit had always been this synchronized.

Avery kept her face composed. Warm smile. Donor posture. The posture that said I belong here and I am unbothered.

Her pulse disagreed.

"Two minutes," Miles murmured, his mouth barely moving.

Avery kept her eyes forward. "Five."

"Two," he repeated, voice low. "We don't let them set the pace."

The phrasing landed. We.

She hated how much steadier it made her feel.

They reached the terrace doors. A server drifted past with a tray of champagne flutes, and Avery took one with reflexive precision, as if a glass could disguise nerves.

Miles did not take one.

Of course he didn't.

He was the sort of man who could be calm on an empty stomach in a crisis.

Avery pushed the door open.

Cold air swept in, crisp and sharp, stripping away the perfume and warmth of the ballroom. The terrace was dimly lit by soft sconces and the distant glow of the city. A few small tables. A couple of smokers near the far railing. The faint hum of traffic beyond the Montclaire's private quiet.

No Patrick Ames.

No ominous figure waiting in the shadows.

Just... normal.

Avery stepped out anyway, because refusing now would look like fear and she would rather choke than confirm someone else's noise.

Miles followed, the door closing behind them with a quiet, final click.

Avery scanned the terrace with fast, efficient eyes.

No one watching them directly.

No slow clap.

No foundation director with a smug tilt of his glass.

Her grip tightened on the champagne flute.

"This is a trap," she whispered.

Miles's gaze moved across the terrace, calm but alert. "Or it's bait."

Avery's mouth tightened. "Same thing."

"No," he said. "Bait means they want you to move first."

Avery's laugh was small and humorless. "I'm thrilled to be in a game."

Miles angled his body slightly, placing himself between her and the terrace door without making it obvious. It was subtle. Professional. Protective in a way that didn't feel like rescue.

It still made her chest tighten.

Avery pulled her phone from her clutch and checked the message again.

Meet me by the terrace doors in five minutes. Come alone. Or I'll send the next photo to Gerald.

Her fingers went cold.

Miles watched her face. "Any update?"

Avery shook her head once. "Nothing."

They waited.

Thirty seconds.

A minute.

Two minutes.

The only movement was the smokers near the railing and the occasional silhouette passing behind the glass doors inside.

Avery's nerves stretched taut.

Then Miles spoke, voice quiet. "They wanted you alone."

Avery's jaw clenched. "Yes."

"And you didn't do it."

Avery lifted her chin. "I don't make decisions based on threats."

Miles's mouth curved faintly. "You do. You don't call them threats. You call them incentives."

Avery shot him a look that would have ended lesser men.

Miles held it, unbothered.

"Do you want to go back inside?" he asked.

Avery stared at the city lights beyond the railing.

She should. The ballroom was safer. Controlled. Familiar. Public.

But public was exactly where this started.

Public was where the microphone stayed live, where her elbow got caught, where a photographer asked Miles to look like he liked her.

Public was where someone decided they could rewrite her into a story.

And somehow, standing here with cold air in her lungs, she could feel the edge of something else.

Not safety.

Not control.

Space.

Avery lifted the champagne flute to her lips, took a sip, and immediately regretted it because it tasted like expensive grapes and bad decisions.

"We stay," she said.

Miles nodded once. "Okay."

Avery glanced toward the door. "If this is Patrick's doing—"

"It might not be," Miles said softly.

Avery's eyes narrowed. "He slow-clapped."

"That could be intimidation," Miles agreed. "Or it could be performance. People like him collect moments like currency."

Avery's throat tightened. "He told me earlier he wanted to keep things focused on the children."

Miles's gaze stayed steady. "And then he asked you to reassure him."

Avery's laugh was sharp. "As if I'm the risk."

Miles's expression tightened, and for the first time tonight she saw the edge of something not calm in him.

"They're treating you like a problem to be managed," he said quietly.

Avery's pulse flickered. "That's headline pressure."

"That's disrespect."

Avery took another sip of champagne to keep her hands from shaking.

Miles's eyes flicked to the flute. "You don't even like champagne."

"It's liquid," she said. "It's in my hand. That's the point."

He watched her, then nodded like he understood something she hadn't said out loud.

"You're trying not to feel anything," he murmured.

Avery's spine stiffened. "I am trying to assess."

"That's your version of not feeling."

She stared at him. "You do not get to rewrite my coping strategies."

Miles's mouth twitched. "I'm not rewriting. I'm translating."

Avery's laugh came out too loud in the quiet terrace air. "That's worse."

Miles stepped closer, not crowding, narrowing the distance enough that she could see the small details of his face under the terrace lights. The line between his brows that appeared when he was concentrating. The steadiness in his eyes.

Avery hated how much she trusted that steadiness.

"Tell me the truth," he said softly.

Avery's grip tightened on the flute. "About what."

"About why that text mattered."

Avery's mouth opened. Closed.

She tried to shape a practical answer, the kind that didn't bleed.

"Because it threatened my board chair," she said.

Miles's gaze held hers. "That's not the truth."

Avery's jaw tightened.

Miles waited. He didn't push. He didn't fill the silence with words. He stood there, steady, making space for her to decide if she wanted to step into it.

Avery stared past him at the city lights.

Then she said, quietly, "Because it implied I want something."

Miles's voice went even softer. "Do you."

Avery's throat tightened. She took a careful breath, and it felt like stepping onto ice.

"I want control," she said.

Miles's mouth curved, faint. "That's always true."

Avery's eyes flashed. "Don't."

He nodded, the faint smile fading. "Okay. Then tell me what else."

Avery swallowed.

the easy answer. The safe answer.

But the safe answer was what she'd always used, and it had gotten her here: a woman with a viral clip, a gala press line, and a stranger texting threats like a director on set.

Avery lowered the champagne flute, her voice dropping.

"I want to not be... reduced," she said. "To a headline. To a rumor. To a board story. To someone else's interpretation of my life."

Miles's eyes softened. "That's fair."

Avery's laugh was quiet and bitter. "It feels pathetic."

"It doesn't," he said firmly.

"It does to me."

Miles took a slow breath, as if choosing words carefully.

"Avery," he said, "you are the least pathetic person I've ever met."

Avery's eyes narrowed slightly. "That sounds like a compliment wrapped in an insult."

"It's a compliment," he said. "And it's also a warning."

"A warning about what."

"That you've built a life where the only acceptable version of you is the one that never needs anything."

Avery's chest tightened so sharply it almost hurt.

She looked down at her hands.

The champagne flute trembled slightly.

She hated it.

She set it on the nearest table with a controlled motion.

Miles noticed, of course he did. His gaze flicked to her empty hand.

"Avery," he said quietly, "you don't have to prove you're untouchable."

Her throat tightened. "If I'm touchable, I'm vulnerable."

Miles's voice stayed calm, but his eyes were intent. "Yes."

Avery's breath caught. "And vulnerability is leverage."

Miles stepped a fraction closer. "Vulnerability is also intimacy."

The word hit like a sudden change in temperature.

Avery's pulse spiked.

"I did not authorize that topic," she said, too quickly.

Miles's mouth twitched. "You don't authorize most topics that matter."

Avery's eyes flashed, but the anger didn't land cleanly. It fractured into something else.

She stared at him, and the terrace felt suddenly smaller, the cold air sharper in her lungs.

"You keep doing that," she whispered. "Standing there like you're... safe."

Miles's gaze didn't waver. "I am safe."

Avery let out a short laugh. "No one is safe."

Miles's voice softened. "I am."

Avery shook her head once, sharp. "You can't promise that."

"I'm not promising outcomes," he said. "I'm offering consistency."

The phrasing struck her, because consistency was the thing she valued most.

She looked away, toward the railing.

Miles didn't let the moment dissolve. He followed her with his eyes, not his body.

"What did the second text say," he asked quietly, "the one after the slow clap."

Avery's shoulders tensed.

She hadn't told him.

She hadn't wanted to.

But something about the terrace, the quiet, the absence of cameras, that loosened her grip on the parts of herself she kept locked.

"It said," she admitted, voice low, "'Tell him you don't need him. Watch his face.'"

Miles went still.

Not offended.

Not angry.

Just... still.

Avery's throat tightened. "It's ridiculous."

Miles's gaze held hers. "Is it."

Avery's mouth opened, closed.

"It's manipulative," she said.

"Yes," Miles agreed. "But it only works if it's targeting something real."

Avery's hands curled at her sides.

She wanted to deny it.

She wanted to say she didn't need him, didn't want him, didn't feel anything that could be weaponized.

But denial had been her packaged for years and it had never made her feel free.

Avery's voice dropped to a whisper.

"I don't like needing anyone," she said.

Miles's expression softened in a way that made her chest ache. "I know."

Avery's eyes narrowed. "You say that like it's... familiar."

"It is," he said quietly. "I used to be you."

Avery blinked. "No, you didn't."

Miles's mouth curved faintly, but no humor in it. "I did. in a different suit."

Avery's breath caught.

She hadn't considered that. She'd assumed his calm was natural, that his steadiness was effortless.

"What changed," she asked, quieter than she meant to.

Miles's gaze moved to the city lights, then back to her.

"I got tired of winning things that made me lonely," he said.

The words landed softly and still hit hard.

Avery's throat tightened. "That sounds like a tagline."

Miles's mouth twitched. "Trust me, it wasn't."

Avery looked at him, and for a brief, dangerous moment she saw him not as a consultant, not as an spotlight problem, not as a variable.

A man.

A man who was standing here with her when someone else tried to isolate her.

A man who didn't ask for anything from her except honesty.

It was... unsettling.

Because it felt like relief.

Avery's voice was barely audible. "You're doing too much."

Miles stepped closer, slow, like he was giving her time to decide if she wanted to retreat.

"I'm doing what I said I'd do," he replied. "I'm not letting anyone rewrite you."

Avery's laugh was quiet. "You keep saying that."

"Because it's true."

She looked up at him.

His face was close enough now that she could see the warmth in his eyes.

Her pulse hammered.

She hated her body's timing. Hated that her breath hitched. Hated that her brain offered images she did not ask for: his hand at her waist, his mouth against hers, the sound she might make if she stopped being perfect.

Avery's voice came out strained. "This is dangerous."

Miles's gaze dropped briefly to her mouth, then back to her eyes, as if he was forcing himself to stay disciplined.

"Yes," he said quietly. "It is."

Avery swallowed. "Because I can't control it."

Miles's voice softened. "Then don't."

Her chest tightened.

She could say no.

She could step back, return to the ballroom, let Natalie handle the donors, let Gerald manage headline pressure, let the texter have their fun.

She could do what she always did.

Or...

She could do the one thing she'd almost never done in her entire life.

She could choose.

Avery's voice was almost a whisper. "If you move closer—"

Miles didn't touch her. He didn't rush.

He said, softly, "Tell me to stop, and I will."

Her mind flashed to the unknown text.

Tell him you don't need him. Watch his face.

She looked at Miles.

He wasn't performing.
no bravado.
patience.
steadiness.

Avery's voice was shaky in a way she despised. "I don't need you."

Miles didn't flinch.

His eyes softened, and in that softness she saw something that made her stomach twist: not hurt, not anger.

Understanding.

He nodded once. "Okay."

Avery's chest tightened harder.

That wasn't the reaction the texter wanted.

It wasn't the reaction she expected either.

Miles took a slow breath. "You don't need me," he said gently. "But you can want me."

The words hit like a door unlocking.

Avery's lips parted.

She didn't answer.

Miles didn't wait for permission beyond what he'd already offered. He lifted his hand slowly, stopping short of touching her cheek, letting her choose whether to lean in.

Avery leaned in.

It was small. Unmistakable.

Her skin brushed his fingers.

Miles's hand cupped her cheek with a tenderness that didn't ask for anything, held.

Avery's breath shuddered.

His thumb brushed the edge of her jaw.

Avery's eyes closed, and the world narrowed to cold air and warmth and the terrifying relief of being held without being handled.

Miles's voice was barely a murmur. "Avery."

Her eyes opened.

His face was close.

Close enough that she could feel his breath.

Close enough that one more inch would change everything.

Avery's pulse hammered like a warning.

And she still didn't move away.

Miles shifted, slow.

Avery's breath caught, and she lifted her hand to his wrist as if to steady herself, as if to anchor him there.

Then the terrace door behind them opened.

Light spilled out. Voices. Laughter.

Natalie's voice, sharp as a blade. "Absolutely not."

Avery and Miles snapped apart like they'd been caught doing something illegal.

Natalie stepped onto the terrace, eyes wide and furious. "Avery, Gerald is looking for you. And I swear to God if I interrupted you two doing something I cannot unsee, I will quit and move to an island where men don't exist."

Avery's face burned.

Miles's ears went pink.

Avery's voice came out too crisp. "We were talking."

Natalie stared at both of them. "You were about to talk with your mouths."

Miles coughed. "Natalie—"

Natalie held up a hand. "No. Don't speak. You'll make it worse."

Avery grabbed her champagne flute off the table like a shield. "Why is Gerald looking for me."

Natalie's expression shifted from comedic outrage to tactical dread. "Because Midtown Pulse posted again."

Avery's stomach dropped. "What."

Natalie stepped closer, lowering her voice. "They posted a new photo. It's not the elbow one. It's from the press line."

Avery's chest tightened. "What did they caption."

Natalie's eyes flicked to Miles. "It's... suggestive."

Avery's throat tightened. "Show me."

Natalie held up her phone.

Avery saw the photo: Avery and Miles standing close, camera flashes exploding around them, Avery's chin lifted, Miles angled toward her with a look that could be interpreted in a hundred ways.

The caption read:

"LOOK AT HIM. That's not a consultant. That's a man in love."

Below it, comments poured in. Heart emojis. Speculation. People tagging friends. People making up backstories like they'd been invited to write fanfiction.

Avery's pulse spiked.

Natalie added, voice tight, "Gerald saw it. He's with Patrick Ames and two donors who think they're matchmaking you like it's a charity auction."

Avery's jaw clenched. "This is insane."

Miles's voice stayed calm, but steel under it now. "The texter escalated."

Natalie's eyes widened. "Texter."

Avery's voice went flat. "They told me to meet on the terrace alone."

Natalie's face drained of color. "Okay. That's not spotlight anymore. That's a person."

Miles's gaze scanned the terrace door and the ballroom beyond. "They're watching. They want you rattled."

Avery's fingers tightened around the champagne flute. "I'm not rattled."

Natalie raised an eyebrow. "You were ninety seconds from kissing him."

Avery's cheeks burned. "That is not relevant."

Natalie's stare was merciless. "It is the most relevant thing that has happened all night."

Miles's jaw tightened, but he didn't argue.

He looked at Avery. "We don't give them a spiral."

Avery swallowed hard. "We don't."

Natalie's voice sharpened. "Gerald. Now."

Avery nodded once, lifting her chin and sliding the mask back into place. Warm. Credible. Controlled.

She turned toward the terrace door.

Miles stepped beside her, not behind her this time.

Natalie noticed and didn't comment, which meant she was truly stressed.

They walked back into the ballroom together.

Avery's phone buzzed in her clutch the moment they stepped into the light.

She didn't look.

She didn't have to.

She could feel the trap tightening like a wire.

Gerald Whitmore stood near the bar with Patrick Ames and two donors, all of them smiling like sharks.

Patrick's smile was polished. His eyes flicked to Avery, then to Miles, then back.

Gerald lifted his glass. "Avery. Mr. Carter."

"Avery," Patrick said smoothly, "beautiful remarks."

"Thank you," Avery replied, voice steady.

Gerald's gaze sharpened. "We have a problem."

Avery's smile stayed in place. "I'm aware."

Gerald leaned in slightly, voice low. "Your consultant is now a romance headline."

Miles's tone was calm. "Gossip doesn't require confirmation to spread."

Gerald's eyes narrowed. "Correct. Which is why you need to manage it."

Avery's jaw tightened. "I am managing it."

Patrick's smile widened. "It's charming, really. The public loves a story."

Avery's eyes flashed. "The public can fund pediatrics without narrating my personal life."

Patrick chuckled like she'd flirted. "Of course. Of course."

Gerald's gaze flicked to Avery's clutch. "Your phone has been buzzing."

Avery's pulse spiked.

Her face did not change.

"It's calendar reminders," she lied.

Gerald's eyes didn't soften. "Give it to Natalie."

Avery's throat tightened. "No."

Gerald's voice stayed polite and dangerous. "Avery."

Miles shifted slightly closer, a subtle signal of support.

Gerald noticed.

His eyes narrowed.

Avery's phone buzzed again.

She could feel it like a heartbeat.

She made a decision.

Not the safe one.

Not the perfect one.

The effective one.

Avery opened her clutch slowly, pulled out her phone, and looked at the screen.

A new message.

Unknown: He touched your face. I have the photo. Last chance to control the story before I do.

Avery's blood turned to ice.

Miles's voice went low. "What did it say."

Avery held the phone so only he could see.

Miles read it.

His jaw tightened hard, the calm finally cracking at the edges.

Gerald's eyes sharpened. "What is that."

Avery lifted her chin, voice steady even as her pulse roared. "Someone is threatening me."

Gerald froze. Patrick's smile faltered for the first time.

Natalie appeared at Avery's shoulder like a blade drawn.

"What," Natalie whispered.

Avery's fingers curled around her phone.

Then she looked up, directly at Patrick Ames.

Because the slow clap.

The timing.

The way he'd blended into the crowd.

And because the threat was now too personal to be random.

Patrick held her gaze, expression smoothing back into composure.

"Avery," he said softly, "I don't know what you think is happening, but—"

Avery cut him off, voice quiet and lethal. "Then you won't mind if I ask security to pull terrace camera footage from the last ten minutes."

Patrick's smile finally broke.

a fraction.

But it was enough.

Gerald's gaze sharpened. "Terrace footage."

Avery didn't look away from Patrick. "Someone watched me out there. Someone is texting me about it."

Miles's voice was low. "We need to leave."

Natalie whispered, "We need to not die."

Avery's eyes stayed on Patrick. "Are you the one texting me."

Patrick's expression snapped back into polished indignation. "Absolutely not."

Avery's phone buzzed again.

A call this time.

Unknown number.

The same one.

It rang once.

Twice.

Avery stared at it.

Gerald's voice was tight. "Answer it."

Miles's voice was firm. "No."

Natalie whispered, "If you answer, put it on speaker."

Avery's pulse hammered.

Then she did the one thing she never did.

She chose chaos on her terms.

She hit accept.

And put it on speaker.

A voice filled the air, smooth and amused.

"Good evening, Avery," the caller said. "Did you enjoy the terrace?"

Avery's blood ran cold.

Miles's hand tightened around hers under the table line, unseen by everyone but her.

Gerald's face went rigid.

Natalie's eyes widened.

Patrick's smile vanished.

And the voice on the phone continued, soft as silk.

"You can stop pretending now," the caller said. "I already have the photo."

Chapter 10: Damage, Controlled

The ballroom didn't go quiet.

It wasn't dramatic like that. This wasn't a courtroom or a movie where the music drops and everyone turns in unison.

It was worse.

The room kept humming. Glasses kept clinking. The quartet kept playing. People kept smiling as if nothing had happened, because most of them hadn't heard the speakerphone.

But the small circle around Avery did go still in the particular way power does when it senses a threat.

Gerald's expression tightened into something that was almost anger but not quite. The board chair didn't do fear in public. He did outrage. Outrage was respectable.

Natalie looked like a firefighter who'd smelled smoke in a building full of dry wood.

Patrick Ames' face had drained of its polish. Not fully, but enough to reveal something underneath it that Avery couldn't name yet.

And Miles, standing half a step too close now, was no longer simply calm.

He was focused.

His hand was at Avery's lower back, barely touching, a presence more than pressure, as if he were anchoring her to the floor so she didn't float into panic.

Avery kept the phone up, speaker on, her face composed like this was a routine donor question about naming rights.

She tightened her fingers around the device and said, evenly, "Who is this?"

The voice on the line was smooth, amused, intimate in the way strangers should never be.

"You can stop pretending now," the caller repeated. "I already have the photo."

Avery didn't let her gaze flick to anyone else. She didn't look at Gerald. She didn't look at Patrick. She didn't look at Miles.

If she looked, she might show something.

And she would not give them that.

"Describe the photo," she said calmly, as if she were in a deposition and the caller had made a claim.

A slight laugh through the speaker. "Oh, Avery. You know exactly which one."

Her stomach tightened anyway.

Natalie leaned closer, whispering without moving her lips. "Keep them talking. Don't give them anything usable."

Miles murmured, even lower, "Short. We keep it short."

Gerald hissed, quiet but sharp. "Turn it off."

Avery ignored him.

"Where are you," Avery asked, her voice still smooth. "In this building?"

Another soft laugh. "Does it matter? You're surrounded by people who want to own you. I'm honest about it."

The words landed like a cold hand around her spine.

Miles's fingers flexed slightly at her back.

Avery continued, "What do you want?"

"Truth," the caller said. "And an end to your little performance."

Avery's smile stayed in place, though it likely looked like she was reacting to a donor compliment. "My performance?"

"The warm executive. The martyr with the mic. The woman who holds everyone else's life together and won't admit she needs anything."

Miles's posture went infinitesimally rigid.

Natalie's eyes widened.

Gerald's mouth tightened hard.

Patrick's gaze darted to the side, then back.

Avery's pulse hammered. She kept her tone steady. "If you intend to extort me, you should know I don't respond well to threats."

Another laugh, slightly sharper. "Extort? No. I'm not asking for money."

Avery held her phone with a firm grip so no one could see her hand shake, because it didn't. It would not.

"Then what," she said, "are you asking for?"

A beat.

Then the voice softened into something quieter, almost... pleased.

"I'm asking you to choose. In front of all of them."

Avery's throat tightened.

Miles leaned in, his mouth near her ear. "End it."

Avery's eyes stayed on Patrick, because she could feel him watching her now, too carefully.

"Choose what," Avery asked.

The caller's voice dropped, intimate and cruel. "The story you control, or the one they write for you. The chair thinks he owns you. The foundation thinks you're a packaged. And your consultant..."

A pause, like the speaker was smiling.

"Your consultant thinks he's protecting you."

Miles's hand slipped from Avery's back to her elbow, not gripping, grounding her in a way no one could see unless they were looking for it.

Avery's stomach twisted.

"You're saying I'm unprotected," she said, voice cool.

"Oh, you're protected," the caller replied. "You're not free."

Avery forced air into her lungs. "I don't know who you are."

"You will," the caller said.

Then, lighter again, like a party guest changing the topic: "Smile, Avery. You're at a gala."

Avery's teeth clenched behind her smile.

Natalie's voice was a whisper. "Avery."

Gerald's voice was low and furious. "End it. Now."

Avery stared at the phone, then said calmly, "If you send anything to Gerald, you'll be dealing with counsel, security, and the Montclaire's own legal team."

A faint hum of amusement. "Counsel. Always counsel. Your favorite religion."

Avery's pulse spiked, but she kept her voice even. "Last chance. Who are you."

A pause.

Then the caller said, "Someone who hates watching you get used."

Avery's chest tightened.

The line went dead.

Avery stared at the screen for one half-second too long.

Then she lowered the phone.

The noise of the room rushed back in, unchanged. Laughter, music, the clink of money on crystal.

As if nothing had happened.

As if everything had.

Gerald exhaled sharply and stepped closer, eyes hard. "Give me the phone."

Avery lifted her chin. "No."

Gerald's mouth tightened. "Avery, this is now board-level."

Avery's smile sharpened into something that looked polite and would have cut glass. "Everything is board-level when it inconveniences you."

Natalie made a tiny sound that might have been a prayer.

Gerald leaned in, voice controlled. "Do not do this here."

Avery's gaze flicked to Patrick, because she needed to see if he was relieved or threatened.

Patrick's expression was composed again, but his eyes were too bright. He looked like someone who'd witnessed a private scene in public.

Miles spoke, calm but firm. "Chair Whitmore, Avery's not staying for more questions in the middle of the ballroom."

Gerald's eyes snapped to Miles. "Mr. Carter, I did not ask for your opinion."

Miles didn't flinch. "You asked for my help."

Gerald's jaw tightened.

Natalie stepped in with the smile of a woman who could weaponize hospitality. "We should move to a private room, Gerald. This is not a conversation for donors."

Gerald's gaze cut to her. "And you are?"

Natalie beamed. "The person who keeps your COO from stabbing people with champagne flutes."

Avery didn't look at Natalie, because if she did, she might laugh.

Gerald blinked, then forced control back into his face. "Fine. Private room. Now."

Patrick cleared his throat, stepping back with smoothness that read as innocence. "I should return to the donors. Avery, again, beautiful remarks."

Avery's gaze stayed on him. "Thank you."

Patrick's smile held. "We'll speak."

It wasn't a promise. It was a warning dressed as charm.

Patrick disappeared into the crowd.

Gerald moved toward a side corridor, Natalie following, and Avery started to follow too.

Miles didn't move.

His hand caught Avery's wrist lightly.

Not stopping her.

Asking her to look.

Avery turned her head.

Miles's eyes were steady. "Not with him," he murmured. "Not right now."

Avery's jaw tightened. "This is my job."

"It's also your life," he said quietly. "And he's going to turn that call into a weapon."

Avery's chest tightened. "Everything is a weapon."

Miles's voice was lower now. "Not everything has to be."

Avery stared at him.

She felt the old reflex: return to Gerald, manage the board, smooth the headline pressure. Prove she was in control.

She also felt something new: a boundary, forming under her ribs like bone.

She glanced toward the corridor where Gerald had gone.

Natalie glanced back, eyes sharp, reading Avery's hesitation like a headline.

Natalie mouthed, Two minutes.

Avery's pulse hammered.

She made a decision.

"Five minutes," Avery said to Natalie, voice calm. "Then I'll meet Gerald."

Natalie nodded once like she'd expected it and vanished down the corridor like a smoke bomb.

Gerald didn't look back.

Miles guided Avery toward a small alcove near a service hallway, partially shielded by a tall floral arrangement that smelled aggressively expensive.

No cameras.

No donors.

quiet and the faint, faraway violin.

Avery leaned a hand against the wall, posture perfect even when her heart was not. "That was reckless."

Miles's voice was soft. "You were brave."

Avery's eyes flashed. "Do not romanticize this."

"I'm not," he said. "I'm naming it."

Avery's throat tightened. "I put it on speaker. In front of Gerald."

Miles nodded. "You did."

"That was—"

"Effective," he said calmly. "Because now he knows it's real."

Avery's mouth tightened. "Now he'll use it."

Miles's gaze held hers. "Only if you let him."

Avery swallowed. The air was cooler here, less perfumed. She could think.

Barely.

"He said I'm influenced," Avery whispered.

Miles's expression tightened. "Yes."

Avery's voice went flat. "He thinks I'm weak."

Miles's eyes sharpened. "He thinks you're human and he's terrified that the board might like it."

Avery's laugh was short and bitter. "They liked it until it got complicated."

Miles stepped closer, careful. "Avery. That caller didn't want money. That's important."

Avery's breath caught. "They wanted me to choose."

Miles nodded.

Avery's fingers curled against the wall. "Choose what."

Miles's gaze dropped to her hand, then back to her face. "You already did."

Avery blinked. "When."

"When you didn't go alone," Miles said.

Avery's chest tightened. "That was strategy."

Miles's mouth curved faintly. "Sure."

Avery glared. "Don't do that."

"Don't do what?"

"Make me sound like I'm capable of feelings."

Miles's eyes softened. "You are."

Avery's pulse jumped.

And then her phone buzzed again inside her clutch.

Avery froze.

Miles's gaze snapped to it.

"Don't," he said quietly.

Avery didn't reach for it. She didn't want to give it the power of her attention. She wanted to crush it. She wanted to throw it into the fountain outside and watch it sink.

The buzzing stopped.

Avery exhaled slowly.

Miles's voice was calm. "He said he has the photo."

Avery's throat tightened. "He does."

Miles's jaw tightened. "The face touch."

Avery's cheeks warmed. "Yes."

Miles's eyes held hers. "That wasn't staged."

Avery swallowed. "No."

"Do you regret it," he asked softly.

Avery's mind flashed back to the terrace: cold air, quiet, his hand on her cheek, the terrifying relief of being held without being handled.

"No," she admitted, and her voice was barely more than breath.

Miles's eyes softened further, and the look on his face was so gentle Avery almost didn't recognize it as desire.

Not the sharp kind.

The steady kind.

"I don't either," he said.

Avery's pulse hammered. "Miles—"

He didn't move closer. He didn't take advantage of the moment. He watched her, like he was waiting for her to choose again.

It was infuriating.

It was also the safest she'd ever felt around a man she could ruin her career for.

Avery's voice went crisp, defensive. "We have to deal with Gerald."

Miles nodded. "We do."

"And Patrick."

"Yes."

"And the press."

"Yes."

Avery's throat tightened. "And whoever that is."

Miles's expression hardened slightly. "Yes."

Avery forced her breath even. "I don't want you hurt by this."

Miles blinked once. "I'm not the one at risk."

"You are," Avery said sharply. "Because this noise is... sticky. And you're leaving in twenty-six days."

Miles's gaze held hers. "Twenty-five."

Avery's jaw tightened. "Stop counting."

Miles's mouth twitched. "I can't."

Avery stared at him, then looked away, jaw clenched so hard it hurt.

Miles's voice softened. "Avery."

She didn't answer.

Miles continued, quietly, "If you keep pushing me away to protect me, you're still letting other people write your choices."

Avery's throat tightened.

She looked back at him.

His expression was steady, but his eyes were not casual. He was in this. Fully.

And Avery could feel herself standing at the edge of something that would change the rest of the book.

The rest of her life, if she were being honest.

Avery's voice was low. "I don't know how to do this."

Miles took a slow breath. "Then let's not do it perfectly."

Avery's laugh was shaky. "That's a nightmare."

Miles's mouth curved faintly. "That's a life."

Avery stared at him.

Then, because she was tired of being managed, tired of being watched, tired of reacting to threats like a trained machine, she made a decision that was not about spotlight.

She stepped closer.

Miles didn't move.

He waited, like he always did.

Avery lifted her hand and placed it on the front of his suit jacket, above his heart.

It was steady.

Of course it was.

"You're too calm," she whispered.

Miles's voice was low. "I'm not calm."

Avery's breath hitched. "Then what are you."

Miles's eyes held hers. "Trying not to move first."

Avery's throat tightened.

She could stop. She should stop. This wasn't the place. Not the time. Not with Gerald waiting, and cameras, and threats.

But the caller had said choose.

And Avery was done letting fear make her choices for her.

She leaned in and kissed him.

It wasn't frantic.

It wasn't performative.

It was deliberate.

A single, clean decision.

Miles froze for half a second, like his body had to confirm he wasn't imagining it.

Then his hand came up to her jaw, gentle, familiar, as if the terrace had been practice for the real thing.

His mouth softened against hers, warm and steady, and Avery felt something inside her unclench that she hadn't known was locked.

He didn't take more than she gave.

He matched her.

And when Avery deepened the kiss, slightly, his hand tightened at her jaw as if to say, Okay. I'm here.

Avery's heart pounded. Her skin heated.

the gala vanished.

only breath and choice and the shock of how right it felt.

Then Avery pulled back, because she still needed air and because she still had a job and because she was Avery Sloan.

Miles didn't chase.

He stayed close, forehead almost touching hers.

His voice was rougher than she'd ever heard it. "Avery."

Avery's breath shook. "That doesn't mean—"

Miles's hand stayed at her jaw, thumb brushing lightly as if to calm her without making a show of it. "I know."

Avery's throat tightened. "I'm not promising anything."

Miles nodded once. "I'm not asking."

Avery stared at him, stunned.

"You're not asking," she repeated.

Miles's mouth curved faintly. "You kissed me in a hallway outside a ballroom full of donors and your board chair."

Avery's cheeks burned. "I did."

"I'm not going to ruin it by negotiating it," he said softly.

Avery's chest tightened. The steadiness of him was unbearable.

"I hate you," she whispered.

Miles smiled slightly. "No, you don't."

Avery exhaled, shaky. "Don't be smug."

"I'm not smug," he said. "I'm... relieved."

Avery's heart squeezed.

She glanced toward the corridor, reality snapping back. "Gerald."

Miles nodded. "We go."

Avery's voice went crisp again, armor returning piece by piece. "We do not look like anything happened."

Miles's mouth twitched. "That's ambitious."

Avery shot him a look.

Miles sobered. "Okay. Professional faces. We can do that."

Avery adjusted her dress collar, smoothed a nonexistent wrinkle, lifted her chin.

Miles lowered his hand slowly, like he didn't want to let the contact go but would.

Then, in the same soft voice that made her furious, he said, "You chose."

Avery's throat tightened. "Don't."

Miles nodded. "Noted."

They walked toward the corridor.

Avery's pulse steadied with each step, control returning like muscle memory.

Natalie met them at the entrance of a small private lounge, eyes sharp.

She took one look at Avery's face, then at Miles, and her expression shifted into something between triumph and dread.

"Oh," Natalie said softly. "You idiots."

Avery's eyes narrowed. "Natalie."

Natalie held up a hand. "Nope. Not now. Later. After we survive Gerald."

Avery inhaled slowly.

They stepped into the lounge.

Gerald stood near the window, phone in hand, expression tight. Two board members sat on a small sofa, watching like they were at a private preview screening.

Patrick was not here.

That was noteworthy.

Gerald turned. "Finally."

Avery offered a controlled smile. "We needed a moment."

Gerald's gaze sharpened. "A moment for what."

Miles spoke smoothly. "For a risk assessment."

Gerald blinked, then looked pleased in the way men like him looked pleased when something could be filed and managed. "Good. Then tell me what you know."

Avery sat, posture perfect. "Unknown caller. Masked number. They referenced a photo from the terrace."

Gerald's eyes narrowed. "A photo that doesn't exist."

Avery's mouth tightened. "We don't know that."

Gerald's voice sharpened. "Then we assume it doesn't. We do not validate threats."

Miles said, calm but firm, "Assuming it doesn't exist is how you lose control of the story."

Gerald's gaze snapped to him. "I am not losing control."

Avery's smile stayed in place. "Gerald, you're already behind. Midtown Pulse posted again."

One board member cleared his throat. "We saw."

Avery nodded once. "Then you know this is not going away by pretending it's nothing."

Gerald's mouth tightened. "No. It goes away by smothering it with the right story."

Avery's jaw clenched. "The right story is pediatrics."

Gerald's eyes flashed. "The right story is stability."

Avery's pulse kicked. "Stability is not pretending I'm not being threatened."

Gerald's voice dropped. "Threatened by what. A gossip account and a voice on the phone."

Avery's throat tightened. "By someone who can access private spaces and knows my patterns."

Gerald's eyes narrowed. "And you put it on speaker in public."

Avery's smile sharpened. "Yes."

One board member leaned forward slightly. "Why."

Avery met his eyes. "Because secrecy is leverage. I removed the leverage."

Silence.

Miles's gaze flicked to her with something like pride, but he didn't say anything.

Gerald's face tightened. "You removed the leverage and gave the room a show."

Avery's eyes cooled. "A show would have been a scene. I gave them an incident. We can manage incidents."

Natalie coughed softly, as if hiding a laugh.

Gerald ignored her.

The other board member spoke, cautious. "What do you want to do."

Avery's breath steadied. "We treat it as harassment. Quietly. We request Montclaire's terrace footage. We ask IT to monitor my number for spoofing attempts. We do not go public."

Gerald's lips pressed together. "And we keep Mr. Carter at your side."

It was phrased as an order.

Avery kept her face neutral. "We keep our team aligned."

Miles's jaw tightened slightly at the possessive implication, but he stayed smooth. "I'll coordinate with Montclaire security."

Gerald nodded once, then fixed Avery with a look. "And you will not deviate from the plan."

Avery's smile was polite. "Gerald, the plan is changing in real time."

Gerald's eyes flashed. "Avery."

Avery held his gaze. "I'm still here."

A beat.

Gerald exhaled through his nose like he didn't like that he respected her.

"Fine," he said. "We proceed. You return to the room. Smile. Be warm. Do your donor rounds. We will not look rattled."

Avery's stomach tightened. "And if the caller contacts me again."

Gerald's gaze sharpened. "You give the phone to Natalie."

Avery's jaw clenched.

Natalie's face went blankly professional. "I can do that."

Miles's eyes flicked to Avery, quiet question.

Avery gave the smallest nod.

Not surrender.

Delegation.

Gerald checked his watch. "We are done here."

Avery rose.

Miles rose beside her.

Natalie followed, already typing on her phone.

As they reached the door, Gerald's voice stopped them.

"Avery."

Avery turned.

Gerald's expression was controlled. "Do not let this... situation become personal."

Avery's smile didn't falter.

"It became personal the moment someone threatened my autonomy," she said.

Gerald's eyes tightened, but he said nothing.

Avery left the lounge.

The corridor outside felt cooler, quieter.

Miles walked beside her, close enough that she could feel the heat of him without touching.

Natalie moved ahead, a tactical missile in heels.

Avery inhaled slowly, then exhaled.

She had kissed Miles.

She had said no promises.

He had accepted that without complaint.

And now she had to return to a ballroom full of cameras and pretend her life wasn't rearranging itself.

Her phone buzzed again.

Natalie's head snapped back. "Give it."

Avery didn't argue. She handed over the phone.

Natalie glanced at the screen, then went still.

"What," Avery asked, voice low.

Natalie swallowed. "It's a text. From the unknown number."

Avery's pulse spiked. "Read it."

Natalie hesitated, then held the screen so Avery and Miles could see.

Unknown: Good. Now you've chosen. Let's see if he survives the story you're about to become.

Avery's blood turned cold.

Miles's jaw tightened.

Natalie whispered, "Okay. That's... unhinged."

Avery's voice went flat. "They saw."

Miles's gaze hardened, scanning the ballroom entrance ahead. "Yes."

Avery's stomach tightened. "They saw the terrace. They saw the hallway."

Natalie's eyes widened. "Wait. How would they see the hallway."

Avery's pulse hammered.

Because the hallway had been shielded.

Because the floral arrangement had blocked the view.

Because it shouldn't have been visible.

Unless someone was closer than they thought.

Miles's voice was low. "Cameras."

Avery's throat tightened. "Montclaire has cameras."

Natalie's face drained. "Oh my god. If the Montclaire security feed is compromised—"

Miles cut in, calm but edged. "We don't spiral. We act."

Avery forced her breath even.

She lifted her chin and walked toward the ballroom entrance.

Miles matched her pace.

Natalie stayed tight at Avery's side.

And as the music rose and the donors turned their smiles toward her again, Avery felt the weight of the night settle onto her shoulders like a cloak.

Only now, she wasn't wearing it alone.

Miles's hand brushed hers briefly at her side, a tiny contact, invisible to everyone else.

A reminder.

Choice.

Then Avery stepped back into the light, smile in place, and thought one clear, furious thought:

If someone wanted a story, she was going to make sure it was hers.

Chapter 11: The Morning After

Avery woke up before her alarm because her brain had decided sleep was optional and consequences were not.

For a few disorienting seconds, she lay still, staring at the ceiling, waiting for her body to catch up to what had happened.

The gala.

The call on speaker.

The board room behind velvet curtains.

The text that proved someone was watching.

And then, in the quiet corridor outside the private lounge, the softest sound of all: her own breath breaking when she kissed Miles Carter like it was a decision she was allowed to make.

Avery rolled onto her side and reached for her phone.

Bad idea.

Her notifications lit up like a warning flare.

She sat up, hair falling forward, and forced her eyes to focus.

Midtown Pulse had posted at 12:47 a.m.

Then again at 7:03 a.m.

And someone had tagged St. Catherine's official account under both posts with the same two-word comment:

"Thoughts?"

Avery stared at the screen until her pulse steadied enough to function.

She clicked.

There it was: a press-line photo, the one from last night. The one where the photographer had told Miles to look like he liked her.

He had looked like he liked her.

The caption had evolved overnight from playful to predatory. "EXECUTIVE ROMANCE OR PR COVERUP? The COO and her 'consultant' are giving main character energy."

The comments were worse.

Not because they were cruel. Because they were confident.

People were sure they knew her.

Sure they knew Miles.

Sure they knew the story.

Avery's mouth tightened.

She scrolled, jaw locked, and found the real problem buried halfway down.

A second image, grainier.

Taken from a distance.

From inside the ballroom.

Toward the terrace doors.

Her and Miles near the archway. Not kissing. Not touching. But close enough to imply intimacy. Close enough to invite interpretation.

The caption underneath:

"Terrace time?"

Avery exhaled slowly and locked her phone.

She did not throw it across the room.

Progress.

Her own reflection in the black screen looked... normal. Bare face. Slightly rumpled. A woman in an expensive apartment who had apparently decided to ruin her own peace.

She set the phone down and stared at it like it might bite.

Then it buzzed again.

A text from Natalie.

Natalie: War room. 8:00. Bring coffee. Also bring your soul, we may need to barter.

Avery's mouth twitched.

She was relieved. Irritated. Weirdly grateful.

All at once.

A new text came through immediately after.

Miles: You awake?

Avery stared at it.

Her thumb hovered.

She could say yes. She could say no. She could say nothing.

She was not afraid of admitting she was awake.

She was afraid of admitting she wanted him to know.

She typed anyway.

Avery: Yes. I saw Midtown Pulse.

Three dots appeared.

Miles: I did too. I'm on my way to the office early. You're not handling this alone.

Avery's chest tightened.

She stared at the words.

Not handling this alone.

It sounded like help.

It sounded like intimacy.

It sounded like risk.

Avery typed.

Avery: We need a plan.

Miles: Already building one. See you at 8.

Avery set the phone down again as if it were hot.

And then she stood up, because if she stayed still she would start thinking about his mouth.

That was not productive.

She showered in record time.

She dressed in her most precise suit, the one that made her shoulders look like they could hold a board meeting and a hurricane. She considered, briefly, the dress from last night.

Then she put it out of her mind before she made a mistake.

She left her apartment with controlled steps, the city air cold against her cheeks, and reminded herself of a few basic facts:

    1. She was the COO of a major hospital system.

    2. She had survived worse scrutiny than a gossip account.

3. She had kissed Miles Carter.

4. She could not, under any circumstances, let the order of those facts change.

The St. Catherine's executive floor had always been quiet in the early morning. Controlled. Polished. The sort of quiet that said important work happened here and everyone should feel slightly nervous about it.

Today it felt like the building itself was holding its breath.

Avery stepped off the elevator and saw Natalie standing outside Avery's office with a rolling cart of supplies like she was preparing for a siege.

Two laptops. Three chargers. A stack of printed screenshots. A legal pad full of notes. A packet of breath mints. A bottle of ibuprofen.

And, as promised, coffee.

Natalie looked up and nodded sharply. "Good. You're alive."

Avery glanced at the cart. "What is all this."

Natalie's expression was grim. "Evidence. Fuel. Emotional support mints."

Avery's mouth tightened. "We don't need emotional support."

Natalie pointed at her like a prosecutor. "You kissed him."

Avery froze.

Natalie's eyes narrowed. "Don't lie. I know what you look like when you've made a choice you want to deny."

Avery's cheeks warmed. "I did not kiss him."

Natalie's stare didn't move. "Okay. You didn't kiss him. You turned into someone who has discovered color exists."

Avery stepped around her and opened her office door. "We have work."

Natalie followed. Of course she did.

She set the coffee down and started talking immediately, brisk and terrifying.

"Here's the situation: Midtown Pulse is trending locally. Not national. Yet. Their post got boosted because someone with a larger following reshared it. I am trying to find who, but my thumbs can only move so fast."

Avery sat behind her desk, forced herself to unclench her jaw, and opened her laptop.

Natalie continued, "Communications is panicking. Gerald is panicking. Donors are curious. Staff are amused. And the internet has decided you are either dating Miles or hiding a corporate scandal."

Avery's eyes narrowed. "We are not hiding a corporate scandal."

Natalie nodded. "Correct. Which means we need to make sure this stays romcom-adjacent and doesn't drift into conspiracy territory."

Avery blinked. "Romcom-adjacent."

Natalie pointed. "Yes. Because the public is already treating you like characters. We either fight that, which makes it bigger, or we shape it, which makes it boring."

Avery exhaled slowly. "What's your plan."

Natalie brightened in the way only a person who loves crisis can brighten.

"Option one: deny everything. Cold. Professional. Statement about mission. This is what Gerald wants. It will not work, because denial is gasoline."

Avery nodded once. "Agreed."

"Option two," Natalie said, holding up a finger, "ignore it completely. Also won't work, because the silence gets interpreted as confirmation."

Avery nodded again. "Agreed."

"Option three," Natalie said, holding up a third finger, "we acknowledge the headline pressure lightly and redirect hard to pediatrics. We do not confirm romance. We do not deny romance. We do not say 'no comment.' We say: 'We're focused on children's care. Our team is aligned.'"

Avery's mouth tightened. "Aligned is Gerald's word."

Natalie shrugged. "We can steal it back."

Avery stared at her. That was... not bad.

The door opened.

Miles stepped in.

He looked like he hadn't slept much either. He'd changed into a suit, but he'd chosen one that was softer than his usual. No tie. Collared shirt. The sleeves were buttoned, but his posture was relaxed, like he was deliberately not escalating the tone.

His eyes went to Avery.

For half a second, something warmed in his expression, so subtle it almost didn't exist.

Then Natalie cleared her throat loudly, and he snapped into professionalism.

"Morning," Miles said.

Natalie waved him in like he belonged here. "Morning. We're building the world's least romantic plan."

Miles's mouth twitched. "Good."

Avery's pulse did something ridiculous.

Miles sat in the chair across from Avery's desk. Close enough to feel like proximity. Far enough to be defensible.

He placed his phone face down on his knee like a man who knew he was being watched. Or like a man who didn't want her to see how many notifications he had.

Natalie slid a printed page toward Avery. "Here. Our proposed statement."

Avery read.

It was short. Calm. Mission-forward.

And it used one phrase that made Avery's stomach tighten:

"Our leadership team is unified."

Unified.

It sounded like a marriage vow.

Avery looked up. "No."

Natalie blinked. "No?"

Avery tapped the phrase. "Unified implies—"

Miles cut in gently. "Coupling."

Natalie's eyes widened. "Okay, yes. True. We swap to 'aligned' or 'coordinated.'"

Avery nodded. "Coordinated."

Miles's mouth twitched again, slightly. "Of course."

Avery shot him a look. "Do not."

He held up one hand. "I didn't say anything."

Natalie stared between them, delighted and stressed. "You two are going to kill me."

Avery exhaled slowly. "We don't have time."

Natalie nodded, then turned toward Miles. "Also, can you confirm that Midtown Pulse doesn't have anything truly compromising besides the press line photos."

Miles's expression tightened. "They don't have the kiss."

Avery's heart stopped for half a second.

Natalie's eyes widened. "So it happened."

Avery's voice sharpened. "Natalie."

Miles's cheeks colored faintly. "We were in a hallway. no cameras."

Natalie stared at him. "Why would you say that."

Miles blinked. "Because it's true."

Natalie pressed two fingers to her temple. "I need a vacation. Or a vow of silence. Possibly both."

Avery forced her voice even. "There may have been cameras."

Miles's gaze went to her. "In that corridor? Unlikely."

Avery's jaw tightened. "We have to assume someone is watching."

Miles nodded once, serious now. "Agreed."

Natalie leaned forward. "We are not turning this into an investigation show. We can quietly ask Montclaire for footage, but we are not doing hacking and spy games. We keep it human-scale. Harassment. Boundary violation. Not a thriller plot."

Avery's mouth tightened. "Agreed."

Miles's eyes held hers too long, as if to say I'm with you without saying it.

Avery broke eye contact first.

She didn't like that she had to.

At 8:17 a.m., Avery's door opened again.

Marla Greene stepped in with her tablet clutched like a shield.

Marla's face was pale. "Avery, I'm so sorry."

Avery's spine straightened. "What."

Marla swallowed. "Someone sent the Midtown Pulse post to a local healthcare reporter. She emailed for comment."

Natalie's head snapped up. "Which reporter."

Marla glanced at her tablet. "Lena Park. City Desk."

Natalie's mouth tightened. "She's not gossip. She's real."

Avery's jaw clenched. "What did she ask."

Marla read, voice trembling slightly. "'Can you confirm whether consultant Miles Carter has been retained for crisis management and whether there is any conflict of interest involving COO Avery Sloan.'"

Conflict of interest.

Avery felt something cold move through her body.

That was how rumors killed careers. Not with scandal. With phrasing.

Miles's jaw tightened, but his voice stayed calm. "There is no conflict of interest."

Natalie snapped, "We do not say that. We say: 'Mr. Carter is contracted through the board for communications support. Ms. Sloan's leadership is focused on patient care and organizational stability.'"

Avery looked at her. "We are not saying organizational stability. That sounds like we're covering."

Natalie sighed. "Fine. Mission and care. But we answer."

Marla's voice was small. "Gerald is asking for you."

Of course he was.

Natalie muttered, "Tell him she's in a war room."

Marla blinked. "He said 'now.'"

Avery stood. "I'll go."

Miles rose too. "I'm coming."

Avery turned sharply. "No."

Miles's gaze held hers. "Yes."

Natalie stepped between them like a referee. "Okay, we're not doing this in front of Marla."

Avery forced herself to breathe.

Miles's voice dropped, calm but firm. "Avery, if Gerald frames you as compromised, you need a witness. You need someone in the room who can push back."

Avery's jaw clenched. "Natalie can do that."

Natalie lifted her hand. "I absolutely can, but I also might say something that gets us sued."

Avery stared at her.

Natalie shrugged. "Truth."

Miles's gaze stayed steady. "Let me come."

Avery's throat tightened.

She hated needing anyone.

She hated that she wanted him there anyway.

"Fine," she said. "But you do not speak unless I signal you."

Miles nodded once. "Understood."

Natalie called after them, "If you two make eye contact for too long, I'm billing you both for emotional labor."

Avery did not respond.

Miles's mouth twitched.

Gerald Whitmore's office felt like a courtroom designed by someone who enjoyed power.

The blinds were closed tighter today. The TV was off, but a printed screenshot of Midtown Pulse sat on Gerald's desk like evidence in a trial.

He looked up as Avery entered, then glanced at Miles, displeased.

"I asked for Avery," Gerald said.

Avery didn't slow. "You asked for the problem. I brought support."

Gerald's eyes narrowed. "Support."

Avery's tone stayed calm. "Professional support."

Gerald looked at Miles. "Sit."

Miles sat.

Avery stayed standing, then sat too, posture perfect.

Gerald slid the printed screenshot toward her. "This is now in the hands of a reporter."

Avery nodded. "I know."

Gerald's voice tightened. "You should not know before I do."

Avery's eyes cooled. "You should have a better system."

Gerald's jaw flexed.

He didn't like being challenged before coffee. That was his personal weakness.

"This," Gerald said, tapping the screenshot, "is an spotlight hazard."

Avery's smile was polite. "The headline pressure hazard is harassment."

Gerald's eyes flicked to her. "Harassment."

Avery kept her voice steady. "An unknown caller contacted me last night. They referenced private moments and threatened to send images to you."

Gerald's face tightened.

"And you put it on speaker," he said.

Avery's chin lifted. "Yes."

Gerald's eyes narrowed. "Why."

Avery held his gaze. "Because secrecy is leverage. I removed the leverage."

Gerald's mouth tightened. "You created a scene."

"I created witnesses," Avery corrected. "That call would have been dismissed as gossip if I handled it privately. Now it is documented."

Gerald exhaled through his nose. "This will require containment."

Avery's jaw clenched. "This will require a boundary."

Gerald's gaze snapped to her. "Avery."

Avery's voice stayed calm. "Do not speak to me like I'm the liability. Someone is targeting me. That is the liability."

Gerald's eyes went sharp.

Miles's posture stayed still, but Avery felt him beside her like a quiet reinforcement.

Gerald leaned back, fingers steepled. "Fine. What is your plan."

Avery spoke evenly. "We respond to the reporter with a mission-forward statement. We request Montclaire security footage from the terrace and surrounding corridors. Quietly. We treat the caller as harassment. We do not validate romance speculation."

Gerald's eyes flicked to Miles. "And Mr. Carter."

Miles stayed silent.

Avery continued, "Mr. Carter is retained by the board. He remains. His presence reduces risk."

Gerald's mouth tightened. "His presence increases noise."

Avery's eyes cooled. "The story exists regardless. If you push him away, you make it louder."

Gerald stared at her.

Then he said, "You are not thinking clearly."

Avery's pulse spiked.

Miles's jaw tightened.

Avery leaned forward slightly, voice sharp but controlled. "Gerald, I am thinking clearly. You are thinking about donors and succession. I am thinking about safety and autonomy."

Gerald's gaze hardened. "This is not about autonomy."

Avery's smile sharpened. "Everything is about autonomy."

Gerald held her gaze. Then, slowly, he exhaled.

"Fine," he said. "We keep Mr. Carter involved. But we will not feed the story."

Avery nodded once. "Agreed."

Gerald's eyes narrowed. "And you will be careful."

Avery's voice went flat. "I have been careful my entire career. Someone else has decided careful is entertaining."

Gerald didn't respond to that.

Instead he said, "There's another problem."

Avery's stomach tightened. "What."

Gerald slid a second printout across the desk.

An email.

Subject: Re: Montclaire Gala KickoffFrom: Patrick Ames

Avery's eyes scanned.

Patrick: Chair Whitmore, I wanted to note that Ms. Sloan appeared... distracted after her remarks. I'm concerned about the pressure she's under and the influence of outside consultants during sensitive donor events. Please advise how you'd like Montclaire to proceed on future appearances.

Avery's vision narrowed.

Influence.

Again.

Gerald's voice was quiet. "He's planting a record."

Avery's jaw clenched. "He's undermining me."

Gerald nodded once. "Yes."

Miles's voice, calm, finally broke silence. "Why."

Gerald looked at him, displeased but forced to answer. "Because Patrick's job is to protect donors. If he thinks Avery's unstable, he'll push for someone else to be the face."

Avery's throat tightened. "Someone else."

Gerald's eyes met hers. "Someone who reads as less... complicated."

Avery's pulse hammered.

Miles's hand tightened subtly against the chair arm. Controlled anger.

Avery swallowed hard and forced herself to speak evenly.

"So Patrick is positioning himself," she said.

Gerald nodded. "Yes."

Avery's eyes cooled. "Then we position back."

Gerald's brow lifted. "How."

Avery's voice steadied. "We give him nothing to use. We control the noise. And we stop acting like I'm fragile."

Gerald's gaze sharpened. "You're not fragile."

Avery's smile was tight. "Then stop treating me like a risk."

Gerald stared at her.

Then, quietly, "You were brilliant last night."

Avery blinked.

It was the closest thing to praise she'd ever heard from him.

He continued, "Your microphone recovery line was good. The room liked you."

Avery's throat tightened unexpectedly.

Gerald's eyes narrowed again. "Which is why this must be contained."

Avery nodded once. "We will contain it."

Gerald leaned forward. "And Avery."

Avery met his eyes.

Gerald's voice was controlled. "Do not let this become emotional."

Avery's smile was polite. "It already is, Gerald. not in the way you think."

She stood.

Miles stood with her.

They left Gerald's office without looking back.

In the hallway, the silence between them was thick.

Miles spoke first, voice low. "Patrick is targeting you."

Avery's mouth tightened. "Yes."

Miles's gaze stayed on her. "And Gerald is watching for weakness."

Avery's eyes cooled. "Yes."

Miles hesitated, then said softly, "And you kissed me anyway."

Avery stopped walking.

Miles stopped too.

Avery's throat tightened. "Don't."

Miles held his hands up slightly. "I'm not pushing. I'm... acknowledging."

Avery exhaled slowly.

"Last night," she said quietly, "I chose one thing that was mine."

Miles's eyes softened. "I know."

Avery swallowed. "It might cost me."

Miles's voice was steady. "Then we make sure it doesn't."

Avery's jaw clenched. "That's not realistic."

Miles leaned slightly closer. "Then we make sure the cost is worth it."

Avery's breath caught.

She looked at him, truly looked, and realized the terrifying part wasn't the gossip.

It was how quickly he had become a place she wanted to stand.

Avery forced her voice even. "War room."

Miles nodded. "War room."

Back in Avery's office, Natalie was pacing like a general.

Marla sat rigidly on the couch, clutching her tablet as if it could save her life.

Natalie looked up. "Okay. Gerald done yelling."

Avery set the Patrick email printout on her desk. "Patrick is positioning himself to undermine me."

Natalie's eyes narrowed as she skimmed. "Oh, I hate him."

Marla looked startled. "We can't say that."

Natalie smiled sweetly. "We can think it."

Avery's voice was calm. "We need to respond to Lena Park."

Marla nodded quickly. "Yes."

Natalie snapped into tactical mode. "Okay. Statement draft. Two sentences. Mission-forward. Zero romance denial. We say: 'Mr. Carter is retained by the board to support communications fit. Ms. Sloan remains focused on St. Catherine's mission and pediatric expansion.'"

Avery nodded. "Good."

Miles added, "And we offer Lena a tour of the pediatric site next week. Controlled context. Redirect."

Natalie blinked, then grinned. "Okay, that's smart."

Avery's mouth tightened. "We cannot appear like we're bribing press."

Miles shook his head. "It's transparency. It keeps the story in patient care, not gossip."

Avery hesitated, then nodded. "Fine."

Natalie scribbled. "Done."

Marla exhaled shakily. "Okay."

Avery looked at Natalie. "Now the internal threat."

Natalie's face tightened. "We request Montclaire footage."

Miles nodded. "I'll call Montclaire security. Quietly."

Avery's eyes narrowed. "Patrick will find out."

Miles said, "Let him."

Natalie pointed at Miles. "I like when you get firm. It's… stabilizing."

Avery shot Natalie a look.

Natalie lifted her hands. "Sorry. It's true."

Avery ignored her and looked at Miles. "No solo moves."

Miles nodded. "No solo moves."

Avery's phone buzzed.

Natalie's hand shot out instantly. "Give it."

Avery handed it over without argument.

Natalie glanced at the screen and went still.

Avery's stomach dropped. "What."

Natalie swallowed. "It's... Midtown Pulse again."

Avery's pulse spiked. "What did they post."

Natalie held up the screen.

A new post.

Not a photo.

A poll.

"Should Avery Sloan and Miles Carter admit it already?" Options: YES / THEY'RE OBVIOUSLY IN LOVE / WHO CARES, SAVE THE KIDS / THIS IS A COVERUP

The comments were already rolling.

Some were funny. Some were annoying. Some were cruel.

One stood out.

A newly created account with no profile picture wrote:

"Wait until lunch today. She'll choose wrong."

Avery's blood chilled.

Miles's gaze sharpened. "That's not a fan."

Natalie's voice was tight. "That's our texter."

Marla whispered, "Lunch?"

Avery's jaw clenched. "They know my schedule."

Miles's voice went low. "Then we change it."

Avery's instinct screamed no. Schedules were control.

Her newer instinct, the one she hated, whispered: changing plans doesn't mean weakness. It means strategy.

She exhaled slowly.

"We don't cancel lunch," Avery said.

Natalie stared. "Avery."

Avery lifted her chin. "We move lunch. We make it public. We put it in the cafeteria with cameras and people and no private corners."

Miles's eyes held hers, admiration flickering. "You're taking away their stage."

Avery's voice was steady. "Yes."

Natalie's expression shifted into delighted terror. "Okay. That is spicy. I like it."

Avery shot her a look. "Do not say spicy."

Natalie grinned. "You kissed him. Everything is spicy now."

Avery's cheeks warmed.

Miles's mouth twitched.

Avery ignored both reactions and turned to Marla. "Coordinate with comms. We invite Lena Park to cover a pediatric update in the cafeteria. Casual. Mission-forward."

Marla blinked. "In the cafeteria."

Avery nodded. "Yes. We make the story boring."

Marla nodded slowly. "Okay."

Natalie looked at Avery, eyes sharp. "This is you leaning in."

Avery's jaw tightened. "This is strategy."

Natalie's smile softened. "Sure."

Miles's gaze stayed on Avery, quiet and steady.

Avery felt her pulse settle.

Not because the problem was solved.

Because she wasn't alone in the room with it.

She looked at Natalie. Then Marla. Then Miles.

"Here's what happens next," Avery said, voice calm and clear. "We stop reacting. We act. We hold the story. We focus on pediatrics. And we do not let anyone isolate me again."

Miles's voice was soft. "Agreed."

Natalie nodded briskly. "Agreed."

Marla swallowed and nodded too. "Agreed."

Avery's phone buzzed in Natalie's hand again.

Natalie glanced at it, then looked up, eyes wide.

"It's a text," Natalie whispered. "From the unknown number."

Avery's stomach tightened. "Read it."

Natalie hesitated, then held up the screen so Avery and Miles could see.

Unknown: Cafeteria is smart. But you can't hide forever. Today I'll show you what "influence" looks like.

Avery's blood turned cold.

Miles's jaw tightened.

Natalie whispered, "Okay. That's not funny anymore."

Avery lifted her chin, voice steady even as her pulse roared.

"Then we make sure," she said quietly, "that when they show themselves, the whole hospital is watching."

And for the first time, the idea didn't feel like fear.

It felt like a plan.

It felt like war.

And Avery Sloan, for all her reluctance, had never been bad at war.

Chapter 12: The Choice, On Camera

By 11:42 a.m., Avery had already made three decisions she would have mocked herself for a week ago:

1. She wore a softer suit. Not soft, exactly. Just... less like armor and more like a person who could exist outside a boardroom.

2. She let Natalie plan her lunch. Which meant she was now eating in the cafeteria like a normal human instead of at her desk like a machine.

3. She stopped pretending the internet wasn't writing fanfiction about her life, and started treating it like weather: unavoidable, manageable, occasionally catastrophic.

The cafeteria at St. Catherine's was bright, loud, and relentlessly alive.

It smelled like coffee and fry oil and disinfectant. Nurses moved in clusters, laughing with the exhausted joy of people who'd earned every breath. Residents hovered over trays like sleep-deprived moths drawn to fluorescent light. An orderly argued cheerfully with a barista about whether "extra espresso" was a medical necessity.

Avery had spent years avoiding this exact sort of chaos.

Today, she walked into it on purpose.

Natalie flanked her on the left like a protective little missile. Marla trailed behind with a tablet and the haunted expression of someone whose job description had recently expanded into "public crisis witness." Miles walked on Avery's right, close enough to be seen, far enough to be plausible.

Avery felt eyes. Staff eyes. Curious eyes. The gentle kind, the amused kind, the Is that him? kind.

She kept her posture steady. She did not speed up. She did not lower her gaze.

This was her building. Her people. Her mission.

And if someone wanted a stage, she was going to choose the lighting.

Natalie whispered without moving her lips, "Lena's here."

Avery scanned and spotted Lena Park near a corner table, notebook open, coffee untouched, expression calm in that dangerous journalist way that suggested she'd already written three versions of the story and was waiting to see which one the world deserved.

Lena met Avery's eyes and gave a small, professional nod.

No fangirl energy. No gossip hunger.

attention.

Good.

Avery angled her body slightly toward Lena as she approached the service area where a small cluster of staff had gathered around a rolling poster board that read: Pediatric Expansion: What's Next.

This was the pretense. The shield. The truth, too.

The pediatric wing was real. The families were real. The need was real.

If anyone tried to reduce Avery Sloan to a romance headline, the best counter was to remind them she was building something that mattered.

Avery lifted her voice slightly, warm but controlled. "Good afternoon."

Heads turned. Conversations softened. Someone in scrubs whispered, "That's her."

Avery smiled. Held it longer than she wanted. Natalie would be proud.

"I'm not here to interrupt your break," Avery said. "I'm here because you deserve to hear the next steps directly, not through a press release."

A few faces relaxed.

Avery continued, "The pediatric expansion isn't a PR line. It's an operational reality. Staffing needs, scheduling, training, equipment, workflow. Real work, done by real people."

A nurse near the front lifted her chin, skeptical but listening.

Avery took a breath. "We've already secured the first phase of donor commitments. That means we can move into design finalization and hiring plans sooner than projected."

A ripple. Not applause. Approval. The kind that mattered more.

Avery felt a slight shift beside her.

Miles had stepped half a step back, exactly as planned. Support, not dominance. But his presence still read. It always did.

Natalie angled herself to the side, scanning the room with the focus of someone who'd once survived middle school and never forgot the tactics.

Marla hovered, ready to faint at any moment.

Avery smiled. "I'll take questions."

A hand went up. A resident with tired eyes and a tray balanced on one forearm.

"Is this going to mean more overnight coverage?" he asked. "Because we're already—" He paused, then tried to soften it. "We're stretched."

Avery nodded. "It's a fair concern. The expansion doesn't work without staffing. Which is why the hiring plan is phased and backed by secured funding. Not hope."

The resident blinked, surprised by the bluntness.

Avery added, "And we're reviewing overnight support models so you're not carrying risk alone."

A few heads nodded. Someone murmured, "Finally."

Avery's gaze flicked briefly toward Lena Park.

Lena's pen moved, quick and precise.

Good. Write that. Not "who kissed who." Write that.

Another hand went up. A nurse with a messy bun and the expression of someone who had seen executives say pretty words and then disappear.

"Are we going to see you down here more," she asked, voice neutral but loaded. "Or is this a... lunch cameo."

Avery held her gaze.

It would have been easy to deflect. Easy to give a vague statement about "visibility."

Avery didn't.

"You'll see me," she said simply. "Not as a performance. As part of my job. If I can't stand in the building I'm responsible for, then I'm not doing leadership. I'm doing theater."

The nurse stared, then nodded once, sharp and approving.

Natalie's shoulders eased slightly.

Miles's expression didn't change much, but Avery felt the quiet heat of his attention anyway, like sunlight on a locked door.

Avery opened her mouth to call on the next question—

And felt it.

A shift.

Not in the staff.

In the air.

Avery's gaze lifted.

Patrick Ames stood near the far entrance to the cafeteria, immaculate in a charcoal suit that didn't belong in a room that smelled like fries. He looked like he'd walked in from a different world.

Beside him was Gerald Whitmore.

Of course.

Gerald's presence pulled focus without asking for it. He didn't need to raise his voice. He didn't need to smile. He simply existed in a way that told people he was used to rooms rearranging around him.

Patrick smiled at Avery like he was pleased to find her right where he expected.

Avery's stomach tightened.

Natalie whispered, "He followed."

Miles's voice was low. "Let him."

Avery's face stayed warm. Her spine stayed straight.

Patrick moved forward through the cafeteria like he owned the air, Gerald behind him like a shadow with an agenda.

Staff watched them approach with the same wary curiosity they reserved for visiting surgeons and surprise audits.

Patrick stopped near the front cluster, close enough to be heard.

"Ms. Sloan," he said smoothly. "This is… charming."

Avery smiled. "Mr. Ames."

Patrick's gaze flicked to Lena. "Ah. Press."

Lena's expression remained calm. "Lena Park."

Patrick offered a smile meant to charm and disarm. "Montclaire Foundation. We work closely with St. Catherine's."

Lena nodded once, noncommittal.

Gerald stepped forward, his presence adding weight to the moment like an anchor dropped into the room. "Avery."

"Gerald," Avery said, voice steady.

Gerald's gaze swept the cafeteria, and Avery saw the calculation behind his eyes: staff, press, spotlight, risk.

He would have preferred this conversation behind closed doors.

That was exactly why Avery had moved it here.

Patrick clasped his hands. "It's wonderful to see leadership engaging so directly. Donors love accessibility."

Avery's smile sharpened slightly. "So do staff."

Patrick's smile didn't falter. "Of course."

Then he did it.

He let his eyes drift—once—to Miles.

"Mr. Carter," Patrick said pleasantly. "Still on duty, I see."

Miles returned the smile with professional calm. "Always."

Patrick's eyes gleamed. "Helpful, having outside perspective during sensitive moments."

Avery felt Natalie stiffen.

Felt the room lean in without realizing it.

Patrick was laying track. Quietly. Politely. Publicly.

Gerald's mouth tightened. "Patrick," he warned, voice soft.

Patrick ignored the warning with the ease of someone who knew Gerald needed him.

Patrick turned back to Avery. "I'm curious, Ms. Sloan. With the chatter this morning, have you considered how... perception may affect donor confidence."

Avery's pulse remained even.

She tilted her head. "Perception of what."

Patrick smiled. "Oh, you know. The story people want."

Lena's pen paused for half a beat.

Staff shifted subtly. Interested now. Protective, too. Avery could feel it. They might not love executives, but they hated being used as props.

Avery's voice stayed warm. "The story people want is that children get care. That's the story we're building."

Patrick's smile widened. "A noble frame. But donors do respond to stability."

Gerald's eyes narrowed.

Patrick continued, "And sometimes stability is undermined by... blurred lines."

Avery felt Marla suck in a small breath.

Natalie's eyes went bright.

Miles's jaw tightened once, controlled.

Avery smiled, calm. "You mean conflict of interest."

Patrick's expression stayed smooth. "I mean influence."

There it was.

The word again.

The texter's favorite.

Avery's body went still in a way only she could feel. Like a door locking.

She looked at Patrick.

And she realized something with sudden clarity:

Patrick didn't know the whole threat.

Patrick was not the caller.

Patrick was opportunistic. He was maneuvering. He was collecting.

But the caller... the caller was enjoying this.

Someone had wanted this moment to happen here, under fluorescent lights, with staff and press and Gerald watching.

Avery felt the impulse to retreat. To deny. To smooth.

To make herself small enough to be safe.

She didn't.

She turned her head slightly, meeting Gerald's gaze.

His eyes were tight. His jaw flexed.

He wanted her to shut this down. Quick. Clean. Cold.

Avery turned back to Patrick.

Then she did what the unknown caller said she couldn't do.

She chose.

Avery's voice stayed warm, clear enough for the room. "If you're concerned about influence, Patrick, let's define it."

Patrick's smile didn't move. "By all means."

Avery gestured lightly toward the pediatric expansion board. "Influence is a donor pushing for a vanity project instead of a functional wing. Influence is a board chair asking me to sound 'warm' so the public likes me while staff carries the weight. Influence is a foundation director planting a record to undermine a hospital leader because she didn't smile the way he preferred."

The room went quiet.

Not dramatic quiet. Real quiet. Staff quiet.

Lena's pen started moving faster.

Patrick's smile finally tightened at the edges.

Gerald's eyes widened slightly, then sharpened.

Avery continued, steady as a metronome. "Influence is not collaboration. It's control."

Natalie looked like she was about to explode with pride and fear.

Avery's gaze swept the staff. "What we're doing here today is collaboration. It's operational planning. It's listening. It's building something that works."

Then Avery looked at Miles.

Not a glance. A decision.

She turned her body slightly, placing him in the frame with her, not behind her.

The cafeteria didn't gasp, but Avery felt the collective attention tilt. The room understood instinctively when someone stepped into partnership.

Avery lifted her chin. "Mr. Carter is here because the board retained him. He is here because St. Catherine's needed clarity in a moment of public scrutiny."

Patrick's voice stayed smooth. "And the headline pressure."

Avery didn't flinch. "And yes, the spotlight. Because spotlight are part of leadership now whether we like it or not."

Gerald's mouth tightened. He hated hearing that stated aloud. It made it real.

Avery went on, "He's not here to influence me. He's here to keep me from being managed by people who mistake control for stability."

That landed like a strike.

Patrick's face went carefully blank.

Gerald's gaze hardened, but he didn't interrupt. Not with staff watching. Not with press writing.

Avery kept her tone calm, almost conversational. "If donors feel unsettled because I have a consultant helping the hospital communicate effectively, that's not donor confidence. That's donor entitlement."

A murmur rippled through the staff cluster, quiet but approving.

Patrick's smile returned, thinner now. "You're direct."

Avery smiled. "It saves time."

Patrick's eyes flicked toward Lena. "And what about the... romantic noise."

Avery didn't look away. "That's not our mission."

Patrick's smile widened. "But it is a story."

Avery's pulse remained steady.

She heard the caller's voice in her head: Choose. In front of all of them.

Avery turned slightly toward Lena Park, then back to the staff.

"Here's the truth," Avery said, voice warm enough to hold a room. "You're going to see a lot of stories about me. Some will be flattering. Some will be ugly. Some will be ridiculous. But none of them change what matters here."

She gestured to the cafeteria, to the staff, to the building itself. "This hospital runs because of you. The pediatric expansion happens because you do the hard work every day. I will not allow anyone to distract from that with rumors."

She paused, then added, eyes steady, "And I will not allow anyone to isolate me so they can control me."

There it was.

A boundary, spoken out loud.

Avery felt the air shift.

It didn't feel like weakness.

It felt like authority.

Patrick's smile didn't reach his eyes. "Avery, no one is trying to control you."

Avery's smile was soft and lethal. "Then you'll have no objection to me asking Montclaire security to preserve terrace and corridor footage from last night."

Patrick's face flickered. The smallest crack.

Then Gerald spoke, voice calm and cold. "We've already requested it."

Avery didn't turn to him, but she felt the weight of that statement.

Gerald had moved without telling her. Or Gerald was lying for headline pressure.

Either way, it meant something.

Patrick recovered quickly. "Of course. Transparency is important."

Avery nodded. "Yes. It is."

She looked at Lena Park again, then back to the staff. "Now. If anyone has further questions about pediatrics, staffing, or workflow, I'm here."

A nurse raised her hand immediately, as if refusing to let Patrick and Gerald hijack the cafeteria.

"Will there be more pediatric mental health resources?" the nurse asked.

Avery's shoulders eased fractionally. "Yes. And we're partnering with two local programs to expand coverage."

The cafeteria exhaled, returning to the real work.

Patrick and Gerald stood there, suddenly irrelevant.

Patrick's eyes stayed on Avery as if she'd surprised him.

Gerald's expression was unreadable.

Natalie leaned in close to Avery's shoulder, whispering, "That was... feral. In a good way."

Avery murmured back, "Natalie."

Natalie grinned. "You ate him."

Miles didn't speak. But Avery felt him close. Felt his presence as a silent reinforcement.

And she hated, in a way that made her chest ache, that she wanted to reach for him.

Instead, she kept answering questions. Calm. Clear. Warm.

She did her job.

Twenty minutes later, the crowd had shifted. Staff drifted away, returning to work. The cafeteria regained its noisy rhythm. Lena Park closed her notebook and approached Avery with a measured expression.

"Thank you," Lena said. "For doing this here."

Avery nodded. "The hospital should be visible."

Lena's gaze flicked briefly to Miles, then back. "You're aware the internet will interpret what happened."

Avery's mouth tightened. "Yes."

Lena studied her. "Your statement about isolation. That was... pointed."

Avery held her gaze. "It was honest."

Lena nodded slowly. "Okay. I'm going to write this as a leadership story. Not a romance story."

Avery felt her shoulders loosen by half a centimeter. "I appreciate that."

Lena's eyes sharpened. "But be aware. Someone wants the romance story. Someone is feeding it."

Avery's blood cooled. "We know."

Lena lowered her voice. "Then treat it like a source. Not like a troll."

Avery blinked.

Lena continued, "A source with an agenda. Which means they'll escalate."

Avery nodded once. "Understood."

Lena stepped back. "Good luck."

Then she walked away.

Avery stood still, letting the fluorescent light hum above her like a warning.

Natalie appeared at her side, phone in hand, eyes wide. "Okay, so... we have a problem."

Avery's stomach tightened. "What."

Natalie held up her phone.

Midtown Pulse had posted again.

A video this time.

Short. Grainy. Clearly taken from the cafeteria's far side.

Avery on camera. Patrick in frame. Gerald behind him. Miles beside Avery. Avery turning her body to include Miles, choosing him in the frame.

The caption:

"SHE PICKED HIM. LIVE. IN THE CAFETERIA. ARE WE WATCHING A ROMCOM OR A COUP?"

Avery's jaw clenched.

Miles leaned in, voice low. "We didn't give them romance."

Natalie's eyes were sharp. "They'll take whatever we give."

Marla appeared behind them, pale. "Gerald is calling."

Natalie groaned. "Of course he is."

Avery took a slow breath. Control returned like muscle memory.

"Fine," Avery said. "We'll talk to Gerald."

Miles's voice stayed steady. "Together."

Avery nodded once.

They started walking toward the elevator bank.

Halfway there, Avery's phone buzzed in her pocket.

Natalie's hand shot out automatically, then stopped. She looked at Avery. "Do you want me to—"

Avery shook her head. "No."

She pulled out her phone herself.

A text.

Unknown number.

Avery's fingers went cold as she read it.

Unknown: Good speech. Wrong enemy.Unknown: Check your email. Ethics complaint filed. Timestamp: two minutes ago.

Avery's stomach dropped.

She lifted her gaze to Miles, then to Natalie.

Natalie saw her face and went still. "What."

Avery didn't answer. She opened her email.

There it was.

A system notification.

New Report Submitted: Ethics & Compliance HotlineSubject: Conflict of Interest – Consultant Relationship / Executive InfluenceStatus: Under ReviewSubmitted: 12:14 p.m.

Avery's throat tightened.

Miles's jaw set.

Natalie's eyes flashed. "Oh, they're going nuclear."

Avery stared at the screen as if staring could force it back into nothing.

This wasn't gossip.

This was a weapon.

And it had been fired the moment she chose, on camera, to stand beside him.

Avery lifted her chin slowly, breath steadying.

"Okay," she said quietly.

Miles's voice was low. "Avery—"

Avery cut him off gently, eyes hard now. "No. This is what they wanted. Pressure. Isolation. Panic."

Natalie whispered, "What do we do."

Avery looked from the email to the elevator doors, then back to her team.

She felt the old version of herself—the perfect, controlled executive—rise like a shield.

But underneath it was something new.

Something stubborn.

Something that had kissed Miles Carter in a hallway and then refused to be moved in a cafeteria.

Avery's voice was calm, almost cold. "We respond like leaders. We don't hide. We don't flinch. And we do not let them define what influence means."

She slid the phone back into her pocket.

The elevator doors opened with a soft chime.

Avery stepped in first.

Miles and Natalie followed.

And as the doors closed, sealing them into a small mirrored box, Avery met her own reflection and realized the real midpoint truth:

She hadn't chosen Miles.

She had chosen a life where she could be seen.

And whoever was playing this game had decided to punish her for it.

Chapter 13: Elevator Rules

The elevator doors slid shut with a soft, indifferent chime, sealing Avery inside a mirrored box with the two people most capable of ruining her life.

Avery's voice came out too flat. "Or a person with access."

Avery's mouth tightened. "An ethics complaint doesn't feel human."

Natalie's eyes narrowed. "It's human in the worst way. It's someone weaponizing policy to embarrass you."

Miles added, steady, "And to separate us."

Avery's pulse jumped at the word us, which was ridiculous. It was also true.

Avery looked at Natalie. "Stop narrating."

"Okay," Avery said, voice controlled. "We respond calmly. We notify counsel. We comply."

Natalie made a choking sound. "You said comply like it's a dirty word."

"It is a dirty word," Avery said.

Miles's gaze stayed on her. "Avery."

She didn't look at him.

Miles's voice softened. "This isn't about policy."

Avery finally turned her head, meeting his eyes in the mirrored reflection.

His expression wasn't dramatic. He wasn't angry or wounded or heroic.

He was simply... present.

"It's about pressure," Miles continued. "They want you to believe that choosing me publicly created consequences you can't control."

Avery's jaw flexed. "It did create consequences."

Miles nodded once. "Yes. But the goal is the same as last night."

Natalie's brows lifted. "Isolation."

Miles glanced at Natalie. "Exactly."

Natalie let out a slow breath. "Okay. So we don't isolate. Great. How do we do that when the entire building has the internet in their pocket."

Avery stared at her reflection again. The elevator felt smaller.

Her phone buzzed in Natalie's hand. Natalie looked at it and hissed like it had insulted her mother.

"Midtown Pulse again," Natalie said.

Avery's stomach tightened. "Don't show me."

Natalie blinked. "Are you sure."

Avery's voice was calm. "Yes."

Natalie squinted at the screen anyway because Natalie was incapable of not knowing. "Okay. It's not a post. It's a comment. Under their own cafeteria video."

Avery's throat tightened. "What does it say."

Natalie hesitated. Then, because they were trapped in an elevator with nowhere for Avery to hide, she read it out loud.

"'If she wants to play leadership in public, let's see her answer questions in public.'"

Avery's spine stiffened.

Miles's gaze sharpened. "That's a prompt."

Natalie nodded grimly. "That's a dare."

Avery swallowed. "From a burner account?"

Natalie checked. "New account. No profile picture. No followers. Username is something like... 'CafeteriaTruth.'"

Miles's jaw tightened. "They're trying to bait a reaction."

Avery stared at the closed elevator doors as the floor numbers ticked downward far too slowly.

"I'm not reacting," Avery said.

Natalie's eyes flicked to her. "You're reacting right now. You're doing it silently."

Avery shot her a look.

Natalie held up both hands. "Okay. Sorry. But my point stands."

Miles spoke, calm, "We don't meet this on their terms."

Avery's voice was clipped. "We can't pretend it's not happening."

"No," Miles agreed. "But we can choose where it happens."

Natalie's mouth twitched. "Avery's new hobby. Choosing stages."

Avery stared at Natalie. "You're enjoying this."

Natalie's eyes widened. "I am not enjoying it. I am thriving in a crisis because it's the only time people listen to me without interrupting."

Miles said mildly, "That's fair."

Natalie pointed at him. "Do not validate me. It makes me emotional."

Avery pressed her lips together. A laugh threatened and she refused it on principle.

The elevator chimed and the doors slid open onto the executive floor.

Avery stepped out first, because if she didn't, she might hesitate.

Natalie and Miles followed.

The hallway smelled like lemony floor polish and tension.

"Avery," Marla blurted. "Gerald is on line one."

Natalie groaned. "Of course he is."

Marla's eyes flicked to Natalie, then to Miles, then back to Avery. "Also, Lena Park is downstairs."

Avery's stomach dropped. "Why."

Marla swallowed. "She says she's here for a pediatric follow-up."

Natalie's expression sharpened instantly. "Good. That's good. We want that."

Avery exhaled. "And what else."

Marla hesitated. That hesitation was a complete sentence.

Avery's voice stayed level. "Marla."

Marla blurted, "Midtown Pulse is outside."

Natalie froze. "Outside where."

Marla swallowed. "The main entrance. Not officially. But there are two people filming. One looks like a freelance social guy with a ring light."

Avery's pulse spiked.

Miles's gaze sharpened. "They're trying to get you leaving the building."

Natalie hissed, "They are trying to force a public reaction."

Avery closed her eyes for half a second, then opened them.

"Okay," she said softly. "Then we don't give them what they want."

Miles nodded. "We choose the stage."

Natalie's eyes were bright with adrenaline. "We absolutely choose the stage."

Avery turned to Marla. "Tell Gerald I'll call him back in ten minutes."

Marla looked terrified. "He said now."

Avery's voice went colder. "Ten minutes."

Marla nodded and nearly sprinted away.

Natalie grabbed the coffee cup off Avery's desk like a prop. "Okay. We need a plan that is public enough to defang the complaint but human enough to stay in romcom land."

Avery stared. "Romcom land."

Natalie nodded seriously. "Yes. The land where people can be messy and still lovable."

Avery's lips pressed together. "I don't live there."

Miles's voice was quiet. "You can."

Avery looked at him, and the air in the room shifted.

Not because he was being intense.

Because he wasn't.

He said it like it was a fact, not a flirtation.

Avery hated how much she wanted to believe him.

Natalie cleared her throat loudly. "Okay! So. We have Lena Park downstairs. We have random influencers outside. We have an ethics complaint inside. We have you two making eye contact like you're in a romance novel."

Avery snapped, "Natalie."

Natalie held up a hand. "I'm sorry. But I'm right."

Miles coughed once and looked away, ears faintly pink.

Avery's cheeks warmed. She ignored it. "We do the pediatric tour. We answer Lena's questions. We keep it mission-forward."

Natalie nodded. "Yes. And we do it with witnesses."

Miles added, "In a space where you're comfortable."

Avery's laugh was short. "No space is comfortable anymore."

Miles's gaze stayed steady. "Then we pick the least bad one."

Natalie grabbed her legal pad. "Okay. Here's what we do. We stage a quick, controlled 'walking Q&A' with Lena. Pediatric wing planning board. Some nurses. A couple of residents. You talk about staffing and mental health resources. Miles is present as your comms support. Natalie is present as your chief of sanity."

Avery stared. "Chief of sanity."

Natalie nodded solemnly. "I accept this title."

Miles's voice was calm. "And if Lena asks about the ethics complaint."

Natalie's smile turned sharp. "We say: 'We take compliance seriously. We welcome review. Mr. Carter's contract is board-approved. Our focus remains pediatric care.'"

Avery nodded. "No defensiveness."

Natalie nodded back. "Exactly. Calm. Confident. Boring."

Miles's gaze flicked to Avery. "And if someone asks if we're together."

Avery's pulse jumped.

Natalie leaned in eagerly. "Oh my god yes, what do we say."

Avery shot her a look that promised consequences.

Natalie grinned, unrepentant.

Miles didn't smile. He watched Avery, waiting.

Avery's throat tightened.

The safe answer was: No comment.

The right answer for a romcom? Something that acknowledged the human without handing over her autonomy.

Avery exhaled. "We say: 'We're focused on the work.'"

Natalie made a face. "That's... sterile."

Avery stared. "Natalie."

Natalie sighed. "Fine. But can we make it less 'I'm allergic to joy'?"

Miles's voice was quiet. "Maybe: 'We're focused on the mission. And we work well together.'"

Avery's stomach tightened at the softness in his tone.

Natalie pointed at him. "That's good. That's bit of romance without confessing love in the pediatric hallway."

Avery's mouth tightened. "We are not confessing love."

Miles's expression was unreadable. "Understood."

Natalie clapped once. "Okay. Shoes on. Faces on. Let's go be boring."

Avery's jaw tightened. "I hate being boring."

Natalie grinned. "No you don't. You love being boring when boring equals control."

Avery opened her mouth to argue.

Then stopped, because arguing would mean Natalie had a point.

Which she did.

The pediatric wing planning board was set up in a conference space near the clinical side, a room with large windows and the faint hum of the hospital beyond. It was less glossy than the executive floor. More real.

Avery felt her shoulders loosen by a fraction the moment she stepped inside.

Nurses and residents were already gathered, along with a facilities manager, a pediatric social worker, and someone from IT who looked like he hadn't slept since 2022.

Good. Witnesses.

Lena Park stood near the board, notebook in hand, expression calm.

She looked up as Avery entered. "Thank you for making time."

Avery nodded. "Thank you for focusing on pediatrics."

Lena's pen paused. "That was your point in the cafeteria."

"Yes," Avery said evenly. "It remains my point."

Natalie hovered at Avery's shoulder, smiling like a polite shark. Miles stood to Avery's other side, a quiet presence that did not read as showy, even if Avery could feel the low awareness of him like static under her skin.

Lena glanced at Miles briefly, then back to Avery. "Do you want him here for this."

Avery's pulse jumped at the directness.

Natalie stepped in smoothly. "Miles is retained by the board to support communications and ensure clarity. We're keeping the messaging consistent."

Lena nodded. "Understood."

Avery appreciated that Lena didn't smirk.

She also appreciated that Lena didn't pretend she hadn't noticed.

They began walking along the planning board.

Avery answered questions with the quiet confidence of someone who did the work, keeping the focus on pediatrics instead of headlines.

As she spoke, she felt the noise shift back to the thing that mattered.

The work.

The people.

The lives.

It steadied her.

Then Lena asked, softly, without looking up from her notebook, "There's an ethics complaint."

Avery's stomach tightened, but she didn't pause.

"Yes," Avery said calmly. "We received a notice."

Lena looked up. "Conflict of interest."

Avery met her gaze. "We welcome review. Mr. Carter's contract is board-approved. The board retained him to support communications plan after a viral incident. My focus remains pediatric care."

Lena's eyes held hers, then she nodded once.

"Okay," Lena said. "That's your statement."

Avery's jaw tightened. "Yes."

Lena's gaze flicked to Miles. "Anything to add."

Miles didn't move. He didn't smile. He didn't perform.

He simply said, calmly, "I'm here to help the hospital communicate with integrity. That's it."

Avery felt the simplicity land like a weight.

Not heavy.

Anchoring.

Lena's pen moved again.

A nurse nearby muttered quietly to another, "At least that's honest."

Avery kept her posture steady.

Then, because the universe was not finished with her, the conference room door opened.

Gerald Whitmore stepped in.

He didn't knock.

Of course he didn't.

He carried himself like a man who thought doors were suggestions.

Avery felt the room tighten around him.

Lena looked up, calm. "Chair Whitmore."

Gerald offered a tight smile. "Ms. Park. I understand you're here for pediatrics."

"Yes," Lena said. "And for comment on the ethics complaint."

Gerald's smile tightened. "We take compliance seriously. St. Catherine's will follow all protocols."

Avery kept her face neutral.

Miles's jaw tightened slightly.

Natalie's eyes flashed. She stayed quiet, for once.

Gerald's gaze settled on Avery. "Avery."

Avery met his eyes. "Gerald."

Gerald's voice was low, controlled, meant for her. "You're inviting press into sensitive spaces."

Avery's voice remained even. "This space is about pediatrics. That's not sensitive. That's mission."

Gerald's jaw flexed. "You need to be careful."

Avery's smile sharpened. "I am being careful. I'm being visible."

Gerald's gaze flicked to Miles. "And you're keeping him close."

The air in the room shifted.

Staff attention sharpened.

Lena's pen paused.

Natalie looked like she was about to leap.

Avery's pulse spiked, but her voice stayed warm. "Mr. Carter is part of the team retained by the board. He's present because communication is part of leadership now."

Gerald's eyes narrowed. "And the romance story."

Avery's spine stiffened.

This was not a press question.

This was Gerald testing her.

Lena watched, expression unreadable.

Staff watched too.

Avery felt the moment press against her ribs.

This was the choice again.

Not Miles, exactly.

Autonomy.

Avery smiled, calm enough to be boring. "We're focused on the mission," she said. "And we work well together."

Natalie exhaled quietly through her nose like she'd won a bet.

Miles's gaze flicked to Avery, something warm passing across his expression before he forced it down.

Gerald's smile did not reach his eyes. "That's all."

Avery held his gaze. "That's enough."

Silence.

Gerald looked away first, then turned to Lena. "I trust you'll be responsible with your framing."

Lena's smile was polite. "Always."

Gerald nodded once, then left the room like he'd done them a favor by appearing at all.

The conference room exhaled.

Avery felt her shoulders loosen. She hadn't realized how tight she'd been holding herself until the pressure eased.

Natalie leaned close and whispered, "That was... annoyingly good."

Avery murmured, "Stop praising me."

Natalie grinned. "No."

Lena closed her notebook. "Thank you. I have what I need."

Avery nodded. "Please keep pediatrics front and center."

Lena's gaze held hers. "I will."

Then Lena's eyes flicked to Miles and back to Avery. "One more thing."

Avery's stomach tightened. "Yes."

Lena lowered her voice slightly, professional but not unkind. "Someone is feeding this. The ethics complaint isn't policy. It's noise shaping."

Avery nodded. "We know."

Lena's expression softened by a fraction. "Then take care of yourself. The internet doesn't care if you bleed."

Avery's throat tightened.

She hated that it landed.

Lena left.

Avery stood alone, staring at the planning board.

Miles stayed beside her, quiet.

When the room finally emptied, Miles spoke softly.

"You did well."

Avery's voice was clipped. "Don't start."

Miles's mouth twitched faintly. "Okay."

Avery exhaled, then looked at him. "Gerald was trying to make me pull away from you."

Miles's expression softened. "Yes."

Avery's jaw clenched. "I didn't."

Miles nodded. "No."

Avery's throat tightened with something dangerously close to emotion.

"Why does it feel like every choice I make is now public property," she whispered.

Miles's gaze held hers. "Because someone is trying to convince you that you don't get to have a private self anymore."

Avery swallowed. "They're succeeding."

Miles stepped a fraction closer, voice low. "No. They're trying."

Avery stared at him.

He didn't touch her. He didn't press. He simply stood there, steady, like he would wait as long as she needed.

Avery's breath shook. "I don't want you hurt by this."

Miles's eyes softened. "I'm not fragile."

Avery's laugh was small and humorless. "That's not the point."

Miles hesitated, then said quietly, "If you need me to step back, I will."

The words hit harder than the ethics complaint.

Avery's chest tightened.

She stared at him, trying to find the angle, the manipulation, the PR strategy.

There wasn't one.

He meant it.

He would step back if she asked.

Because he wasn't here to own her.

He was here to support her.

And that made her want to do the opposite of what fear demanded.

Avery's voice came out rougher than she wanted. "Don't offer that like it's easy."

Miles's gaze held hers. "It isn't."

Avery swallowed. "Then why offer it."

Miles's voice stayed steady. "Because you deserve choice. Real choice."

Avery's throat tightened so sharply she had to look away.

She stared at the planning board again, at the words quiet rooms and family space and mental health resources, and the absurdity of her own life nearly made her laugh.

She turned back.

Her voice was quiet. "I don't want you to step back."

Miles's breath caught, subtle.

His eyes softened. "Okay."

Avery's pulse hammered. "But I also can't... I can't let you become collateral."

Miles's voice was low. "Avery, I'm already in it."

Avery's jaw clenched. "You're leaving."

Miles nodded. "Yes."

Avery's throat tightened. "In twenty—"

"Twenty-four," Miles corrected gently.

Avery glared. "Stop counting."

Miles's mouth twitched. "I can't."

Avery exhaled sharply, then gave up on pretending she wasn't human.

"Last night," she said quietly, "I kissed you because for once I wanted something without asking permission."

Miles didn't move. He watched her, eyes steady.

Avery continued, voice softer, "Today, I stood beside you because Gerald wanted me to look ashamed."

Miles nodded once. "I saw."

Avery's chest tightened. "And now there's a complaint, and people are filming outside, and I can feel my life being... pulled."

Miles stepped closer, still not touching, but near enough that she could feel warmth.

His voice was low. "Then we pull back."

Avery blinked. "How."

Miles's gaze held hers. "We decide what's ours. And we protect it."

Avery's throat tightened. "That sounds like a romance novel."

Miles's mouth curved faintly. "Maybe you need one."

Avery's laugh broke free, small and real, and she hated that it felt like relief.

Miles smiled softly, then sobered. "Let me help."

Avery looked at him.

, she wanted to kiss him again.

Not because she needed comfort.

Because she wanted to.

She didn't.

Not here. Not now.

Instead, she said quietly, "Okay."

Miles nodded, serious. "Okay."

Avery's phone buzzed.

She flinched before she could stop herself.

Miles's gaze sharpened. "Don't look at it yet."

Avery swallowed. "It could be Gerald."

"It won't be," Miles said softly.

Avery's stomach tightened. "How do you know."

Miles's expression tightened, and for the first time, his calm looked like effort.

"Because Gerald doesn't text," Miles said. "He summons."

Avery let out a short, startled laugh.

Miles's mouth twitched. "And because Natalie would have told you if it was internal. This feels... timed."

Avery stared at her pocket, then pulled out her phone anyway, because she was still Avery Sloan and she still needed information to breathe.

Unknown number.

Of course.

Avery's fingers went cold as she opened it.

Unknown: Nice performance. You looked brave.Unknown: Now let's see how brave you are without your script.Unknown: Go to the main entrance. Alone. Two minutes.

Avery's blood chilled.

Miles watched her face change. "What."

Avery held up the phone.

Miles read it once. His jaw tightened hard. "No."

Avery's throat tightened. "They're outside."

Miles's voice went low. "Yes. And they're baiting you into isolation again."

Avery's pulse hammered. "If I don't go, they'll escalate."

Miles's eyes held hers. "If you go alone, they win."

Avery's jaw clenched. "So what do we do."

Miles's gaze sharpened, thinking quickly, but not like a spy. Like a man who understood people.

"We go," he said.

Avery blinked. "Together?"

Miles nodded. "Together. With Natalie. With witnesses. We do not give them alone."

Avery's throat tightened. "They said alone."

Miles's mouth turned grim. "They don't get to set the terms."

Avery stared at him.

Then she did something she hadn't done a month ago.

She trusted him.

Avery inhaled slowly. "Okay."

Miles nodded once. "Okay."

He stepped back, pulled his phone out, and texted Natalie with quick, efficient taps.

Avery's own phone buzzed again, a follow-up message.

Unknown: If he's with you, I'll make sure everyone knows what he wants.

Avery's chest tightened.

Miles looked up from his phone, eyes sharp. "Another message."

Avery didn't answer. She showed him.

Miles read it, then went still.

Not scared.

Focused.

He looked at Avery and said quietly, "Whatever happens, you do not let them make you ashamed."

Avery swallowed. "I'm not ashamed."

Miles's gaze held hers. "Good. Because I'm not either."

Avery's pulse hammered.

She didn't know if he meant the kiss, the partnership, or something deeper.

Maybe all of it.

The door opened.

Natalie rushed in, eyes blazing. "Okay. I got your text. What fresh hell."

Avery held up her phone.

Natalie read it, then made a noise between a laugh and a growl.

"Oh," Natalie said. "Oh, absolutely not."

Miles's voice stayed calm. "We're going to the main entrance. Together."

Natalie nodded immediately. "Yes. And I'm calling security. And I'm bringing Marla, because Marla cries on command and that's useful."

Marla appeared in the doorway as if summoned by the mention of her name. "I heard crying."

Natalie pointed at her. "See. Prepared."

Avery couldn't help it. She laughed once, short and disbelieving.

Natalie looked at her. "Good. Laugh. It reminds your nervous system we're not dying."

Avery exhaled slowly.

They moved.

Down the corridor. Into the elevator. The same mirrored box, but this time it was crowded with purpose.

Natalie stood like a general. Marla clutched her folder like a shield. Miles stood close enough that Avery could feel his presence without touching.

Avery's phone buzzed again, but she didn't look.

The elevator descended.

The doors opened onto the lobby.

Noise hit them: voices, footsteps, the hospital's constant motion.

And near the main entrance, beyond the revolving doors, Avery saw them.

Two people.

One holding a phone on a stabilizer.

The other adjusting a ring light like the hospital lobby was a red carpet.

They spotted her immediately.

The one with the ring light lifted his hand and called, too loudly, "Avery Sloan! Quick question!"

Avery's spine straightened.

Natalie stepped forward, smile bright and deadly. "Hi! This is a hospital."

The man grinned. "We're here to ask about the ethics complaint. People deserve transparency."

Avery felt her stomach drop. It was already spreading.

Miles's jaw tightened.

Marla made a small, distressed sound on cue.

Natalie whispered without moving her lips, "Marla, dial it to eleven."

Marla's eyes widened, then immediately watered.

Avery stared at the influencer, then at the ring light, then at the phone stabilizer.

This was the stage.

This was the trap.

Avery kept her voice calm, warm enough to sound reasonable. "This is a healthcare facility. I won't discuss internal processes in the lobby."

The influencer nodded like he respected boundaries and then crossed them anyway. "Are you in a relationship with Miles Carter."

Avery's pulse jumped.

Natalie's eyes widened in outrage.

Miles didn't move.

He watched Avery.

Waiting.

Choice.

Avery lifted her chin. "We work together."

The influencer grinned. "That's not a no."

Avery's smile sharpened. "It's not an answer you're entitled to."

The other person, filming, zoomed in.

Natalie leaned in, voice sweet. "If you'd like, I can give you the number for our press office."

The influencer laughed. "The press office won't tell the truth."

Avery's skin went cold.

Because the influencer wasn't the real threat.

He was the delivery system.

The real threat was the person who had orchestrated him, timed him, and now wanted Avery to react on camera.

Avery felt Miles shift closer, not touching, but present.

Then the revolving doors spun again.

A third figure stepped into the lobby, moving with purpose.

Not an influencer.

Not a staff member.

Someone in a tailored coat, hair neat, posture confident.

Someone who walked like they belonged in any room.

Avery's breath caught.

Patrick Ames.

He smiled as he approached, too calm for coincidence.

"Ah," Patrick said smoothly, as if this were an accidental encounter. "Avery. What a surprise."

Natalie's face tightened like she'd tasted poison.

Miles's jaw set.

The influencer turned eagerly. "Mr. Ames! Great timing. Can you confirm there's an ethics complaint about Avery Sloan and her consultant."

Patrick's smile widened, polished and lethal. "I'm afraid I can't comment on internal matters."

Avery's stomach dropped.

Because Patrick had legitimized the question by answering it.

He'd stepped into the frame.

He'd made it real.

Patrick looked at Avery, voice soft enough to sound caring. "I hope you're taking care of yourself."

Avery's pulse roared.

Miles's voice went low. "Patrick."

Patrick's gaze flicked to Miles and sharpened with something like satisfaction. "Mr. Carter."

The influencer's phone stayed trained on them.

The ring light glared.

The lobby hummed around the scene.

And Avery realized, with sudden clarity, that the "lunch" threat hadn't been about the cafeteria at all.

It had been about forcing a confrontation where the wrong people could define the story.

Avery lifted her chin slowly, eyes locking on Patrick.

Then her phone buzzed in her pocket one more time.

Avery didn't need to read it to feel the intent.

But she did anyway.

Unknown: There he is.Unknown: Now choose. On camera.

Avery's blood turned to ice.

Miles's gaze flicked to her phone, then to her face.

Natalie's whisper was barely audible. "Oh my god."

Patrick smiled, waiting.

The influencer leaned closer, hungry. "Avery, are you resigning."

Avery's throat tightened.

This was the moment.

Choice, on camera.

And she could feel the entire romcom hinge creak under the weight of it.

Because whatever she said next would either pull Miles into the storm with her...

...or push him out to save herself.

Avery took one slow breath.

Then opened her mouth.

Chapter 14: Ma'am, This Is a Hospital

Avery had been in front of cameras before.

Press conferences, donor galas, ribbon cuttings, the occasional "celebrate our nurses" photo-op where she smiled until her cheeks ached and then went back upstairs to put out fires.

This was different.

This was a hospital lobby with fluorescent lights, a ring light that had no business being within fifty feet of an emergency department, and a man asking if she was resigning like he was ordering coffee.

Avery took one slow breath.

Then another.

And because she refused to let a stranger with a stabilizer dictate her nervous system, she looked directly into the phone camera and said, clearly:

"No."

The influencer blinked. "No... what."

Avery's smile turned polite, the kind she used on vendors who tried to upsell her on printer ink.

"No, I'm not resigning," she said. "I'm going back to work. You know. At the hospital."

Behind the influencer, the ring light guy shifted, trying to angle for better lighting. The light flared across the floor like an interrogation lamp.

Avery's eyes flicked to it, then back to the camera. "Also, for the record, this is a healthcare facility. The lighting in here is bad on purpose. It's called 'not being a studio.'"

Natalie made a sound that was either a laugh or a battle cry.

The influencer recovered quickly, eager. "So you deny the ethics complaint."

Avery blinked slowly. "I didn't say that."

He leaned in. "So you admit it."

Avery held his gaze, then glanced past him at the steady stream of people moving through the lobby: a man pushing a wheelchair, a mother with a toddler on her hip, an orderly guiding a confused older patient toward radiology.

Then she looked back at the influencer and said, warmly, "I'm sorry, are we doing a choose-your-own-adventure right now."

Natalie snorted.

Miles stayed still at Avery's side, calm enough that it almost looked like he didn't want to laugh too.

Patrick Ames watched with a small smile that looked like approval. Or amusement. Or both. His presence in the frame was deliberate, and Avery hated how well he understood spotlight.

The influencer tried again, louder. "People deserve transparency."

Avery nodded like she accepted the premise. "Agreed. Here's transparency: you are filming in a hospital lobby with a ring light. That's... not a great look."

The influencer scoffed. "It's public."

Natalie stepped forward, beaming like a woman about to become a viral meme on purpose.

"Hi," Natalie said brightly. "Natalie Kim. Crisis communications. Also, unofficially, the person who prevents adults from doing dumb things in front of sick children."

The influencer blinked. "Who are you."

Natalie smiled wider. "Excellent question. Who are you."

He pointed at himself. "I'm with Midtown Pulse."

Natalie's smile froze in place, sweet and deadly. "No, you're not. Midtown Pulse is an account. You're a man with a ring light, a haircut that suggests you own a podcast, and absolutely no hospital credentials."

A few people nearby slowed to watch.

A nurse at the coffee kiosk murmured, "Ooh."

Avery's cheeks warmed. This was not how she wanted to be famous.

Natalie gestured at the revolving doors with her whole arm like she was escorting someone out of a nightclub. "If you'd like to speak to press, we have a press office. It is not located in the lobby next to radiology. Follow me."

The influencer dug in. "We're not leaving until we get answers."

Avery's pulse stayed steady. "Then you'll be here a long time, because I have a meeting. And a hospital. And I am not a reality show."

He swung the camera toward Miles. "What about you. Are you sleeping with her."

Avery's heart did something stupid.

Natalie inhaled sharply like she was about to lunge.

Patrick's eyebrows lifted, pleased, as if the moment had finally become messy enough to be useful.

Miles moved half a step forward.

He didn't raise his voice.

He didn't threaten.

He simply said, calm and clear, "Turn it off."

The influencer laughed. "Why."

Miles's gaze stayed level. "Because you're filming patients and staff in a medical facility without consent. You're interfering with patient flow. You can keep filming if you want. Security will escort you out. And your video will be you getting escorted out of a hospital. Make that your content."

The ring light guy's smile wobbled.

Natalie's grin returned, triumphant.

Avery felt a flicker of relief so sharp she could have kissed Miles again for that line.

She didn't.

Because she was still standing in a lobby under a ring light.

Patrick clucked softly, stepping closer, voice smooth enough to sound concerned. "Let's not escalate."

Avery turned her head slowly, eyes sharp. "You're right. Let's not."

Patrick's smile widened. "I'm only here because I heard ... commotion."

Natalie made a sound like she'd bitten into something sour. "You heard."

Patrick's gaze flicked to Natalie, then back to Avery. "Donors are asking questions. I thought I might help calm things down."

Avery's pulse stayed even, but her mind sharpened. "You heard in under ten minutes that influencers in our lobby."

Patrick's smile didn't falter. "News travels."

Avery nodded slowly. "Interesting."

Patrick's eyes narrowed slightly. "Avery."

Avery's smile softened into something that looked friendly, but wasn't. "Patrick."

The influencer, sensing drama, swung the camera toward Patrick. "Mr. Ames, should Avery Sloan resign."

Patrick's smile turned sympathetic. "I'm not in a position to comment on St. Catherine's internal leadership decisions."

Avery's jaw clenched.

He'd done it again.

Legitimized the question by treating it like a reasonable one.

Natalie stepped in with a bright, weaponized smile. "Great. Then please stop standing in the frame like you're auditioning for an exposé."

A few people nearby laughed.

Patrick's smile tightened.

Avery felt the crowd's attention shift, not toward Patrick, but toward her.

Staff weren't cheering. They weren't clapping.

They were watching the way people watch to see if someone will be bullied in public.

Avery took another slow breath.

She looked directly at the influencer's camera and said, calm, warm, and tired:

"If you want transparency, here it is: There is a compliance process for everything in a hospital. We welcome review. We follow policy. We keep working. That's the story."

She gestured subtly toward the corridor where transport was moving a patient bed. "And if you want a real story, interview the nurses who keep this place running. They save lives. I mostly schedule meetings."

Natalie whispered, "That's cute."

Avery shot her a look without turning her head.

The influencer hesitated, then tried one last time, hungry. "Are you in love with Miles Carter."

Avery blinked slowly, then let out a small laugh she couldn't stop.

It wasn't hysterical.

It was the laugh of someone who could not believe this was happening in the same building where trauma surgeons were sewing people back together.

Avery looked into the camera and said, "I am not answering that question in a hospital lobby."

Then, because she was apparently losing her mind, she added, "Also, I'm pretty sure the hospital cafeteria has better lighting than you do."

Natalie choked on a laugh.

Miles's mouth twitched once, almost a smile, then he looked away as if he didn't trust himself.

The ring light guy frowned like he'd been personally insulted.

Avery turned slightly toward Natalie, voice low. "Where is security."

Natalie lifted her hand like she'd been waiting for this cue her whole life. "On their way."

As if summoned, two security officers appeared near the entrance, walking with calm purpose.

One of them looked at the ring light, then at Natalie, then at Avery.

"Ms. Sloan," he said, respectful. "We've got it."

Natalie beamed. "Thank you. Please escort the ring light out of my life."

The officers moved in.

The influencer tried to protest, but his energy deflated the moment he realized he wasn't in control of the room anymore.

As security guided them toward the doors, the ring light guy hissed, "This is censorship."

Natalie waved cheerfully. "It's healthcare."

The revolving doors swallowed them.

The lobby exhaled.

People resumed walking. Phones lowered. The ordinary rhythm returned.

Avery realized, with a jolt, that her hands were slightly cold.

Miles stepped closer, voice low. "You okay."

Avery's throat tightened. "I'm... fine."

Natalie, still vibrating with adrenaline, said, "You were not fine. You were hilarious, though."

Avery stared at Natalie. "I was not hilarious."

Natalie nodded solemnly. "You were. 'Choose-your-own-adventure.' Iconic."

Avery rubbed her forehead. "I hate my life."

Miles's voice was soft. "No, you hate being watched."

Avery's chest tightened.

Natalie glanced between them, then abruptly clapped her hands. "Okay. We need to debrief. Somewhere that doesn't smell like disinfectant and doom."

Marla, who had been hovering behind them like a fragile ghost, whispered, "I cried. Did that help."

Natalie nodded seriously. "Yes, Marla. You were a star."

Marla looked pleased and terrified.

Natalie turned to Avery. "Come on. Conference room. Two minutes. Then we call Gerald before he summons us like we're in medieval court."

Avery exhaled and started walking.

Miles moved with her.

Natalie walked ahead, still muttering things like "ring light" under her breath as if it had personally betrayed her.

They made it into a small conference room off the hallway, a neutral space with a long table and a whiteboard that still had someone's half-erased flow chart about parking.

Natalie shut the door and leaned against it, breathless. "Okay. We handled that. We stayed in the genre. We did not become a corporate thriller."

Avery dropped into a chair. "Barely."

Miles sat beside her, not too close, but close enough that Avery could feel his presence in the way she had started to rely on without admitting it.

Natalie pointed at Avery. "You were warm. You were funny. You were human. That matters."

Avery's jaw tightened. "I don't want to be human on camera."

Natalie nodded. "I know. But it played well. Midtown Pulse wanted a meltdown. They got boundaries."

Avery's phone buzzed on the table.

Avery's stomach tightened, reflexively.

Natalie grabbed it before Avery could, read the screen, then frowned.

"It's your mom," Natalie said.

Avery blinked. "My... mom."

Miles's eyebrows lifted.

Natalie held up the phone. "It's a text."

Avery stared like the words might rearrange themselves into something less humiliating.

Avery's mother rarely texted her in the middle of the day.

Which meant this was either an emergency or a catastrophe.

Natalie read it aloud because Natalie was apparently determined to kill Avery today.

"'Avery Elizabeth Sloan. I saw a video of you in a hospital lobby telling a man with a ring light that you're not a reality show. Proud of you. Also... who is Miles?'"

Avery stared.

Miles's mouth twitched.

Natalie's eyes widened in delight. "OH MY GOD."

Avery's face warmed. "Do not."

Natalie was already grinning like Christmas morning. "Your mom has seen him. Your mom is asking. This is escalation."

Avery pressed her fingers to her temple. "This is mortifying."

Miles's voice was gentle. "It's sort of sweet."

Avery shot him a look. "You would say that."

Miles's mouth curved faintly. "I would."

Natalie slid into a chair across from them, still smiling. "Okay. Here's the deal. We can't pretend this is going away. They're outside, they're posting, they're baiting. We have two options."

Avery's shoulders stiffened. "Natalie."

Natalie held up a hand. "Hear me out. Option one: we keep deflecting and the story keeps writing itself. Option two: we surf it."

Avery's jaw clenched. "Surf."

Natalie nodded, eyes sharp now. "We pick a controlled public moment. One. Where you and Miles appear together deliberately. Not romantic. Not denial. Just... competent partnership. We make it boring in the most polished way."

Miles's gaze flicked to Avery. "Avery decides."

Avery's pulse hammered.

She could feel how close this was to fake dating territory. To headlines. To being used.

She also felt the other truth: the more she tried to hide, the more power it gave them.

Avery exhaled slowly. "We do not fake date."

Natalie nodded. "Agreed. No fake dating. But we do controlled visibility."

Avery's eyes narrowed. "One moment."

Natalie smiled. "One moment. One photo. One statement."

Miles said quietly, "It gives you agency."

Avery stared at him.

Agency.

Choice.

The words had started showing up in her life like they belonged there.

For thirty minutes, they managed to exist like normal people.

Avery hid in her office with the blinds half-closed, Natalie posted herself outside the door like a stylish security system, and Miles leaned against the window ledge, tie loosened, watching the city as if it could be reasoned with.

Natalie insisted on ordering dinner, even though it was barely five. "Your blood sugar is an HR violation waiting to happen," she declared. "Also, if the internet is going to ruin your life, it can at least do it while you have dumplings."

Avery didn't argue. That was also new.

When the food arrived, Natalie spread containers across Avery's coffee table like she was setting out evidence. "Okay," she said, tapping her chopsticks against the lid of the soy sauce. "On my scale, today's lobby encounter was a misdemeanor. If anyone tries to corner you with a ring light again, we're officially at felony."

Miles glanced at Avery. "She has a scale."

"It's calibrated," Natalie said, offended. "I'm a professional."

Avery sank to the floor instead of the sofa, back against the cabinet. She told herself it was because the sofa was too stiff. The truth was simpler: the floor felt honest.

Miles sat down across from her without making it a thing. No comment about posture. No executive coaching tone. a container of dumplings and the quiet presence of someone who didn't need her to perform competence to stay.

Avery took a bite and, for the first time all day, felt her shoulders loosen.

And then, as if the universe wanted to test her, the drawer under the coffee table stuck halfway open with a squeak.

Avery stared at it, irrationally irritated. "That drawer has been doing that for months."

Miles set his food down, leaned forward, and slid the drawer out with careful hands. He ran a thumb along the track, then reached into his pocket.

Miles shrugged slightly. "Sometimes it's one small adjustment."

The line landed in her chest like a quiet echo of everything they weren't saying.

Natalie, abruptly soft, cleared her throat. "Okay. This is the part where I pretend I'm not witnessing intimacy. I'm going to take my felony scale and go intimidate someone in procurement."

Avery looked up. "Natalie—"

Natalie's eyes flicked to Avery's face, gentle for once. "You did good today," she said simply. "Not the clip. Not the headline pressure. You."

Avery's throat tightened.

Natalie waggled her chopsticks. "Also, your mom texted me asking if he's cute. I told her yes and that she should behave."

Avery groaned. "Natalie."

Natalie grinned, and then she was gone, door clicking shut behind her.

Silence settled. The office felt smaller without Natalie filling it with jokes.

Avery took another bite, then looked at Miles over the rim of her container. "You didn't have to fix that."

Miles's gaze stayed steady. "I wanted to."

Avery's voice went quieter. "You make it hard to keep pretending I don't need anything."

Miles's expression softened. "Good."

Her phone buzzed again in Natalie's hand.

Natalie's face changed. "Okay. New problem."

Avery's stomach dropped. "What."

Natalie turned the screen so Avery and Miles could see.

Midtown Pulse had posted another clip.

Not from the lobby.

From the cafeteria earlier.

The moment Avery turned her body to include Miles.

Freeze-framed.

Zoomed.

Captioned in neon text:

"SHE PICKED HIM. NOW ETHICS IS COMING. WHO WINS?"

And beneath it, a new comment from the burner account:

"Tonight. 7 p.m. Fundraiser planning meeting. Bring him. Or lose him."

Avery's blood went cold.

Miles's jaw tightened.

Natalie whispered, "Okay. That's... absolutely a romcom curse."

Avery stared at the words.

Tonight. Seven. Fundraiser planning meeting.

A meeting Avery had not scheduled.

A meeting that suddenly felt like a trap wrapped in a calendar invite.

Avery lifted her chin slowly, eyes hard.

"Well," she said quietly, "they picked the stage for us."

Miles's gaze held hers. "We can still choose how we show up."

Avery nodded once.

Natalie grinned, equal parts thrilled and horrified. "Okay. Fine. If they want a scene, we're going to give them one."

Avery's phone buzzed one more time, a final text from her mother.

"'Also, if Miles is cute, tell him I said hi.'"

Avery closed her eyes.

Miles's quiet laugh filled the room.

Natalie slapped the table. "We are so back in the genre."

Avery opened her eyes, staring at the ceiling like she could escape through it.

She couldn't.

But she could choose.

And tonight at seven, someone was going to learn the difference between controlling her story... and underestimating her.

Chapter 15: The Meeting That Definitely Wasn't a Date

At 6:12 p.m., Avery Sloan stood in front of her bedroom mirror and told herself the same lie three different ways.

This is not a date.

She wore a fitted navy dress that could pass as "fundraiser appropriate" and "executive competent" while still letting her breathe like a human. She had chosen it on purpose because it made her look unbothered.

Avery adjusted the neckline by half an inch, then stopped, because she could feel herself spiraling into micro-control. She did not need to perfect the neckline. She needed to survive a "fundraiser planning meeting" that felt suspiciously like a stage someone else had picked for her.

The intercom buzzed.

Her doorman's voice came through, professional and too polite to be real. "Ms. Sloan? Your... guest is here."

Guest. Right.

Avery's pulse jumped at the word in a way that made her furious.

She exhaled slowly and reached for her coat.

The intercom buzzed again immediately.

"This is also not a date," Natalie said through the speaker.

Avery closed her eyes.

Of course Natalie had arrived.

Avery pressed the intercom button. "How did you even get in."

Natalie's voice was cheerful. "Your doorman is terrified of me. Also, I brought cookies."

Avery stared. "Cookies."

Natalie sighed dramatically. "Avery. I know you're allergic to joy, but I'm trying to introduce it into your ecosystem like a probiotic."

Avery opened her door.

"You're early," Avery said.

Natalie breezed past her into the apartment. "I'm not early. I'm on time. You're chronically emotionally delayed."

Avery locked the door with more force than necessary. "We are going to a meeting."

Natalie nodded solemnly. "Yes. The meeting that is not a date. With the man you kissed in a hallway like you were auditioning for a medical drama."

Avery's cheeks warmed. "It was one kiss."

Natalie turned, eyes bright. "One kiss can start a war. Have you ever read history."

Avery turned toward the mirror again, smoothing her hair. Her hands felt too cold. Her stomach felt too tight.

Natalie leaned against the dresser and watched her like she was watching a friend pretend she wasn't nervous about a first day of school.

"You're doing the thing," Natalie said, gentler.

Avery didn't look at her. "What thing."

"Pretending you're made of granite," Natalie said. "You're not. You're... like marble. Expensive, beautiful, and still capable of cracking if someone drops you."

Avery's throat tightened. "That's not comforting."

Natalie shrugged. "It's accurate."

Avery exhaled. "This meeting is a trap."

Natalie nodded. "Yes. And also: it's a fundraiser planning meeting. Which means the donors will be there, and so will the board's favorite hobby, which is watching you in rooms."

Avery stared at her.

Natalie shrugged. "If you cancel, they'll assume you're rattled. If you show up, you remind everyone you're still the person who runs this place. And if anyone tries to turn it into a spectacle, I'm bringing cookies as a distraction weapon."

Avery exhaled once, sharper, then softer. "That is not a weapon."

"It absolutely is," Natalie said. "People will forgive anything if you give them sugar and a purpose."

Natalie stepped closer and made a tiny adjustment to Avery's necklace, turning the pendant so it sat properly in the hollow of her throat.

"There," Natalie said. "Now you look like someone who has a life."

Avery's voice went dry. "I do have a life."

Natalie's eyebrows rose. "Do you."

Avery glared.

Natalie grinned. "Okay. Fine. You have a life. It's mostly spreadsheets and trauma responses."

Avery's phone buzzed on the dresser, face down.

Both women froze.

Avery didn't reach for it.

Natalie, who had no self-preservation instincts, reached for it immediately.

Avery snapped, "Natalie."

Natalie flipped it over anyway.

Then her expression changed.

Avery's stomach dropped. "What."

Natalie held up the screen.

Miles: Downstairs. Whenever you're ready. And for the record, you don't have to do tonight alone.

Avery's throat tightened in that ridiculous way her body had started doing around him.

Natalie's grin returned, bright and annoying. "Oh, he's good."

Avery took the phone from her and slid it into her purse like she was handling evidence. "We're leaving."

Natalie grabbed her tote bag. "Lead the way, marble statue."

They rode the elevator down in silence until the doors opened to the lobby.

Miles was waiting near the entrance, hands in his coat pockets, posture relaxed like he belonged there. He wore a dark suit and a charcoal coat, no tie, and that same steady expression that made Avery feel both safe and furious.

He looked up as she approached, and for one beat, his gaze softened.

Not enough to be obvious to anyone else.

Enough for Avery to feel it in her ribs.

Natalie appeared at her side like a chaperone with an agenda. "Miles Carter," Natalie said brightly. "Tonight's theme is: don't die."

Miles blinked once. "Noted."

Natalie leaned in, stage whispering. "Also, Avery insists this is not a date."

Avery's cheeks warmed. "Natalie."

Miles's mouth twitched. "Understood."

Miles stepped slightly closer, voice low enough only Avery could hear. "You okay."

Avery's spine straightened. "Fine."

Miles's gaze held hers. "That's not an answer."

Avery swallowed. "I'm... ready."

Miles nodded once. "Okay."

He didn't touch her. He didn't lead her. He simply matched her pace as they walked out to the waiting car.

And Avery hated, in a way that made her heart ache, how much that felt like partnership.

The fundraiser planning meeting was being held at a private event space attached to the Montclaire Foundation's Midtown offices. The sort of place that had a "lobby concierge" and tasteful art that looked expensive without ever being interesting.

Avery stepped inside and immediately felt the shift in air.

Natalie's shoulders squared as if she'd entered battle.

Miles's expression stayed calm.

Avery's spine straightened instinctively. This space had rules. Unspoken, cruel rules. And Avery had spent years mastering them.

A staffer approached with a practiced smile. "Ms. Sloan. Mr. Carter. Ms. Kim. Thank you for coming."

Natalie blinked. "They know my name."

The staffer smiled politely. "Yes, ma'am."

Natalie leaned toward Avery. "That's either respect or a warning."

Avery murmured, "Both."

They were ushered into a meeting room that looked like it had been designed by someone who'd never experienced mess.

Long table. Bottled water in glass. Notepads with embossed logos. A platter of bite-sized pastries arranged like jewelry.

Around the table sat the fundraiser planning committee: three donors, two Montclaire staff members, one hospital development director, Gerald Whitmore, and Patrick Ames, positioned near the head of the table like a man who had never once questioned whether he deserved the head of anything.

Patrick rose as Avery entered, smiling with smooth warmth. "Avery. Thank you for joining us."

Avery returned a calm smile. "Patrick."

Gerald's gaze flicked to Avery, then to Miles, then to Natalie, and tightened as if he'd realized the room contained too many uncontrollable variables.

Natalie offered Gerald a bright smile that made Avery nervous. "Chair Whitmore. Lovely to see you not on a speakerphone in a crisis."

Gerald's mouth tightened. "Ms. Kim."

Natalie took a seat without waiting to be invited, as if she'd been born at a board table and refused to pretend otherwise.

Miles sat beside Avery, not too close, but close enough that the room read them as a unit.

Avery could feel it. The subtle shift. The quiet interest.

Like a room full of wealthy adults about to watch a reality show they insisted they didn't watch.

Patrick clasped his hands. "Tonight's goal is to finalize the public-facing structure for next month's pediatric gala. We want it inspiring. Warm. Community-centered."

A donor in pearls nodded enthusiastically. "We want it joyful."

Natalie whispered, "They always want it joyful when they're not the ones in the building at three a.m."

Avery shot her a look.

Natalie mimed zipping her lips.

Patrick continued, "We've also had... increased public attention on St. Catherine's leadership."

Gerald's jaw tightened.

Patrick's eyes flicked briefly to Avery, then to Miles. "Which means spotlight are, unfortunately, part of our planning."

Avery's pulse stayed steady. "headline pressure are always part of planning."

Patrick smiled. "True. But now the audience is louder."

Avery's throat tightened.

Gerald looked displeased, like he didn't enjoy staff validation when it didn't come through him.

Patrick's smile held. "Yes. Well. That's why we're here. We want the gala to reinforce trust."

Natalie murmured, "Trust is always a fun word because no one uses it when they're already trusting."

Avery pressed her lips together to keep from laughing.

Miles's mouth twitched once, as if he'd heard it too.

Patrick glanced at a packet in front of him. "First agenda item: keynote structure. Avery, the committee would like you to speak again. Your remarks last night were... effective."

Avery nodded. "I can do that."

A donor with a silver watch smiled. "With Miles at your side."

Avery's pulse jumped.

Miles stayed still.

Patrick's eyes gleamed faintly. Gerald's gaze sharpened.

Avery kept her expression neutral. "Miles is contracted for communications support. Whether he stands near the stage is a logistical decision."

The donor waved a hand. "Oh, I don't mean literally. I mean... symbolically."

Natalie leaned forward, cheerful. "Symbolically, she's at her strongest when she has competent support and men stop trying to manage her."

The room went still.

Avery's soul briefly left her body.

Gerald's eyes narrowed.

Patrick's smile tightened.

Then the donor in pearls laughed, delighted. "Oh! You're funny."

Natalie beamed. "Thank you. I am."

Avery inhaled slowly through her nose.

Miles looked at Natalie like he was trying to decide whether she was a genius or a hazard.

Natalie mouthed, Both.

Patrick cleared his throat smoothly. "Yes, well. Symbolism aside, the point is public confidence. Which brings us to... guest pairing."

Avery's stomach tightened. "Guest pairing."

Patrick slid a paper forward. "We've had donors request a 'leadership table' that includes Avery and Miles together."

Natalie choked softly. "Of course they did."

A donor in pink looked thrilled. "It's charming."

Avery's jaw clenched. "This is a pediatric fundraiser."

The donor smiled. "Exactly. People love a story. It makes them give."

Gerald's voice was cold. "We are not using personal narratives to raise money."

Natalie blinked at him. "Oh. We're not. That's adorable."

Gerald's eyes flashed.

PUBLIC IMAGE, PRIVATE HEART

Miles spoke calmly, cutting through tension. "We can structure the leadership table without implying anything personal. It's a seating plan, not a statement."

Patrick's smile warmed. "Exactly."

Avery's mind sharpened. Patrick was pushing. Gentle. Polished. Publicly reasonable.

Patrick continued, "Also, to avoid speculation, the committee suggests Avery and Miles arrive together. Coordinated. Controlled."

Avery's pulse ticked upward.

Natalie leaned toward Avery and whispered, "This is fake dating with a tux on."

Avery's jaw tightened. "No."

Miles's voice stayed calm. "That seems unnecessary."

Patrick's gaze flicked to Miles. "Not if we want to prevent rumors from shaping the evening."

Avery felt the trap tightening.

Rumors were already shaping everything. Patrick wanted to own the shape. Gerald wanted to crush it.

Neither option felt like hers.

Avery lifted her chin. "We will not design hospital strategy around gossip accounts."

Patrick smiled, warm and reasonable. "Of course not. But we do design around public trust. And right now, perception is part of trust."

Natalie murmured, "I hate that sentence because it's true and evil."

Avery's throat tightened. She felt eyes on her. Donors. Gerald. Patrick. Even the development director looked anxious.

Miles's presence beside her felt steady.

Avery turned slightly toward the committee, voice calm. "If the goal is trust, then we focus on pediatrics. Not on my personal life."

Patrick's smile didn't move. "Then perhaps it would help if your personal life stopped intersecting with leadership spotlight."

Avery's blood cooled.

There it was. The implication.

Influence. Conflict. Shame.

Avery's pulse hammered once. She kept her face warm.

She looked at Patrick. "My personal life is not your fundraising asset, Patrick."

A few donors blinked, surprised.

Patrick's smile tightened. "I didn't say it was."

Avery's tone stayed even. "You implied it. And I'm clarifying."

Gerald's gaze sharpened like he might speak.

Natalie, sensing danger, reached for a pastry and took a bite with the casualness of someone trying to remind the room they were still human.

Miles spoke quietly, steady. "We can accomplish the committee's goals without turning Avery into a storyline."

Patrick's eyes gleamed. "And can we accomplish that while you remain attached to her side."

The room went still again, that delicious, awful stillness of wealthy people watching conflict.

Avery felt her stomach tighten.

Miles didn't flinch. "Yes."

Patrick's smile widened. "Then prove it."

Avery's jaw clenched.

Natalie whispered, "Oh my god, he's doing it. He's turning a meeting into a duel."

Avery shot her a look.

Natalie swallowed her pastry and mouthed, Sorry.

Miles's voice remained calm, but his words were precise. "We prove it by being transparent. My contract is board-approved. My role is communications strategy. We welcome compliance review. And we keep the gala focused on pediatric outcomes."

Patrick's smile held, but his eyes sharpened. "A clean statement."

Miles nodded. "Clean is usually the goal in a hospital."

A donor laughed, delighted. Another nodded approvingly.

Patrick's mouth tightened for half a beat.

Then he recovered with smooth ease. "Excellent. Then let's move to program elements."

Miles leaned slightly closer and murmured, "If you laugh, they'll think you're approachable."

Avery whispered back, "God forbid."

Miles's mouth twitched. "Exactly."

Avery felt the warmth of that exchange under her ribs, small and dangerous.

Not because it was romantic.

Because it was easy.

Halfway through the meeting, Patrick called for a short break.

Avery stood immediately, needing air.

Natalie followed, carrying her tote bag like it contained emergency supplies for emotional disasters. "You're doing great," Natalie whispered.

Avery's voice was low. "He's baiting me."

Natalie nodded. "Yes."

Avery's jaw tightened. "He wants me to push Miles away in front of donors."

Natalie's eyes flashed. "Yes."

Avery stared at her. "And you're agreeing."

Natalie shrugged. "Because it's true. And because we're not doing what he wants."

Avery exhaled slowly.

Miles approached quietly, holding two waters. He offered one to Avery without fanfare.

Avery took it. Their fingers brushed, brief and electric.

Natalie saw it and made a pained noise like someone stepping on a Lego.

Avery glanced at her. "Stop."

Natalie whispered, "Your hands linger. It's sick."

Avery's cheeks warmed. "They did not linger."

Miles looked amused. "They lingered."

Avery stared at him. "You are not helping."

Miles's smile was faint. "Sorry."

Natalie clapped quietly. "Okay, I'm leaving you two for sixty seconds to be normal. Don't ruin my life."

Natalie turned and walked away toward the hallway like she was fleeing a romantic explosion.

Avery watched her go, then looked back at Miles.

Silence settled.

Not awkward. Not quite.

Heavy, in a quiet way.

Miles's voice softened. "You're holding up."

Avery's laugh was small and humorless. "I'm performing."

Miles nodded. "Yes."

Avery's throat tightened. "And I hate that it works."

Miles's gaze held hers. "It doesn't have to be performance every time."

Avery swallowed. "In rooms like that, it does."

Miles stepped slightly closer, voice low. "Then we make sure you have spaces where it doesn't."

Avery's chest tightened.

She hated that her body believed him.

Avery looked down at her water bottle. "They filed an ethics complaint because I stood next to you."

Miles's jaw tightened. "They filed it because you stopped letting them isolate you."

Avery exhaled. "I can't tell which is worse."

Miles's voice was gentle. "You being seen isn't worse. It's new."

Avery's throat tightened. "And dangerous."

Miles paused, then said softly, "If you want me to step back tonight, I will."

Avery's chest tightened with that same painful reaction as before.

She looked up sharply. "Stop offering that."

Miles didn't flinch. "Why."

Avery's voice came out rougher than she wanted. "Because it makes it feel like I'm the one making you leave."

Miles's gaze softened. "You're not making me do anything."
Avery swallowed. "You're leaving in… twenty-three days."
Miles's mouth twitched. "Twenty-three."
Avery glared. "Stop counting."
Miles's eyes softened. "I can't."
Avery stared at him, then looked away, jaw clenched.
Miles's voice lowered. "Avery. I'm here now."
Avery's throat tightened.

She wanted to kiss him. Not because she needed comfort. Because she wanted to stop thinking.

Instead, she said quietly, "I'm scared this will become my story."

Miles's gaze held hers. "Then we make sure your story stays yours."

Avery swallowed. "How."

Miles's mouth curved faintly. "By choosing each other on purpose. Not because we're forced. Not because someone's watching."

Avery's breath caught. "That sounds like…."

Miles's smile was soft. "Romcom logic."

Avery huffed a laugh. "I hate romcom logic."

Miles's eyes warmed. "No you don't."

Avery started to argue.

Then she felt it.

A touch at her neckline.

Miles reached up, gentle, and adjusted her necklace pendant again, the same way Natalie had earlier, except Miles did it without commentary or pride, like he was simply fixing something that mattered.

His fingers brushed the skin at her throat.

Avery's breath caught.

Miles's hand dropped immediately, like he was aware of every boundary. "Sorry. It was crooked."

Avery stared at him. "It was fine."

Miles's mouth twitched. "It wasn't."

Avery's cheeks warmed. "You're… absurd."

Miles's eyes softened. "I know."

Avery's heart hammered. She could feel herself standing too close to the edge of something that would not be easily undone.

Natalie returned at that exact moment, eyes widening as she clocked their proximity.

"Oh my god," Natalie whispered. "He touched your necklace. That's like... Regency romance behavior."

Avery snapped, "Natalie."

Natalie held up a hand. "I'm sorry. It's that you two are becoming unbearable."

Miles looked mildly amused. "Noted."

Natalie leaned toward Avery. "Okay. Back in. Patrick is about to propose a 'power couple' photo op. I can feel it in my bones."

Avery's stomach tightened. "We refuse."

Natalie nodded briskly. "We redirect. We do pediatrics. We do not do couples content."

Miles's voice was steady. "Agreed."

Avery exhaled. "Let's go."

They walked back into the meeting room.

Patrick looked up as they entered, eyes gleaming faintly, as if he'd been watching the break through a window.

Avery's jaw clenched.

Fine.

If Patrick wanted to watch her life like a show, she could star in it without giving him the ending.

The meeting resumed.

Patrick shifted to "closing decisions," which meant he started assigning roles like a man handing out scripts.

"And for the gala's opening," Patrick said smoothly, "I propose a brief on-stage welcome. Avery, with Miles beside you. A symbol of stability."

Avery's pulse spiked.

The donor in pearls smiled. "That would be lovely."

Gerald's voice went cold. "No."

Patrick tilted his head. "Chair Whitmore."

Gerald's gaze flicked to Avery. "We are not feeding narratives."

Natalie murmured, "Gerald is accidentally on the right side of history. Mark the calendar."

Avery shot her a look.

Miles stayed quiet, watching Avery.

Avery lifted her chin. "I'll do the welcome. Miles will not be on stage as a symbol."

Patrick's eyebrows rose. "Then why have him present at all."

Avery's smile was warm. "Because he's good at his job."

A few donors nodded approvingly. It was hard to argue with competence when it looked calm.

Patrick's smile tightened. "And the headline pressure."

Avery's gaze sharpened. "The spotlight will be pediatrics. If you want to raise money, put the children in the story."

Patrick stared at her.

Then he smiled again, smooth. "Of course."

Gerald looked relieved. Natalie looked proud. Miles looked... quietly impressed, which was the most dangerous look he could give her.

Patrick turned to the development director. "Fine. We'll adjust."

He flipped a page.

"And now," Patrick said, voice almost too casual, "final item. Media. There's a local morning show interested in covering the pediatric gala kickoff. They requested Avery and Miles together for a pre-event interview."

Avery's stomach dropped.

Natalie whispered, "There it is."

Gerald's jaw tightened. "That's not happening."

Patrick smiled. "It's a strong opportunity."

Avery's pulse hammered. She could feel the trap. A public pairing. A noise cemented.

And underneath it, the burner account's dare: Bring him. Or lose him.

Avery forced her breath even.

She looked at Miles.

His expression was calm, waiting. No pressure. No push.

Choice.

Avery turned back to Patrick, voice steady. "We'll do the interview."

Natalie choked.

Gerald's eyes snapped to Avery. "Avery."

Avery held his gaze. "On our terms."

Patrick's eyebrows lifted. "And what are your terms."

Avery's smile sharpened. "Pediatrics. Staffing. Outcomes. Not my personal life."

Patrick's smile widened. "Of course."

Avery continued, "Natalie will be present. We control the questions. And if the host tries to pivot into gossip, we pivot back."

Patrick nodded slowly, as if impressed. "well."

Gerald looked furious, but he couldn't argue without looking like he was blocking pediatrics coverage.

Natalie leaned toward Avery, whispering through her teeth, "You agreed to a joint interview."

Avery whispered back, "On our terms."

Natalie's eyes narrowed. "You're surfing."

Avery's jaw tightened. "I'm choosing."

Natalie blinked, then smiled, unexpectedly soft. "Okay."

Patrick glanced at his phone, then looked up, smile smooth. "Wonderful. We'll confirm details tomorrow."

The meeting wrapped with donor chatter and fake warmth and promises of future generosity.

Avery stood, gathering her things.

As she did, she noticed something that made her stomach turn cold.

A small black device clipped to the underside edge of the conference table.

Not a microphone. Not exactly.

A meeting recorder.

Avery's pulse spiked.

Natalie saw it too. Her eyes widened.

Miles's gaze sharpened.

Patrick's expression didn't change.

Avery felt a chill.

Then Patrick said, lightly, "Thank you all. This was productive."

Avery's throat tightened.

Was the device always there? Was it standard? Was it a trap?

She forced herself not to spiral.

Romcom.

Stay in romcom.

But the presence of the recorder did one thing: it made Avery aware that anything said in this room could become content.

Avery turned toward Miles, voice low. "We're leaving."

Miles nodded. "Yes."

Natalie stepped in close, whispering, "Do not look at the recorder. Do not acknowledge the recorder. We will pretend it is normal and then we will set it on fire emotionally later."

Avery exhaled. "Natalie."

Natalie smiled. "Too much."

Avery nodded. "Too much."

They moved toward the exit corridor.

Behind them, Patrick's voice carried, polite and warm to donors.

In front of them, the hallway was quiet.

Natalie's phone buzzed.

She checked it, then went still.

Avery's stomach dropped. "What."

Natalie held up her screen.

Midtown Pulse had posted.

A clip.

From inside the meeting.

Not long. Not clear. enough.

Avery's voice, caught mid-sentence: "We'll do the interview."

Caption: "SHE SAID YES. JOINT INTERVIEW CONFIRMED. THIS IS NOT A DRILL."

Avery's blood turned cold.

Natalie whispered, "Okay. That recorder was not standard."

Miles's jaw set. "We didn't announce that publicly."

Avery's pulse hammered. "Someone is leaking in real time."

Natalie's eyes flashed. "Or broadcasting."

Avery forced her breath even, though her ribs felt tight. "Romcom," she whispered to herself like a prayer. "This is a romcom."

Miles leaned slightly closer, voice low, steady. "Then we play it like one."

Avery looked up at him. "How."

Miles's gaze held hers. "We don't hide. We don't flinch. We show up. Together. On purpose. And we keep it about kids."

Avery's throat tightened.

Natalie swallowed. "Okay. I hate that he's right."

Avery's phone buzzed in her purse.

Avery froze.

Then pulled it out.

Unknown number.

Her fingers went cold as she opened it.

Unknown: Good.Unknown: Now the whole city gets to watch you choose.Unknown: Smile, Avery. It plays better on camera.

Avery stared at the screen, heart pounding.

Natalie whispered, "Tell me you're not going to throw up."

Avery's jaw clenched. "No."

Miles's voice was soft. "Avery."

Avery looked up.

Miles's eyes were steady, warm, unshaken.

Avery took one slow breath and did the only thing she could do if she wanted to stay in control of her own story.

She lifted her chin.

She slid the phone back into her purse.

And she said, calm enough to surprise even herself, "Fine."

Natalie blinked. "Fine?"

Avery nodded. "They want a show. They're going to get one."

Miles's mouth twitched faintly. "On our terms."

Avery's eyes locked on his. "On our terms."

Natalie exhaled slowly, a grin breaking through her fear. "Okay. Romcom war it is."

They walked toward the exit.

And behind them, somewhere in the Montclaire's polished hallways, someone was counting down to the moment Avery Sloan would be asked, again, to choose on camera.

Only this time, Avery wasn't planning to survive the question.

She was planning to own the answer.

Chapter 16: Hot Mic, Cold Hands

Avery Sloan had faced down hostile attorneys, hostile board members, and once, a hostile decorative fern that someone insisted belonged in a waiting room despite the fact it looked like it had been watered with spite.

None of those things had ever tried to contour her cheekbones.

The makeup artist tapped a sponge under Avery's left eye with cheerful ruthlessness. " brightening. You've got great bone structure."

Avery stared straight ahead into the mirror and said, flatly, "I slept seven hours."

Natalie hovered behind the stylist like a stage manager with a clipboard and a vendetta. "That's adorable. The camera thinks you slept four."

Avery kept her face still, because the sponge was now near her nose and she did not trust herself to speak without inhaling powder. Her hands rested in her lap, fingers interlaced, knuckles white.

The studio dressing room smelled like hairspray and lemon wipes. Bright bulbs lined the mirror, so unforgiving they made even the air look judgmental. On a small table beside Avery sat a cup of lukewarm coffee and a folder labeled ST. CATHERINE'S: PEDIATRIC GALA TALKING POINTS in cheerful font, like this was an elementary school book fair and not the current public battle for her dignity.

Across the room, Miles sat in a chair that looked built for someone smaller and less annoyed. A production assistant had attempted to powder his face and he had reacted with polite confusion, as if someone had offered to varnish him.

"I'm fine," he'd said.

"No one is fine on HD," the assistant had replied, and then dabbed his forehead anyway.

Miles now looked exactly the same, except faintly betrayed.

He caught Avery's gaze in the mirror and his mouth twitched like he was fighting a smile.

Avery did not smile back.

Not because she didn't want to.

Because smiling would mean admitting she was nervous, and she was absolutely not nervous.

She was... strategically aware.

Natalie leaned in closer to Avery's ear. "I want you to remember something important."

Avery murmured without moving her lips. "If you say 'breathe' I'm going to fire you."

Natalie whispered, "If you say 'we're focused on pediatrics' one more time, I'm going to throw myself into traffic."

Avery's eyes flicked to her. "It's the mission."

"It's also your emotional support phrase," Natalie said. "And I respect that. But the host is going to try to drag you into romance content. You need a fun pivot."

Avery stared at herself in the mirror. "I'm not fun."

Natalie's eyes widened in mock horror. "Excuse you. You were fun in the lobby. You told a man with a ring light that you weren't a reality show."

Avery's cheeks warmed. "That was not fun. That was survival."

Natalie nodded seriously. "Exactly. Survival, but with jokes. That's romcom."

The makeup artist smiled politely, clearly pretending she wasn't listening to a conversation that sounded like a group therapy session for people allergic to vulnerability.

Avery's phone buzzed in her purse.

Avery's stomach tightened.

Natalie's hand shot out automatically, then she stopped herself, palms up like she was restraining an instinct. "I won't. I won't touch it."

Avery glanced at Miles.

He watched her calmly, a quiet anchor in a room that felt too bright and too loud even when no one was speaking.

Avery exhaled slowly and forced herself to focus on what mattered.

This was not a date.

This was not a confession.

This was a pediatric gala interview with a morning show host who would absolutely try to turn it into a "power couple" moment because the internet was incapable of minding its business.

And Avery was going to walk out of this studio with her dignity intact.

Even if the makeup artist tried to glue it to her face with setting spray.

Five minutes later, a producer appeared at the door with a headset and the energy of someone who ran on adrenaline and half-finished protein bars.

"We're up in twelve," she announced. "Ms. Sloan, Mr. Carter, we'll mic you in the green room."

Natalie stood immediately. "Great. We'll be there. Also, quick question: are we doing this like a normal interview or like a public execution."

The producer blinked once. "Normal."

Natalie nodded. "Perfect. Love that for us."

Avery rose, smoothing her dress. Her hands were still cold. She hated that detail. She hated feeling like her body was conspiring with the internet.

Miles stood too, offering Avery a steady look. "You're good."

Avery's voice was clipped. "I'm prepared."

Miles nodded as if those were the same thing, or as if he understood the difference and didn't want to fight her on it.

Natalie fell into step beside Avery. "Remember: pediatrics first, charm second, and if the host says 'chemistry' I will tackle him."

Avery stared at her. "Natalie."

Natalie smiled sweetly. "I'm joking. Mostly."

They followed the producer down a corridor lined with framed photos of smiling anchors. Everyone looked friendly and approachable and impossibly rested, as if morning shows ran on sunshine instead of sleep deprivation and caffeine.

The green room was exactly as Avery feared: soft couches, a bowl of fruit no one ate, and a television playing their segment preview on loop.

On screen, Avery's face appeared next to Miles's.

A split-screen still from the cafeteria.

The headline beneath it read:

ST. CATHERINE'S LEADERSHIP UNDER THE SPOTLIGHT

Natalie made a strangled sound. "Under the spotlight. That's polite. They mean 'being hunted for sport.'"

Avery's jaw clenched. "Ignore it."

Miles's gaze flicked to the screen, then back to Avery. "We control what we can."

Avery's chest tightened at the quiet steadiness of his voice.

A sound tech approached with two wireless mic packs and the brisk efficiency of someone who had clipped microphones to every type of human emotion.

"Ms. Sloan first," he said, already reaching.

Avery stiffened instinctively.

Miles stepped closer, voice low. "Do you want me to take it."

Avery's eyes narrowed. "No."

Natalie whispered, "Let him. It's intimate. It's romantic."

Avery shot her a look that promised consequences.

Miles held Avery's gaze, then stepped back half a step, hands up in surrender. "Okay."

The sound tech clipped the mic pack at the back of Avery's dress and threaded the wire upward.

Avery held her posture rigid, staring straight ahead as if she could disassociate through professionalism.

"Can you lift your hair," the tech asked.

Avery lifted her hair.

The tech's fingers brushed the nape of her neck as he positioned the mic.

Avery's skin went cold, then hot.

Her pulse jumped.

This was ridiculous. She was a CEO. She had survived worse than a microphone.

Natalie watched with the intensity of a woman who believed every romantic beat needed to be documented for future blackmail.

Then it was Miles's turn.

The tech clipped the pack onto Miles's waistband and threaded the wire under his jacket.

Miles remained calm, but Avery noticed the slight tension in his shoulders, the subtle discomfort of someone who hated feeling manipulated by equipment.

Avery should have found it funny.

She did.

Which made her hate herself more.

The tech stepped back. "All set. You're hot in sixty seconds."

Natalie's head snapped up. "We are not calling it that."

The tech blinked. "Hot mic."

Natalie pointed at Avery like she was presenting evidence to a jury. "See. This is what I mean. Everything is phrased like it's about sex or shame."

Miles coughed once, a laugh he tried to swallow.

Avery's cheeks warmed. "Natalie, stop."

Natalie smiled. "I will not. I am your emotional airbag."

The producer reappeared. "We're ready."

Avery's stomach tightened.

Miles's gaze met hers, steady. "Hey."

Avery looked at him.

"On air," Miles said quietly, "I won't speak over you. I won't answer for you. If they push, you lead."

Avery's throat tightened.

She had spent her life surrounded by men who believed leadership was something they could manage around her.

This man was offering her the opposite.

Avery's voice came out softer than she intended. "Thank you."

Miles nodded once, calm. "Always."

Natalie pretended to gag. "Ugh. Healthy communication. Disgusting."

Avery elbowed her, lightly. Natalie yelped dramatically and then grinned.

The producer opened the studio door.

"Let's go," she said.

Avery stepped forward.

Lights hit her like a wave.

The set was bright and cheerful in a way Avery found deeply suspicious.

A soft blue backdrop. A couch. Two chairs. A coffee table with a decorative plant that looked like it had never experienced hardship. Two anchors sat across from where Avery and Miles were directed to sit, both smiling like they genuinely enjoyed waking up at four in the morning.

The host, a man with perfect hair and the energy of someone who had never been told "no" in a public setting, stood to greet them.

"Avery Sloan," he said warmly. "Thank you for being here."

Avery shook his hand, smile controlled. "Thank you for having us."

"And Miles Carter," he added, smiling as if he'd been waiting his whole career for this exact pairing.

Miles shook his hand, calm. "Morning."

Natalie sat off-camera on a stool, arms crossed, expression sharp enough to cut glass.

The female anchor smiled brightly at Avery. "We've been hearing so much about the pediatric expansion. This is exciting."

Avery's shoulders eased by a fraction. Good. Start there.

The host sat and angled toward Avery with a practiced warmth. "We do have to ask, Avery. The internet has been... lively."

Avery smiled, polite. "It has."

"And we've all seen the cafeteria clip," the host continued, leaning in. "You were incredibly composed. But you've also had an ethics complaint filed. How are you handling that?"

Avery felt her spine straighten.

Calm. Warm. Mission.

"We take compliance seriously," Avery said, voice even. "We welcome review. And we keep doing the work. My focus is pediatric care and staff support. That's what matters."

The female anchor nodded, impressed. "That's a grounded response."

Avery held her smile.

The host tried again, smoothly. "And Miles, what do you say to people who think you're... influencing Avery."

Natalie's face off-camera went lethal.

Miles kept his expression calm and said simply, "I'm here to help the hospital communicate clearly. Avery leads. I support. That's it."

Avery felt a flicker of relief in her chest.

Good.

Clean.

No drama.

The host's smile widened, hungry. "But you can see how people might interpret it. You're both in high-profile roles, you're working closely, and there's been a lot of speculation."

Avery's jaw clenched slightly.

She kept her smile warm. "Speculation doesn't build pediatric wings. Donations do."

The host blinked, thrown off for half a beat.

Then the female anchor laughed softly, delighted. "That's fair."

Avery continued, leaning enough into humor to stay human. "Also, I'd like to remind everyone that this is a hospital. We're here to talk about kids and care, not my facial expressions in a cafeteria."

Natalie made a quiet approving sound off-camera.

Miles's mouth twitched.

The host chuckled, but Avery could see him recalibrating. He wasn't going to get the "tell us about your relationship" segment without trying harder.

He turned to the pediatric gala talking points on the table. "Okay, let's talk about the gala. What will the funds support."

Avery's shoulders loosened. "Pediatric mental health resources, family support rooms, and staffing expansion for overnight coverage. We want families to feel held, not treated."

The female anchor softened. "That's beautiful."

Avery nodded. "It's necessary."

Miles added, briefly, "And it's measurable. Not a slogan."

Avery glanced at him.

He didn't look at her like he was trying to steal the moment.

He looked at her like he was making sure the mission stayed anchored.

Avery felt something warm and strange under her ribs.

Then the host struck again, smiling.

"And you two will be appearing together at the gala kickoff, correct?"

Avery kept her expression smooth. "We will both be present, yes."

The host leaned in, voice playful. "Together together."

Natalie inhaled sharply off-camera.

Avery kept her smile. "We work well together."

The host grinned. "That's not a no."

Avery laughed lightly, the way she'd practiced in rooms full of people who wanted a reaction. "It's not an answer you're entitled to."

The female anchor's eyes widened in delighted surprise.

Then she laughed. "Okay, that's incredible."

The host chuckled, but Avery could tell he'd been gently slapped with a boundary on live television, and it was not a sensation he enjoyed.

He pivoted quickly. "Well, we can respect privacy. But viewers are rooting for you both, I'll say that."

Avery smiled politely, refusing to validate the premise.

Miles, calm, added, "Viewers can root for pediatric mental health too."

Natalie's eyes off-camera went wide with pride.

Avery almost smiled for real.

Almost.

The segment continued for another four minutes: pediatric needs, donor engagement, staff gratitude. Avery answered questions with warmth and specificity. Miles supported without dominating. Natalie sat off-camera like a vigilant hawk, occasionally mouthing "NO" when the host tried to drift into gossip.

By the end, the female anchor looked genuinely moved.

"This is important work," she said. "Thank you both for being here."

Avery nodded. "Thank you for keeping it focused."

The host smiled, camera-ready. "All right, we'll be right back."

A light above the camera blinked off.

Commercial break.

Avery exhaled for what felt like the first time in an hour.

Natalie immediately stood and hissed from off-camera, "That man is obsessed with the phrase 'together together.' I want him arrested."

Avery whispered, "Natalie."

Natalie leaned closer. "You did great. Also, your face does this thing when you look at Miles—"

Avery cut her off. "Natalie."

Miles's mouth twitched. "She's not wrong."

Avery turned sharply. "Do not encourage her."

Miles looked mildly amused. "I'm not encouraging. I'm... acknowledging."

Avery pressed her lips together, cheeks warm.

Natalie whispered, "Okay. One more rule: your mics are off. You can be human for thirty seconds."

Avery's shoulders loosened. "Thank God."

Miles leaned slightly closer, voice low, warm. "You were good."

Avery looked at him. His eyes were steady, soft, and annoyingly kind.

Avery's breath caught.

She heard herself say, quieter than she meant, "Stop looking at me like that."

Miles blinked. "Like what."

Avery swallowed.

This was the exact moment her brain should have kicked in and reminded her she was on a set, with people, and that the universe hated her.

Instead, Avery said the truth, because she was tired and human and apparently had lost her grip on self-preservation.

"Like I'm..." She hesitated, then forced the words out, voice low. "Like I'm yours."

Miles went still.

The air between them tightened.

Not heavy. Not dark.

charged.

Miles's gaze held hers, and his voice was quieter than the bright studio could justify.

"I'm not claiming you," he said. "I'm... choosing you."

Avery's chest tightened.

Natalie made a small strangled sound.

Avery started to speak—

And the host's voice boomed from nearby, cheerful and loud. "Folks, we are still hot!"

Natalie froze.

Avery froze.

Miles froze.

The sound tech, wearing a headset, snapped his fingers and pointed at their mic packs like he was trying to warn them through interpretive dance.

Avery's blood turned to ice.

Hot.

Hot mic.

Not "off." Not "safe." Not "private."

The red light above one of the cameras blinked.

Not the live broadcast camera, but a behind-the-scenes digital recorder used for social clips.

Natalie's eyes went huge.

Avery's soul left her body and checked into a different hotel.

Miles's jaw tightened.

The host laughed, waving. "kidding! But seriously, our digital team loves grabbing little moments for social. You guys are great."

Avery stared, frozen.

Natalie whispered, through her teeth, "We are going to die."

Miles leaned toward Avery, voice low, calm. "Don't panic."

Avery whispered back, rigid, "I can't believe I said that."

Miles's mouth twitched, almost a smile. "It was honest."

Avery stared at him. "It was catastrophic."

Natalie hissed, "It was viral."

The producer rushed in, breathless. "We're back in ten! Everyone reset!"

Avery forced her face into composure with sheer willpower. She lifted her chin, turned toward the set, and smiled like she hadn't offered the internet the most delicious phrase of its life.

Miles sat back, calm again, as if his nervous system had an off switch Avery could not locate.

The host returned to his chair, laughing lightly. "All right! Back in three, two..."

The light blinked on again.

Avery delivered the last portion of the segment like a woman performing surgery on herself: steady hands, controlled breath, no visible bleeding.

When it ended, the anchors thanked them again.

The camera light blinked off.

Avery smiled until the exact second it was safe to stop.

Then she stood.

Miles stood with her.

Natalie practically sprinted onto the set, grabbing Avery's arm.

"We're leaving," Natalie whispered. "Immediately. Before I burn down this studio."

The producer approached, bright and oblivious. "You guys were fantastic! Our social team is going to clip some behind-the-scenes moments, so keep an eye out."

Natalie's smile was wide and terrifying. "We will."

Avery's legs felt numb.

Miles leaned in slightly, voice low. "Hey."

Avery turned to him.

His gaze was steady, warm. No panic. No shame.

"We'll handle it," he said.

Avery swallowed. "How."

Miles's mouth curved faintly. "Romcom rules."

Avery let out a short, disbelieving laugh. "I hate romcom rules."

Miles's eyes softened. "No you don't."

Avery stared at him, heart thudding.

She did.

She hated them because they were real.

Because they required her to be seen.

Natalie tugged her arm. "Come on. Before the building posts it with a heart emoji."

They moved quickly through the corridor toward the exit.

Avery's phone buzzed.

Avery froze.

Natalie reached for it automatically, then stopped herself. "Do you want me to look."

Avery's throat tightened. "No."

Miles's gaze sharpened. "Let Natalie look."

Avery stared at him. "Traitor."

Miles's mouth twitched. "Practical."

Avery handed Natalie the phone.

Natalie's eyes flicked over the screen.

Then her face went blank.

Avery's stomach dropped. "What."

Natalie slowly turned the screen toward Avery and Miles.

Midtown Pulse.

Posted one minute ago.

A clip.

Grainy, behind-the-scenes, pulled from the studio's digital camera feed.

Avery's voice, unmistakable:

"Stop looking at me like that." Miles: "Like what." Avery: "Like I'm yours." Miles: "I'm not claiming you. I'm choosing you."

Caption, in neon text:

"HOT MIC ROMCOM CONFIRMED. SHE SAID 'YOURS.' HE SAID 'CHOOSING.' WE ARE NOT OKAY."

Avery's breath stopped.

Natalie whispered, "We are trending."

Miles's jaw tightened. Not angry. Focused.

Avery's hands went cold again.

She stared at the clip, at her own mouth moving on screen, at Miles's steady eyes, at the way the moment looked intimate and real and devastatingly romantic.

She had wanted privacy.

She had given the city a love confession by accident.

Natalie's phone buzzed too. She glanced at it and let out a low whistle. "Avery. Your mother commented."

Avery's throat went tight. "Of course she did."

Natalie read it aloud, horrified and delighted.

"'HELLO MILES. THIS IS AVERY'S MOTHER. I LIKE YOUR VIBES.'"

Avery closed her eyes. "I'm going to move to a cave."

Miles's voice was soft, warm. "Your mother seems... supportive."

Avery opened her eyes and glared at him. "Do not encourage her."

Miles's mouth twitched. "I'm not encouraging. I'm... acknowledging."

Natalie pointed at him. "Stop stealing my lines."

Miles looked mildly amused. "Sorry."

Avery's phone buzzed again.

A text this time.

From Gerald Whitmore.

Avery's stomach clenched before she even opened it.

She did anyway.

Gerald: My office. Now.

Natalie made a low sound. "Here comes the lecture."

Miles's gaze sharpened. "We go."

Avery stared at the message, then looked up at Miles.

Her heartbeat was loud in her ears.

"Together?" she asked quietly.

Miles's eyes held hers. "On purpose."

Natalie exhaled, half laughter, half panic. "Okay. This is either romantic growth or the beginning of my stress ulcer."

Avery slid the phone back into her purse, lifted her chin, and let the fear settle into something like resolve.

She'd been forced onto stages she didn't choose.

But now, at least, she could choose how she walked onto the next one.

Avery looked at Miles. "Fine."

Miles nodded once. "Fine."

Natalie fell into step beside them. "For the record, if Gerald says 'headline pressure' I'm going to scream."

Avery's mouth twitched despite herself. "Try not to."

Natalie grinned. "No promises."

They headed for the elevator.

And on the screen behind them, Midtown Pulse's clip kept looping, feeding the city's appetite with the exact thing Avery had never planned to give anyone:

Proof that she wasn't made of granite.

Proof that she could be chosen.

And proof that, for better or worse, the whole world had heard it.

Chapter 17: The Price of Being Seen

Gerald Whitmore's office had a view of the city that made other people stand straighter the second they walked in.

Avery had always hated that about it.

Not because it was impressive. It was. Floor-to-ceiling glass, skyline cut like a serrated edge, the sort of altitude that suggested you were above consequences.

She hated it because Gerald believed the view meant something.

Like the higher you stood, the less you were allowed to feel.

Avery stepped into the office and kept her face neutral, even though her stomach was still tight from the studio clip replaying in her head in an endless loop.

Like I'm yours. I'm choosing you.

Natalie had insisted they take the service elevator up, as if avoiding the main elevator would somehow stop half the hospital from watching them get summoned like criminals.

Miles walked in at Avery's side, calm in a way that made her both grateful and quietly furious. Not at him. At the fact that his calm made her want to lean on him. She didn't want to need leaning. She wanted to be the one people leaned on.

Natalie followed, clutching her tote bag like it contained either weapons or snacks, which in Natalie's case meant the same thing.

Gerald stood behind his desk, hands braced on the edge, suit immaculate, face controlled. He wasn't red with rage. He wasn't shouting.

That was how Avery knew it was serious.

He didn't look up right away. He stared at the tablet on his desk as if reading it could reverse the last hour of Avery's life.

Finally, he lifted his gaze.

"Avery," he said.

Then, to Miles, without warmth: "Mr. Carter."

Miles nodded once. "Chair Whitmore."

Natalie chirped, "Gerald."

Gerald's eyes flicked to Natalie like she was a loud siren he didn't have the authority to unplug. "Ms. Kim."

Natalie smiled brightly. "I'm here to make sure no one says anything unhinged."

Gerald's mouth tightened. "Then you'll be busy."

Avery inhaled slowly.

Gerald looked at her again, and his expression shifted, slightly.

Not anger.

Something worse.

Disappointment, dressed up in control.

"You went on television," Gerald said.

Avery kept her tone calm. "To talk about pediatrics."

Gerald's gaze flicked down to the tablet. "And you talked about pediatrics."

Avery waited. She could feel Natalie vibrating behind her like a live wire.

Gerald lifted the tablet and turned the screen toward them.

The clip was paused on the frame where Avery's mouth was mid-word and Miles's gaze was steady and infuriatingly gentle.

The caption screamed in bright letters.

Avery's jaw clenched.

Gerald tapped the screen once. Audio played.

Avery heard her own voice, low and unguarded:

"Stop looking at me like that."

She heard Miles:

"Like what."

She heard herself again, the words falling out like a confession she'd never agreed to make:

"Like I'm yours."

Then Miles's reply, quiet and ruinous:

"I'm not claiming you. I'm choosing you."

Gerald muted it before it finished.

The silence afterward was thick.

Natalie whispered, "I hate that it's adorable."

Avery shot her a look.

Natalie mouthed, Sorry.

Gerald set the tablet down carefully, as if it might break. Or as if Avery might.

"Avery," Gerald said again, and his voice had softened by half a degree. "Do you understand what this does."

Avery's throat tightened. "It's a viral clip. It will burn itself out."

Gerald's eyes narrowed. "That's what you said about the cafeteria."

Avery's pulse ticked upward. "The cafeteria clip was—"

"Not the point," Gerald cut in, but his tone stayed controlled. He looked at her for a long beat, then exhaled, slow.

When he spoke again, his voice wasn't sharp.

It was weary.

"That clip," Gerald said, "is now the story."

Avery's stomach tightened. "The story is pediatric care."

Gerald's gaze held hers. "That should be the story."

Avery flinched internally, though her face stayed still.

Gerald continued, quieter, like he was speaking to someone he'd once believed would never put him in this position. "Avery, you have been building trust for years. Not with donors. With staff. With the city. With the board."

Avery's jaw clenched. "I still am."

Gerald nodded once. "Yes. But you've also handed the public a story they can consume without thinking."

Natalie muttered, "The public does love that."

Gerald ignored her. His gaze didn't leave Avery's.

"What happens when a donor writes a check because they think they're buying a love story," Gerald said, "and not a pediatric wing."

Avery's voice stayed even. "We redirect them."

Gerald's eyes softened slightly, the way a mentor's eyes soften right before they say something that hurts.

"You can't redirect a story once it's been fed," Gerald said. "You can only choose whether you're in control of it."

Avery's throat tightened. "I didn't choose that clip."

Miles spoke calmly, measured. "The studio's digital team clipped it. They posted it. Midtown Pulse boosted it."

Gerald's gaze flicked to Miles. "And you said it on a hot mic."

Miles didn't flinch. "Yes."

Avery's pulse jumped.

Miles wasn't defending himself. He was owning it.

Avery hated how much she respected that.

Gerald's attention returned to Avery. "That's what concerns me."

Avery held his gaze. "That I'm human."

Gerald's mouth tightened. He didn't deny it.

His voice softened. "That you're vulnerable."

Avery's chest tightened at the word. She hated it. She hated how it sounded in his mouth.

Natalie made a small sound, like she wanted to argue but knew this wasn't a room where arguing would help.

Gerald stepped out from behind his desk and moved toward the window, looking out at the skyline like he needed distance from the words he was about to say.

"When I brought you in," he said quietly, "you were young and brilliant and angry in a way that made you dangerous."

Avery's jaw clenched. "I wasn't angry."

Gerald's smile was brief and dry. "You were furious. You packaged it like ambition."

Avery's throat tightened.

Gerald continued, voice still calm. "You learned how to win in rooms like this. You learned how to be respected even by people who wanted to diminish you."

Avery's fingers curled slightly at her sides.

Gerald turned back, and his expression was not cold.

It was almost... protective.

Which was the problem.

"I'm not asking you to be less human," Gerald said. "I'm asking you to understand the price of being seen."

Avery's stomach tightened. "What are you saying."

Gerald looked at her for a long beat.

Then he said it.

The emotional knife.

"You can have the hospital," Gerald said softly. "Or you can have the story."

Avery's pulse stopped for a fraction of a second.

Gerald's gaze did not waver. "But you don't get both."

Avery's chest tightened hard enough it almost hurt.

Natalie whispered, "Okay, that's... brutal."

Miles's posture stayed steady, but Avery felt him go still beside her, the way a person goes still when they're trying not to flinch.

Avery forced air into her lungs. "This is not a choice."

Gerald's voice stayed calm. "It is."

Avery's jaw clenched. "You're telling me I have to choose between leadership and... my personal life."

Gerald's gaze held hers. "I'm telling you the world will force that choice on you."

Avery's throat tightened. "Then we push back."

Gerald's eyes softened again, and Avery hated that she could see the weariness behind them. "You can push back, Avery. But pushing back still costs you something."

Natalie stepped forward, voice bright but controlled. "With respect, Gerald, the world is not a board meeting. People are allowed to fall in love without forfeiting their competence."

Gerald's eyes narrowed slightly. "This is not about love."

Natalie's mouth tightened. "Sure."

Gerald's gaze returned to Avery. "You hired Carter to help you navigate spotlight. And now spotlight are consuming you."

Avery's voice went cold. "The board hired him."

Gerald's jaw flexed, but he didn't argue.

Instead, he said quietly, "Avery. I'm going to ask you something, and I need you to answer honestly."

Avery's stomach tightened. "Fine."

Gerald looked at her. "Do you want him here."

Avery's pulse jumped.

The room went tight around the question.

Miles's gaze stayed on Gerald, but Avery could feel his awareness shift to her, quiet and steady.

Natalie's eyes widened slightly, then she looked at Avery as if she would physically hold her upright if she needed it.

Avery's mouth went dry.

If she said no, she would be safe. The story would lose fuel. Gerald would relax. The board would stop sharpening knives behind smiles.

If she said yes...

She would be choosing being seen again.

On purpose.

Avery forced her voice steady. "He's doing his job."

Gerald's eyes narrowed. "That's not an answer."

Avery's cheeks warmed with anger. "It is an answer."

Gerald held her gaze. "Do you want him here, Avery."

Avery swallowed.

Her throat felt tight, not with fear, but with something worse.

Truth.

She could lie. She was good at lying. She could keep everything in categories, keep every piece of her life in its assigned box.

But she was tired.

And she could still hear Miles's voice in the studio, quiet and unshaken.

I'm choosing you.

Avery lifted her chin. "Yes."

Natalie exhaled sharply, like she'd been holding her breath the whole time.

Miles didn't move. He didn't smile. But Avery felt the shift in him, subtle, like warmth.

Gerald stared at her for a long beat.

Then his expression softened in a way that made Avery's chest ache.

Not approval.

Understanding.

"That," Gerald said quietly, "is what I was afraid you would say."

Avery's jaw clenched. "Because you think it makes me weak."

Gerald's eyes hardened slightly. "Because I know how people will use it against you."

Avery's voice went low. "Then let them try."

Gerald's gaze held hers, and, Avery saw something in him she rarely saw.

Regret.

He said quietly, "You don't know what it costs until it's already taken something from you."

Avery swallowed. "I'm not asking for permission."

Gerald nodded once, almost imperceptibly. "I know."

He looked at Miles. "Mr. Carter. You're good at what you do."

Miles nodded once. "Thank you."

Gerald's voice remained calm, but steel under it. "If you care about this hospital, you will not let your presence become the headline."

Miles's gaze didn't waver. "I won't."

Avery's throat tightened.

Gerald looked back at Avery. "Then here are the boundaries."

Natalie muttered, "Here we go."

Gerald ignored her. "No more unscheduled media appearances. No more improvisation. Any interview goes through our press office and compliance team. And if you are asked a personal question on camera, you answer like a CEO."

Avery's jaw clenched. "I did answer like a CEO."

Gerald's gaze flicked to the tablet. "You said 'yours.'"

Avery's cheeks warmed. "That was off camera."

Gerald's voice softened. "It wasn't."

Silence.

Natalie whispered, "This is why I hate microphones."

Gerald continued, "We have a gala in three weeks. Donors are watching. Staff are watching. The board is watching. You need to decide what you want to be remembered for."

Avery's voice went cold. "I want to be remembered for building pediatrics."

Gerald nodded. "Then act like it."

Avery's jaw tightened. "I am."

Gerald's gaze held hers. "Good. Then don't let them turn you into entertainment."

Avery swallowed.

Because she didn't know how to stop the world from watching her, now that it had discovered she could be human.

Gerald moved back behind his desk and picked up the tablet again. "Now. One more thing."

Avery's stomach dropped. "What."

Gerald tapped the screen. "The gala committee met after your segment aired."

Natalie's eyes narrowed. "Why do I feel dread."

Gerald looked up. "They're thrilled."

Avery's pulse spiked. "Thrilled about pediatrics."

Gerald's mouth tightened. "Thrilled about engagement."

Natalie made a small gagging sound.

Gerald continued, calm. "They want to capitalize on attention."

Avery's jaw clenched. "No."

Gerald's gaze sharpened. "They're donors, Avery. They don't understand boundaries unless you give them a reason to respect them."

Avery's voice went low. "What are they proposing."

Gerald looked at the tablet and read, "They want you and Carter to close the kickoff event."

Avery froze. "Close."

Gerald nodded. "On stage. Together. Live."

Natalie's eyes went wide. "Absolutely not."

Gerald lifted a hand. "It's already being discussed publicly."

Avery's stomach tightened. "By whom."

Gerald's gaze flicked toward the window, as if he could see Patrick in the skyline. "Montclaire. And several committee members who love being first to hint at something."

Natalie muttered, "Nothing says 'for the children' like romantic performance art."

Miles's posture stayed steady, but Avery saw the slight tension in his jaw.

Avery forced her voice calm. "We are not doing couples theater."

Gerald's gaze held hers. "Then you need to give them something else."

Avery's jaw clenched. "Like what."

Gerald's voice softened, almost careful. "Like leadership."

Avery stared. "That's what I've been giving."

Gerald nodded. "Then give it louder. Make it impossible for them to reduce you to a clip."

Avery's chest tightened.

She didn't want louder. She wanted quieter. She wanted a life where she could care about someone without a ring light appearing like a demon.

Gerald looked at her for a long beat, then said, softer, "Avery. I'm not your enemy."

Avery swallowed. "I know."

Gerald's gaze softened again, and the disappointment in it didn't feel like punishment. It felt like fear.

Fear for her.

Fear of what the world did to women who let themselves be seen wanting anything.

Gerald exhaled slowly. "I'm trying to protect you from a fight you don't realize you're in."

Avery's throat tightened. "I'm already in it."

Gerald nodded once. "Yes."

Silence held.

Then Natalie cleared her throat and stepped forward, voice brisk. "Okay. Here's the plan. We do the close, but we make it about pediatrics, not romance."

Avery's head snapped toward her. "Natalie."

Natalie held up a hand. "Hear me out. We control it. We script it. We make it so boring for gossip people that they choke."

Natalie turned to Gerald. "No flirting. No 'together together.' impact numbers and staff voices and a clear donor ask."

Gerald's expression didn't change, but Avery saw him considering it.

Natalie turned to Avery. "And if someone tries to pivot it into romance on stage, you do the thing you do best."

Avery's jaw clenched. "What thing."

Natalie smiled. "You kill them politely."

Avery's mouth twitched despite herself.

Miles spoke quietly, measured. "If we do it, we do it on our terms."

Avery looked at him.

His gaze held hers, calm and steady.

Not pushing.

Not claiming.

Offering partnership without demand.

Avery's chest tightened.

Gerald watched the exchange, and something in his face softened further, like he saw what Avery didn't want to admit out loud.

That this wasn't headline pressure.

It was real.

Gerald said quietly, "If you agree to close together, the board will see it as a statement."

Avery's pulse spiked. "Statement of what."

Gerald's voice stayed calm. "That you're willing to tie your leadership spotlight to him."

Avery's jaw clenched.

Miles said quietly, "I won't let it be about me."

Gerald's gaze flicked to Miles, assessing. "You'd better not."

Natalie muttered, "Gerald, you're being dramatic."

Gerald's eyes flicked to her. "I'm being realistic."

Natalie shrugged. "Same thing in this building."

Avery inhaled slowly.

She could feel the decision hovering.

If she said no, she would look like she was afraid. Like she was running. Like the rumors owned her.

If she said yes, she was stepping into the story again.

On purpose.

And the unknown number would be watching.

Avery swallowed. "If we do it," she said slowly, "it's pediatrics. It's staffing. It's families. It's outcomes."

Natalie nodded eagerly. "Yes."

Miles nodded once. "Yes."

Gerald's gaze tightened, then softened. "And you."

Avery's jaw clenched. "And me."

Gerald exhaled slowly. "Fine."

Natalie blinked. "Fine?"

Gerald's eyes sharpened. "Fine. But if you do this, Avery, you do it with a spine. You do it with boundaries. You do it without apologizing for existing."

Avery's throat tightened at the last part.

Because Gerald never spoke like that unless he was scared for someone.

Avery's voice went quieter. "I don't apologize."

Gerald's gaze held hers. "You do. not out loud."

Avery went still.

Natalie's expression softened, unexpectedly.

Miles's gaze stayed steady, warm.

Gerald picked up his tablet again and tapped. "The committee wants confirmation tonight."

Natalie groaned. "Of course they do."

Gerald looked at Avery. "So decide."

Avery's pulse hammered.

This was it again.

Choose.

Not on camera this time, but in the rooms that mattered.

Avery looked at Miles.

His gaze didn't demand. It didn't plead.

It simply stayed.

Avery felt something settle in her chest, not soft, not weak.

Stubborn.

She turned back to Gerald.

"Yes," Avery said. "We'll close together."

Natalie exhaled loudly, like she'd been holding her breath for five chapters.

Miles's jaw loosened slightly.

Gerald stared at Avery for a long beat, then nodded once.

"Then make it count," Gerald said quietly.

Avery's voice was calm. "We will."

Gerald's gaze lingered on her longer, and the disappointment in it shifted into something else.

Acceptance.

Maybe even pride.

He said softly, "Avery. Don't confuse being seen with being owned."

Avery's throat tightened. "I won't."

Gerald nodded once. "Good."

Natalie clapped her hands, brisk and nervous. "Okay. Great. We're all emotionally damaged now. Can we go."

Gerald's eyes flicked to Natalie. "Yes."

Natalie grabbed Avery's arm and started steering her toward the door like she was evacuating a building.

As they stepped into the hallway, Avery's phone buzzed in her purse.

Avery froze.

Natalie hissed, "Don't."

Miles's gaze sharpened. "You should look."

Avery's stomach tightened anyway, because phones had become tiny portals to other people's opinions.

She pulled it out and saw not a number, but a push notification from Montclaire's official account.

NEW POST: "Avery Sloan, live in rehearsal. Steady leadership. Real heart."

Natalie leaned over, read it, and made a strangled sound. "They made you a limited-edition collectible."

Avery stared. "They posted rehearsal."

"They posted rehearsal," Natalie confirmed, like she was naming a crime.

Miles's jaw tightened. "We told them no behind-the-scenes."

Natalie's eyes flashed. "Patrick told them yes behind-the-scenes. Patrick would livestream your dental cleaning if it tested well."

Avery exhaled through her nose. "Okay."

Natalie blinked. "Okay?"

Avery slid the phone back into her purse and forced her voice calm. "If they want a finale, we give them a finale."

Miles's mouth twitched faintly. "On our terms."

Avery met his gaze. "On our terms."

Miles's voice was low. "Avery."

Avery looked up at him.

His gaze was steady, warm, anchored.

Whatever was happening outside them, the thing between them was real. It was the only thing that felt like it belonged to her.

Avery inhaled slowly.

Then she slid the phone back into her purse and forced her voice calm.

"Okay," she said.

Natalie blinked. "Okay?"

Avery nodded, eyes hard. "If they want a finale, we'll give them one."

Miles's mouth twitched faintly. "On our terms."

Avery met his gaze. "On our terms."

Natalie exhaled, half laughter, half panic. "Cool. Great. I'm going to need a snack and a therapist."

Avery started walking again, shoulders squared.

Because the gala was coming.

The city was watching.

And Avery Sloan was done letting anyone else decide what her story meant.

Chapter 18: Rehearsal in an Empty Room

The gala ballroom looked like a place where joy was rented by the hour.

Avery stood at the edge of the stage with a folder of talking points in her hands and tried not to feel like she was about to be graded.

Miles arrived a minute later, calm in a way that made Avery resentful and relieved at the same time. They ran the opening once. Natalie stopped them twice. "Less TED Talk," she warned. "More human being who has seen parents cry in fluorescent light."

Avery adjusted one line, and it landed.

They ran the handoff. It felt disturbingly natural. That was the problem.

On the third pass, Avery stumbled anyway, throat closing as her own leaked voice echoed in her head.

Avery stopped mid-sentence.

Miles's gaze sharpened. "Hey."

Avery forced a breath. "I'm fine."

Natalie made a low sound from her chair. "You are not fine."

Avery shot her a look. "Stop."

Miles spoke softly. "Take a second."

Avery pressed her lips together. She hated that her eyes burned. She hated that her body was doing the thing where it threatened tears when she was trying to be competent.

She gripped the podium edge harder than she needed to.

Miles stepped closer, voice low enough that it didn't echo. "Is it the clip."

Avery's throat tightened. She didn't answer.

Natalie, who had no self-preservation, blurted, "It's the clip."

Avery glared.

Natalie held up her hands. "I'm sorry. But it's obvious. You're the sort of woman who can handle a hospital crisis but gets derailed by... feelings."

Avery's voice went flat. "Thank you."

Natalie shrugged. "It's a talent."

Miles's gaze stayed on Avery. "Avery."

Avery exhaled, finally letting the truth out because she was tired of lying to everyone, including herself.

"It's not the clip," she said quietly.

Natalie's expression softened, surprising Avery. "Okay."

Avery swallowed. "It's the fact that I didn't know I could be heard."

Miles's jaw tightened slightly. "You didn't consent."

Avery's chest tightened. "And now... everyone thinks they get to be in my head."

Natalie nodded slowly. "That's real."

Avery forced herself to continue, voice low. "I hate that it worked. I hate that people liked it. I hate that I'm now... a story."

Miles's gaze didn't waver. "You're still you."

Avery's laugh was small and humorless. "Apparently, I'm also content."

Natalie muttered, "We all are. It's a nightmare."

Miles stepped closer, careful. "Look at me."

Avery didn't want to. She did anyway.

Miles's eyes were steady, warm. He didn't look like he was judging her for being shaken. He looked like he was simply there.

"You don't have to perform right now," Miles said quietly.

Avery's throat tightened. "I don't know how to stop."

Miles's voice softened. "Then don't stop completely. Just... let it be smaller."

Avery swallowed. "Smaller."

Miles nodded. "You can be strong and still be affected. Those aren't opposites."

Avery's chest tightened hard enough it felt like pain.

Natalie whispered, "Okay, I hate this because it's true and also because it's tender."

Avery shot her a look.

Natalie immediately pretended to zip her mouth again, dramatically.

Avery exhaled slowly and looked down at her notes.

"Again," Avery said, voice steadier. "From the handoff."

Miles nodded. "Okay."

They started again.

This time, Avery didn't stumble.

She kept her cadence warm. Human enough to land. Controlled enough to feel safe.

Miles followed, timed perfectly.

When they finished, Natalie clapped once, sharp. "Okay. That's it. That's the close. It's clean. It's mission. It's not couples theater."

Avery exhaled. "Good."

Natalie grabbed her tote bag and went to harass the AV team, muttering about fonts like it was a personal feud.

Avery watched her go, then looked at Miles.

He was watching her with that same calm expression that made her want to scream.

Avery's voice went clipped. "She's being dramatic."

Miles's mouth twitched faintly. "She's often right."

Avery huffed. "Annoyingly."

Miles nodded. "Yes."

Silence settled.

Not empty. Not awkward.

Just... quiet.

Avery didn't like how symbolic that felt.

She looked down at her folder again, flipping pages unnecessarily to keep her hands busy.

Miles's voice was soft. "Are you okay."

Avery's mouth tightened. "Yes."

Miles didn't move. "That's not an answer."

Avery's chest tightened. "I'm fine."

Miles's gaze stayed steady. "Avery."

Avery exhaled sharply, then said the truth because it was easier than pretending.

"I'm worried."

Miles nodded. "About the slide."

Avery's jaw clenched. "About... all of it."

Miles didn't push. He waited.

Avery's throat tightened. "I agreed to close with you because I'm tired of being forced into choices by people who don't know me."

Miles's gaze softened. "Okay."

Avery swallowed. "But I also..."

She stopped.

Miles's voice was quiet. "But you also what."

Avery looked at him, then looked away again, furious at her own vulnerability.

"I don't want to be managed," Avery said, voice low. "Ever."

Miles nodded. "I know."

Avery's eyes snapped back to his. "Do you."

Miles didn't flinch. "Yes."

Avery's pulse hammered. "Because right now, everyone is talking about me like I'm... a headline. A character. Like I'm someone's project."

Miles stepped slightly closer, careful. "You're not."

Avery's throat tightened. "Then why does it feel like I'm losing control."

Miles's voice softened. "Because you've never let yourself be seen wanting something."

Avery's chest tightened. She hated that he could say that without cruelty. Without accusation.

Miles continued, quietly, "You've controlled your life so well that you confuse control with safety."

Avery's jaw clenched. "Control is safety."

Miles shook his head slightly. "Control is... management. Safety is trust."

Avery stared at him.

That word again.

Trust.

She hated it. She wanted to throw it out a window.

She wanted it anyway.

Avery's voice came out rougher than she intended. "And what if trust gets used against me."

Miles's gaze held hers. "Then we deal with it. Together."

Avery's pulse jumped at the word together.

It was a normal word.

It felt loaded now.

Avery forced her voice steady. "I can't afford to lose the hospital because I became a story."

Miles nodded. "You won't."

Avery's laugh was small. "How do you know."

Miles's voice was quiet, sure. "Because you're not weak. And because wanting someone doesn't make you less competent."

Avery's chest tightened.

Natalie's voice echoed faintly from the hallway, shouting something about "slides" and "I will commit emotional arson."

Avery almost laughed.

Miles's mouth twitched. "She's intimidating."

Avery huffed. "She's a menace."

Miles nodded. "Yes."

The silence returned.

Avery looked at Miles.

Avery's throat tightened.

She said softly, "When you said 'choosing'... you didn't have to."

Miles's gaze softened. "I meant it."

Avery's pulse hammered.

She hated how much she wanted to step closer.

She hated that she could feel the moment tipping toward something.

Miles's gaze dropped briefly to her mouth, then returned to her eyes. His breathing shifted, subtle.

Avery's heart hammered.

She took one small step closer without meaning to.

Miles didn't move, but his focus sharpened as if he was asking permission with his eyes.

Avery's breath caught.

The ballroom felt too quiet.

Too large.

Too full of light for something private.

Avery's voice came out barely above a whisper. "This is a bad idea."

Miles's mouth curved faintly. "Probably."

Avery's fingers tightened on her folder like it was a shield she was about to drop.

Miles's voice was quieter. "Tell me to stop."

Avery swallowed.

She should.

She knew she should.

Instead, she looked up at him and didn't say anything.

Miles leaned in, slow, like he was giving her a thousand chances to step back.

Avery's breath caught. She felt the warmth of him before he touched her. The closeness. The promise.

Then her phone buzzed in her purse.

The vibration felt like a slap.

Avery froze.

Miles stopped instantly, pulling back without complaint, without frustration, as if he'd been trained to respect the moment's boundary.

Avery's chest tightened, heat flooding her cheeks.

Natalie returned from the hallway at that exact second, eyes wide and triumphant. "I FOUND THE SLIDE GUY," she announced. "And I have a spreadsheet."

She stopped when she saw Avery and Miles.

Her eyes narrowed.

Then widened.

Then narrowed again.

"Oh," Natalie said slowly. "We were almost doing something."

Avery's face burned. "We were not."

Miles cleared his throat softly. "We were... interrupted."

Natalie pressed her lips together, trying not to smile. She failed. "God. This is excellent."

Avery glared. "Natalie."

Natalie lifted a hand. "Okay. Fine. Business. Slides."

Avery's phone buzzed again, insistently.

Unknown, probably.

Avery's stomach tightened. She didn't look. She shoved the purse deeper against her side like hiding it could make it less real.

Natalie held up a printed sheet. "Here's the issue. The slide deck has been updated since your approval."

Avery's pulse spiked. "Updated by whom."

Natalie's eyes flashed. "Exactly. That's what I asked. The slide guy said 'committee.' Which is not a person. It's a fog."

Avery's jaw clenched. "What changed."

Natalie lifted the sheet like she was presenting evidence in court.

"It's the closing slide," Natalie said, voice sharp. "The one behind you when you do the final donor ask."

Avery's stomach tightened. "Show me."

Natalie turned the page.

There it was in bold, elegant font:

LEADERSHIP IN PARTNERSHIP

Under it, in smaller text:

Avery Sloan & Miles CarterTogether for St. Catherine's Children

Avery's blood went cold.

She stared at the words, unable to breathe.

Miles's jaw tightened beside her.

Natalie whispered, "I told you."

Avery's voice came out flat. "I did not approve this."

Natalie nodded. "No. You approved a version without this. This was added after."

Avery's pulse hammered. She felt the room tilt again, not into romance this time, but into something sharper.

This wasn't donors being cute.

This was someone shaping a noise deliberately.

Avery's throat tightened. "Who approved it."

Natalie's mouth tightened. "Patrick."

Avery went still.

Miles's gaze sharpened. "Patrick approved the slide?"

Natalie nodded grimly. "The slide guy said Patrick emailed the update 'for cohesion.'"

Avery's stomach turned. Cohesion. Sure.

Natalie looked at Avery, eyes hard. "This is not an accident."

Avery's jaw clenched. "He's trying to make it official."

Miles's voice was low. "He's trying to make it unavoidable."

Avery's breath shook. She hated how quickly her body went cold.

Natalie stepped closer. "Okay. We can fix it. We tell them to remove the slide."

Avery's voice was tight. "And then it looks like I'm panicking."

Natalie's eyes flashed. "Better panic than being packaged."

Avery's throat tightened. Packaged. That was the word.

Miles's voice was quiet. "Avery. We remove it."

Avery looked at him.

His gaze was steady. Firm. Protective in a way that didn't feel like control. It felt like a boundary he was willing to hold with her.

Avery swallowed. "Fine. We remove it."

Natalie exhaled, relieved. "Yes. Okay. Great. I will go yell politely."

Natalie spun toward the doors, ready to charge.

Avery's phone buzzed, and her body reacted on instinct, not fear so much as exhaustion with being reachable.

She glanced at the screen and saw Natalie in all caps: I AM WALKING TOWARD THE AV EQUIPMENT LIKE I AM ABOUT TO COMMIT A FELONY.

Miles read it over her shoulder and let out a quiet breath that might have been a laugh.

"She's going to be fine," he said. "Terrifying. But fine."

Her fingers went cold as she pulled the phone out.

Unknown number.

Of course.

She opened it.

Unknown: Nice try.Unknown: Partnership looks good on you.Unknown: Don't fight the story. It fights back.

Avery's blood turned to ice.

Natalie read it over her shoulder and whispered, "Nope."

Miles's jaw tightened hard. "It knows about the slide."

Avery's pulse hammered. "It knows everything."

Natalie's eyes flashed. "Someone is feeding it in real time."

Avery's breath caught. "From inside."

Natalie nodded grimly. "Yes."

Miles went still, focus sharpening. "Avery, we need to be careful about what we say in rooms like this."

Avery's throat tightened.

Careful.

The word landed wrong.

Not because it wasn't true.

Because it sounded like management.

Because it sounded like fear.

Avery's chest tightened, heat rising behind her eyes.

Natalie looked between them, sensing the shift. "Okay. Let's not do this here."

Avery's voice went sharp. "Do what."

Natalie's voice softened. "The thing where you spiral into control because you feel cornered."

Avery's jaw clenched. "I'm not spiraling."

Miles spoke gently. "You're tense."

Avery turned on him, faster than she meant to. "Of course I'm tense."

Miles didn't flinch. "Okay."

Avery's chest tightened. "This is exactly what I didn't want."

Miles's brow furrowed slightly. "What."

Avery's voice came out rough. "I didn't want to be handled. By Patrick. By Gerald. By the board. By the internet. By anyone."

Miles's gaze held hers. "I'm not handling you."

Avery's laugh was sharp. "You told me to be careful about what we say."

Miles's voice stayed steady. "Because people are watching. Because someone will always be ready to turn a private moment into a headline."

Avery's pulse hammered. "And now I have to police every word around you too."

Miles went still.

Natalie made a small sound. "Okay, Avery, that was... not fair."

Avery saw it the second the words left her mouth: the hurt that flickered in Miles's expression before he locked it down. Not dramatic. Not angry. quiet.

"I'm not asking you to shrink," Miles said softly. "I'm asking you to let me stand next to you."

Help felt like control. Partnership felt like risk.

Natalie clapped once. "Pause. Water. Everyone remember we are on the same team. Also: this is a fundraiser rehearsal, not a spy movie. If anyone tries to make it a spy movie, I will personally unplug the WiFi."

Avery didn't look up. "I'm fine."

Miles didn't let it go. "That's not an answer."

Avery exhaled and finally looked at him.

His expression was calm, but something in his eyes that made her chest tighten.

Not pressure.

Concern.

Avery hated that her throat burned.

"I don't want to lose the hospital," Avery said quietly.

Miles nodded. "You won't."

Avery's laugh was small, bitter. "You keep saying that like it's guaranteed."

Miles's voice softened. "Nothing is guaranteed. But you're not alone."

Avery's chest tightened. "That's the part that scares me."

Miles went still. "Because you don't trust people."

Avery's jaw clenched. "Because people use proximity like leverage."

Miles's gaze sharpened slightly. "I'm not leverage."

Avery's throat tightened.

She wanted to say: I know.

She didn't.

Instead, her eyes flicked past him.

Toward the ballroom doors.

Because movement had caught her attention.

Someone had entered the ballroom again.

Avery's spine stiffened.

Patrick Ames walked in with his phone in his hand and a polished smile on his face, as if he'd been invited.

Avery's blood went cold.

Patrick's gaze flicked to Avery, then to Miles, then back to Avery.

"Perfect," Patrick said smoothly. "You're both here."

Miles's jaw tightened.

Avery's voice went cool. "Patrick."

Patrick's smile widened, friendly and infuriating. "I wanted to catch you before you left."

Avery's pulse hammered. "Why."

Patrick lifted his phone slightly. "The clip is still trending. Donors are engaged. The gala kickoff has a momentum we didn't anticipate."

Avery's jaw clenched. "We anticipated it."

Patrick laughed lightly. "Not this level."

He stepped closer, gaze moving to Miles. "Miles. Excellent composure this morning. Strong messaging."

Miles's tone was calm. "Thank you."

Avery's stomach tightened at Patrick's comfort with praising Miles like he owned the scoreboard.

Patrick looked back at Avery. "I approved a small change to the closing deck. It's cohesive. It aligns your presence with stability."

Avery's blood cooled. "You added 'Leadership in Partnership.'"

Patrick's smile didn't falter. "Yes."

Avery's jaw clenched. "Remove it."

Patrick's eyes flicked briefly to Miles, then back to Avery. "Avery, donors love it. It's warm. It's human."

Avery's voice went colder. "It's manufactured."

Patrick's smile tightened slightly. "It's packaged."

Avery's pulse hammered. Branding. He said it like a compliment.

Miles spoke calmly, measured. "Patrick, it wasn't approved by Avery."

Patrick looked at Miles, smile smooth. "It's a committee deck. It's not personal."

Avery felt heat rise in her chest. "It is personal when it uses my name."

Patrick's gaze returned to Avery, voice gentle, as if he were soothing her. "Avery, you are fighting the thing that is helping you right now."

Avery's jaw clenched. "Helping me or helping Montclaire."

Patrick's smile tightened. "Helping pediatrics."

Avery stared at him.

Then she felt it: the subtle shift of Miles beside her, the way his posture went a fraction more alert.

Like he was bracing.

Not against Patrick.

Against Avery's reaction.

As if he expected her to explode.

As if he was managing the scene.

Avery's stomach tightened.

Patrick turned slightly, angling his body so he could speak to Miles more directly.

"Miles," Patrick said smoothly, "we should talk."

Avery's pulse jumped.

Miles glanced at Avery briefly, then nodded once. "Okay."

Avery's chest tightened.

Natalie wasn't back yet.

Avery stood alone on the stage with the two men who were now stepping slightly aside, speaking in low voices.

Avery could see Patrick's mouth moving. Could see his hand gesture once, small, as if he were emphasizing a point.

Miles listened.

Miles nodded once.

Natalie barreled back in, triumphant, and took one look at their faces. "Okay," she said, softer. "Everybody inhale. Nobody implode. We are not giving Patrick the satisfaction."

Avery turned.

Natalie's expression was sharp, but not unkind. "You're scared. That's normal. But don't punish him for trying to stand between you and Patrick."

Avery's throat tightened. "I'm not punishing him."

Natalie's eyebrows lifted. "You're pulling back. That's your punishment."

Avery went still.

Miles's gaze didn't waver, but Avery could feel the tension under his calm now.

Natalie continued, quieter, "You asked for partnership and now the moment it shows up, you treat it like a trap."

Avery's chest tightened. "Because partnership is being used as a headline."

Natalie nodded. "Yes. And that sucks. But Miles didn't make that slide."

Avery looked at Miles.

He watched her steadily, face open.

Not defensive.

Not angry.

Just... there.

Avery's throat tightened painfully.

She said quietly, "I need a minute."

Miles nodded once. "Okay."

Natalie stared at her. "Avery."

Avery's voice was tight. "Natalie."

Natalie exhaled, frustrated. "Fine. Take a minute. But don't take a week."

Avery stepped off the stage, moving toward the back of the ballroom where the shadows were deeper under the chandelier light.

Her phone buzzed again in her purse.

Avery's stomach dropped.

She pulled it out.

Unknown number.

Of course.

She opened it.

Unknown: You saw it.Unknown: Men always talk. Even the nice ones.Unknown: How long until you realize you're still being managed?

Avery's blood went cold.

Her hand shook slightly.

She stared at the message until the words blurred.

Then she slid the phone back into her purse like hiding it could protect her.

When she turned back toward the stage, Miles was watching her from a distance.

Natalie stood between them, arms crossed, eyes narrowed like she was about to fight the entire universe.

The ballroom felt massive again.

Avery walked back slowly, forcing her posture steady.

Miles met her halfway.

His voice was low. "What did it say."

Avery swallowed. "Nothing."

Miles's gaze sharpened. "Avery."

Avery forced a breath. "It's just... trying to get inside my head."

Miles nodded. "It's succeeding."

Avery's throat tightened. "Because it knows exactly what scares me."

Miles's voice softened. "Then we name it."

Avery's chest tightened. "Name what."

Miles held her gaze. "That you're afraid someone will turn you into a project."

Avery's jaw clenched.

Miles continued, quietly, "And that you're afraid I'll be part of that."

Avery's throat burned.

Natalie stepped closer, voice sharp. "He won't."

Avery swallowed. "I know."

But the truth was, Avery didn't know anything anymore. Not in the way she liked knowing. Not in the way she could control.

Miles's voice stayed steady. "Avery. I won't talk about you like you aren't here."

Avery's chest tightened.

Miles continued, "If Patrick tries again, we shut it down. If donors push, we redirect. If the board postures, we focus on pediatrics. But you don't have to fight this by making yourself alone again."

Avery's throat tightened.

Natalie whispered, "Please don't choose loneliness. It's boring and you deserve better."

Avery's mouth twitched despite herself.

Miles's gaze softened. "Are we okay."

Avery hesitated.

Her instinct was to say yes. To smooth. To control.

Instead, she said the truth.

"I'm... not sure," Avery whispered.

Miles went still.

Natalie made a small distressed noise.

Avery forced herself to continue. "Not because of you. Because of me. Because this is... getting under my skin."

Miles's voice softened. "Then let me be under it with you."

Avery's breath caught.

Natalie squeezed her eyes shut like she was enduring something emotionally loud.

Avery's throat tightened. "I can't... I can't afford to lose control."

Miles's gaze held hers. "Then don't lose it. Share it."

Avery stared at him.

Sharing control felt like jumping without checking the ground.

Natalie cleared her throat and stepped back, giving them space without announcing it.

The ballroom was quiet again, but the quiet felt different now. Less like emptiness. More like a pause.

Avery looked at Miles.

He looked back.

Steady. Present.

And Avery realized with a jolt that she didn't want to step away. She didn't want to be alone.

She wanted to stop feeling watched.

Avery exhaled slowly. "Okay."

Miles nodded once. "Okay."

Avery's voice was quiet. "We finish rehearsal."

Miles's mouth curved faintly. "Yes."

Natalie clapped once, relieved. "Thank God. Okay. Back on stage before I start crying and ruining my packaged."

Avery shot her a look.

Natalie shrugged. "I'm emotional. It's a disease."

They returned to the stage and ran the close one more time.

This time, their rhythm locked. Avery's voice steadied. Miles's cadence matched hers. The final donor ask landed clean.

When they finished, Natalie nodded. "That's it. That's the close."

Avery exhaled. "Good."

Natalie lifted her phone. "Now we confirm the deck is updated."

Avery's stomach tightened again.

Natalie's phone buzzed almost immediately, as if the universe was listening.

Natalie glanced at it, then frowned. "Okay. The updated deck is in."

Avery held out her hand. "Show me."

Natalie walked closer, holding the phone so Avery and Miles could see.

The slide thumbnail loaded.

Avery's pulse spiked.

Because the title was still there.

LEADERSHIP IN PARTNERSHIP

Avery's blood went cold.

Natalie blinked rapidly. "No. No no no."

Miles's jaw tightened. "He said it was removed."

Natalie tapped, scrolling frantically. "It's... it's still in the deck. It's still the closing slide."

Avery's chest tightened hard.

Then Natalie's eyes narrowed. "Wait. It's different."

Avery leaned in.

Under the title, the names were gone.

Now it read:

LEADERSHIP IN PARTNERSHIPAvery Sloan & Miles CarterTogether for St. Catherine's Children

It was the same.

It was not removed.

It was confirmed.

Avery's stomach dropped.

Natalie whispered, horrified, "He lied."

Miles's voice went low. "Or someone re-added it."

Avery stared at the slide, throat burning.

Her phone buzzed in her purse again, as if timed.

Avery didn't even want to look.

But she did.

Unknown number.

She opened it.

Unknown: You can delete it.Unknown: But you can't delete what people already believe.Unknown: See you on stage.

Avery's blood turned to ice.

She looked up at Miles, then at Natalie.

Natalie's face had gone pale with rage.

Miles's jaw was set, eyes sharp.

And Avery stood in the empty ballroom under rented chandeliers and realized the city wasn't watching her anymore.

Someone inside her orbit was directing the lights.

And in three weeks, she would be standing under that slide, whether she wanted to or not.

Chapter 19: The Line Between Help and Control

Avery Sloan did not throw her phone.

This should have been noted as character growth.

Instead, she stared at the screen in Natalie's hand until the words LEADERSHIP IN PARTNERSHIP began to feel like they were physically pressing against her ribs, and then she did something far more dangerous than throwing a phone.

She smiled.

It wasn't a warm smile. It wasn't the kind she used in donor meetings.

It was the smile she used when she was about to cut someone neatly in half with a sentence and then walk away looking polite.

Natalie took one look at it and whispered, "Oh no. We're in CEO execution mode."

Miles's jaw tightened. "Avery."

Avery didn't look at him. She kept her gaze on the slide thumbnail.

"Patrick said it was removed," Avery said, voice smooth enough to sound calm. "And it wasn't."

Natalie's voice went sharp. "I would like to personally fight PowerPoint."

Miles's gaze stayed steady. "It may not have been Patrick. Someone could have re-added it."

Avery's smile held. "Of course someone could have re-added it."

She turned and started walking off the stage.

Natalie scrambled after her. "Where are we going."

Avery's voice stayed even. "To find the person who can tell me who touched the deck."

Natalie nodded briskly. "Great. I love interrogations. It's my love language."

Miles fell into step beside Avery without trying to stop her. That was one of the things she liked about him. He didn't block her. He didn't grab her elbow. He didn't tell her to calm down like she was a child holding a match.

He simply moved with her, like he understood the speed at which anger turned into purpose inside her.

They crossed the ballroom toward a side corridor where a staff member in a headset was taping down cables with the meticulous focus of someone who had never once asked the question, Why are we doing this, and was therefore happier than everyone else.

Natalie cut in front like a bodyguard. "Hi. Love your vibes. Quick question: who controls the slide deck."

The staffer blinked. "Uh... the committee."

Natalie smiled brightly. "The committee is not a person. The committee is a fog. I need a human name."

The staffer looked panicked, eyes darting to Avery as if Avery could revoke his ability to breathe.

Avery stepped closer, voice calm. "Who has access. Who can edit it. Who can approve changes."

The staffer swallowed. "Patrick Ames. And... and the Montclaire media team."

Avery's smile sharpened. "Who in the media team."

The staffer hesitated.

Natalie leaned in, still smiling. "If you tell us, I will compliment you on Yelp. If you don't, I will haunt your nightmares with spreadsheet formulas."

The staffer blinked, confused. "Yelp?"

Natalie nodded. "I will find a way."

Miles said quietly, "We're not here to threaten anyone."

Natalie looked offended. "I'm not threatening. I'm... motivating."

Avery kept her tone gentle, terrifying. "Please."

The staffer exhaled. "Elena. Elena Fray."

Avery's pulse ticked. She didn't recognize the name.

"Where is she," Avery asked.

The staffer pointed down the corridor. "Production office. Second door."

Avery nodded once, then walked.

Natalie followed, whispering, "Elena Fray sounds like someone who owns a ring light and a soul contract."

Miles murmured, "Natalie."

Natalie looked at him. "What. I'm right."

Avery didn't speak. She didn't need to. The hallway was too bright, too quiet, and her anger had become a clean line inside her chest.

Second door.

Avery knocked once and entered without waiting.

The production office looked like a controlled disaster: laptops, cables, printouts, a half-eaten salad that had given up.

A woman in her thirties with a neat ponytail looked up, startled.

"Elena," Avery said.

Elena's eyes widened slightly. "Ms. Sloan. Hi. I— I wasn't expecting—"

Avery smiled, still polite. "I'm sure you weren't."

Natalie stepped in behind Avery like she was part of the furniture now. "Hello, Elena. Love the ponytail. Quick question: why do you keep trying to packaged my friend's nervous system."

Elena blinked. "I... what."

Miles stepped in last and shut the door gently behind them. "We need clarity. The slide deck."

Elena's mouth tightened. "Oh. That."

Avery placed her folder on the desk, voice calm. "That slide was removed. Then it wasn't. I would like to know which version is going live."

Elena glanced at her laptop. "The version that's scheduled."

Avery's smile sharpened. "Which one is scheduled."

Elena hesitated, then clicked something, turning the laptop slightly. The deck was open.

There it was again.

LEADERSHIP IN PARTNERSHIPTogether for St. Catherine's Children

Avery's chest tightened. "Who approved that version."

Elena's eyes flicked to Miles, then back to Avery. "Patrick."

Natalie made a noise like a kettle. "Patrick is going to be the reason I end up on a watch list."

Miles's jaw tightened. "Elena, Patrick said he removed it."

Elena's mouth tightened. "He requested a revision. Then he requested the original tagline be restored. He said—" she stopped herself.

Avery's voice stayed calm. "He said what."

Elena swallowed. "He said donors respond to warmth. He said it was... cohesive."

Natalie's eyes narrowed. "Cohesive is what you call wallpaper. Not people."

Avery inhaled slowly. "When did he request it be restored."

Elena glanced at the timestamp. "Twenty minutes ago."

Avery's blood cooled. "After he told us it was removed."

Elena winced.

Natalie whispered, "That's slimy."

Miles's jaw tightened, but his voice stayed even. "Elena. Did anyone else request changes."

Elena hesitated, then said carefully, "The Montclaire account team asked for... social assets."

Avery's pulse spiked. "Social assets."

Elena nodded once. "They want the teaser graphic to match the stage slide."

Natalie's face went blank. "Oh no."

PUBLIC IMAGE, PRIVATE HEART

Avery felt the floor tilt slightly.

Not because of the deck.

Because of what that meant.

Someone wasn't trying to put words behind her on a screen.

Someone was building a story ahead of her.

Avery's voice was controlled. "Who asked for that."

Elena glanced down. "Patrick."

Natalie leaned toward Avery and whispered, "Okay, so we're at the point where I can legally bite him."

Avery didn't move. "Elena. Remove it."

Elena's eyes widened. "I can't. Patrick—"

Avery's voice stayed calm, but something in it sharpened. "Elena."

Elena swallowed hard. "He's committee chair. He—"

Natalie stepped forward, smiling brightly. "Elena, if you keep it, you are complicit in emotional terrorism. Do you want that on your résumé."

Miles said quietly, "Natalie."

Natalie shrugged. "What. It's accurate."

Avery's gaze held Elena's. "This is my hospital. This is my name. If you keep that slide, you are choosing his noise over my consent."

Elena's throat bobbed. "I... I'm doing my job."

Avery's smile softened by a fraction. "So am I."

Elena stared at Avery for a long beat, then looked down at her laptop again. Her fingers hovered over the trackpad like she was about to cross a boundary.

Then she clicked.

The slide disappeared, replaced by a neutral one: THANK YOU FOR SUPPORTING PEDIATRIC CARE.

Elena exhaled shakily. "Okay."

Natalie whispered, "Thank you for choosing peace."

Miles nodded, calm. "Thank you."

Avery's chest loosened slightly.

Then Elena swallowed and added, quietly, "But Patrick will notice."

Avery's smile returned, cold and clean. "Good."

They left the production office and walked back down the corridor, the ballroom lights still glowing like nothing had happened, like a fundraiser couldn't hold violence behind its scenes.

Natalie marched at Avery's side, muttering, "I hate him. I hate him. I hate him."

Miles walked on Avery's other side, quiet.

Avery could feel his silence like pressure.

Her phone buzzed in her purse.

Avery didn't look.

Natalie did.

Natalie's hand moved toward Avery's bag like a reflex, then she stopped herself. "Sorry. I'm... addicted to chaos."

Avery exhaled. "It's fine."

Miles's voice was low. "It's not fine."

Avery's jaw tightened. "It's a text."

Miles's gaze held hers. "It's someone monitoring you."

Avery felt heat rise. "And I'm handling it."

Miles nodded once. "You're handling it by not looking."

Avery's chest tightened. "Because looking doesn't help."

Miles's voice stayed calm. "Sometimes it does."

Avery's throat tightened. There it was again. The tone that sounded like strategy. Like management.

She didn't want to feel that from him.

Natalie, sensing danger, stepped between them slightly as they passed a staff station.

"Okay," Natalie said briskly, "we're leaving. We are going to eat something. We are going to hydrate. We are going to pretend we're not one more notification away from joining a convent."

Avery shot her a look. "I am not joining a convent."

Natalie nodded. "Fine. A bunker."

They entered the elevator.

Of course two nurses inside.

Of course.

One of them looked up, smiled brightly, and said, "Oh my god. It's you guys."

Avery's stomach tightened.

Natalie's face rearranged into polite delight at record speed. "Hi!"

The nurse grinned at Avery. "That clip was so cute."

Avery's mouth went dry. "Thank you."

The second nurse leaned in conspiratorially. "We're all rooting for you."

Avery's cheeks warmed. "We're... focused on pediatrics."

Natalie made a choking sound.

Miles's mouth twitched.

The first nurse smiled. "Of course. But also... you deserve happiness. You work so hard."

Avery felt her throat tighten unexpectedly.

Because the nurse wasn't being nosy.

She was being kind.

Avery forced a smile. "Thank you."

Natalie leaned closer to Avery and whispered, "If you cry in this elevator I will need you to pay for my therapy."

Avery shot her a look, but her eyes burned anyway.

The elevator doors opened.

The nurses stepped out, still smiling, still carrying their lives like they weren't under a microscope.

Avery watched them go.

Natalie whispered, "Okay. That was sweet. And also horrifying."

Avery exhaled slowly.

Miles's voice was quiet. "They care."

Avery's jaw clenched. "They care about a clip."

Miles's gaze held hers. "Maybe they care about you."

Avery's chest tightened again.

She didn't answer.

The elevator doors slid closed.

Silence pressed in.

Natalie looked between them like she was watching two people try not to touch a live wire.

Natalie cleared her throat. "Okay. I'm going to the café. I'm getting something with carbs. Anyone who tries to speak about 'partnership' will be stabbed with a fork."

Avery stared. "Natalie."

Natalie smiled sweetly. "Metaphorically."

Miles's mouth twitched. "Noted."

Natalie jabbed the lobby button, then said quickly, "Also, I'm leaving you two alone for five minutes. Please do not emotionally combust."

Avery's cheeks warmed. "We're not—"

Natalie pointed at her. "You are. I can feel it."

The elevator doors opened.

Natalie slipped out like a woman escaping a crime scene and waved without looking back.

Avery and Miles remained inside as the doors closed again.

The elevator hummed upward, empty now, the hospital's quiet machinery carrying them like it didn't know it was moving a bomb.

Miles's voice was low. "Avery."

Avery kept her gaze on the elevator numbers. "What."

Miles exhaled slowly. "You're pulling away."

Avery's jaw clenched. "I'm not."

Miles's voice stayed calm, but firmer. "You are."

Avery's throat tightened. "I'm handling a situation."

Miles's gaze sharpened. "By controlling everything around you."

Avery's chest tightened. "That's what leadership is."

Miles shook his head slightly. "Leadership isn't shutting people out."

Avery's pulse jumped. There it was. The tone. The implied correction.

Avery's voice went colder. "Don't tell me how to lead."

Miles went still. "I'm not."

Avery turned sharply. "You are."

Miles's jaw flexed. "No. I'm telling you how you're treating me."

Avery's chest tightened. "This is not about you."

Miles's gaze held hers. "It is if you're making it about me."

Avery laughed once, sharp. "I'm making it about you."

Miles's voice was quiet, steady. "You watched Patrick and me speak and you started rewriting the story in your head."

Avery's stomach twisted.

Miles continued, softer but blunt. "You didn't ask what he said. You assumed. And now every time I try to help, you hear control."

Avery's pulse hammered. "Because it looks like control."

Miles's brows lifted slightly. "Because I offered to be careful about what we say with a leak happening."

Avery's jaw clenched. "It's not that."

Miles waited.

Avery's throat tightened. She hated that the words were already there, ready to be weaponized.

She exhaled and said them anyway.

"Do you understand how it feels," Avery said quietly, "to have your life negotiated around you."

Miles's gaze softened. "Yes."

Avery's voice went sharper. "No. You don't."

Miles went still. "Avery."

Avery's chest tightened. "You keep saying 'partnership' like it's safe."

Miles exhaled slowly. "It can be."

Avery's pulse jumped. "It can also be a headline."

Miles's voice stayed calm. "That's not my doing."

Avery's throat tightened. "But it's convenient."

The moment the word left her mouth, she knew she'd crossed the line.

Miles's expression tightened.

Not anger.

Hurt, controlled.

"Convenient," Miles repeated quietly.

Avery's jaw clenched. "You came here to build your consultancy. You're leaving soon. And now you're trending with me.

People love you. Donors love you. The board loves you because you make me look warm."

Miles went still.

Avery's chest tightened, but she didn't stop, because fear had grabbed her tongue and wouldn't let go.

"And you keep saying you're choosing me," Avery said, voice low, "but what if you're choosing the storyline."

Silence.

The elevator hummed.

Miles's jaw flexed hard enough to show muscle.

When he spoke, his voice was steady, but something in it had changed.

"That's what you think I'm doing," Miles said quietly.

Avery's throat tightened. "I didn't say that."

Miles's gaze held hers. "You did."

Avery's chest burned. She hated herself. She hated the way fear made her cruel.

Miles continued, voice low, controlled. "I didn't come here to become your headline."

Avery swallowed.

"I came here because the board hired me to do a job," Miles said, "and because I saw you drowning in expectation and still refusing to ask for air."

Avery's throat tightened.

Miles's gaze didn't waver. "I came here to help you keep your voice."

Avery's chest tightened, pain blooming.

"And now," Miles added quietly, "you're telling me my presence is convenient."

Avery's breath shook.

She wanted to take it back.

She didn't know how.

Miles exhaled slowly. "Avery. I'm not trying to manage you. I'm trying to stand beside you."

Avery's throat burned. "And what if I don't know where my voice ends and your strategy begins."

Miles went still.

Then he said quietly, "Then you ask me."

Avery's jaw clenched. "I shouldn't have to."

Miles's gaze sharpened slightly. "You shouldn't have to, but you do. Because you don't trust anyone with the messy parts of you."

Avery's chest tightened.

Miles continued, voice low. "You want love that doesn't cost you power. But you treat power like it's the only thing that's ever protected you."

Avery's breath caught.

The elevator chimed softly, arriving at Avery's floor.

The doors slid open.

Avery didn't move.

Miles didn't move.

The hallway waited.

Avery swallowed hard. "I didn't mean it like that."

Miles's gaze held hers. "How did you mean it."

Avery's throat tightened. She didn't have an answer that wasn't still fear dressed up as logic.

Miles exhaled slowly and stepped out of the elevator.

Avery followed, heart hammering.

They walked down the corridor in silence.

Avery unlocked her office door with hands that felt too cold.

They stepped inside.

The door clicked shut behind them.

The quiet felt heavy.

Avery turned to face Miles, chest tight. "Miles—"

Miles held up a hand, not harsh. Just... a boundary.

"Avery," he said softly. "I need you to hear me."

Avery went still.

Miles's voice was steady, but a tremor under it now, a human crack.

"If you want me to step back," Miles said, "I will. But I'm not going to be in your life as a tool you pick up when you need stability and put down when you feel exposed."

Avery's throat burned. "That's not—"

Miles's gaze held hers. "That's what it feels like."

Avery's breath caught.

Miles continued, quieter. "You deserve someone who doesn't compete with your ambition. You also deserve someone you don't punish for caring."

Avery's eyes burned.

Miles's jaw flexed. "And I deserve to not be treated like I'm secretly rooting for you to fall."

Avery swallowed. "I don't think that."

Miles's gaze didn't waver. "You did, for a minute. And that's enough to hurt."

Avery's chest tightened hard enough she almost couldn't breathe.

Her phone buzzed in her purse again.

Avery didn't reach for it.

Miles's eyes flicked to her bag, then back to her face. "It's still texting you."

Avery's throat tightened. "Yes."

Miles's voice was quiet. "What does it say."

Avery shook her head. "It doesn't matter."

Miles's gaze sharpened. "It does if it's feeding your fear."

Avery's chest tightened. "Stop."

Miles went still. "Stop what."

Avery's voice cracked slightly. "Stop trying to fix this like it's a messaging problem."

Miles's expression softened. "It's not a messaging problem."

Avery's throat tightened. "Then what is it."

Miles held her gaze.

And his voice came out low, painfully honest.

"It's a trust problem," Miles said.

Avery's breath caught.

The room felt too small.

Avery's eyes burned.

She hated that her body wanted to cry when she was trying to fight.

Avery whispered, "I'm trying."
Miles's gaze softened. "I know."
Avery's voice was tight. "And I hate that I'm failing."
Miles exhaled slowly. "You're not failing. You're scared."
Avery's throat tightened. "I am not scared."
Miles's mouth twitched, sad. "Avery."
Avery swallowed.

Then, because her life was a cruel joke, her phone buzzed again. Louder this time, like the universe wanted an audience.

Avery's hand went to her purse.

Miles watched.

Avery pulled it out, not because she wanted to, but because not knowing felt worse.

Unknown number.

Avery opened it.

Unknown: There it is.Unknown: You can't keep him and keep control.Unknown: Choose.

Avery's blood went cold.

She stared at the screen, breath shallow.

Miles's eyes narrowed. "What."

Avery swallowed. "It's... telling me to choose."

Miles's jaw tightened. "Avery."

Avery looked up at him, chest tight, eyes burning.

"It's right," Avery whispered, and she hated herself for saying it.

Miles went still.

Avery's throat tightened. "Because I don't know how to do both."

Miles's expression softened, hurt flickering again.

Then his phone buzzed.

Miles pulled it out, glance quick.

His jaw tightened.

Avery's stomach dropped. "What."

Miles hesitated.

Avery's chest tightened. "Miles."

Miles exhaled slowly, then turned the screen toward her.

A message from the board's legal counsel.

Board Counsel: Your exit clause can be executed immediately. Paperwork ready. Confirm.

Avery's throat closed.

It wasn't what she thought it was.

And it was exactly what she feared anyway.

Avery's breath caught. "You're... leaving."

Miles's gaze held hers, steady. "No."

Avery's voice went sharp, panic bleeding through. "That's an exit clause."

Miles swallowed. "It's an option."

Avery's chest tightened hard. "An option you didn't tell me about."

Miles's jaw tightened. "It came in now."

Avery's breath shook. "It's ready. That means someone arranged it."

Miles's gaze sharpened. "Yes."

Avery's stomach twisted. The anonymous texter. Patrick. Gerald. The board. The slide.

Everything converged into one sick story in her head: he can leave whenever he wants. He can choose to disappear the moment it becomes hard.

Avery's throat tightened. "So you can walk away."

Miles's voice was low. "Avery, look at me."

Avery stared at him, chest tight.

Miles's gaze held hers. "I'm not walking away."

Avery's laugh was sharp and broken. "Then why do you have an exit clause ready to execute."

Miles's jaw flexed. "Because I'm a contractor and this is how boards work."

Avery's eyes burned. "No. Because they want you gone. Or they want you to threaten to go so I'll behave."

Miles went still.

Avery's breath shook. "Do you see it. Do you see how it works."

Miles's voice was quiet. "Yes."

Avery's throat tightened. "And you're still telling me this is not control."

Miles stepped closer, careful. "Avery. Don't do this."

Avery's voice cracked. "I can't... I can't be managed."

Miles's eyes softened. "I'm not managing you."

Avery's breath caught. "But you could leave."

Miles's jaw tightened. "Yes."

Avery flinched.

Miles continued, voice low, steady. "I could leave. And I'm choosing not to."

Avery's throat burned.

Miles's gaze didn't waver. "But if you keep treating me like the enemy, I won't be able to stay and still be myself."

Avery's eyes burned.

She whispered, "So this is it."

Miles's expression tightened. "No."

Avery's voice broke slightly. "It feels like it."

Miles exhaled slowly, then looked down at his phone again, thumb hovering over the reply.

Avery's heart hammered.

Miles looked up at her, voice quiet. "Tell me what you want."

Avery stared at him.

Everything inside her screamed for control. For safety. For the hospital.

And a softer part of her screamed for him.

Avery's mouth opened.

No words came out.

Miles's gaze softened, pain flickering. "Avery."

Avery's throat burned. "I don't know."

Miles nodded once, small. "Okay."

He looked down again and typed one short reply.

Avery watched his thumb move like it was a guillotine.

Miles turned the phone slightly so she could see.

Miles: Not executing. Hold.

Avery's breath released in a shaky exhale she didn't know she'd been holding.

Miles slipped the phone into his pocket.

Then he looked at Avery with that same steady gaze.

"I chose," Miles said quietly. "Now you choose what you want to believe about me."

Avery's chest tightened painfully.

She couldn't answer.

Miles's voice softened, quieter. "I'm going to give you space."

Avery's throat tightened. "Miles—"

Miles shook his head slightly, not unkind. "Not tonight."

He walked toward the door.

Avery stood frozen, heart pounding, trying not to fall apart in her own office like she was someone who didn't know how to handle pressure.

Miles paused at the door and looked back.

His voice was quiet. "For the record... I meant what I said."

Avery's throat tightened. "What."

Miles's gaze held hers. "I'm choosing you."

Then he left.

The door clicked shut.

Avery stood alone in the quiet.

Her phone buzzed again.

Avery didn't look.

She didn't need to.

Because the real cliffhanger wasn't the message.

It was the empty space Miles had left behind.

And the awful realization that for the first time in her life, Avery Sloan wanted something she couldn't force into compliance.

Chapter 20: The Shape of Distance

By morning, the hospital had done what it always did.

It moved on.

Not because anything was solved, but because patient care didn't pause for viral clips or broken hearts. The elevators still chimed. The overhead announcements still crackled. The smell of disinfectant still hugged the air like a permanent apology.

Avery walked into the executive corridor with a folder in her hand and a spine that felt too tight. She wore the same armor she wore every day: tailored jacket, neutral expression, pace that suggested she had never once been rattled by anything a human being could say to her.

It worked.

Mostly.

Until she saw Miles.

He was already outside her office.

Not leaning against the wall like he belonged there.

Not waiting with that quiet patience that made her feel steadier by proximity.

He stood a respectful distance away from her door, hands at his sides, posture perfectly neutral.

Professional.

He looked up when she approached.

His expression was calm, polite.

And empty.

"Avery," Miles said.

her name.

No warmth.

No soft edge.

No private meaning.

Avery's chest tightened, sharp.

"Miles," she replied, voice controlled.

Natalie was with her, holding a coffee like it was a weapon. Natalie's eyes narrowed the moment she registered Miles's tone.

Natalie gave Avery a look that said, Oh, we're doing this now.

Miles nodded toward the folder Avery carried. "Board update meeting at nine."

Avery kept her voice even. "I know."

Miles's gaze flicked to Natalie briefly, then back to Avery. "I'll be in the conference room."

Avery swallowed. "Fine."

Miles nodded once, then turned and walked away.

like that.

No pause.

No lingering.

No moment where he looked like he wanted to say something and didn't.

He was a man who had taken her at her word and given her what she claimed she wanted.

Distance.

Avery watched him go, throat tight.

Natalie took one slow sip of coffee and whispered, "I would like to kill the concept of professionalism."

Avery didn't answer.

Natalie leaned closer. "That hurt, didn't it."

Avery's voice was flat. "No."

Natalie rolled her eyes. "Okay, cool. So your heart is made of granite and your eyes are just... watering because they're patriotic."

Avery shot her a look.

Natalie held up a hand. "Noted. We're pretending you're fine."

Avery opened her office door and stepped inside.

The quiet hit her like a weight.

The space was orderly. Controlled. Clean.

And suddenly it felt like a room built for a person who didn't let anyone in.

Avery set the folder on her desk.

Her phone buzzed.

Avery froze.

Then, because she was apparently a glutton for punishment, she checked it.

Montclaire PR account.

A new notification.

Avery's stomach dropped before she even opened it.

She did anyway.

A polished teaser graphic filled the screen.

A warm-toned photo of her and Miles from the morning show—both of them looking composed, both of them looking like the sort of attractive, competent people the internet liked to project stories onto.

And across the image, in elegant font:

LEADERSHIP IN PARTNERSHIPKickoff Friday. Live.

Caption:

"Join St. Catherine's as Avery Sloan and Miles Carter share a vision for pediatric care. Together."

Together.

Again.

Avery's blood went cold.

Natalie, who had apparently developed a sixth sense for impending nonsense, leaned over Avery's shoulder.

Natalie stared at the graphic, then whispered, "Oh, absolutely not."

Avery's jaw clenched. "They posted it."

Natalie's voice went sharp. "They posted it after we removed it from the deck."

Avery's pulse hammered. "It's public now."

Natalie made a low growl. "I want to throw a stapler into the sun."

Avery's throat tightened.

This was the part she hated most: not the gossip, not the speculation, not the teasing.

The feeling of being moved.

Placed.

Packaged.

Natalie pointed at the screen. "We report the account."

Avery's voice was tight. "It's Montclaire. We can't report the account."

Natalie's eyes narrowed. "We can absolutely report the account. For emotional violence."

Avery exhaled slowly. "It will look defensive if we react."

Natalie's mouth tightened. "You are allowed to react when someone is rewriting your life."

Avery swallowed.

Natalie's gaze softened slightly. "Okay. What do we do."

Avery stared at the graphic, the words burning into her chest.

"We don't give them fuel," Avery said quietly.

Natalie's eyes widened. "So we... do nothing."

Avery's jaw clenched. "We stay focused. We deliver a perfect kickoff. We talk pediatrics. We ignore the headline."

Natalie stared at her. "Avery."

Avery's voice went colder. "Natalie. This is how you win."

Natalie's mouth tightened. "This is how you survive."

Avery didn't respond.

Because that was the truth.

The board update meeting was exactly as miserable as Avery expected.

The conference room was all glass and polished wood, designed to make every conversation feel like a power play. Board members sat with their coffee and their careful faces. Gerald Whitmore sat at the head of the table, expression controlled.

Patrick Ames sat two seats down, looking annoyingly pleased with himself.

Avery took her seat, spine straight.

Miles sat beside her, a chair's width away.

Not close.

Not distant enough to be rude.

Exactly the sort of distance that said, We are not together together.

Avery's chest tightened.

Gerald opened with pediatrics metrics.

Avery contributed cleanly.

Miles spoke when addressed, brief and efficient.

Patrick, of course, took every opportunity to mention momentum.

"The public response is positive," Patrick said smoothly. "Engagement is strong. Donor interest is up. This is an opportunity we shouldn't waste."

Avery kept her expression neutral. "We will not center the noise over the mission."

Patrick smiled. "The story can serve the mission."

Avery's jaw clenched. "Or swallow it."

Patrick's smile didn't falter. "Only if we let it."

Avery's fingers tightened on her pen.

Gerald's gaze flicked between them, tired.

One board member, a woman with a pearl necklace and the expression of someone who believed emotions were tax fraud, leaned toward Avery.

"Ms. Sloan," she said, voice mild, "the public enjoys your... warmth."

Avery's stomach tightened. "My warmth."

The woman nodded. "It humanizes leadership."

Avery's voice stayed calm. "Leadership does not require humanizing. It requires competence."

Patrick chuckled lightly. "And connection."

Avery turned her gaze toward Patrick, smile polite. "Connection with families. Not headlines."

Patrick's smile sharpened. "Sometimes it's both."

Avery felt Miles shift slightly beside her. She didn't look at him. She didn't want to see his face. She didn't want to see him bracing again, ready to manage the room.

She wanted him to be on her side.

She wanted him to stay.

She wanted too much, apparently.

Gerald ended the meeting with his usual controlled efficiency.

"Kickoff remarks will be finalized by Thursday," Gerald said. "We keep it mission-focused. We keep it clean. Understood."

Patrick nodded. "Understood."

Avery nodded. "Understood."

Miles nodded. "Understood."

The board members filed out, satisfied enough to pretend they were in control of something.

Patrick lingered.

Of course.

He approached Avery's chair with his polished smile.

"Avery," Patrick said, voice warm, "that graphic is doing well."

Avery's jaw clenched. "It's unauthorized."

Patrick's smile stayed. "It's effective."

Avery's voice went colder. "Remove it."

Patrick's gaze flicked to Miles, then back to Avery. "Avery, don't fight it. People respond to authenticity."

Avery's eyes narrowed. "That's not authenticity. It's packaging."

Patrick's smile tightened slightly. "It's storytelling."

Avery's pulse hammered.

Miles spoke quietly, controlled. "Patrick, it's not approved."

Patrick held up a hand. "Miles. We talked about this. Warmth wins donors."

Avery's stomach twisted.

We talked about this.

The phrase landed like a bruise.

Avery's chest tightened.

Patrick turned back to Avery. "You can let this carry you. Or you can keep pushing against it and look like you're ashamed."

Avery's blood went cold. "I'm not ashamed."

Patrick's smile sharpened. "Then act like it."

Avery's fingers curled.

Miles's voice was low. "Patrick, enough."

Patrick's gaze flicked to Miles, smile smooth. "trying to help."

Avery's throat tightened.

Help.

Help that felt like control.

Patrick walked away like he'd done a good deed.

Avery sat still, breathing through her anger.

Miles's voice was quiet. "Avery."

Avery didn't look at him. "Don't."

Miles went still.

Avery's throat tightened. She stood, gathering her folder.

Miles stood too, maintaining that careful distance.

They walked out of the conference room together.

Not together.

A pair of people aligned by headline pressure, separated by fear.

Natalie was waiting in the hallway, arms crossed, eyes bright with contained fury.

Natalie took one look at Avery's face and said, "Don't tell me he posted it and then called it 'authentic.'"

Avery's jaw clenched. "He did."

Natalie whispered, "I hate him."

Miles murmured, "Same."

Natalie blinked. "Oh. He speaks."

Miles's expression was calm. "I speak when necessary."

Natalie pointed at him. "Do you realize you're doing the professional thing again."

Miles's gaze stayed on Avery. "I'm trying to give her space."

Natalie made a frustrated sound. "Space is a lie. Space is how people lose each other."

Avery's chest tightened.

Natalie turned to Avery, voice softening. "Avery. Say something."

Avery's throat tightened. "What."

Natalie's eyes held hers. "Tell him you don't want space."

Avery's jaw clenched. "Natalie."

Natalie's mouth tightened. "Avery. You don't hate being partnered. You hate needing someone."

Avery's chest tightened hard.

Miles's gaze sharpened slightly, but he didn't move. He didn't speak.

He simply waited.

Avery hated waiting.

She hated that he was giving her the dignity of choice when she'd spent her whole life thinking choice was a luxury.

Avery swallowed. "This isn't the time."

Natalie's eyes narrowed. "It's always the time if you're about to lose something."

Avery's breath caught.

Miles's voice was quiet. "Natalie."

Natalie threw her hands up. "Fine. I'm leaving. But if you two destroy my faith in love, I will start a cult."

Natalie turned and stalked down the hall.

Avery and Miles stood alone in the corridor.

The hospital buzzed around them like nothing was happening.

Miles's voice was low. "Are you okay."

Avery's laugh was short. "No."

Miles's gaze softened. "Then tell me."

Avery's throat tightened. "I can't."

Miles's jaw tightened slightly. "Because it feels like losing control."

Avery stared at him.

He was too perceptive. It was unfair.

Avery's voice went quiet. "Because I don't know what's mine anymore."

Miles went still.

Avery swallowed. "My reputation. My story. My name. Even my... words."

Miles's gaze held hers. "Your words are still yours."

Avery's eyes burned. "They're not. They're content now."

Miles stepped slightly closer, careful. "Avery."

Avery flinched, then forced herself not to.

Miles's voice softened. "I'm sorry."

Avery's jaw clenched. "You didn't leak it."

Miles nodded. "I know. But it happened around me."

Avery's throat tightened.

Miles continued, "And I know you watched Patrick and me and it looked wrong."

Avery's pulse spiked.

Miles's gaze held hers. "It looked like I was deciding things around you."

Avery swallowed. "It did."

Miles nodded once. "I'm sorry."

Avery's chest tightened at the word.

Sorry meant he saw her.

Sorry meant he cared.

Avery hated how much she wanted to reach for him.

Miles continued, quietly, "I'm trying to not push you."

Avery's throat tightened. "And you're succeeding."

Miles's mouth twitched, sad. "It hurts."

Avery's chest tightened.

She whispered, "It hurts me too."

Miles's gaze softened, warmth flickering, then he tamped it down again like he was protecting them both from hope.

Avery hated that.

Avery's voice went quiet, raw. "I don't want to be managed."

Miles's gaze held hers. "I'm not managing you."

Avery swallowed. "But everyone else is trying."

Miles nodded. "Yes."

Avery's throat tightened. "And I can't tell where it ends."

Miles's voice softened. "Then let's name it. Patrick is pushing noise. The board is opportunistic. Donors are enthusiastic. That's the noise."

Avery's chest tightened. "And the texts."

Miles's jaw tightened. "Yes."

Avery exhaled. "And you."

Miles went still.

Avery's throat burned. "Because you're the only part of this that feels... real."

Miles's eyes softened.

Avery's breath caught.

Miles stepped closer, one step. Not demanding. Not claiming.

Avery didn't move away.

Miles's voice was low. "Avery."

Avery's voice shook slightly. "I don't know how to do this."

Miles nodded once. "Then we learn."

Avery's chest tightened.

Then her phone buzzed.

Again.

Avery froze.

Miles watched her, face unreadable.

Avery pulled the phone out with fingers that felt numb.

Unknown number.

Avery opened it.

Unknown: He's leaving.Unknown: He always was.Unknown: Watch.

Avery's blood went cold.

She stared at the screen, breath shallow.

Miles's gaze sharpened. "What."

Avery swallowed. "It says... you're leaving."

Miles's jaw tightened. "I'm not."

Avery's throat tightened. "Then why does it keep saying it."

Miles's voice was low. "Because it knows what scares you."

Avery's chest tightened hard.

Miles's phone buzzed.

Miles glanced down.

His jaw tightened.

Avery's stomach dropped. "What now."

Miles hesitated.

Avery's voice went sharp. "Miles."

Miles turned the phone toward her.

A new message.

From Board Counsel again.

Board Counsel: Reminder: exit clause remains executable. Board prefers resolution before kickoff.

Avery's throat closed.

Miles's voice was low. "They're pressuring me."

Avery's breath shook. "To leave."

Miles's gaze held hers. "To create a lever."

Avery's chest tightened painfully.

Because it was exactly what she'd feared.

Not that Miles was a villain.

That the world would weaponize him anyway.

Avery's voice was quiet. "They want you to threaten to go so I'll behave."

Miles nodded once. "Yes."

Avery's eyes burned.

Miles's gaze softened. "Avery. Look at me."

Avery forced herself to.

Miles's voice was steady. "I'm not leaving. Unless you tell me to."

Avery's throat tightened.

She wanted to say, Don't leave.

She wanted to say it so badly it hurt.

Instead, she heard her own voice, careful and controlled.

"I can't be the reason you lose your future," Avery whispered.

Miles's brows knit slightly. "My future isn't a consultancy. It's... being able to live with myself."

Avery's chest tightened.

Miles continued, voice low, earnest. "I came here because I wanted to build something ethical. And because I wanted—"

He stopped himself.

Avery's pulse jumped. "Because you wanted what."

Miles's jaw flexed, eyes steady. "Because I wanted you."

Avery's breath caught.

The hallway felt too bright.

Too public.

People walked past, not looking, but Avery felt watched anyway.

Avery's throat burned. "You shouldn't."

Miles's mouth twitched, sad. "Too late."

Avery's eyes burned.

She didn't know how to do this without breaking something.

Miles's voice softened. "Avery. You don't have to earn love by being untouchable."

Avery's chest tightened.

She whispered, "I don't know how to be anything else."

Miles's gaze held hers. "Then let me be close while you figure it out."

Avery's breath caught.

She took one small step toward him before she could stop herself.

Miles didn't move. He let her choose.

Avery's fingers brushed his sleeve, barely touching.

It felt like stepping onto a bridge over open air.

Miles's voice was a whisper now. "Tell me to stay."

Avery's throat closed.

Say it.

say it.

Avery's lips parted—

And then Patrick's voice cut through the corridor.

"Avery. Miles."

Avery jerked back like she'd been caught stealing.

Miles went still, expression neutral again, armor snapping into place.

Patrick approached with that polished smile, holding his phone out like it was a gift.

"I wanted you to see this," Patrick said brightly.

Avery's stomach dropped.

Patrick turned the screen toward them.

A new post.

From Montclaire.

A slicker version of the earlier teaser. More polished. More official.

Their faces side by side.

And now, in bold text:

LEADERSHIP IN PARTNERSHIPFeaturing Avery Sloan & Miles CarterKickoff Friday. Live.

Under it, a line in smaller font:

"A conversation about care, leadership, and what it means to choose each other."

Avery's blood went cold.

Natalie appeared from nowhere at the end of the hall like a summoned demon.

Natalie stared at the screen and whispered, "Oh my god."

Patrick smiled. "It's getting incredible traction."

Avery's voice went low. "Remove it."

Patrick's smile didn't falter. "Avery, why. This is—"

Avery's eyes flashed. "Remove it."

Patrick's smile tightened slightly. "The board wants this momentum."

Miles's voice was calm, sharp. "Patrick. This is not consent."

Patrick's gaze flicked to Miles, smile cool. "It's publicity. It's not a marriage license."

Avery's chest tightened hard.

Then Patrick, apparently deciding he was the hero of this story, added with a friendly laugh, "Plus, it's not like either of you can deny the chemistry now. The city's watching."

Avery's stomach twisted.

Miles's jaw tightened.

Avery felt something in her snap, quiet but decisive.

She was tired of being moved.

Tired of being packaged.

Tired of people acting like her life was a campaign.

Avery's voice came out calm, lethal. "Patrick. If you don't take that down, I will call Montclaire's board and explain, in detail, how you are using pediatric care as a romance marketing asset."

Patrick blinked, smile faltering. "Avery—"

Avery held his gaze. "Try me."

Patrick swallowed. "That's... unnecessary."

Avery's smile sharpened. "So is that post."

Patrick's eyes flicked between Avery and Miles, then he exhaled like he was the one being inconvenienced.

"Fine," Patrick said, tapping his phone. "I'll ask them to adjust the wording."

Avery's voice went colder. "Take it down."

Patrick's jaw tightened. "Avery, you're overreacting."

Miles's voice was low. "She's not."

Patrick's smile returned, sharp. "Miles, you're getting emotionally involved."

Miles's gaze didn't waver. "I'm getting ethically involved."

Patrick's face tightened.

Natalie whispered, "Eat him alive."

Avery held Patrick's gaze. "Take it down."

Patrick stared at her longer, then finally nodded once, curt.

"Fine," Patrick said, tapping again. "It's down."

Avery didn't relax. She didn't trust him.

Patrick pocketed his phone with a tight smile. "You're making this harder than it needs to be."

Avery's voice was quiet. "And you're making it uglier than it needs to be."

Patrick's smile faltered.

Then he recovered and walked away, shoulders stiff, like a man who'd been told no for the first time in his life.

Natalie exhaled loudly. "Okay. That was hot."

Avery shot her a look.

Natalie shrugged. "What. It was."

Miles's gaze stayed on Avery.

Avery's chest tightened again.

Because she could feel the moment still there, hovering between them.

Patrick had interrupted.

The world had interrupted.

But the question remained.

Miles's voice was low. "Avery."

Avery swallowed. "Yes."

Miles's gaze held hers. "Tell me to stay."

Avery's throat closed.

Natalie stepped back, suddenly quiet, like she understood this wasn't her scene anymore.

The corridor felt too bright, too public, too risky.

But Avery was tired of living only in safe rooms.

Avery lifted her chin and looked at Miles, looked.

Not as a strategist. Not as a headline. Not as a threat to her control.

As a man who had been steady when she was shaking.

As a man who had chosen her even when she didn't know how to choose back.

Avery's voice came out barely above a whisper.

"Stay," Avery said.

Miles's breath released, slow.

His gaze softened.

He didn't smile like a man who'd won.

He smiled like a man who'd been holding his breath and finally got air.

Natalie turned away and pretended to study a wall.

Avery's chest tightened, warmth flooding.

Miles stepped closer, careful.

"Okay," Miles said quietly. "I'm staying."

Avery's throat tightened. "But... not as a lever."

Miles's gaze sharpened. "Never."

Avery exhaled slowly.

For the first time in days, something loosened in her chest.

Not the problem.

Not the pressure.

But the loneliness.

Miles's voice was soft. "We still have to handle the board."

Avery nodded. "I know."

Miles's gaze held hers. "And the texts."

Avery swallowed. "Yes."

Miles's voice was quiet, firm. "We don't let them control the story."

Avery's jaw clenched, resolve settling.

"No," Avery said.

Miles's mouth curved faintly. "No."

Avery looked down the corridor where Patrick had disappeared, then back at Miles.

Avery's voice was low. "Friday."

Miles nodded. "Friday."

Avery's chest tightened.

Because Friday wasn't a kickoff.

It was a stage.

A trap.

A spotlight.

And now, it was theirs.

Avery's phone buzzed again.

Avery didn't look.

She didn't need to.

Because she'd already answered the only message that mattered.

Chapter 21: The Calm Before the Spotlight

Avery didn't sleep.

Not because she was panicking.

Not because she was spiraling.

Because her brain refused to stop drafting speeches at three in the morning like it was a hobby.

She lay on her back in her apartment, staring at the ceiling, running through the kickoff remarks again and again until each line felt like a wire pulled too tight.

Pediatrics. Outcomes. Staffing. Family space. Donor impact.

No fluff.

No story.

No love story.

And yet she could feel it in her bones: the city was going to show up for the love story anyway.

Her phone sat face down on her nightstand.

Miles had asked her not to let it control her.

She was trying.

Trying meant she had left it face down like it was a live grenade.

At 3:14 a.m., it buzzed.

Avery didn't move.

At 3:16 a.m., it buzzed again.

Avery exhaled slowly and forced herself to stay still.

At 3:18 a.m., a third buzz.

Avery's jaw clenched.

She reached for it with deliberate calm and flipped it over.

Unknown number.

Of course.

She stared at it, then tapped.

Unknown: Friday is going to be perfect.Unknown: Don't mess it up.

Avery's blood went cold.

The message wasn't threatening exactly.

It was... familiar.

Like someone who thought they were part of the plan.

Avery's throat tightened.

She didn't reply.

She didn't give it fuel.

She set the phone back down and stared at the ceiling again, wide awake, her pulse too loud in her ears.

Friday is going to be perfect.

That wasn't a villain line.

That was a fan line.

And that realization was somehow worse.

By morning, St. Catherine's was buzzing in a different way.

Not crisis buzzing.

Not emergency buzzing.

The sort of buzzing that happened when a story had gotten loose in the halls.

Avery could feel eyes on her as she moved through the lobby. Not hostile. Not even curious in an unkind way.

Soft.

Hopeful.

Like people were rooting.

Avery hated how much that made her chest tighten.

Natalie met her by the elevators, hair pulled back, coffee in hand, expression already annoyed at the universe.

"You look like you slept," Natalie said immediately.

Avery nodded. "I slept."

Natalie's eyes narrowed. "You're lying."

Avery's jaw clenched. "I'm fine."

Natalie sighed. "Okay. Cool. We're all fine. Everything is fine. The city is building a shrine to your cheekbones and we are fine."

Avery shot her a look.

Natalie held up her phone. "Also, the Montclaire post went down. For now."

Avery's throat tightened. "Good."

Natalie's expression sharpened. "But there are screenshots. And reposts. And TikToks. And someone made a compilation called 'Miles Carter's Micro-Expressions When Avery Sloan Talks.'"

Avery stared. "That cannot be real."

Natalie nodded solemnly. "It's real. And I watched it. For research."

Avery groaned.

Natalie pointed at her. "Don't judge me. It's objectively adorable."

Avery exhaled slowly and stepped into the elevator.

Natalie followed, then leaned in as the doors closed.

"Okay," Natalie said quietly. "We need to talk about the texts."

Avery's jaw clenched. "We already did."

Natalie shook her head. "No. We did the part where you were terrified and Miles looked like a wounded golden retriever."

Avery's cheeks warmed. "Natalie."

Natalie lifted a hand. "I'm not wrong. But now we need to do the part where we stop pretending the texter is a criminal mastermind."

Avery's stomach tightened. "You think it's not."

Natalie stared at her. "Avery. The wording is... enthusiastic. It's not 'I will destroy you.' It's 'Friday is going to be perfect.' That's not a threat. That's a fan."

Avery's throat tightened.

Natalie continued, "Which means it's probably someone who thinks they're helping. Someone who thinks pressure will force a romantic payoff."

Avery's jaw clenched. "That's sick."

Natalie nodded. "Yes. But also stupid. And stupidity is easier to beat than evil."

Avery exhaled slowly.

Natalie's gaze sharpened. "So we find out who it is. Today."

Avery's pulse ticked. "How."

Natalie smiled like a woman about to do something reckless. "We bait them."

Avery stared. "No."

Natalie shrugged. "Okay. Then we do it the boring way. We ask Elena Fray."

Avery's stomach tightened. Elena. The name returned like a small itch.

Natalie nodded as if reading her mind. "She's the only human who admitted the post assets were being requested. She's also the only one who looked like she might cry if you raised your voice."

Avery's jaw clenched. "I didn't raise my voice."

Natalie looked at her. "You don't have to. You have CEO eyes."

Avery exhaled. "Fine. We talk to Elena."

Natalie smiled. "Great. Love a confrontation that ends in awkward tears."

Elena Fray was in the production office again, laptop open, headset around her neck, surrounded by cable chaos.

She looked up when Avery and Natalie entered and immediately tensed like she was about to be executed.

"Ms. Sloan," Elena said quickly. "I— I removed the slide. It's locked. I triple-locked it."

Natalie smiled brightly. "Triple-locking is sexy. Good for you."

Elena blinked.

Avery kept her tone calm. "Elena. We need to talk."

Elena swallowed. "Okay."

Natalie stepped closer, voice gentle in a way that was probably new for her. "Elena, has anyone on your team been... texting Avery."

Elena froze.

Her eyes widened.

Then she looked down at her laptop as if it could save her.

"No," Elena said quickly. "No. I mean— I don't— I don't know."

Avery's chest tightened. "Elena."

Elena's throat bobbed. "I don't have her number."

Natalie tilted her head. "But someone does."

Elena swallowed hard. "It's not me."

Avery watched her face.

Elena wasn't lying the way Patrick lied. Elena looked like someone who was terrified of being in trouble but also genuinely horrified by the question.

Avery's voice softened slightly. "Elena. This isn't about punishment. It's about stopping it."

Elena blinked rapidly. "Stopping what."

Natalie lifted her phone. "The anonymous texts. The posts. The noise pressure. Someone is pushing 'Leadership in Partnership' like it's a religion."

Elena's cheeks flushed. "Oh my god."

Avery's gaze sharpened. "You know something."

Elena shook her head quickly. "No. I mean— yes. I mean— I know who it is."

Natalie's eyebrows lifted. "There it is."

Elena's voice dropped. "Please don't tell Patrick I told you."

Avery's jaw tightened. "Elena."

Elena swallowed. "It's... not Patrick."

Avery's pulse ticked. "Then who."

Elena's cheeks went red. "It's... it's a junior associate. She's in Montclaire's social team. She doesn't mean harm."

Natalie's eyes narrowed. "She means meddling."

Elena nodded quickly. "She's... she's obsessed. She watches all the engagement metrics. She thinks she can 'nudge' stories into place."

Avery's blood went cold. "She's been texting me."

Elena nodded, miserable. "I think so. She bragged about 'direct pressure.'"

Natalie whispered, "Direct pressure. Like you're a bottle of ketchup."

Avery's jaw clenched. "What's her name."

Elena hesitated, then said quietly, "Tessa."

Natalie blinked. "Tessa. That's... so aggressively normal."

Elena nodded, face burning. "Tessa Wren. She's twenty-four. She thinks everything is content. She... she said the hospital needs a 'romance arc' to keep donors emotionally engaged."

Avery's stomach turned.

Natalie looked like she might physically explode. "That is unhinged."

Avery's voice was quiet. "How did she get my number."

Elena swallowed. "She... she pulled it from a contact sheet. The kickoff planning doc. It wasn't supposed to be shared outside, but—"

Natalie's eyes flashed. "It was shared."

Elena nodded quickly. "Patrick forwarded materials. He wanted the assets built quickly."

Avery's throat tightened.

So Patrick hadn't been texting her.

He'd simply opened the door.

Natalie exhaled. "Okay. So Tessa is... what. Shipping you two like it's her job."

Elena nodded miserably. "Yes."

Avery's jaw clenched. "Where is she."

Elena flinched. "In Montclaire. Social suite. Third floor."

Natalie smiled brightly. "Perfect. We're going to go ruin her day."

Elena whispered, panicked, "Please don't ruin her day."

Natalie looked at her. "Elena, she has been texting the CEO of a hospital like it's a fanfic. Her day deserves to be ruined."

Avery exhaled slowly, trying to keep her anger cold.

"Thank you," Avery said to Elena, voice controlled.

Elena nodded quickly. "I'm sorry."

Avery's voice softened by half a degree. "I know."

Natalie grabbed Avery's sleeve as they walked out. "Okay. We go to Montclaire. We confront Tessa. We do it politely but terrifyingly. Then we get Miles to help lock down comms."

Avery's chest tightened at his name.

Natalie glanced at her. "You're thinking about him."

Avery's jaw clenched. "No."

Natalie rolled her eyes. "Sure."

Miles was in a small conference room down the hall, reviewing a stack of kickoff materials with the focused calm of someone who didn't sleep but somehow still looked better than everyone else.

He looked up when Avery entered.

warmth in his eyes this time.

Not guarded.

Not empty.

But careful, as if he didn't want to spook her.

"Avery," Miles said softly.

Avery's chest tightened, relief and fear colliding.

Natalie barged in behind her. "We found the texter."

Miles went still. "You did."

Avery nodded, voice controlled. "It's not Patrick. It's a junior associate at Montclaire. Tessa Wren."

Miles's jaw tightened. "How did she get your number."

Avery's throat tightened. "From planning documents."

Miles's expression hardened. "That's a breach."

Natalie clapped once. "Thank you. Yes. Breach. That word. Use it."

Miles looked at Avery, voice low. "Are you okay."

Avery's mouth tightened. "No."

Miles nodded once, calm. "Okay. We deal with it."

Natalie leaned forward. "We're going to Montclaire."

Miles blinked. "We."

Natalie nodded. "We. Avery needs witness energy. Also, you have ethical backbone. And I want to watch someone get gently destroyed."

Miles's mouth twitched faintly. "Natalie."

Natalie shrugged. "What. I'm honest."

Miles's gaze returned to Avery, steady. "Do you want me there."

Avery's throat tightened.

Yes.

Avery nodded once. "Yes."

Miles's expression softened, relief flickering.

"Okay," Miles said quietly. "Then we go together."

Natalie whispered, satisfied, "Together. But not in a packaged way."

Avery shot her a look.

Natalie held up her hands. "Sorry."

Montclaire's offices were the sort of sleek that felt designed to make you feel slightly less important the second you walked in.

Glass walls. Minimalist signage. A lobby that smelled like expensive citrus and quiet judgment.

Natalie marched in like she owned the building.

Avery walked beside her, spine straight, face neutral.

Miles moved on Avery's other side, calm and steady.

Avery could feel the difference it made, having him there. Not because he was protecting her. Because he reminded her she wasn't alone.

A receptionist smiled too brightly. "Hi. Can I help you."

Avery's voice was calm. "We're here to see Tessa Wren."

The receptionist blinked. "Do you have an appointment."

Natalie smiled. "We have a problem."

Miles held up his badge from St. Catherine's, voice controlled. "This is related to your team's communications with our CEO."

The receptionist's smile faltered. "One moment."

They waited.

Avery stared at a wall art piece that looked like someone had framed a stock photo of confidence.

Natalie whispered, "If I ever work in a place like this, please stage an intervention."

Avery whispered back, "I already did."

Miles's mouth twitched faintly.

The receptionist returned, nervous. "She's in the social suite."

Natalie smiled brightly. "Great."

They rode the elevator up.

Avery's pulse hammered. Not fear of confrontation. Fear of what the confrontation meant.

It meant she hadn't been targeted by a mastermind.

She'd been targeted by someone who thought she was a story.

Avery hated that.

The social suite was louder than the rest of the building.

Screens everywhere. Trend charts. People wearing headphones and tapping like their fingers were on fire.

A woman with long hair and bright eyes looked up from a laptop, startled.

"Tessa," the receptionist said quickly. "These people are—"

Avery stepped forward, voice calm. "Avery Sloan."

Tessa's eyes widened. "Oh my god."

Natalie leaned in, smiling with surgical precision. "Yes. Oh my god is correct."

Miles's gaze stayed steady on Tessa. "We need to discuss your communications."

Tessa's cheeks went pink. "Wait— are you—"

Avery's voice stayed even. "You've been sending me messages from an anonymous number."

Tessa froze.

Her face went pale.

Then she laughed nervously. "I— no— I mean—"

Natalie's smile sharpened. "Don't."

Tessa swallowed hard. "Okay."

Avery's chest tightened. "Why."

Tessa's eyes darted between them, then down. "I thought... I thought it would help."

Natalie blinked. "Help."

Tessa nodded quickly, words spilling out. "The engagement was insane. People were invested. And pediatric fundraising is hard, like, emotionally hard. People scroll past sad stories. But when there's a romance arc—"

Avery's blood went cold. "A romance arc."

Tessa nodded, frantic. "Not like fake. You're real. You're both real. I could tell. And I thought if I just... nudged it, the momentum would carry. Donors would stay. The kickoff would blow up. Pediatrics would win."

Natalie stared at her like she was looking at a raccoon holding a credit card.

Miles's voice was low, controlled. "You understand you breached privacy."

Tessa nodded rapidly. "Yes. I realize that now. I'm sorry."

Avery's chest burned. "You've been texting me at three in the morning."

Tessa's face crumpled. "I— I thought you were awake. You're always awake."

Natalie made a strangled sound. "That's not a justification. That's a cry for therapy."

Avery's voice was quiet. "You told me to choose."

Tessa swallowed. "I... I thought you needed it."

Avery's eyes narrowed. "You thought I needed pressure."

Tessa nodded, miserable. "I thought you were scared and he was leaving and—"

Miles's jaw tightened. "He wasn't leaving."

Tessa looked at him, then down. "I didn't know. I assumed... because it was dramatic."

Natalie whispered, "I hate the internet."

Avery stared at Tessa, feeling something strange in her chest.

Not fear.

Not even anger anymore.

Disbelief.

"You don't know me," Avery said quietly.

Tessa's eyes filled. "I know. I know. I'm sorry. I got... carried away."

Miles spoke calmly, firm. "You will stop. Immediately."

Tessa nodded rapidly. "Yes. Yes. I will."

Natalie leaned in. "And you will never use the phrase 'Leadership in Partnership' again unless you are talking about an actual PowerPoint template."

Tessa sniffed. "Okay."

Avery's voice was low. "And you will take down any remaining posts or assets using my name in that context."

Tessa nodded quickly. "Yes."

Miles's gaze sharpened. "We also need confirmation of how you obtained her number, and we need it documented."

Tessa nodded, panicked. "Okay. Yes."

Natalie whispered to Avery, "He's so hot when he's ethical."

Avery's cheeks warmed. "Natalie."

Natalie shrugged. "I'm stating facts."

Avery took one slow breath.

Then she looked at Tessa again.

"This isn't a show," Avery said, voice controlled. "It's a hospital. People come here with their children and they trust us. You don't get to turn that into entertainment."

Tessa's eyes spilled tears. "I didn't mean—"

Avery's voice softened by half a degree. "I know. But you did."

Tessa nodded, wiping her cheeks. "I'm sorry."

Avery held her gaze. "Stop."

Tessa nodded. "I will."

Miles's voice was calm. "Now."

Tessa reached for her laptop, hands shaking, and began clicking rapidly.

Natalie watched, arms crossed, satisfied.

Avery stood still, chest tight.

Because even though it wasn't a mastermind, it still proved something Avery hated:

The world would take whatever pieces of her it could reach.

Avery's phone buzzed.

One final time.

Unknown number.

Avery looked at it.

Tessa looked up, face flushing. "That's me."

Avery opened the message.

Unknown: Okay. I'm stopping.Unknown: Please don't hate me.

Avery stared at the screen.

Then she typed one reply.

Avery: Stop means stop. Pediatrics is not content.

Avery hit send.

Then she blocked the number.

It felt like cutting a wire.

Natalie exhaled, relieved. "Thank god."

Miles's gaze stayed on Avery, soft. "You did that."

Avery swallowed. "I shouldn't have had to."

Miles nodded. "You shouldn't."

Natalie clapped once. "Okay. Great. We solved the internet."

Avery shot her a look.

Natalie grinned. "Kidding. The internet is unkillable."

On the drive back to St. Catherine's, the city looked the same.

Taxis, streetlights, the river like a dark ribbon.

But Avery felt different.

Not fixed.

Not safe.

Just... clearer.

Miles sat beside her in the backseat, quiet. Natalie sat up front, narrating traffic like a sportscaster.

At a red light, Avery felt Miles's hand brush hers on the seat between them.

Not grabbing.

there.

Avery's throat tightened.

She didn't pull away.

Miles's voice was soft. "Are you okay."

Avery exhaled slowly. "I'm... less trapped."

Miles nodded once. "Good."

Avery stared out the window. "She thought she was helping."

Miles's voice was low. "People do that."

Avery's jaw clenched. "I hate it."

Miles's gaze stayed steady. "I know."

Avery swallowed. "And I hate that part of me still feels ashamed."

Miles went still. "Ashamed of what."

Avery's voice came out quiet. "Of being seen wanting you."

Miles's breath caught slightly.

Natalie, from the front seat, muttered, "Oh my god."

Avery shot her a look. "Natalie."

Natalie held up her hands without turning around. "I'm silent."

Miles's voice was soft. "You don't need to be ashamed."

Avery's throat tightened. "The board—"

Miles shook his head slightly. "The board doesn't get to decide what you deserve."

Avery's chest tightened.

Miles's hand stayed near hers, not forcing.

Avery let her fingers slide closer, touching his lightly.

Not a declaration.

Not a headline.

A choice, made quietly, where no one could package it.

Miles's gaze softened. "Friday."

Avery nodded, throat tight. "Friday."

Miles's voice was a whisper. "We do it on our terms."

Avery's jaw clenched, resolve settling.

"Yes," Avery said.

Natalie whispered loudly, "Finally."

Avery exhaled, almost smiling.

Because Friday was coming.

The spotlight was waiting.

And for the first time, Avery Sloan wasn't bracing for it.

She was planning to take it back.

Chapter 22: Under the Lights

Friday arrived with the sort of cold, bright clarity that made everything feel sharper.

The city looked freshly scrubbed, as if Manhattan itself had decided to behave for once. The streets outside St. Catherine's were lined with black cars and camera rigs and people in coats that probably cost more than Avery's first year of med school.

The gala kickoff wasn't technically a gala yet.

This was the opening night, the press-forward, donor-heavy event designed to create momentum for the month-long campaign. The actual big fundraiser would come later.

But this night was the stage.

This night was the headline.

And Avery could feel it in the air the moment she walked through the staff entrance and heard the soft hum of a crowd gathering like a storm.

Natalie met her backstage with a garment bag slung over one arm and a look on her face that could have powered the hospital if they hooked her up to a generator.

"Okay," Natalie said immediately. "We have a situation."

Avery's stomach dropped. "What."

Natalie's eyes widened. "Not a bad situation. A stupid situation. Which is, arguably, worse."

Avery exhaled slowly. "Natalie."

Natalie pulled a folded printout from her tote bag and slapped it into Avery's hands.

Avery unfolded it.

It was the event program.

Glossy. Elegant. The sort of thing donors took home as a souvenir of their own generosity.

At the bottom, under Closing Remarks, it read:

Avery Sloan & Miles CarterLeadership in Partnership

Avery's blood went cold.

Natalie hissed, "I told you. Wallpaper people. They never stop."

Avery's jaw clenched. "We removed it."

Natalie nodded. "We removed it from the deck. Not from the printed program. Which was printed yesterday. Because of course it was."

Avery's chest tightened hard.

The phrase had become a hydra.

Cut it off in one place and it grew in another.

Avery's fingers tightened on the program. "Who approved this."

Natalie's eyes flashed. "Patrick."

Avery's throat tightened. "Of course."

Natalie leaned in. "Okay. Here's the good news. The program is already printed. We can't unprint it. The bad news is that if one more person says 'partnership' to me tonight, I may commit a felony."

Avery's voice went quiet. "Natalie."

Natalie exhaled, then softened. "Okay. Listen. You can't stop people from trying to write your story tonight. So you do what you do best."

Avery blinked. "What."

Natalie's mouth tightened. "You take the microphone and you rewrite it yourself."

Avery's chest tightened.

That was the plan, wasn't it.

Reclaim the story.

But reclaiming meant stepping into the light. It meant being seen doing it.

Avery's fingers trembled slightly.

Natalie caught it and squeezed her forearm once, quick and grounding. "You've got this."

Avery swallowed. "Where is Miles."

Natalie's mouth twitched. "Ah. There we go. That's the real question."

Avery shot her a look.

Natalie held up both hands. "Okay, okay. He's in the greenroom. Doing the thing where he pretends he's fine but looks like he wants to fight a board member."

Avery exhaled slowly and handed the program back. "I need to see him."

Natalie's grin sharpened. "Yes you do."

The greenroom was a small conference space turned into a staging area.

bottled waters, a tray of fruit no one would touch, and two staff members with headsets who looked like they'd been born with clipboards.

Miles stood by the window, jacket off, sleeves rolled, tie loosened.

He looked up when Avery entered.

His gaze softened instantly.

Not performative.

Not professional.

Just... him.

"Avery," Miles said quietly.

Avery's chest tightened at the sound of her name in his voice.

Natalie stayed at the door, clearly pretending she was not eavesdropping while actively eavesdropping.

Avery stepped closer, lowering her voice. "The program."

Miles's jaw tightened. "I saw."

Avery's throat tightened. "Patrick."

Miles nodded once. "Patrick."

Avery exhaled slowly. "I can't stop it."

Miles's gaze held hers. "You don't have to."

Avery blinked. "What."

Miles stepped closer, careful. "You don't have to stop them from trying to write you. You have to refuse to read from their script."

Avery's throat tightened.

Miles's voice softened. "Tonight is yours. Not his."

Avery swallowed. "The board is going to be watching."

Miles nodded. "Yes."

Avery's chest tightened. "The press will be watching."

Miles nodded again. "Yes."

Avery's voice went quieter, raw. "Everyone will be watching."

Miles's gaze softened. "Then give them something real."

Avery's breath caught.

Natalie made a small choking noise at the doorway, as if the emotional content had physically struck her.

Avery shot her a look.

Natalie whispered, "Sorry. Allergies."

Avery turned back to Miles.

Miles's voice was low. "Still want me beside you."

Avery's throat tightened hard.

She didn't hesitate this time.

"Yes," Avery said.

Miles's breath released slowly, relief flickering.

Avery's chest tightened. "But not as... that."

She nodded slightly toward the printed program, toward the phrase that had haunted her all week.

Miles's mouth twitched, soft. "Not as a slogan."

Avery swallowed. "Not as a lever."

Miles's gaze sharpened. "Never."

Avery's throat tightened.

, they stood there, close enough that Avery could feel the warmth of him without him touching her.

Miles's voice softened. "You're shaking."

Avery's jaw clenched. "I'm not."

Miles's mouth twitched. "You are."

Avery exhaled, annoyed. "Fine."

Miles's gaze held hers, quiet. "Breathe."

Avery inhaled slowly, then exhaled.

Miles watched her like he was anchoring her with his eyes.

Avery swallowed. "I don't know what I'm going to say."

Miles's voice was calm. "Yes you do."

Avery blinked. "I do."

Miles nodded. "You're going to say the truth."

Avery's chest tightened.

Miles continued, softly, "You're going to talk about pediatrics. You're going to talk about care. And if anyone tries to turn you into a headline, you're going to remind them that leadership isn't performance."

Avery's throat tightened. "Leadership isn't performance."

Miles nodded. "Exactly."

Natalie whispered from the doorway, "Yes. Drag them."

Avery shot her a look.

Natalie held up a hand. "Sorry. I'm not here."

Avery turned back to Miles.

Miles's voice went lower, intimate. "Whatever happens tonight, I'm with you."

Avery's chest tightened, warmth flooding.

Avery whispered, "I don't want to lose you."

Miles's eyes softened. "You won't."

Avery's throat tightened. "You keep saying that like you're sure."

Miles's mouth curved faintly. "I am."

Avery's breath caught.

Miles's gaze flicked to her mouth, then back to her eyes.

, Avery thought he might kiss her.

Backstage.

Under fluorescent lights.

With Natalie watching like a gremlin.

He didn't.

He simply lifted his hand and brushed his knuckles lightly against her wrist.

Grounding.

A promise that didn't need cameras.

Avery's breath shook.

A staff member in a headset appeared at the doorway like a summoned omen. "Ms. Sloan. Mr. Carter. Two minutes."

Avery's pulse spiked.

Miles's hand fell away.

Avery's throat tightened.

Natalie stepped forward, suddenly all business. "Okay. Showtime. You're going to walk out there and be hot and ethical."

Avery stared. "Natalie."

Natalie nodded, serious. "It's the only way."

Miles's mouth twitched.

Avery exhaled slowly. "Two minutes."

Miles nodded. "Two minutes."

Backstage was a narrow corridor behind the ballroom.

The noise of the crowd bled through the walls: laughter, clinking glasses, the murmur of people who believed money made them safe from consequences.

Avery could feel her heartbeat in her throat.

Natalie walked with them, posture sharp, eyes scanning like she was looking for threats. She had her phone out, which in Natalie's hands was a weapon.

"Okay," Natalie whispered, "Patrick is stage left. Gerald is front row. Board chair is wearing pearls and disappointment. Also, there's a journalist from the Times. Don't panic."

Avery's jaw clenched. "I'm not panicking."

Natalie nodded. "Great. Then stop breathing like you're in labor."

Avery shot her a look.

Natalie grinned. "Love you."

Miles moved closer, not touching, but present.

Avery whispered, "If I freeze—"

Miles's voice was low. "You won't."

Avery swallowed. "If I do—"

Miles's gaze held hers. "Look at me."

Avery's breath caught.

Natalie whispered, "Okay. I'm going to stand in the shadows and be proud and also ready to commit arson if necessary."

Avery stared. "Natalie."

Natalie smiled. "Metaphorically."

Then Natalie slipped away.

Avery and Miles stepped to the edge of the curtain.

The host's voice carried over the speakers, warm and practiced.

"And now, please welcome the CEO of St. Catherine's, Avery Sloan, alongside crisis strategist Miles Carter."

Avery's stomach tightened.

The phrase crisis strategist made her want to laugh and vomit at the same time.

Miles looked at Avery, quiet. "Ready."

Avery swallowed.

"No," Avery whispered.

Miles's mouth twitched faintly. "Same."

Avery almost smiled.

Miles's gaze softened. "But we go anyway."

Avery exhaled slowly.

Then she stepped forward.

The curtain opened.

The ballroom lights hit her like a wave.

, Avery saw only glare.

Then shapes.

Faces.

Tables.

People in expensive clothes, eyes bright with curiosity.

And cameras.

Always cameras.

Avery forced her shoulders down, spine straight.

She walked to the podium, Miles a pace behind, slightly to her right.

The crowd applauded.

Too loud.

Too eager.

Avery smiled politely and waited until the applause dipped. Then she began.

"Good evening," Avery said, voice clear. "I'm Avery Sloan, CEO of St. Catherine's."

Her voice echoed slightly.

She paused and let the room settle.

"Thank you for being here," Avery continued. "Not for the headlines. Not for the story that the internet wants to write. But for the children and families who walk into our hospital every day and trust us with everything."

A ripple moved through the room.

Avery could feel people leaning in.

Good.

She kept going.

"Pediatric care is not a viral clip," Avery said, voice steady. "It's a nurse staying past her shift so a parent can get five minutes of sleep. It's a social worker holding a teenager's hand while they admit they're scared. It's a doctor making hard choices and then going home and carrying those choices anyway."

The room was quiet now.

Avery's throat tightened.

She didn't look at the cameras.

She looked at the faces.

"Tonight, you'll hear a phrase repeated," Avery said calmly. "Leadership. Partnership. Warmth. Story."

Avery paused.

Her pulse hammered.

"Let me be clear," Avery said, voice calm, controlled. "Leadership isn't about appearing together for applause."

A hush.

Avery's chest tightened.

"It's about choosing who stands beside you when the cameras are off," Avery continued, voice softening slightly. "It's about integrity when no one is watching."

Avery felt Miles's presence beside her, steady.

Avery's breath caught.

"I choose pediatric care," Avery said, voice clear. "I choose this hospital. I choose our staff who show up every day with courage. And I choose honesty over packaging."

A ripple ran through the crowd.

Avery's chest tightened.

She shifted, slightly, turning her head toward Miles.

Not theatrically.

Not dramatically.

Just... real.

"And I'm grateful," Avery said quietly, "for people who remind me that strength doesn't have to mean isolation."

Miles's breath caught.

The room held still.

Avery looked back to the crowd, voice steady again. "If you give tonight, give because you believe children deserve more than survival. They deserve care that sees them fully. They deserve a hospital that fights for them when the world moves on."

Avery's throat tightened.

She finished the ask cleanly: numbers, programs, impact.

Then she stepped back from the podium and turned toward Miles.

Miles moved forward.

He didn't smile too much.

He didn't perform.

He looked out at the room with the calm steadiness of someone who had learned the difference between spotlight and truth.

"Good evening," Miles said, voice warm. "I'm Miles Carter."

He paused.

"And I'm not here to sell you anything," Miles continued, dry enough to draw a small laugh from the crowd. "Except maybe the idea that integrity can still be compelling."

Avery's chest tightened.

Miles's gaze swept the room, then returned to Avery for half a beat, grounding her.

"You've heard a lot of noise this week," Miles said. "A lot of opinions. A lot of projections."

He paused.

"But here's what I've learned," Miles said, voice quiet, sincere. "You don't have to destroy yourself to deserve success."

A hush.

Avery's chest tightened hard, heat rising behind her eyes.

Miles continued, voice steady. "And you don't have to be perfect to be worthy of care."

He glanced toward the crowd again.

"This hospital deserves support because it changes lives," Miles said. "And because the people inside it choose courage every day, whether anyone applauds or not."

Miles finished with a clean donor call, then stepped back.

The room was quiet.

Then applause.

Not polite applause.

Not the shallow clapping of donors who were pleased with themselves.

Real applause.

Standing, in places.

Avery's chest tightened.

She looked down briefly, blinking hard.

Natalie was in the shadows near the curtain, eyes bright, hands pressed to her mouth like she was trying not to cry in public.

Avery almost laughed.

Patrick Ames sat at a table near stage left, his smile tight, applause measured.

Gerald sat front row, expression unreadable, but his eyes held something that looked like reluctant respect.

Avery exhaled slowly.

She had done it.

Not perfectly.

But honestly.

Avery turned toward Miles again.

He looked at her, eyes warm, soft.

No slogan.

No lever.

him.

Avery's throat tightened.

The host returned to the mic, voice bright. "Thank you, Ms. Sloan and Mr. Carter."

The crowd applauded again.

Avery and Miles stepped away from the podium and moved toward the curtain.

As they walked, someone in the front row called out, half-joking, "Kiss!"

A laugh rippled.

Avery's cheeks burned.

Miles's mouth twitched, but he kept walking.

Avery's pulse hammered.

They slipped backstage.

The curtain closed behind them.

The noise dimmed.

, Avery stood there, breathing.

Then Natalie surged toward them like a proud gremlin.

"Oh my god," Natalie whispered fiercely. "You were magnificent. You were ethical. You were hot. You dragged the noise and then fed it to pediatrics."

Avery exhaled, shaky. "Natalie."

Natalie grabbed her shoulders briefly. "I'm so proud I might explode."

Miles's mouth twitched faintly. "It was good."

Avery's chest tightened at his voice.

Natalie nodded briskly. "Okay. Now. Here's the problem."

Avery's stomach dropped. "What."

Natalie held up her phone.

Avery's pulse spiked.

Natalie's eyes widened. "Montclaire posted again."

Avery's blood went cold. "What did they post."

Natalie turned the screen toward Avery.

A short clip.

From the ballroom.

Avery's speech, mid-pivot.

The line: Leadership isn't about appearing together for applause...

Then the camera cut, slightly zoomed.

Not on the donors.

Not on the stage.

On Avery turning her head toward Miles.

On that quiet look.

That real look.

And the caption, already live:

"She chose. Now it's his turn."

Avery's breath caught.

Miles went still beside her.

Natalie whispered, "They're still trying to force a moment."

Avery's chest tightened.

Because she could feel it now:

The story hadn't died.

It had adapted.

And the spotlight wasn't done with them yet.

Chapter 23: Off Script

The ballroom doors hadn't even fully closed before the noise shifted.

Not applause.

Not donor chatter.

Phones.

Everywhere.

Buzzing. Flashing. Vibrating like the city itself had decided to weigh in.

Natalie stood in the backstage corridor with her phone in both hands and the look of someone trying to hold back a tidal wave with sarcasm.

"Okay," she said briskly. "So. Good news. Donations are up thirty-eight percent in the last twelve minutes."

Avery blinked. "That's... good."

Natalie nodded. "Yes. Love that. Fantastic. The pediatrics fund is thriving."

She lifted her phone higher.

"Less fantastic," Natalie continued, "is that Montclaire's clip is trending under three separate hashtags."

Miles leaned slightly closer. "Which ones."

Natalie read from the screen.

"#SheChose. #NowHisTurn. And my personal favorite, #HospitalHeart."

Avery closed her eyes for half a second.

Miles's jaw tightened. "They're trying to force a response."

Natalie nodded. "Yes. The internet is currently demanding you either kiss, propose, or dramatically declare lifelong devotion in the next twenty-four hours."

Avery opened her eyes slowly. "No."

Natalie shrugged. "I know. But they're loud."

Avery exhaled slowly, trying to keep her pulse even.

She had expected pressure.

She hadn't expected it to feel so personal.

Miles's voice was calm. "What's the board doing."

Natalie smirked. "Smiling."

Avery's stomach turned.

"Gerald already sent a message," Natalie added, reading from her phone. "'A compelling and authentic moment tonight. Excellent fit.'"

Avery's jaw tightened. "plan."

Natalie looked up. "You pivoted the noise, but you didn't kill it. You made it more romantic."

Avery swallowed.

Miles's voice softened slightly. "That wasn't the point."

Natalie shrugged. "I know. But perception doesn't care about intention."

A staff member passed them carrying a tray of empty glasses, whispering to another employee, "Did you see the way she looked at him?"

Avery felt heat climb her neck.

Miles heard it too.

He didn't react.

But Avery felt the air change slightly between them.

Natalie stepped closer. "Okay. Strategy question. Do we issue a statement."

Avery blinked. "About what."

Natalie lifted a brow. "About you two."

Avery's chest tightened. "No."

Natalie nodded once. "Good. That's what I thought."

Miles looked at Avery. "What do you want."

Avery hesitated.

The honest answer rose immediately.

"I want it to stop," Avery said quietly.

Natalie snorted softly. "That's not happening."

Avery's jaw clenched.

Miles's gaze stayed steady on her. "Then what do you want."

Avery swallowed.

She didn't answer immediately.

Because the real answer had nothing to do with press cycles.

Or board headline pressure.

Or hashtags.

It had to do with him.

"I want this to be ours," Avery said finally.

Miles's breath shifted slightly.

Natalie went still.

Avery continued, voice low but firm, "Not theirs. Not Patrick's. Not Montclaire's. Not the internet's."

Miles nodded slowly. "Okay."

Avery met his eyes. "I don't want to perform it."

Miles's mouth softened faintly. "Then don't."

Natalie held up a hand. "Okay. I'm going to do something mature and give you two space before I become an accidental third wheel in an emotional breakthrough."

Avery shot her a look.

Natalie squeezed her shoulder once. "You were extraordinary tonight."

Then she disappeared down the hallway, phone already back at war.

The corridor felt quieter without her.

Avery became acutely aware of the sound of her own breathing.

And of Miles standing close enough that she could feel the warmth radiating off him.

The ballroom noise filtered through the walls again, muffled.

Miles's voice was gentle. "You were extraordinary."

Avery's throat tightened. "You said that already."

Miles's mouth twitched. "Worth repeating."

Avery exhaled.

Then the tension she had been holding all night slipped slightly.

"Did I make it worse," Avery asked quietly.

Miles shook his head immediately. "No."

Avery's jaw tightened. "They're still pushing."

Miles nodded. "They will."

Avery's chest burned. "I'm tired of being a story."

Miles stepped half a pace closer.

Not touching.

But there.

"You're not a story," he said softly. "You're a person."

Avery's breath caught.

She looked up at him.

"I don't know how to do this," Avery admitted.

Miles's brows pulled slightly. "Do what."

"This," Avery whispered. "Us. Without losing control."

The word us hung between them.

Miles didn't flinch from it.

"I don't want to become the headline," Avery said. "I don't want to be reduced to someone's story arc. I don't want to be the CEO who fell in love and got soft."

Miles's eyes sharpened slightly.

"You think loving someone makes you soft," he said gently.

Avery swallowed. "It makes me vulnerable."

Miles nodded once. "Yes."

Avery's throat tightened.

"And I've spent my entire career proving that vulnerability doesn't get to cost me power," Avery continued.

Miles studied her carefully.

Then he spoke.

"I stayed in PR longer than I should have," Miles said quietly.

Avery blinked. "What."

Miles exhaled slowly. "I was good at it. I could control perception. Manage risk. Spin disaster into something survivable."

Avery's chest tightened.

"But it was easier to manage other people's stories than build my own," Miles continued.

Avery watched him carefully.

"I told myself I was building something ethical," he said. "And maybe I was. But I was also hiding."

Avery's breath caught.

"Hiding from what," she asked.

Miles met her eyes.

"From wanting something steadier," he said.

Avery's pulse thudded.

"I didn't think I was allowed to want that," Miles admitted. "Not with the career I built. Not with the reputation I had."

Avery swallowed hard.

"And then I met you," he said quietly.

The air seemed to shift.

Avery's throat tightened painfully.

"You don't bend," Miles continued. "You don't shrink. You don't soften for applause."

Avery's voice was barely there. "You think that's good."

"I think it's brave," Miles said.

Avery felt something in her chest crack slightly.

"And I don't want to be a headline either," Miles added. "I don't want to be the strategist who 'won' the CEO. I don't want to be your prop."

Avery flinched slightly. "You're not."

Miles's gaze softened. "I know. But that's what they're trying to make it."

Avery exhaled slowly.

"They're saying it's your turn," Avery said quietly.

Miles's mouth curved faintly. "The internet loves symmetry."

Avery's lips twitched despite herself.

"They want a gesture," she said.

Miles nodded. "They always do."

Avery looked up at him.

"I don't want a gesture," she said.

Miles held her gaze.

"Good," he said.

Silence fell between them.

Not uncomfortable.

honest.

Avery's chest tightened.

"I'm scared," she admitted.

Miles didn't hesitate.

"Me too."

Avery blinked.

"Of what," she asked.

Miles's voice was steady.

"Of losing this because we let them rush it," he said.

Avery's throat tightened.

"Of you deciding that it's easier to close the door than risk being seen wanting me," Miles added gently.

Avery's breath hitched.

He wasn't accusing.

He was naming the fear.

Avery's eyes stung.

"I don't want to close the door," she whispered.

Miles stepped closer.

enough that the space between them felt intentional.

"Then don't," he said softly.

Avery's chest rose and fell quickly.

"It's not that simple," she said.

Miles's gaze stayed steady. "It can be."

Avery shook her head slightly. "I have a board. I have staff. I have—"

"You have a life," Miles interrupted gently. "You're allowed to have one."

Avery swallowed.

"I don't know how to do that without feeling like I'm compromising something," she said.

Miles's voice was quiet. "Then we do it slowly."

Avery blinked.

"No announcements," Miles said. "No statements. No performance."

Avery's pulse ticked.

"We don't deny it," he continued. "But we don't packaged it."

Avery's throat tightened.

"We let it be ours," Miles said.

The words landed somewhere deep.

Avery searched his face.

"You're not leaving," she said.

It wasn't a question.

Miles didn't look away.

"I'm not leaving," he said.

Avery's breath caught.

"You're not choosing between me and the hospital," he added gently. "And I'm not choosing between you and whatever comes next."

Avery's eyes burned.

"I don't want to be the woman who can't have both," she said.

Miles's mouth softened.

"You're not," he said.

Avery stepped forward without fully thinking about it.

Her hand found his jacket, gripping lightly.

Miles inhaled sharply.

Avery looked up at him.

"I want this," she said.

The word felt enormous.

Miles didn't smile big.

He didn't grandstand.

He simply said, "I know."

Avery's breath trembled.

"And I want you," she added, voice barely steady.

Miles's composure cracked slightly at that.

"I want you too," he said.

No flourish.

No speech.

truth.

Avery's pulse thundered.

Avery's phone buzzed again, persistent, like the building itself had opinions.

She looked at the screen and saw three missed calls from numbers she didn't recognize and one text from Natalie that read: PLEASE DO NOT LET ANYONE HAND YOU A RING LIGHT.

Miles saw it over her shoulder and exhaled through his nose. "She's having fun."

"She's in pain," Avery said. "That's her love language."

Miles's mouth twitched. "Mine is apparently walking into chaos and choosing you anyway."

Avery swallowed hard, heat rising to her cheeks. "Don't say things like that in hallways. Someone will quote you."

"Then let's not be in the hallway."

He glanced down the corridor, toward a small alcove with a vending machine and a door marked STAFF ONLY.

Avery followed his look and, to her own surprise, nodded.

They slipped into the alcove. The vending machine hummed like a small, judgmental refrigerator. The fluorescent light above it flickered as if it also wanted to weigh in on the situation.

"Romantic," Avery murmured.

Miles leaned closer to the machine and squinted at the options. "Nothing says emotional breakthrough like a Snickers and a malfunctioning light."

Avery huffed a laugh, then immediately felt a rush of relief at the sound. Laughter made everything feel less like it might shatter.

Miles pressed a few buttons. The machine whirred, paused, then did nothing.

"Of course," Avery said.

Miles tried again. The machine whirred, then dropped a tiny bag of pretzels with all the drama of a curtain call.

"There," Miles said, solemn. "We have been blessed."

Avery picked up the pretzels and held them between them like an offering. "Should we split them?"

Miles nodded gravely. "We must. It's a bonding ritual."

Avery rolled her eyes, but the warmth stayed. She tore the bag open and offered him one.

Miles took it, fingers brushing hers. The touch was small, but it steadied her more than any speech ever had.

Avery leaned lightly against the wall, the cool surface grounding her. "I hate that they think they own everything."

"They don't," Miles said, voice low. "They think attention equals permission. It doesn't."

Avery's gaze lifted. "What if the board decides I was too..." She searched for the word. "Soft."

Miles's expression sharpened. "Then your board doesn't deserve you."

Avery blinked. "That's not how this works."

"It is if you decide it is," he said. "You're allowed to write your own terms."

Avery felt her chest tighten. "I'm used to surviving by anticipating the terms other people write."

Miles nodded, understanding without pity. "And you are very good at that. But you don't have to do it every minute of your life."

Avery looked down at the pretzels, absurdly grateful for something to focus on that wasn't her pulse.

"What if I can't learn," she asked quietly.

Miles stepped closer. "You already are."

Avery's laugh was soft. "Because I shared snacks with you by a vending machine?"

Miles's mouth curved. "Because you came in here with me instead of staying out there where you could perform safety."

Avery's throat tightened. She hated that he saw her so clearly.

"And because you said you want this to be ours," Miles added, gentle. "That's not a small thing for someone who has spent her whole life being careful."

Avery swallowed. "Careful is what keeps me employed."

"Careful keeps you armored," Miles said. "It doesn't always keep you happy."

Avery's eyes stung, annoying and inconvenient. "I don't know how to be happy without feeling like I'm missing something."

Miles's gaze softened. "Then let it be simple for a minute."

Avery looked up. "Simple like what."

Miles gestured toward the pretzel bag. "Simple like sharing a snack because you're hungry. Simple like holding my hand because you want to."

Avery's breath caught.

"Simple like this," Miles continued, voice steady. "We don't deny it. We don't monetize it. We don't run from it. We just... choose it."

Avery stared at him, the word choose echoing in her chest like a note finally hitting the right pitch.

"I want to," she whispered.

Miles's eyes held hers. "Then do."

Avery's voice was barely there. "I want you."

"I want you too," he said, and it didn't sound like a line. It sounded like a decision.

Then, slowly, carefully, like they were defusing something fragile instead of igniting it, Miles lifted his hand and cupped her jaw.

Not for the cameras.

Not for the internet.

For her.

Avery leaned in.

The kiss wasn't dramatic.

It wasn't hungry.

It was steady.

Warm.

Certain.

The sort of kiss that said, We're choosing this, not performing it.

When they pulled apart, Avery's forehead rested lightly against his.

"Still terrified," she whispered.

Miles huffed softly. "Same."

Avery almost laughed.

Her phone buzzed in her clutch.

She ignored it.

It buzzed again.

Miles glanced down. "Probably Natalie."

Avery exhaled and pulled it out.

It was Natalie.

Avery answered.

"Yes."

Natalie's voice came through, barely contained. "Okay. The internet is now arguing whether that was a proposal."

Avery closed her eyes.

Miles exhaled softly beside her.

Natalie continued, "Half of them think he's about to drop to one knee. The other half think you're about to announce a secret engagement."

Avery leaned her head back slightly and laughed.

Not sharp.

Not brittle.

Real.

Miles watched her, warmth in his eyes.

Natalie paused. "Wait. Are you laughing."

"Yes," Avery said.

Natalie's tone shifted. "Oh. That's new."

Avery smiled slightly. "Let them argue."

Natalie went quiet.

Then she said, softly, "Okay."

Avery ended the call.

She slipped her phone back into her clutch.

Miles studied her.

"What," he asked gently.

Avery's lips curved.

"I think," she said slowly, "for the first time in my life, I don't care if they're watching."

Miles's mouth softened.

Avery looked at him.

"Because I know what this is," she said.

Miles nodded once.

"And it's not theirs," he said.

Avery stepped closer again, her hand sliding into his.

"No," she agreed.

Outside the corridor, applause swelled again as another speaker took the stage.

, Avery considered going back into the ballroom and pretending none of it had happened. That was her old reflex: re-enter the room, reclaim the posture, outlast the moment.

Instead, she took Miles's hand and tugged him down the service corridor toward the staff elevator. "Five minutes," she said. "Fresh air. Then we go back in."

Miles's mouth curved. "Avery Sloan requesting fresh air. Mark the date."

"Don't," she warned, but it came out softer than she meant.

The staff elevator smelled like disinfectant and someone's peppermint gum. They rode down in silence, shoulders nearly touching. Not because they were hiding. Because the world didn't get to sit between them.

"Okay," she said. "That helped."

Miles leaned against the wall beside her. "See. Humans need air."

"I'm aware," Avery said. "I just forget to schedule it."

Miles's eyes warmed. "I can write you a memo. The Ethics of Oxygen."

Avery huffed a laugh. "Do you ever stop."

"Only when bribed with dumplings," he said.

Miles nodded once, as if that confirmed everything he suspected about her relationship with basic needs. "There's a bodega across the street."

Avery blinked. "You want to cross the street."

"Wild idea," he said. "Pizza. Five minutes. We come back."

Avery's first instinct was to veto it on principle. Then she pictured the ballroom again: the smiles, the questions, the looming proximity of people who thought they were entitled to her story.

"Fine," she said. "But if anyone recognizes us, this never happened."

Miles's mouth twitched. "Your list is getting longer."

They crossed the street like two people trying to look normal while being deeply aware they were bad at it.

Miles watched her, amused. "Good."

They'd almost made it out without incident.

Almost.

A woman near the refrigerated drinks turned, stared, then gasped softly. "Oh my god. You're... you're them."

Avery froze mid-bite.

Miles went still beside her.

The woman's eyes darted between them, delighted. "I saw the clip. The look. The speech. Are you—"

Avery swallowed hard, then did the only thing she could think of.

She held up her pizza slice like it was a shield. "Ma'am," she said, calmly, "this is a bodega."

The woman blinked.

Miles made a low sound that was dangerously close to laughter.

The woman recovered. "I just— I love you two. It's so romantic."

Avery's cheeks warmed. "It's... pediatrics."

The woman nodded vigorously. "Yes! That too. But also... him." She pointed at Miles like he was the romantic lead in a streaming series. "He looks like he gives good advice."

Miles's mouth twitched. "I do my best."

Avery shot him a look.

The night wasn't over.

The campaign wasn't finished.

The board would still maneuver.

The internet would still speculate.

But for the first time since that viral press conference cracked her perfect image, Avery didn't feel like she was bracing for impact.

She felt steady.

And beside her, Miles squeezed her hand lightly.

No spotlight.

No slogan.

a choice.

Made off script.

Chapter 24: Terms of Engagement

By Monday morning, the headlines had moved on.

Mostly.

still think pieces circulating. Still tweets dissecting "that look." Still one particularly dramatic blog insisting Miles had "missed his moment."

But the city had a short attention span.

A celebrity divorce had broken overnight. A mayoral candidate had said something regrettable. A subway incident had gone viral.

The internet had found something shinier.

And for the first time in weeks, Avery walked into St. Catherine's without feeling like she was stepping onto a stage.

The lobby felt normal.

Coffee in paper cups. Scrubs rustling. A nurse arguing gently with a delivery driver about where to park.

Normal was underrated.

Natalie fell into step beside her, already mid-scroll.

"Okay," Natalie announced, "pediatrics is officially trending for the right reasons."

Avery raised a brow. "Meaning."

Natalie held up her phone. "Donation goal? Surpassed. By twelve percent."

Avery stopped walking.

"Twelve," she repeated.

Natalie grinned. "Twelve. Turns out integrity sells."

Avery exhaled slowly, relief settling somewhere deep in her ribs.

"And," Natalie added casually, "the board meeting is in twenty minutes."

Of course it was.

Avery straightened automatically.

Natalie studied her. "You're not nervous."

Avery adjusted her blazer. "No."

Natalie blinked. "You're not."

Avery considered it.

"I'm clear," she said finally.

Natalie's mouth twitched. "Hot."

Avery shot her a look.

Natalie shrugged. "What. Authority looks good on you."

They reached the executive corridor.

Miles was already there, leaning lightly against the wall outside the boardroom, jacket on, expression thoughtful.

He looked up when Avery approached.

The warmth in his eyes was quieter now.

Not the charged electricity of a crisis week.

Something steadier.

"Morning," he said.

Avery's chest softened slightly. "Morning."

Natalie glanced between them, then at her phone. "I'm going to stand inside and glare at Patrick preemptively."

She slipped into the boardroom without waiting for a response.

Avery faced Miles.

"You don't have to stay," she said.

Miles tilted his head slightly. "I know."

Avery's throat tightened faintly.

"I want to," he added.

Avery held his gaze.

No cameras.

No captions.

choice.

"Okay," she said softly.

Miles's mouth curved faintly.

"Still terrified," he asked.

Avery considered.

"No," she said.

Miles nodded once. "Good."

Avery stepped past him and into the boardroom.

The long table was already half full.

Gerald sat at the head, hands folded. Pearl-necklace board chair to his right. Patrick Ames near the middle, posture composed, smile thin.

The atmosphere was polite.

Too polite.

Avery took her seat.

Miles remained near the wall, not at the table, not central. Present, but not positioned.

Gerald cleared his throat.

"Congratulations," he said smoothly. "The pediatrics campaign has exceeded its initial benchmark."

Avery nodded once. "The staff did exceptional work."

Gerald's lips curved slightly. "Your speech resonated."

Avery held his gaze. "Good."

A pause.

Then Patrick leaned forward slightly.

"There's an opportunity here," he began, voice measured. "Momentum like this is rare. We should consider capitalizing on—"

Avery didn't let him finish.

"No," she said calmly.

The room stilled.

Patrick blinked. "I'm sorry?"

Avery folded her hands on the table.

"We will not capitalize on personal noise," she said evenly. "The campaign remains mission-first."

Patrick's smile thinned. "With respect, the public response indicates—"

"The public response indicates that people value integrity," Avery interrupted gently. "Not spectacle."

A ripple moved down the table.

Patrick shifted. "We can guide perception without compromising values."

Avery's gaze sharpened slightly.

"Perception is not our product," she said. "Care is."

Silence.

Gerald leaned back slightly, studying her.

Patrick tried again, softer this time.

"Montclaire has already drafted a follow-up content series. Short interviews. A behind-the-scenes—"

"That won't be necessary," Avery said.

Her voice was calm.

Not sharp.

Not angry.

Certain.

Patrick held her gaze.

, it felt like a chessboard.

Then he leaned back slowly.

"As you wish," he said.

Avery nodded once.

Gerald cleared his throat again.

"And Montclaire's contract," he said carefully.

Avery met his eyes.

"Will not be renewed," she said.

A quiet intake of breath from somewhere down the table.

Gerald didn't look surprised.

"Do you have an alternative strategy," he asked.

Avery glanced briefly toward Miles.

Not for permission.

For confirmation.

He met her gaze steadily.

Avery turned back to the board.

"Yes," she said. "We build internal communications capacity. Transparent. Direct. No story packaging without executive approval."

Gerald considered this.

"And Mr. Carter," he said, eyes flicking toward Miles. "Will his role continue."

Avery didn't hesitate.

"Mr. Carter's role concludes as scheduled at the end of the month," she said.

A faint tightening in Patrick's jaw.

"But," Avery continued calmly, "we are exploring an ethics-focused consultancy partnership model for future crisis advisory."

Miles didn't move.

Didn't react.

watched.

Gerald's brows lifted slightly. "Interesting."

Avery held his gaze.

"We don't need spin," she said. "We need clarity."

A long pause.

Then Gerald nodded once.

"well," he said.

The tension shifted.

Not gone.

But redirected.

Patrick gathered his papers neatly, expression controlled.

The meeting moved on to budget allocations and staffing numbers.

Avery answered cleanly.

Efficiently.

Unshaken.

And when the meeting adjourned, no applause.

No drama.

the quiet acknowledgment that something had shifted.

Not in spotlight.

In power.

Outside the boardroom, Natalie exhaled like she'd been holding her breath for an hour.

"Oh," she whispered. "You ended him."

Avery blinked. "No."

Natalie stared at her. "Yes."

Miles's mouth twitched faintly.

Avery adjusted her sleeve. "We adjusted strategy."

Natalie snorted. "Sure."

Gerald passed them in the corridor, offering Avery a measured nod.

"Strong leadership," he said.

Avery met his eyes. "Consistent leadership."

Gerald's lips curved faintly.

He moved on.

Patrick exited next, avoiding eye contact.

Natalie watched him go.

"Moment of silence," she whispered.

Avery suppressed a smile.

Miles stepped closer.

"You were clear," he said quietly.

Avery exhaled slowly. "I was."

Miles studied her.

"You didn't compromise," he said.

Avery met his eyes.

"I didn't," she agreed.

A pause.

Then Natalie clapped once, brisk.

"Okay," she announced. "I have to go wrangle the pediatrics expansion timeline and possibly fight someone in procurement. You two look emotionally stable. Try to stay that way."

She disappeared down the hall.

Avery and Miles made it three steps before a volunteer in a crisp blazer appeared like a pop-up ad.

"Dr. Sloan," the volunteer said brightly, clutching a tote bag full of packaged water bottles. "A quick photo with the donors? Just one. They're very excited."

Avery's reflex was immediate: comply, smile, get it over with. The old muscle memory twitched in her face.

Then she heard Miles's voice, quiet at her shoulder. "You can say no."

Avery looked at the volunteer and smiled, warm but firm. "Not today. Thank you for helping."

The volunteer blinked, then recovered. "Of course. Absolutely. Thank you." She retreated, slightly stunned, like she'd watched gravity change direction.

Avery exhaled slowly. Her shoulders felt lighter by a fraction.

Miles's mouth curved. "That was clean."

"I'm practicing," Avery said.

They passed a small group of nurses near the elevators. One of them recognized Avery, then noticed Miles, then did the sort of eyebrow lift that should have required a license.

Avery's cheeks warmed. The nurse smiled. "We liked your speech."

Avery nodded once. "Thank you."

The nurse added, deadpan, "Also, for the record, if you ever need to hide, pediatrics has a supply closet behind the mural. We protect our own."

Avery blinked, then laughed before she could stop herself.

Miles's quiet laugh followed. "Noted."

And like that, the hospital felt less like a boardroom and more like a place full of people who understood exactly what mattered.

Silence settled.

Avery looked at Miles.

"So," she said.

Miles tilted his head. "So."

Avery folded her arms lightly. "End of the month."

Miles nodded.

"You're leaving Montclaire," she said.

"Yes."

Avery's chest tightened faintly.

"And starting your consultancy," she added.

Miles's mouth curved faintly. "That's the plan."

Avery hesitated.

"Are you sure," she asked quietly.

Miles studied her.

"I stayed in a structure that didn't fit me for too long," he said. "I'm not doing that again."

Avery's throat tightened.

"Good," she said.

Miles stepped closer.

"Are you sure," he asked gently, "that you're not going to try to overwork yourself into emotional numbness now that the crisis is over."

Avery exhaled softly.

"I might try," she admitted.

Miles's mouth twitched. "I suspected."

Avery's lips curved slightly.

"But," she added, "I don't think I need to."

Miles's gaze softened.

Avery looked down the hallway toward pediatrics.

"Come with me," she said.

Miles followed without question.

The pediatrics floor was brighter than the executive corridor.

Walls painted in soft blues and yellows.

Artwork taped slightly crooked at child height.

The air smelled faintly of antiseptic and crayons.

Avery slowed as they stepped into the main hallway.

A small girl in fuzzy socks waved from a doorway.

Avery waved back automatically.

Miles watched her.

Not the CEO.

Not the headline.

her.

A nurse approached, smiling.

"Dr. Sloan," she said warmly.

Avery smiled. "It's Avery."

The nurse laughed softly. "The new infusion chairs arrived."

Avery's chest tightened. "Already."

"Yes," the nurse said. "And the playroom renovation starts next week."

Avery nodded slowly.

This.

This was the point.

Miles stepped beside her, quiet.

"You did this," he said softly.

Avery shook her head slightly. "We did."

Miles studied her.

"Still afraid," he asked gently.

Avery considered the question.

still risks.

Still headline pressure.

Still noise.

But the fear felt... different.

Manageable.

"No," she said slowly. "Not like before."

Miles nodded once.

Avery looked at him.

"I don't want to hide this," she said.

Miles's pulse shifted slightly.

"But I don't want to perform it either," she added.

Miles's mouth softened.

"Then we don't," he said.

Avery's chest tightened warmly.

She reached for his hand.

Not dramatic.

Not secretive.

natural.

He took it.

A nurse glanced over.

Smiled.

Moved on.

No gasp.

No whisper.

normal.

Avery exhaled slowly.

"I think," she said, voice softer now, "I finally understand something."

Miles tilted his head.

"What."

Avery looked at the children's drawings on the wall.

"I don't have to destroy myself to deserve success," she said quietly.

Miles's hand tightened slightly around hers.

"And I don't have to choose between power and love," she added.

Miles's gaze held hers.

"No," he said gently. "You don't."

Avery felt the truth of it settle deep.

The hospital hummed around them.

Not a stage.

Not a spectacle.

work.

And life.

And possibility.

Avery squeezed his hand once.

"Okay," Miles said, glancing down at their hands as if confirming it was real. "Where do you want to go?"

Avery opened her mouth, then paused because her brain immediately tried to turn lunch into a logistical plan with contingencies. She could feel it happening: the instinct to optimize. To schedule. To control.

Miles watched her with quiet amusement. "Say the first place that doesn't involve a reservation spreadsheet."

Avery huffed a laugh. "The cafeteria."

Miles blinked. "That was not what I expected."

"It's five minutes away," Avery said. "It has soup. And no one can claim it's a power lunch."

Miles's mouth curved. "You underestimate the political power of soup."

Avery led him toward the elevators anyway, and the fact that she didn't look around first to see who might be watching felt like a small rebellion.

Avery grabbed a tray and reached for a bowl without thinking.

Miles hesitated, then followed, eyes scanning options like he was negotiating with an unfamiliar country.

They ended up with two bowls of tomato basil and one grilled cheese to split, because Miles insisted on balance and Avery insisted on efficiency.

They found a small corner table near the window. It wasn't private. It wasn't romantic in the glossy way romance tried to sell romance.

It was real.

Avery sat down and immediately felt her shoulders drop, like her body had been waiting for permission to stop bracing.

Miles looked up, dead serious. "I respect their structural integrity."

Avery laughed, surprised at how easy it came.

A nurse at the next table glanced over, smiled, then went back to her conversation without whispering or taking a photo.

It was the smallest kindness. Avery felt it anyway.

Miles dipped his spoon into the soup. "So," he said, "what does a normal week look like for you now?"

Avery stared at him. "Define normal."

Miles's mouth curved. "A week where you are not one push notification away from spiraling."

Avery blew out a slow breath. "I'm not sure I've ever had that."

"Then we build it," Miles said.

Avery's throat tightened. "You make it sound like a project plan."

"It is," Miles said. "But it's a nice one. Low risk. High reward."

Avery's lips curved. "You're making fun of me."

"Gently," he corrected. "With affection."

Avery's pulse skipped. The word affection still felt like stepping onto an unexpected floor and discovering it could hold her.

Before she could respond, a young resident stopped beside their table, tray clutched to his chest, expression caught between admiration and terror.

"Ms. Sloan," he blurted.

Avery looked up. "Yes?"

The resident swallowed. His gaze flicked to Miles, then back to Avery. "I just wanted to say... the town hall clip. And then the pediatrics campaign. My mom donated. She never donates to anything. She said you sounded like a person and that made her trust the hospital."

Avery's chest tightened.

"Tell your mom thank you for me," she said softly.

Miles's voice was warm. "It's not a thing unless we make it one."

Avery lowered her hand. "They're going to make it a thing anyway."

"Then let them," Miles said.

Avery blinked. "Let them."

Miles nodded once. "We can't control what people project. We can control what we do."

Avery looked down at the grilled cheese, then back at him. "And what do we do?"

Miles's gaze held hers. "We eat lunch. We do our jobs. We go home at a reasonable hour at least twice a week."

Avery's mouth twitched. "Twice."

"I'm negotiating," Miles said. "Start high."

Avery shook her head, but the warmth stayed.

"I don't want to be a story," she said quietly.

"Then don't be," Miles said. "Be a person."

Avery swallowed. "And you."

Miles's mouth curved. "Me."

"Are you going to be okay?" Avery asked, meaning the consultancy, meaning leaving Montclaire, meaning the freedom that also looked like a cliff.

Miles nodded. "I'm scared. But it's the right scared."

Avery felt something loosen inside her.

"Then," she said, voice steady, "I'll be your loudest reference."
Miles laughed. "Deal."
"Lunch," she said suddenly.
Miles blinked. "Lunch."
"Yes," Avery said. "Not a board lunch. Not a donor lunch. Just... lunch."
Miles's mouth curved.
"I can do lunch," he said.
Avery nodded once.
"Good," she said.
They turned down the hallway together.
Not rushing.
Not hiding.
Not announcing.
walking.
On their terms.

Epilogue: The Cameras Are Off

Six months later, St. Catherine's smelled like fresh paint and lemon polish.

Avery noticed it the second she stepped off the elevator and onto the pediatrics floor. The corridor looked familiar, but sharper around the edges, like someone had taken an already good place and decided it deserved to feel kinder. New lighting warmed the walls. The playroom doorway had been widened. The family lounge had actual couches that didn't look like they'd been designed to punish spine fit.

And the mural.

The mural was enormous. A sweep of bright sky across one entire wall, painted with floating kites and tiny constellations tucked into the corners. Kids' handprints dotted the base in messy color, like proof that joy had been physically installed here.

Natalie stood under it with a clipboard and the expression of someone trying to hold a ribbon-cutting ceremony together with pure force of personality.

"Avery," Natalie called the moment she saw her. "Please don't get kidnapped by donors. We are starting in eight minutes."

Avery adjusted the lapel of her coat. "I'm not getting kidnapped."

Natalie stared at her. "This is Manhattan. Anything can happen."

Avery's mouth twitched. "You've been watching too much true crime."

Natalie blinked. "I work in healthcare administration. The true crime watches me."

Avery started toward her, then paused when she saw the line of photographers setting up near the entrance. Not as many as the kickoff. Not the frenzy of that week.

Still enough to remind her the world loved a story.

Avery felt the old reflex rise anyway: the desire to straighten, polish, perform.

Then a small hand slipped into hers.

Avery looked down.

girl in purple leggings and a glittery headband stared up at her with the serious confidence of someone who had never worried about reputation a day in her life.

"Are you the boss?" the girl asked.

Natalie made a choked sound.

Avery blinked once. "I work here."

The girl considered that. "My dad says you're the boss."

Avery glanced up and saw a tired man hovering a few steps back, mortified, holding a paper cup of coffee like it was a shield.

"I'm sorry," he mouthed.

Avery crouched so she was level with the girl. "What's your name?"

"Ruby," Ruby said, then immediately added, as if it mattered to the record, "I'm six and a half."

"That's important," Avery said gravely.

Ruby nodded. "And I like the kites."

Avery followed Ruby's gaze to the mural. Bright, bold, impossible to miss. Proof that the money had landed where it was supposed to land.

"I'm glad," Avery said softly. "We made it for you."

Ruby frowned. "Did you paint it?"

Natalie made another noise, like her soul was leaving her body.

Avery glanced at Natalie. Natalie's eyes begged her to say anything except the truth.

Avery smiled at Ruby. "No. Someone else did. Someone who is weirdly good with paint and also refuses to take credit for things."

Ruby's eyes widened. "Like a superhero."

"sort of," Avery said.

Ruby giggled, delighted, and ran back to her dad with the confidence of someone who had secured insider information.

The dad mouthed thank you.

Avery stood, warmth spreading through her ribs in a way that no board approval ever had.

"Noted," Avery said.

Natalie stared at her.

Natalie exhaled and shoved the clipboard at her. "Here's the order. Smile. Wave. Say the mission. Mention the donors. Do not flirt with your boyfriend in front of a Nikon."

Avery arched a brow. "He's not my—"

Natalie's eyes narrowed. "Avery. Don't make me say it in front of God and this child-filled hallway."

Avery opened her mouth, then closed it again because she could hear Miles's voice in her head: We can't control what people project. We can control what we do.

Across the hall, a familiar laugh sounded, low and warm.

Avery turned.

Miles walked toward her with a small bundle in his arms and the expression of a man who had made a questionable choice on purpose.

Miles appeared with a bright red balloon dragon in his hands, looking pleased with himself.

boy nearby gasped and pointed. "Dragon!"

Miles immediately knelt, offering it like a peace treaty. The boy took it with reverence, then hugged it to his chest like it was the only stable thing in the universe.

Miles stood, looking satisfied. "Okay. I have fulfilled my civic duty."

Avery stepped closer, lowering her voice. "You did that on purpose."

Miles's eyes softened. "Maybe."

Avery's throat tightened. Six months ago, she would have been furious about the spotlight. She would have listed risks and contingencies.

Now she felt... steady.

"Are you ready?" Miles asked.

Avery glanced at the photographers. The ribbon. The donors lining up with rehearsed smiles.

Then she looked back at the mural, at Ruby's handprints, at the boy clutching the balloon dragon.

"Yes," she said.

Natalie clapped once, brisk and bossy. "Okay. Places. Everyone pretend to be normal. This is a medical center, not a Netflix premiere."

Miles leaned in toward Avery as they walked to the ribbon. "Do you know what's funny?"

Avery glanced at him. "Dangerous question."

Miles smiled. "You're still competent. You didn't explode. And you didn't disappear."

Avery swallowed. "Neither did you."

Miles's hand brushed hers, brief and grounding. "Told you. Steady."

Avery stepped up to the ribbon, the scissors placed in her hand like a prop she used to fear.

The cameras lifted.

She looked out at the small crowd and felt the familiar pressure...

Then felt it ease, because Miles was beside her, Natalie was behind her, and the floor under her feet was her own.

Avery smiled. "Thank you for coming," she began, voice clear. "This space exists because people decided kids deserve more than survival. They deserve joy."

Natalie made a satisfied sound behind her.

Avery continued, not performing, not apologizing, telling the truth.

And when the ribbon finally fell, the applause rose, warm and real, Avery didn't feel owned.

She felt chosen.

And for once, that was enough.

Avery's gaze drifted to the new donor plaque mounted near the family lounge.

THE SLOAN FAMILY PEDIATRIC RENEWAL PROJECTMade possible through community support

other names beneath it, dozens of them, etched neatly.

The goal had been met.

Surpassed.

Turned into something tangible.

Avery felt her throat tighten unexpectedly, and she forced herself to inhale slowly.

Natalie noticed anyway. She always did.

"Don't you cry," Natalie warned, voice low. "My mascara isn't waterproof and I refuse to be the only emotionally stable person in this hallway."

Avery shot her a look. "You're not emotionally stable."

Natalie nodded. "Correct. But I'm functioning."

Avery's mouth curved faintly. "Fine. No crying."

Natalie's eyes narrowed. "Liar."

Avery's phone buzzed.

Avery didn't flinch.

That was another change.

She glanced down.

A single text.

Miles: On my way. Don't let Natalie stage a coup.

Avery's chest warmed.

She typed back without thinking:

Avery: If she stages a coup, it's because you're late.

Natalie leaned in, eyes sharp. "You're smiling. Who are we blaming for that."

Avery slid her phone back into her pocket. "No one."

Natalie scoffed. "That's Miles. I can tell because your face looks like you remembered sunlight exists."

Avery's cheeks warmed. "Natalie."

Natalie grinned. "It's fine. I'm happy for you. In a way that makes me furious."

Avery huffed a soft laugh.

The hall filled with motion: staff in clean uniforms, volunteers holding small gift bags, a pediatric nurse shepherding two kids in matching superhero capes toward the playroom.

One of them stopped, stared at Avery, then waved with serious intensity.

Avery waved back automatically.

The child grinned, then bolted off again.

Natalie watched Avery's face soften and muttered, "Okay, yes. That's why we did all of this. Not for hashtags."

Avery's throat tightened. "No."

Natalie's phone rang. Natalie answered with the speed of a woman used to disaster.

Natalie snapped her clipboard closed. "Okay. Miles is late. The board is arriving. Gerald is here. Pearl Necklace is already looking disappointed. We have seven minutes."

Avery nodded once, calm. "We'll start on time."

Avery's eyes flicked to the glass wall at the end of the corridor where families could see into the new lounge. A young father sat on a couch with a sleeping toddler tucked against his shoulder, their bodies finally relaxed in a way Avery hadn't seen enough in this building.

"I'm the person who's learned the world doesn't end if I don't control every second," Avery said quietly.

Natalie blinked.

Miles arrived with two minutes to spare, of course.

Avery saw him before she fully registered she was looking for him.

He stepped off the elevator in a suit that looked like it had been tailored for confidence without arrogance, hair slightly wind-tousled, expression calm. He scanned the hallway like he was assessing a room for risks out of habit.

Then he saw her.

And the calm in him shifted into something warmer.

Not flashy.

present.

Avery's chest eased in a way that still surprised her sometimes.

Miles walked toward her, and Natalie immediately materialized in his path like a bouncer.

"You're late," Natalie said.

Miles stopped. "I'm two minutes early."

Natalie pointed at her clipboard. "I live in eight-minute increments. In my world, you're late."

Miles's mouth twitched. "Fair."

Natalie leaned in. "Don't mess this up. This is Avery's day. This is pediatrics. This is not a packaged moment. If you propose in front of donors, I will tackle you."

Miles blinked. "Was I planning to propose in front of donors."

Natalie narrowed her eyes. "I don't know. Men do stupid things when nervous."

Miles glanced at Avery with quiet amusement. "Am I nervous."

Avery's lips curved. "No."

Natalie scoffed. "He's not nervous because he's a menace."

Miles smiled faintly. "Noted."

Natalie stepped back, satisfied. "Okay. Proceed. But remember I'm watching."

Miles turned to Avery, voice softer. "You okay."

Avery nodded. "Yes."

Then she added, honest, "I'm... happy."

Miles's eyes softened.

"Good," he said quietly.

Avery's gaze flicked to the photographers. "They're here."

Miles followed her look, then back to her. "We let them take pictures. We don't give them a show."

Avery's chest warmed. "Agreed."

Miles's mouth curved. "Also, Natalie threatened to tackle me."

Avery huffed a soft laugh. "She would."

Miles leaned slightly closer, voice low. "so you know, I'm not doing anything today that makes you feel like you're onstage."

Avery's throat tightened with gratitude. "Thank you."

Miles's eyes held hers. "Always."

He offered his hand.

Avery took it without hesitation.

Not secretive.

Not defiant.

Normal.

And that still felt like the most radical thing she'd ever done.

Avery stepped to the small podium, microphone in hand.

, the old instinct flashed: perform, control, make it perfect.

Then she looked at the mural.

At the handprints.

At the father still in the lounge, now sipping coffee while a nurse spoke quietly with him.

She felt her shoulders drop.

Avery leaned into the mic.

"Thank you for being here," she began.

Her voice carried steady, clear.

"But before I thank you for the funds, I want to thank you for something harder to quantify."

She paused.

"For choosing care," Avery said. "Not in the abstract. Not as a concept you donate to and then forget. But as something that belongs in a place like this. In the chairs parents sit in at three a.m. In the quiet rooms where nurses speak softly. In the play spaces that remind kids they're still kids even when they're scared."

The crowd went quiet.

Avery continued, voice warm but controlled. "Six months ago, this hospital became a story in ways I didn't expect. The internet did what it does. People projected. They packaged. They tried to turn something real into something easy."

A few soft laughs in the crowd.

Avery's eyes flicked briefly to Miles. He was a few feet back, hands clasped loosely, gaze steady on her.

Avery looked back to the audience.

"But the truth," Avery said, "is that the only story that matters here is the one we live every day. Staff choosing courage. Families choosing hope. A community choosing to support a place that holds people on their worst days."

She paused.

"So today," Avery said, voice firm, "we cut a ribbon. We open doors. We build something better."

Her throat tightened slightly.

"And we do it," she added softly, "because success shouldn't cost you your humanity."

A hush.

Avery exhaled and smiled.

Then she stepped back, gesturing to Gerald, to the nurse manager, to a small child in a cape holding oversized ceremonial scissors like it was the greatest honor imaginable.

The ribbon was cut.

The crowd applauded.

The child swung the scissors triumphantly and shouted, "WE DID IT!"

Laughter burst out, genuine and bright.

Natalie wiped at her eyes and hissed, "Okay, fine. That's adorable."

Avery's chest loosened as if something inside her had finally unclenched.

People flowed forward into the renovated space.

Cameras clicked.

Staff guided donors politely.

Kids ran straight to the new play corner and immediately began arguing about whose cape was more powerful.

Avery stepped aside near the mural, breathing it in.

Miles moved to her quietly.

"Good speech," he said.

Avery's mouth curved. "Not too much story."

Miles's eyes softened. "The right amount."

Avery glanced at him. "Was it... enough."

Miles studied her.

"It was you," he said simply.

Avery's throat tightened.

She didn't look away.

"Thank you," she said quietly. "For... steadying me."

Miles's mouth curved faintly. "I don't compete with your ambition. I want to be near you while you build."

Avery's chest warmed.

Then Natalie appeared like a summoned force.

Avery shot him a look. "Don't encourage her."

Miles's eyes crinkled. "I'm sorry. That was good."

Natalie beamed. "Thank you. Finally, someone appreciates my genius."

Avery exhaled and looked at Miles.

He was smiling.

Not the polished PR smile.

A real one.

Warm.

Easy.

Avery felt something settle in her chest.

Not the end of pressure. Not the end of leadership. Not the end of a life that demanded things from her.

the end of the belief that she had to carry it all alone.

Miles's eyes softened. "What was."

Avery looked at him.

"Choosing," she said simply.

Miles's hand found hers.

No flash.

No announcement.

contact.

Avery squeezed back.

Somewhere down the hall, a child laughed again, bright and unburdened.

Natalie appeared at the end of the hall, scanning for them like she was hunting fugitives. When she found Avery, she stopped, lifted a hand in a small wave, and then did something rare: she didn't make a joke.

She walked up and pressed a folded piece of paper into Avery's hand. "From the playroom," she said quietly. "A kid drew the new mural and labeled it 'The Place Where Grown-Ups Don't Yell.'"

Avery's throat tightened as she opened it. The drawing was messy, bright, and absolutely devastating in the best way.

Natalie cleared her throat and made a valiant attempt to recover her personality. "Also, before you say anything, I'm officially reclassifying today as a non-crime. No misdemeanors. No felonies. Just... functional joy."

Miles's mouth twitched. "That's the highest rating."

Natalie nodded once. "Don't make me emotional." Then she stepped back, eyes shiny, and vanished before anyone could comment.

And for once, Avery didn't feel like she needed the world to approve her happiness.

She needed to live it—steadily, honestly, with the cameras off.

Acknowledgements

Every book begins long before the first sentence is written.

Thank you to the professionals who trust me with their stories—attorneys, administrators, strategists, and leaders who navigate pressure with grace most people never see. Your conversations about responsibility, ambition, burnout, and integrity shaped this story more than you know.

To the readers who continue to show up for smart, banter-forward romances with emotionally steady heroes and ambitious women at the center—thank you for proving that love stories don't need chaos to feel electric. Your messages, reviews, and recommendations matter. They keep these stories alive.

To the editors and early readers who challenge me to sharpen the humor, deepen the emotional beats, and cut what doesn't serve the heart of the story—you make every book stronger.

And to anyone quietly questioning whether success has to cost them everything: I hope this book gives you permission to redefine what power looks like.

As always, thank you for reading.

— Trevor Jensen

About the Author

Trevor Jensen writes contemporary romance for ambitious people who are tired of pretending they don't need love.

His stories center on intelligent, capable women and emotionally steady men—characters who navigate pressure, power, and vulnerability without losing themselves in the process. Blending sharp banter with grounded emotional depth, Trevor's novels explore what it means to build success that doesn't come at the cost of connection.

When he's not writing about boardrooms, late-night strategy sessions, and slow-burn tension, he's studying the way modern professionals balance ambition with authenticity—and how the right partner can make both stronger.

He believes the best love stories aren't about rescue.

They're about choosing each other.

To see more of Trevor Jensen's romance-genre publications, please visit his web site at:

http://www.TrevorJensenBooks.com

www.ingramcontent.com/pod-product-compliance
Lightning Source LLC
Chambersburg PA
CBHW022036220526
45357CB00059B/214